CHA...
LAMB
Collection

The
CHARLOTTE
LAMB
Collection

LOVE IN THE DARK

LOVE IN THE DARK

BY
CHARLOTTE LAMB

MILLS & BOON LIMITED
Eton House, 18–24 Paradise Road
Richmond, Surrey TW9 1SR

*All the characters in this book have no existence
outside the imagination of the Author, and have no
relation whatsoever to anyone bearing the same
name or names. They are not even distantly inspired
by any individual known or unknown to the Author,
and all the incidents are pure invention.*

*All rights reserved. The text of this publication or
any part thereof may not be reproduced or transmitted in any form or by any means, electronic or
mechanical, including photocopying, recording,
storage in an information retrieval system, or otherwise, without the written permission of the publisher.*

*This book is sold subject to the condition that it shall
not, by way of trade or otherwise, be lent, resold,
hired out or otherwise circulated without the prior
consent of the publisher in any form of binding or
cover other than that in which it is published and
without a similar condition including this condition
being imposed on the subsequent purchaser.*

First published in Great Britain 1986
by Mills & Boon Limited

© Charlotte Lamb 1986

Australian copyright 1986
Philippine copyright 1987
Reprinted 1987
This edition 1991

ISBN 0 263 77557 7

Set in Times 10½ on 11½ pt.
19–9110–49427

Made and printed in Great Britain

CHAPTER ONE

STEPHANIE STUART handed her key to the woman on the other side of the reception desk, smiling politely. 'I hope you'll be very comfortable here, Mrs Graham. George will bring up your bags immediately. You're on the second floor; take a right turn as you leave the lift, your room is halfway down that corridor.'

'Could I have some tea brought up to my room at once, please?' The grey-haired woman gave a sigh. 'I'm very tired and I'm dying for some tea.'

'Of course, I'll see to that for you at once,' Stephanie nodded, giving the woman a concerned glance. She looked tired; in fact she looked exhausted. 'Is there anything else I can do for you, Mrs Graham? Please don't hesitate to ask, we're here to help our guests.'

'That's very good of you, but all I need is a cup of tea, a warm bath and an hour or two on my bed, then I'll be fine.' Mrs Graham was very thin and pale; her features seemed drawn. Stephanie hoped she wasn't ill. She had seen that look in someone's face before— the bluish lips, the lines of pain. She wouldn't be surprised if Mrs Graham had a heart condition. She watched the woman walk towards the lift, frowning, then wrote on Mrs Graham's private card, PHC. It was the custom of the Wyville Arms to have a careful filing system for all their guests, listing their tastes and preferences, their characters and danger spots. It helped the staff to give a personal service so that if a crotchety retired Army officer arrived he would not be offended by the wrong newspaper in the morning, or by being given China tea when he only drank Indian, or lightly grilled bacon when he liked it crisp.

Stephanie slid Mrs Graham's card into the drawer in which they kept current details. Glancing at her watch, she made a wry face. Anya was late again. It was ten minutes past six; Stephanie should have gone off duty at six, but her replacement, Anya Carter, managed to clip a little time off each end of her shift, arriving late and leaving early unless the manager was around to watch her.

Gill appeared through the door behind Stephanie. 'Coming?' She looked around the lobby. 'Where's Anya?' Catching the expression on Stephanie's face, she groaned. 'Not late again? Really, she is the limit! It's a sauce, she shouldn't be allowed to get away with it.'

'If she isn't here soon I'll have to ring Mr Wood. There's no way I can work late tonight.'

'Of course, you're going to a party, aren't you?'

'Elspeth's engagement party! I'm not missing that. Mrs Cameron would never forgive me.' Stephanie spoke lightly, but she was half serious. Mrs Cameron could be very kind and pleasant, but she had a rigid, unbending sense of what she expected from people and Stephanie was slightly scared of her. She had accepted an invitation to Elspeth's party; Mrs Cameron would expect her to be there.

'Mrs Cameron? Don't you mean Euan?' teased Gill.

Laughing, Stephanie shook her head.

'Oh, I see—you can handle him, but not his mother?'

'Something like that.' Stephanie's blue eyes danced; her wide mouth curving with a happiness which made

Gill smile back at her.

'You're serious about him, aren't you? Think it's *the* one? The real thing?' She sounded half envious; Gill Evans had just broken up with her boy-friend and was going through a trough of depression and self-doubt which made her slightly moody.

Stephanie crossed her fingers behind her back. 'Maybe—who knows? I'm not rushing it.' Her eyes flashed behind Gill and she gave a little sigh of relief, seeing Anya slipping into the reception area. 'Oh, there you are! You're nearly fifteen minutes late—it really isn't on, Anya. I've got an important date tonight.'

Anya had her excuse ready, glib and coaxing. 'Oh, I'm sorry, Stevie, but the bus was running late, it wasn't my fault, honestly.'

Stephanie and Gill exchanged looks. 'You'd better take an earlier bus in future, Anya. That one seems to run late at least once a week.' The mild sarcasm was water off a duck's back, Anya merely smiled, and Stephanie had no more time to waste on her tonight.

She rushed into the staff-room to grab her coat and then she and Gill made their way to the hotel entrance. A taxi drew up and disgorged a new guest. Idly, Stephanie watched him get out, turning his head to glance at the meter in the taxi, the wind whipping his blond hair backwards, revealing a sculptured profile, coolly incisive.

A spasm of shock made her stomach muscles clench. It couldn't be! Fate couldn't do this to her.

Gill was staring too, unashamedly, her lips pursed in a low whistle. 'Isn't he something?' she whispered as her feet slowed so that she could take a longer look. 'I hope he's staying here—were we expecting another guest tonight? You don't know his name, do you?'

Stephanie didn't answer. She was already some feet away, moving so fast she was almost running. She didn't look back, but she didn't have to—she knew his name, and the hotel certainly hadn't been expecting him. She wouldn't have missed that name on the list of expected guests, it would have leapt out at her like a snake from a box.

Gill caught up with her at the car, panting breathlessly. 'You *are* in a hurry to get away!'

You can say that again, Stephanie thought, unlocking the car. What on earth was he doing here? He hadn't booked, it must be a one-night casual, perhaps he was *en route* somewhere, and would move on in the morning. Thank God he hadn't arrived ten minutes earlier when she was on the desk. She slid into the driving seat, angrily aware that she was trembling. The very prospect of looking up, innocently unaware, to find herself staring at him across the reception desk made her blood turn to ice.

'I hope he isn't just a one-nighter,' said Gill, clipping her safety belt. 'He didn't look like a travelling salesman, did he? Let's hope he's still here on Monday.'

Let's hope he isn't, Stephanie thought, starting the engine. As she drove out of the car park she saw the taxi doing a U-turn in the road to drive away. Their new guest had vanished, but they both saw the porter, George, his hands gripping the handles of two very expensive pigskin suitcases, shouldering his way through the swing doors.

'Like the luggage,' Gill commented, peering. 'That's real pigskin, isn't it? He must be loaded. I bet he's married, but then the best men always are.'

She seemed unaware of Stephanie's silence and chattered lightly as they drove through Wyville's Saturday night traffic. The hotel was just off the sea front, but from some of the bedrooms on the upper floors you could get stunning sea views. The little town was not a popular resort now, although it had been at the turn of the century during the heyday of Victorian seaside holidays, a fact reflected in much of the architecture, including that of the Wyville Arms. Solidly built, but with many curlicues; turrets at the corners, high windows, gables on the top floor, a mass of ornamental plasterwork, the hotel was far too large for the custom it got now. They relied heavily on passing traffic; often half the rooms were empty.

Wyville was something of a backwater. Streets of crumbling Edwardian boarding-houses spread out from the sea front; few of them did much business, even in the high season. Now, in early spring, many of them were closed until the start of the summer, their windows blank, their paintwork shabby. The little town had a melancholy air, like a bride deserted at the altar, her finery decaying, her guests long gone, her future bleak.

Stephanie shivered, and Gill stopped talking to give her a sideways frown. 'Hey, are you okay? You look pale, I hadn't noticed.'

'Tired, I suppose,' Stephanie said with a forced smile as she turned into the new housing estate on the edge of town. Gill lived with her parents in one of the timber and concrete boxes set in pocket-handkerchief gardens. Pulling up outside, Stephanie turned towards her passenger.

'Have a good weekend.'

'Same to you. Don't drink too much at the party or

Mrs Cameron will decide you aren't a suitable daughter-in-law!'

Stephanie managed to laugh, although that wasn't really funny. 'I've only been dating Euan for three months—hold on there! Marriage hasn't even been discussed.'

Gill winked. 'Thought about, though, I bet.' She got out, slamming the door with an enthusiasm that made Stephanie wince. Her head had begun to throb; she hoped she wasn't getting the sort of headache that hangs around all evening. That would ruin the party.

It was ruined already, she admitted grimly, driving away. She had been looking forward to tonight all week and now she wished she wasn't going out. She needed to be alone for a few hours to think; her mind was being eaten alive with questions. What was he doing here? Did he know she lived and worked in Wyville? How long was he staying and was it sheer chance that had brought him here or ...

She broke off, taking a deep anxious breath, her face white. It had to be mere coincidence; it mustn't be anything else. She wouldn't even consider the other alternative. Yet she had a sinking sense of uneasiness about seeing him outside the hotel where she worked. Her life was just beginning to hold a new happiness; the old nightmares had faded into memory. Surely fate could not be so cruel as to bring them all back?

She was so obsessed with anxiety that she almost missed the turning which led to her home. Realising it, she braked suddenly, skidding on the wet tarmac. It had been raining that afternoon, obviously. She hadn't noticed, she had been too busy.

As she took the right-hand turn a car behind her hooted noisily. She looked into her driving mirror,

face apologetic, and then saw that it was Robert
following her in his new Ford. She waved and drove
on to park outside the house. Robert turned his car
into the short driveway and pulled up, leaning out of
the window.

'Trying to kill someone? What were you dreaming
about when you should have been keeping your mind
on the road? Or should I say who?' He grinned, brown
eyes teasing, as Stephanie slid out of her driving seat
and came walking towards him.

Strangers might never have guessed that they were
brother and sister. They resembled each other only in
having the same colour hair—a warm, rich dark
brown close to the colour of polished mahogany.
Robert was solidly built, a man of thirty with a rugged
face, individual if not handsome features, and a casual
good humour. Stephanie was slight, her body slender
and supple, innately graceful. Her features had a
delicacy which was faintly deceptive; she was not
quite as vulnerable as she seemed, but her blue eyes
had an occasional sadness, as if something haunted
her, and her long, pale throat made her seem fragile.

'You're early,' she said as Robert joined her.
'Hospital kick you out for killing patients?'

'By some fluke they all survived today,' he replied,
sauntering beside her towards the front door. 'I did my
best, but we had a tough bunch in the theatre, they
kept insisting on staying alive.'

'Gwen's on the night shift, isn't she?'

He nodded. His wife worked in the same hospital
but all too often on a different shift, so that she and
Robert practically had to make an appointment to
meet for lunch once a week. Gwen always said that
they had been able to see more of each other before

they got married than they did now.

'The powers that be have this thing about married couples getting together, you know. Sex scares the hell out of them. They're determined to keep us apart so we can't do anything they don't approve of!'

She laughed. 'Poor Robert, I can see the frustration is murder.'

He made a face at her. 'Okay, laugh. Wait until you've married a doctor. You won't think its so funny then, always being on different shifts.' He unlocked the front door and Stephanie walked into the hall. She had a separate flat on the upper floor, above the garage, but while Gwen was on the night shift Stephanie usually got Robert his evening meal. He always protested that he could manage to put something frozen into the microwave all on his own, but Stephanie preferred to cook a real meal for them, something a good deal more nutritious than an instant TV dinner.

'I wish everyone would stop marrying Euan and me off,' she said irritably, and her brother looked at her with enquiry in his eyes.

'What's up, doc?'

She laughed. 'Oh, nothing.' She couldn't tell him whom she had seen that evening at the hotel; Robert had enough problems on his mind, he didn't need hers too. She owed Robert so much; more than she could ever repay. He had stood by her when she had needed someone to believe in her, someone to lean on—well, that had been five years ago, she had been very young then. Now she felt very old. She was certainly old enough to shoulder her own worries without landing her brother with their burden. He had a wife to take care of now.

'You haven't quarrelled with Euan, have you?'
probed Robert. Stephanie looked amazed and then
laughed.

'Of course not!'

'No, I can't imagine Euan quarrelling with anyone,
he's Mr Cool in person, isn't he? It's that mother of
his, of course—she's so well bred she makes me
nervous. I'm sure Euan was a perfect child; he
wouldn't have dared be anything else.'

Stephanie gave him an anxious look. 'Don't you like
Mrs Cameron?'

'What's there to dislike? Always courteous, always
reasonable—my God, I wouldn't have the nerve to
dislike her, it would be positively ill-mannered.'
Robert walked towards the stairs. 'I'm going to have a
long soak in the bath, a glass of whisky and half an
hour's absolute total idleness. After that I may feel like
going to Elspeth's party, which at the moment I am
not eager to do. Out of the last twenty-four hours I've
worked seventeen. I suppose I ought to be grateful for
the fact that I'm not a surgeon and don't have to stand
on my feet all day. At least the anaesthetist gets to sit
down. Let us give thanks for small mercies.'

His voice trailed up the stairs after his disappearing
figure and Stephanie looked after him with affection
and concern. Robert had been working these hours for
months; how much more could he take? His salary
was derisory, he needed the rent Stephanie paid for
her three rooms, in order to help pay the mortgage on
this house, and all the money Gwen earned as a staff
nurse went into a special fund intended to make it
possible for her to give up work in two years' time in
order to have a baby. They had planned their life like a
military operation, down to the last detail—but

Stephanie couldn't help wondering if either of them
had realised how exhausting and frustrating these
years were going to be.

She went into the kitchen and prepared the salad
which she was going to serve with a quick cheese
soufflé. While the soufflé was cooking, she ran into her
own flat to get ready for the party. A quick shower,
into her coral-pink silk dress, and ten minutes in front
of her dressing-table mirror, then she was ready to
rush back to the kitchen. She heard the water running
out of Robert's bath and called to him.

'Dinner will be on the table in ten minutes exactly.'

'Right.'

'Don't forget, you're to wear your evening suit. No
excuses. We may go on somewhere afterwards,
dancing, late supper—who knows?'

'Gwen said that if she gets off promptly at ten she
might catch up with us if we go to the Laserlight.'

'In her uniform?' She peered up the stairs at him
and Robert craned over the banisters to grimace at
her.

'No, dummy. She'll change at the hospital. She took
her new dress with her.'

'Get dressed!' she hissed, seeing that he was still in
his damp towelling robe.

'Nag, nag, nag!' Robert vanished and Stephanie
went back into the kitchen to gaze anxiously at the
clock. If he didn't hurry, her soufflé would be ruined.
It had to be eaten the minute it came out of the oven or
all that soaring lightness would collapse into a puddle.

She checked the table by the window for the second
time; she hadn't forgotten anything. Where was
Robert? Then she heard his running feet on the stairs
and with a sigh of relief grabbed up her oven gloves.

An hour and a half later they drove up the hill towards Cameron House, a Victorian extravaganza of turrets and Gothic battlements, built at the same time as the similar houses in Wyville, by a speculative builder from Edinburgh called Hamish Cameron. He had decided to settle here and built himself a large house on a hill overlooking Wyville so that he could contemplate his own achievements from a great height. Hamish Cameron had lived to be ninety-five, married for the third time at the age of sixty, and finally managed to get himself a son and heir, Hamish the Second, who was so dominated by the old man that he grew up a nervous wreck. Hamish the Second had dreamt of becoming an artist. His father had brought a stick down on his head and ordered him to join the firm. He had also ordered him to marry his cousin, Margo. Hamish obeyed, but he died young, collapsing of a heart attack when he was forty-three while swimming in the sea with his own small son, Euan. 'My father had a sad life,' Euan had once told Stephanie. 'Even after his old tyrant of a father died, Dad couldn't give up business and start painting because there was no one to run the firm.'

When her husband died, however, Margo Cameron took over control of the building firm and ran it with immense success, intending to hand it over to her own son when he grew up. Euan had other ideas. He had wanted to be a doctor from the day he saw his father dying on the beach at Wyville. Euan was a quiet, gentle and affectionate boy. His mother didn't imagine she would have any difficulties with him, but Euan had inherited an iron will from her. She couldn't persuade him out of his intention to go to medical school. Euan qualified and got a job in the hospital at

Wyville, working in the cardiology department, specialising in heart operations because his father's death had made that an obsession with him. His mother went on successfully running the family firm.

The party tonight was to celebrate the engagement of Euan's sister, Elspeth, to John Barry, an architect who had worked on the new housing estate with Mrs Cameron. Their marriage would give Johnny a golden future with the firm, but it would also give Mrs Cameron what Euan had denied her—a member of the family to help her run the firm in future. Cynics in the town had murmured that it was an arranged marriage, more business than romance. They didn't know Elspeth. Stephanie did; and knew that Elspeth was deeply in love with Johnny. His feelings were not so obvious; he didn't wear his heart on his sleeve.

As Robert parked in the only space left available on the long driveway up to the house, he looked at the lighted windows and above them the bizarre silhouette of the roof against the moonlit sky. 'Looks like a set for a Hammer horror film, doesn't it? Any minute we'll probably see the bats swooping up from the chimneys.'

'It isn't exactly an ideal home,' Stephanie agreed, sliding her long shapely legs out of the car and standing up.

'You and Euan wouldn't be expected to live here, would you?' enquired Robert, locking the car, and she looked irritably at him across the top of the car.

'Robert! For heaven's sake, stop trying to marry us off. And don't drop any of your loaded hints to Mrs Cameron. Or Euan, come to that. I'll kill you if you do!'

She had enough on her mind tonight without the

added problem of her brother making embarrassing
jokes about wedding bells for her and Euan. She no
longer felt like going to this party: how could she relax
and enjoy herself when she didn't know why Gerard
Tenniel was in town and how long he would be
staying? She had thought she had put all that behind
her, but here he was, a lethal time bomb ticking away,
which might at any moment explode and blow her
carefully built new life to smithereens.

'I'm sorry, kid, don't get so upset—of course I won't
say a word. What do you take me for?'

'Don't tempt me,' she said as they walked towards
the house, but she linked her arm through Robert's to
show that she forgave him.

He pressed her arm against his side, looking down
sideways at her, smiling. 'I just want you to be happy,
Stevie. You had a tough time a few years back, I know
how badly you felt, but all that is over now and
forgotten and I'm glad you're dating Euan, he's a good
man. I don't mean to jump ahead of you, or rush you,
believe me. I'll try to be discreet tonight.' He put a
finger on his mouth. 'My lips are sealed, okay?'

'Okay,' she said, nudging him with her shoulder.
'You are an idiot, you know, but as a brother you're a
bargain.'

He laughed. 'I'm not sure how to take that.'

The front door opened; Euan appeared, framed in
light, his red hair glinting vividly above the formal
evening dress he wore. Mrs Cameron was old-
fashioned in many ways—for special occasions like
tonight she believed in formal dress, and none of her
family would dream of disobeying her.

'Hallo, you look lovely,' said Euan, kissing her
lightly as she moved from her brother to greet him.

'My mother's favourite colour, pink; she has a whole
bed full of roses just that shade, she'll love that dress.'

'They called it coral, in the dress shop,' Stephanie
said, glancing down at the clinging silk. She had
chosen a demure style, one she felt Mrs Cameron
would approve of—the neckline was modestly
scooped a little, the sleeves were puffed, the skirt
covered her knees. She was uneasily aware, though,
that the material adhered a little too closely to her
figure. She might be covered up but somehow the thin
silk gave a very different impression. When she tried
it on in the shop she hadn't noticed how seductively
silk clung, how sensuous an impression it gave, or she
would never have chosen this dress. But perhaps Mrs
Cameron would be too busy with her guests to notice.

'Hallo, Rob. Pretty rigorous day we had, wasn't it?'
Euan said, grinning past her at her brother. 'Do you
feel as whacked as I do?'

'Worse,' said Robert. 'I got that long lecture from
Sister Morris about going to sleep while they were
wheeling in the next patient. I closed my eyes for a
second and Morris hit me like a whirlwind. That
woman is beyond a joke! She's never forgiven me for
marrying Gwen. She hates her theatre nurses to get
married—all they're supposed to have on their minds
is work.'

'Is Gwen going to manage to get here tonight?'

'Doubt it. She hopes to get off at ten, but she may
not manage it if there's an emergency and when she
does she'll be on call until two. Never marry a nurse!'

Stephanie tensed, hoping that her brother wasn't
going to deliver one of his jokey hints, but Robert's
smile was free of any double meaning and Euan
laughed.

'Working in theatre all I ever see is their eyes, and I
don't get turned on by a pair of eyes above a mask.' He
looked at Stephanie thoughtfully, as if just noticing
her eyes. 'You never wanted to be a nurse, Stevie?'

She shook her head. 'Blood makes me faint.'

Both men grinned. 'Most people do pass out, their
first time in theatre,' said Euan, putting an arm
around her to steer her into the house. He looked down
at the parcel she was carrying. 'That for Elspeth and
Johnny?'

She nodded. She had taken most of her lunch hour
to find what she was looking for—a boxed set of
Waterford sherry glasses. She wanted a particular
design which had not been stocked by the first two
shops she visited, but eventually she had tracked these
down in a smaller shop on the edge of town.

Euan looked good in evening dress; it did something for his thin, wiry figure. Although he worked
hard, hours as long as Robert's, he still found time to
keep fit with punishing games of squash and tennis at
the hospital staff sports centre, built with Cameron
money five years ago, at Euan's suggestion. Stephanie
had picked up a strong suggestion of disapproval from
Mrs Cameron, who disliked spending money too
freely, but in that, as in choosing his career, Euan had
had his way. His quiet determination was visible in his
bony, controlled face; patients could read nothing in
his calm smile and steady hazel eyes. Euan wasn't
handsome by any means, but his strength attracted
Stephanie. He was a man you could rely on; someone
you trusted implicitly. That, in her view, was more
important than good looks.

The party had spread throughout the ground floor of
the house. Stephanie knew some of the other guests

but others were complete strangers, many of them
Cameron relatives whom, Euan said drily, even he
barely knew. His mother had organised this party and
drawn up the guest list. Her future son-in-law was on
display to her family and friends. Johnny's family was
here, and several of his friends, but by and large, the
Cameron contingent dominated the gathering.

'Hallo, Stephanie, nice of you to come.' Elspeth
floated over to kiss her, floated being the exact word to
describe the way she moved on very high, silvery
sandals, her pale green and white chiffon dress
drifting around her in a delicious swirl. She was only
five feet tall, even with those high heels; her hair, a
shade lighter than her brother's, had a red-gold
brilliance, and her eyes were mint green. She was
much younger than Euan and her features had a soft,
rounded curve to them, but behind the youth and
smiling sweetness lay the same Cameron determination. Elspeth was no soft touch, as Johnny would
discover after their marriage.

'I hope you and Johnny are going to be blissfully
happy,' said Stephanie, handing over her foil-
wrapped gift.

'Oh, a prezzie!' Elspeth cooed, pulling at the gold
ribbon bow. 'You are an angel, thank you, they're
gorgeous, just what we wanted—how did you
remember?'

Elspeth had spent the last few weeks making lists of
all the things she would need to set up home in the
personally designed house which was now being built
by the firm for her and Johnny. Stephanie hadn't had
to use any imagination; Elspeth knew precisely what
she wanted, and made sure everyone else did too. She
was very like her mother.

Robert had a gift with him, too. While he was giving it to Elspeth, Euan guided Stephanie over to say hallo to his mother, who was holding court from her Queen Anne chair at the other side of the room.

'Good evening, Stephanie.' Mrs Cameron raised her face so that Stephanie could kiss her cheek. She always carried a faint, delicate fragrance of lavender around with her, seeming never to wear any other perfume. The perfume matched her conservative clothes: tonight she wore a cool blue evening dress with long sleeves and a high neckline which hid her finely lined throat. The style and material could have been worn at any time in the last twenty years, Stephanie thought wryly. She wouldn't be surprised to hear that Mrs Cameron had had the dress as long as that, either.

'You look very daring tonight,' Mrs Cameron said with slight reproof, eyeing the clinging silk dress.

'Oh, Mother, really!' protested Euan, laughing. 'Stevie looks marvellous and that's a very pretty colour—you've always said how much you like pink.'

'Yes,' his mother said uncertainly. Her eyes were almost the same colour as her son's and her hair had been auburn. Now it was a becoming silver, softly curled around her very feminine features. She had a small, delicate nose, high cheekbones and a bow of a mouth lightly glossed with pale pink. She must have been very pretty as a girl, Stephanie thought, but all that femininity was deceptive. Under her sweet smile, Mrs Cameron had a backbone of steel. All the same, she was never unkind or spiteful. She had high standards and insisted on maintaining them, insisted everyone around her should maintain them, too. She wasn't easy to live up to, nor, probably, to live with—

but Stephanie respected her, and rather liked her too.

'Find Stephanie a glass of sherry, Euan, but don't monopolise her. No skulking in corners together tonight; this is a family party. Everyone will want to meet her. Your Aunt Jennifer was asking me about her earlier. Where is she?' Mrs Cameron glanced around the crowded room, her eye moving quickly over the little groups of chattering people, until they rested on a couple sitting on a sofa talking. 'Oh, there she is—with Adrian. Doesn't he look well? You would never believe that he was over seventy. He swims before breakfast every day, he tells me. You might try that, Euan, in that expensive sports centre you persuaded me to build. You might as well use it occasionally.'

'I use it every day, Mother. We all do. It's probably done more good than anything else we've added to the hospital facilities in the last fifty years. Preventative medicine is worth . . .'

'Euan, please! No lectures, not tonight. I know your views on preventative medicine. Take Stephanie over to meet Jennifer and your cousin Adrian.'

Euan gave a wry smile. 'I'll get you that drink first, Stevie. You're going to need it. Aunt Jennifer can only be taken in small doses with the help of a stiff drink.'

His mother looked reprovingly at him. 'Really, Euan! That wasn't very kind. And it seems a great pity to shorten Stephanie's pretty name in that way. You make her sound like a boy!'

'In that dress, nobody is going to mistake her for a boy,' a deep, cool voice murmured behind them.

Stephanie swung round, all the colour rushing out of her face, and the tall man who had spoken observed her with a lazy mockery that had the quality of dry ice.

His smile was spiked with menace and Stephanie swallowed in sheer panic. Oh, God, what was he doing here?

'Gerard! How wonderful to see you again. I'm so glad you could come.' Mrs Cameron's voice was warm; she held out her hand, smiling.

'Hallo, Godmother.' He bent his blond head to kiss her hand lightly. 'You look charming, and you haven't changed a hair since I last saw you. How do you do it? Have you discovered the secret of eternal youth?'

Mrs Cameron laughed as he straightened. 'Nonsense, Gerard. Such flattery! I'm past the age for such delightful compliments.'

'I don't believe it.'

Stephanie was fighting for self-control, her hands tensely clasped together. He was Mrs Cameron's godson? His name had never been mentioned by anyone here before. She had no idea. So that was why he had checked into the hotel—he had been invited to this party. Had he known that he would find her here? He hadn't seemed surprised; indeed, his smile had had a twist of satisfaction as he observed her stunned dismay, as though he had been looking forward to that moment when she first set eyes on him. He'd known just how much of a shock that would be, and he had enjoyed watching her face.

Well, he had had his fun. She wished she had been able to hide how she felt, but he had taken her by surprise. She might be five years older than the last time they met; but her control over her emotions was no stronger.

'You remember my son, Euan, don't you?' Mrs Cameron was murmuring. 'Euan, this is Gerard Tenniel—his mother was my best friend at school and he's my godson. You met him several times when you were younger, do you remember?'

'Of course,' said Euan, offering his hand without visible enthusiasm.

He had never heard that name on Stephanie's lips, he couldn't know that she had ever met this man before, but as the two men shook hands they eyed each other with remote courtesy, as though Euan had picked up some vibration in the air. Or perhaps he had never liked Gerard Tenniel much, anyway? She must not read too much into Gerard's presence here. He might not have any intention of revealing her past. He knew Mrs Cameron; he knew just what effect that old story would have—he couldn't be cruel enough to wreck her chance of happiness with Euan.

The blond head turned her way, the cool, grey eyes travelled up and down her body in a speculation which was little short of insolence. 'Aren't you going to introduce us, Godmother?' he drawled, and Stephanie hardly dared to breathe as Mrs Cameron answered.

'Of course, how remiss of me—Gerard, this is Stephanie Stuart, I'm sure I mentioned her when I wrote to your mother with the invitation, she's been seeing a good deal of Euan lately.'

Gerard Tenniel held out his hand. He was pretending that they were strangers. He wasn't going to tell them what he knew about her. She was afraid to hope too much, but her blue eyes reflected fear and pleading as she let her hand be engulfed by his, and he smiled with a mocking satisfaction that made it clear that Gerard Tenniel had a whip poised over her head. He might not plan to tell them yet—but that was no guarantee that she was safe. She could not trust this man.

CHAPTER TWO

STEPHANIE hardly knew how she got through the next hour. It felt as if she had sleepwalked her way round the room. People spoke to her, she smiled at them without really seeing them, nodding. Did she answer? She must have done, yet she couldn't remember anything she said. Her heart was beating with a wild, erratic beat. If she had dared, she would have fled, got away from there, from that house, from Gerard Tenniel. But how could she leave the party? Euan would be puzzled, he might start asking questions and the longer she put off having to answer him the better. If Gerard Tenniel did tell the family what he knew, that would be the end for her and Euan. Stephanie was certain of that.

At least during the time while she and Euan were circulating among his family, she could keep away from Gerard. She didn't look towards him, yet she always knew where he was; from time to time, she picked up the timbre of his deep voice. Five years ago, the sound of that voice made her knees give. Today, it made her feel sick with dread.

'You okay, Stevie? You look a bit green,' said Robert in her ear, and she jumped about ten feet into the air.

'Oh . . .'

'Hey, your nerves are bad! What's up?'

'Nothing, don't be silly,' she said, trying to laugh, but she couldn't fool her brother.

'Quarrelled with Euan?' he asked shrewdly.

'Of course not. I'm just tired.'

'You need to sit down.' Her brother glanced around the room, making a face. 'No empty seats here.' The Cameron relatives were mainly older people who preferred to sit down even at a party. Every chair was taken.

'It doesn't matter, I'm not going to faint.'

'From the look on your face you might, at any minute.' Robert pushed her through the door and across the hall to sit on the stairs.

Stephanie's body collapsed with relief and she gave Robert a wry look.

'Thank you, Doctor.'

'My pleasure. Feel better? It's cooler out here— fewer pairs of lungs using up all the oxygen. That might account for it, you know. People often faint at parties or big gatherings, solely due to lack of air.' He put his hand on the back of her neck. 'Put your head down on your knees, that will bring the blood back to your head in no time.'

She obeyed ruefully. There was no point in telling Robert that it wasn't lack of oxygen making her pale but was a surfeit of Gerard Tenniel. He wouldn't have recognised the name, but Robert knew all about the man and she did not want him to realise who was here tonight. If she could only keep very still and quiet she might be safe. Gerard would go away again and nobody here need ever know about the past. Or was that just wishful thinking? Could anything be buried for ever?

Robert said softly, 'Stay here. I'll get you a glass of water.'

Stephanie closed her eyes, her forehead resting on

her knees. The sound of the party seemed far away. It was sheer bliss to be alone; not to have to smile, talk, pretend. She couldn't stay here long, though—Euan would start wondering where she had got to, and then he would come looking for her.

She heard the door open and the noise of the party grow louder. That must be Euan, coming in search of her. The door shut again as she slowly lifted her head, but it wasn't Euan coming across the dim hall, it was Gerard Tenniel.

She sat up, shaking helplessly, but screwing up her courage to face him. She must not let him see how much he frightened her.

'I wondered where you'd got to,' he muttered, his mouth twisting. 'I thought you might have left altogether.'

'I was hot,' she said, trying not to let her voice tremble. 'I came out here to cool down.'

His grey eyes assessed her, a spark of savagery in their black pupils. 'You look cool enough to me . . . but then you always were deceptive.' He smiled, but the movement of his cold, beautiful mouth made her wince. 'Not to say a bloody little liar,' he added conversationally.

The pretence that they were strangers had vanished; enmity showed in his face and Stephanie looked away, downwards, her lashes fluttering against her cold skin. She couldn't hold that stare; it tortured her.

'Look at me when I'm talking to you!' His hand shot out and caught her chin and she gave a cry of shock at the touch of his fingers. He ruthlessly pushed her head backwards until she was looking up into his icy grey eyes.

'Please . . . my brother will be back any minute,' she whispered, and he stared at her, frowning.

'We've got to talk—if not here, where?'

Stephanie's mind was a blank. She helplessly shook her head and at that second heard Robert's footsteps coming from the kitchen. Gerard heard them, too. He let go of her chin and straightened, pushing his hands into his pockets and taking on a casual air, as though they were having a polite chat: a little small talk between strangers met at a party.

'Come to the hotel,' he hissed so that only she would hear.

Stephanie's pallor increased. 'When?'

'Tomorrow morning, early. We'll have breakfast together.'

His smile made her bite her lower lip. 'I can't . . .'

The smile vanished; his mouth was hard and hostile. 'You'd better be there. Eight o'clock tomorrow morning.'

Before she could answer that, Robert came into sight. He looked surprised when he saw Gerard, but smiled cheerfully. 'Hallo. Did you leave the party for some air, too? It is stuffy in there.' He handed his sister the glass of water; he had dropped a few ice cubes in for good measure, they clinked against the glass as he put it into her hand. 'Here you are, Stevie; feeling any better?'

'Yes, thanks,' she managed huskily, but her brother's professional eye was moving over her and he was frowning.

'You certainly don't look it. I think perhaps I ought to take you home. You may be incubating something.'

The door behind them opened again and Euan came out; his eyes fixing on them in surprise. 'Oh, there you are, Stevie—what's wrong? Aren't you well?'

'She looks to me as if she's coming down with something,' Robert told him.

'I'm fine,' Stephanie insisted, standing up. Gerard took the glass from her and she gave him a quick, nervous glance, but his face was impassive now. He looked calmly sympathetic, indeed. He had accused her of being deceptive—he was more than that, he was a born actor. Nobody would guess that there was anything between them but a brief acquaintance.

'Maybe we shouldn't go on to the club,' said Euan to Robert.

They moved together, stepping slightly apart to have a professional debate, and Stephanie suddenly felt like laughing hysterically. Her emotions were completely out of key.

'The lasers might give her a headache,' agreed Robert, nodding.

'If she hasn't got one already,' Euan said, glancing at her. He came back, put a hand on her forehead. 'Any headache, Stevie?'

'No, I'm fine, of course I'll come on to the club—I don't want to ruin the party.' She had been looking forward to it all week; it wasn't often that they all went out in a group. It wasn't often that Euan had any time off for dancing. Their dates were often a snatched couple of hours at some ridiculous time of the day or evening: a meal somewhere or a cuddle in front of the television in her flat, or merely a walk along the sea front until Euan had to hurry back to the operating theatre to plunge back into work again.

'It seems a little unwise,' Gerard Tenniel murmured coolly.

The two doctors looked at him, professional hackles up. Euan said smilingly, 'I think my mother was asking where you'd got to, Gerard.' His tone said politely that Gerard and his opinions were unwanted.

His mouth crooked with sardonic amusement, Gerard strolled away. Robert stared after him.

'What does he do for a living?'

'Law,' said Euan tersely.

'Solicitor?'

'Barrister.'

Robert shrugged, dismissing Gerard Tenniel. The two men exchanged looks. Who did he think he was? A barrister giving his opinion on a purely medical matter? Typical! Outsiders were always dispensing crazy advice when they knew nothing about the subject. Stephanie knew their views inside out, she had heard them talking impatiently about the nutty ideas people got into their heads about medicine. No other profession was so beset by amateurs interfering in matters best left to the professionals, the trained men and women who knew what they were talking about. At least, that was how Euan and Robert saw it.

They looked back at her, eyes assessing, and she gave them a rueful smile. Now that Gerard was no longer around she felt a little better; her colour was not so deadly and her body was more at ease.

'She's looking better,' they agreed.

'A walk in the fresh air wouldn't do any harm,' Euan said, taking her hand. 'Come on, I prescribe a little exercise.' His eyes teased. 'Accompanied by your private physician!'

Stephanie laughed, letting him draw her towards the front door. 'Your mother will wonder where we are.'

'I'll cover for you,' promised Robert, grinning. 'I'll tell her Stephanie almost fainted and you're dealing with it.'

The night was crisp and cool; the moon laid a silvery wash over trees and houses, giving a magical air to everyday, familiar things. Everything was very still; not a branch moved, not a grass stirred. You could almost hear the sea—a distant murmur as if someone breathed softly across the flat fields.

Euan put his arm around her waist and she leaned on him, her head brushing his shoulder, as they walked, slowly, over the gravel paths and lawns.

He halted to look back at the house, his expression wryly affectionate. 'Crazy old house. I love it, you know. It's a monstrosity, but at least it isn't one of those ticky-tacky boxes we're always building today. They aren't meant to last, you know. They're built to fall down in a few years; cheap materials, run up as fast as possible. There's no pride in workmanship any more, no desire to make a house special or beautiful. That's one reason why I wouldn't go into the firm. Even if I hadn't been set on becoming a heart specialist I would have wanted to find another job. I didn't want anything to do with the sort of houses we were putting up all around Wyville.'

Stephanie watched his thin profile achingly. Euan was a good man, a little stern, at times, high-principled and serious about the things he felt mattered, but a man she respected and admired. He had turned his back on material success to become a doctor because of those high principles. How could she harbour a secret wish that Euan was not quite so serious-minded?

He looked down at her, smiling. 'You look very

sober. Still feeling faint?'

'No, I was thinking . . . when Elspeth has got married, there'll only be you and your mother in the house. Won't you feel like two peas rattling around a giant box?'

His eyes held warmth and amusement. 'My grandfather built this place to hold a big family,' he agreed. 'Stevie . . .' His hand caressed her cheek and she suddenly knew that he was about to propose.

She couldn't let him, not now. She walked on, talking lightly over her shoulder.

'Elspeth's new house isn't ticky-tacky, though, is it? She's obviously going to have a beautiful home. Johnny's a very good architect; I love the way he's designed the layout of the house.'

She had been waiting for Euan to propose for weeks. Everyone around them seemed to regard it as a settled thing, they were the butt of teasing jokes among their friends and it was true that they had something special—a warmth and sympathy which was even more important than the strong physical attraction they had felt from the beginning. Euan wasn't the type to rush into anything, though. He had taken his time to think it out, and Stephanie had approved of that. Marriage was a serious matter; she didn't want to rush into it either. At the same time, she had expected Euan to say something soon, and now she must not let him.

Gerard Tenniel's arrival on the scene had changed everything, wrecked the settled happiness of her life over the past year or so. It had taken her years to get over what had happened, but now that she had, Gerard had crashed into her life again, bringing back all the bad memories.

When Euan heard about what happened five years ago, how would he look at her? Gerard would paint a very black picture. Even if Euan listened to her side of the story, how could he ever feel the same about her again? What he had just said about his house applied equally to his pride in his family name. The Camerons were still the most important people in this little town, not only because of their wealth, but because of their enormous impact in community life over the past century. Cameron money had built the hospital, equipped new wards, helped to finance the construction of a new church. Mrs Cameron was a justice of the peace, as well as employing a large workforce from the town. Euan's work at the hospital was a source of great pride locally: they saw him as their own doctor, born and bred here but with a reputation as a surgeon which was becoming far more widespread. Euan was a brilliant heart surgeon.

Scandal had never touched their name. How could she bear to be the first to bring scandal to the Cameron family? She should have realised from the beginning that this might happen one day. She had thought that by burying herself here in this little backwater she could bury the past, too, but sooner or later every stone is turned, every secret uncovered.

If she had told Euan the truth at the beginning they might have had a chance; if he believed her side of the story. But she hadn't dared risk it. She had been afraid that he wouldn't want to see her again, even if he had believed her. It wasn't just Euan she had to convince, of course. There was his mother. Mrs Cameron would be deeply shocked, horrified, even if she heard the slightest hint of scandal attached to Stephanie's name. Anyone who joined the Cameron family had to be above suspicion, like Caesar's wife.

Euan caught up with her just before they reached the door. He framed her flushed face with his hands and smiled at her, kissing her nose. 'Shy, darling? Don't be. I won't insist on an answer yet. Think about it. I reckon we make a great team.'

She managed a smile; it wasn't easy, but it seemed to convince Euan.

'That's better,' he murmured, kissing her lips, and then they went back into the house, walking straight into Gerard Tenniel who was in the hall, shrugging into his smooth, black cashmere overcoat.

'Going already?' asked Euan, surprised.

The grey eyes held an ironic gleam. 'I have to get up early tomorrow morning. I have an important appointment.'

Stephanie felt her cheeks burn and his smile mocked her, reminded her, warned her not to forget to keep that appointment.

'Oh, this wasn't just a pleasure trip, then? You have business in the town? Legal business, I suppose—I hadn't heard of any exciting legal developments in Wyville.'

'This is . . .' Gerard paused, his face bland, then said, 'more personal than legal.'

Euan laughed. 'Sorry I asked. Then you mustn't keep the lady waiting, must you?'

'I hope she won't keep me waiting,' drawled Gerard. As he turned to go his eyes flickered over Stephanie's face, hardening. Then he was gone and the anxious fire inside her died down, leaving her in a state of weary misery. Robert and Euan noticed; they insisted that she must go home to bed. They went on to the Laserlight club without her to meet Gwen. All the

younger people at the party went in a big group to
dance and drink for several hours; it was the latest 'in'
place in Wyville. Stephanie was relieved not to have to
endure the chatter and brash music, the darkness split
by sudden violent colours as the laser lights cut
through the room. She wouldn't have enjoyed it
tonight; she needed to be alone to think. She went to
bed and lay in the dark, her mind pursuing the past
and wondering what Gerard Tenniel was going to say
to her tomorrow.

She had to go; there was no escape. He knew that;
his eyes had stressed the weakness of her own position.
He had the whip hand and he would use it ruthlessly if
she didn't fall into line.

But why did he want to talk to her? What was there
to talk about? She stared at the ceiling, watching the
moon make delicate lace patterns on the plaster. From
time to time the headlights of a car cut across the
room, making her blink. Robert and Gwen would be
home soon; it was nearly one o'clock. They never
stayed out too late. Their lives were too dedicated. So
was Euan's; he was totally devoted to his career, to his
patients.

She had been living in a fool's paradise, imagining
that she could ever marry Euan. Her background
made that impossible. Why hadn't she seen that? Why
hadn't Robert said something? He must have known;
it must have dawned on him that if anything ever
came out about what had happened five years ago
there would be a scandal which would make life
unlivable for her here.

She closed her eyes and tried to sleep. She had to get
up at first light and drive back to the hotel. She would
try to slip in without being noticed. Nobody must see

her going up to Gerard Tenniel's room.

She heard her brother and his wife drive up, the quiet sound of their front door closing. At least she wouldn't have to sneak out tomorrow past their door, she had her own exit. They would sleep late, they wouldn't hear her. If only she could get to sleep! She was going to be exhausted in the morning.

Perhaps Gerard Tenniel wanted to find out if she was genuinely in love with Euan. Perhaps if he believed she was, he wouldn't tell them anything.

She mustn't harbour wild hopes; he was capable of utter ruthlessness. She turned over, thumping her pillow. She wouldn't think about him any more: tomorrow would come soon enough and she would find out then what was in that tortuous mind of his.

She woke up in the morning with a shuddering start when her alarm went off at six-thirty. For a few seconds she was dazed; wondering why her head banged like a tin drum. Then she remembered and swung out of bed, staggering a little as she went to the bathroom.

She had thought out a plan last night, a way of appearing at the hotel at that early hour without arousing too much surprise.

She showered and combed her hair and dressed in her pastel-pink tracksuit. If she turned up at the hotel saying she had been jogging and wanted to shower and change before she went home her excuse might be accepted.

She let herself out of the house very quietly and drove away, parking on the deserted sea front. She jogged for ten minutes until she felt herself beginning to perspire, then began to run towards the hotel.

The night staff looked up as she came into the

reception lobby. 'Hallo, Stevie—don't tell me you've been up all night?' asked the night desk clerk, grinning at her, then he let his eyes move over her tracksuit. 'You must have energy to burn! I thought you went to a party last night?'

'I did but I had a headache and I thought a little fresh air might clear my head.' She leaned on the desk, breathing heavily. 'Mind if I have a shower and change before I drive home? I'll use one of the bathrooms upstairs, I don't suppose any of the guests will be stirring.' She had brought along a small zip-topped bag in which she had put a change of clothes; she waved it at the night clerk. 'Okay by you?'

'Be my guest,' he laughed and watched her walk unsteadily over to the lift. 'You poor dear, you're hardly able to move a muscle. Want me to come and scrub your back for you?'

Stephanie pretended to laugh as she stepped into the waiting lift. Alone and unseen, her face lapsed into lines of anxiety. She had got over hurdle number one. While she was idly chatting to the desk clerk she had been able to run her eye over the guest book to check which room they had given Gerard Tenniel. Now all she had to do was get inside his room without being seen.

She left the lift at his floor and hovered, glancing around to make sure the coast was clear, then walked quickly to his door and tapped softly.

There was a pause during which Stephanie was on tenterhooks in case someone came out of one of the other rooms, or a member of the staff came up with a breakfast tray for a guest. She was so nervous that when the door did open she hurried into the room without looking at Gerard. Only when he closed the door and leant on it, watching her ironically, did she look round at him.

Her first glimpse was a shock. He wasn't dressed. He was only wearing a short white towelling robe beneath which he was obviously naked. He looked as if he had just had a bath, his blond hair damp, darkened by water, clinging to his scalp, emphasising the razor-edged lines of his face. Stephanie's nervous eyes ran over him and up to his face again.

'Please say what you have to say quickly. I have to get back before I'm missed,' she said flatly.

'What did you tell your family?' Gerard observed her speculatively. 'That you were going out jogging?' His mouth twisted. 'You're good at telling lies.'

Heat burned in her face. 'I didn't tell them anything. I have a flat of my own. I didn't need to explain where I was going, they aren't up yet.'

'Last night I gathered that you lived with your brother and his wife.'

'My flat is over their garage.'

He nodded coolly. 'I see. And your parents? Where are they now?'

She looked away. 'My father died a year ago. My mother is still in Australia, she liked it there, and my sister and her family are nearby, so . . .' She broke off, sighing. 'Can we get to the point? I want to get this over with.'

He turned his head towards the door, his eyes alert. 'That must be Room Service bringing my breakfast. You'd better go into the bathroom, unless of course you don't mind the waiter seeing you here?'

She hated him; hated the mockery and sarcasm in his voice, the way the grey eyes watched her stiffen and understood her alarm. Did it give him pleasure to torture her, play with her like a cat with a mouse?

She could hear the rattle of crockery on the table which the waiter was wheeling along the corridor now. Silently she walked across the room and bolted herself into the bathroom. While she was in here she might as well shower again and dress. She had to keep up the pretence that that was why she was here—she could hardly leave the hotel still wearing her tracksuit.

She stripped off, hearing the tap on the door. 'Room Service, sir! Your breakfast.'

Stephanie ran the shower and stepped under it; tensing as the cool needles of water touched her hot skin. She couldn't hear voices in the room beyond while the water was running. It was a rapid shower, then she stepped out again and began to towel herself angrily. She had brought a neat grey skirt and blue blouse in her bag; she hurriedly dressed in them and spent two minutes combing her hair, putting on a pink lipstick and powdering her nose.

'Are you staying in there all day?' Gerard's voice enquired drily on the other side of the door.

Stephanie unbolted it and pulled it open. He surveyed her with a faint curiosity, his pale brows lifting.

'That was quick.' His gaze sauntered down over her from her head to her feet. 'Very demure.'

She walked past him, ignoring the trace of acid in his tone. The breakfast table had been set up near the window, which had been opened, so that sunshine flooded in and a faint spring breeze brought the salt smell and soft whispering of the sea. It was an idyllic scene: the table was covered with white damask, a yellow rose in a small glass vase standing among the covered dishes and coffee-pots.

'I ordered breakfast for two,' Gerard told her as she stared at the table. 'Room Service were discreetly curious as this is a single suite, but they were far too well-mannered to query it. I took the liberty of ordering a continental breakfast for you: orange juice, croissants and coffee. I hope that was a good guess.'

'I'm not hungry, thanks.'

'After all that jogging?' he mocked. 'Of course you are. Sit down.'

'No, thank you.'

He came up behind her, his hands grasping her slender shoulders, and forced her down into a chair as if she was a child.

Before she could get up again he leaned over and placed the glass of orange juice in front of her. 'Coffee?' He picked up the heavy silver pot and poured some coffee into her cup. 'Cream? No, you still drink it black? No sugar, either, I seem to remember.'

Her agonised eyes shot up to his face and he smiled tightly. 'I have a very good memory. I never forget an important detail, a vital part of my professional training.'

There was no point in pleading with him, begging him to get this over with, deliver his blow and let her stumble away. He would play this his way and her plea would merely increase his enjoyment of having her at his mercy. He never forgot—and he never forgave. She hadn't known him very long, five years ago, but she had learnt that much about him. Gerard Tenniel was a hard man.

With a shaky hand she picked up her glass of orange juice which was served, as the hotel always served it, embedded in a silver goblet of crushed ice, the way their chef had learnt to serve orange juice when he worked in America for some years. The hotel was very lucky to have Joe; he was an excellent head chef and could have got a job in any of the luxury London hotels, but had chosen to come back to Wyville to be near his ageing mother who refused to move from her home of many years.

'You've changed,' Gerard observed thoughtfully as he sat down opposite her and took the cover off his own orange juice. 'Five years is a long time, of course, and you were only eighteen, weren't you?'

Stephanie's blue eyes stayed on his hard-boned face. He said that so coolly, but had he ever stopped to consider what he was saying? She had been eighteen, still half a child. Far too young to know how to cope with the nightmare situation which suddenly exploded around her.

'I've often wondered what became of you. I knew you'd left Australia, but I had no idea you had come to Wyville. An odd coincidence. If my mother hadn't had a letter from Margo Cameron I'd never have found out where you were.' Gerard had sipped some of his juice; now he took the cover off a dish of scrambled egg and tomatoes and began to eat them with a fork.

Stephanie found it hard to swallow. She pushed her own juice to one side and took a croissant and broke it into little pieces. It gave her trembling fingers something to do. Gerard's eyes lifted, observed what she was doing, his mouth twisting.

'Eat something. You look as if you need the blood sugar.'

'You may be enjoying this, but I'm not,' she broke out, her voice hoarse. 'Please Mr Tenniel . . .'

'Mr Tenniel?' he repeated with barbed irony. 'You used to call me Gerard.'

Her pallor became a scalding rush of hot blood and she looked down again. She heard him laugh and felt like throwing her cup of coffee at him. How could he sit there, calmly eating scrambled egg, buttering toast, drinking coffee, while she waited like a convicted criminal to hear her sentence?

'Or don't you remember that?' he mocked.

She didn't even bother to answer. There was no point—it had been a purely rhetorical question, he knew she hadn't forgotten him or their brief relationship before the nightmare started. All this was part of his deliberate torture; he had learnt this slow needling technique years ago when he was training for the bar, no doubt. It worked with witnesses who had something to hide; he was a very successful barrister now. She had occasionally seen his name in newspaper reports of cases and had known that he was back in England—but then at the time he had told her that he was only in Australia for a year on a sabbatical course to study the Australian legal system. She had realised that he would come back to England, too, but he was an ambitious man and a clever lawyer and she had guessed that he would aim for London and get a place in a good chambers there. Their paths had been very unlikely to cross. She had felt safe here in Wyville; it was such a tranquil backwater. She had blithely imagined that Gerard Tenniel could have no connections there, but she had been wrong.

He had finished his breakfast and was leaning back in his chair with his second cup of coffee, studying her with narrowed eyes.

She sat up, too, tensed for the attack, her hands clenched in her lap. She hadn't eaten a thing and had only had a few sips of orange juice. Her coffee was cold; she couldn't bring herself to drink any of it.

Gerard smiled and said calmly, 'Euan doesn't know, does he?'

She didn't answer even then. Anything she said would be used against her.

'And when I tell him, he won't want to know you,' Gerard added, after waiting to see how she would react.

'And you *are* going to tell him!' Stephanie muttered harshly. 'I'm surprised you waited. Why not tell him last night? But then you couldn't have had the fun of playing cat and mouse with me if you had, could you? You didn't want to miss out on that. It's made your day, hasn't it, sitting here laughing at me, sticking your poisoned needles into me, making me wait and suffer, when all the time you knew you were going to tell Euan anyway. I should never have come, I shouldn't have let you put me through this.'

He was staring at her, his face taut, his mouth a straight line. She would never have spoken to him like that five years ago, she had been too shy, too awed by him. Every time he turned those mocking grey eyes on her she had blushed and felt dizzy. She had thought she was in love, but she had been too young to know what love was or she would have realised that Gerard Tenniel was only amusing himself by flirting with her. His eyes had smiled, then, though; they had almost had a tenderness in them. Now they were sharp, cold flint.

'But you did come,' he said through those tight, contemptuous lips, the words a mere thread of sound holding a faint question.

Stephanie answered the question he hadn't asked. 'Not for myself, I didn't come here to plead for myself—I can't stop you telling Euan and his mother, and you're probably right, that will be the end of everything between us then. Euan wouldn't want a wife who'd been mixed up in anything like a murder trial. But none of that matters as much as what this would do to my brother, to Robert. He's a doctor, at the hospital, and it would ruin his life here, wreck his reputation—he might be asked to leave and he likes it here, he'll be shattered if that happens.' She got up, her hands gripping the back of the chair, her face set and white. 'You can't do that to him. I'll go away. I won't marry Euan, I'll never see him again, but please . . . please, promise me you won't tell the Camerons, or anyone here in Wyville.'

CHAPTER THREE

GERARD TENNIEL considered her, one long-fingered hand tapping idly on the edge of his chair. Stephanie waited, hardly breathing, for his answer. Surely he couldn't refuse her? If he went ahead and broke this story it would be so cruelly unfair to Robert and Gwen. He might hate her, but he had no grudge against her brother.

'You say you wouldn't marry Cameron, you'd leave town and not come back?'

She nodded, a heaviness oppressing her at the very prospect.

'How do I know you'd keep your word?' His smile iced her blood; it held such cynicism and contempt. 'We both know what a liar you are—and a cheat. What if you waited a few weeks until I was out of the way and then came back and took up with Cameron again?'

'I wouldn't do that!'

'How do I know that? He's loaded, isn't he? A very eligible bachelor who could give you everything that greedy little mind of yours has always been after.'

She flinched. 'That isn't true! I'm not like that; you have no right to say such things. I'm not interested in Euan's money, I like him for himself.'

He laughed in derision. 'Do you expect me to believe that? You were always interested in money. Why else did you encourage Burgess? A man twice your age, going bald, with the personality of a white

45

rabbit—but he had money, didn't he? He had position, status, a beautiful house, even a yacht. What did it matter to you that he was forty years old to your eighteen? Or that he had a wife already?'

Stephanie's head drooped on that long, slim neck, the sun picking out streaks of gold among the dark brown hair, gilt tips on the thick lashes clustering on her cheek. The man seated at the table watched her, his mouth reined tightly, a slight tic beating beside it, as though he was not quite as in control of himself as he wanted her to believe. The grey eyes blazed with some emotion; rage or distaste, perhaps, or something in which those feelings mingled.

'I can't argue with you, you wouldn't listen to me, just as nobody would at the time, nobody believed me, but I'd done nothing to encourage Theo Burgess. Nothing. I was sorry for him, that was all. It wasn't my fault if . . .'

'You can save your breath. I don't want to hear a speech for the defence from you. We'll take it that you would like me to think you were innocent, but whether you were or not, I know one thing for certain—Margo Cameron wouldn't want you married to her son, part of the family.' Gerard got up slowly, his long, powerful body moving without haste towards her. 'I'll also admit that I have no wish to wreck your brother's life. I imagine he went through enough five years ago. He was still a medical student then, wasn't he? I seem to remember you telling me that he was in his last year at one of the London teaching hospitals.'

Stephanie nodded wearily. His memory was perfect, he had forgotten nothing.

'It must have been tough on him, having to take his final exams just when his sister was involved in a public scandal. I wouldn't want to drag it all up again, but on the other hand, Margo Cameron is my godmother. I couldn't keep silent and let you go ahead and marry her son. She would never forgive me.'

'I've said I'll go away, what more do you want?' she burst out bitterly, her eyes lifting and watching him with bitter hostility. 'Oh, why did you have to come here? I was happy again. I thought I'd forgotten it all, put it behind me, and then you turn up and . . .'

She dropped her head into her hands to hide the tears helplessly welling up in her blue eyes. She wouldn't cry in front of him. He wasn't going to have the pleasure of seeing her break down. Five years ago she had stood in a witness box giving evidence, while from the well of the court Gerard's savage eyes watched her—hated her. It was like being watched from hiding by some wild animal tracking you to pull you down and tear you to pieces.

She had been stricken when she heard that the firm he was attached to for a year had taken Viola's case; she knew it meant that Gerard would be in court. She hadn't seen him throughout the long months before the case was finally given a date for a hearing. It had been nerve-racking enough to face the trial itself; having to face Gerard too made it so much worse.

She had made mistakes, stammered, tried desperately to avoid meeting his eyes. She must have looked the picture of guilt; the evidence was so damning. She hadn't expected that Gerard would stare at her with such crushing contempt, though. She had had to fight for self-control during the hours when she was in the box; first giving her evidence, then under cross-examination followed by a re-examination by the prosecution lawyer who was intent on trying to underline the points in her story which the defence lawyers had tried to destroy. All the time Gerard had watched her from the defence bench with a bitter hostility, and that had been the part of her ordeal which was least tolerable.

She rubbed a hand over her wet eyes. She hadn't broken down in front of him then; she wouldn't now.

He was closer than she had expected; standing right beside her, his face harsh. 'Tears won't work with me, Stephanie.'

'I'm not crying,' she said huskily.

He put out a hand; his finger touched her wet lashes, brushing over them, making her jump. Incredulously, she saw him lick his finger, tasting her tears.

'Real tears,' he said tersely, as she stared, shocked by the strangeness of the little action.

'Are you glad about that?' she asked, close to hysteria. 'Did you want to make me cry? I'm sorry I didn't weep buckets for you. Maybe if you hit me I might—you haven't tried that yet. You've insulted me, threatened me, talked to me as if I was below contempt—what comes next? What do you want to do to me?'

'Don't tempt me,' he said, and with disbelief she saw him laugh; a humourless laughter, low and harsh. 'I thought you were such a little innocent; eighteen, never been kissed, big blue eyes like a baby, skin like a peach—God, I thought you were beautiful, and so sweet. I hardly dared touch you with a finger in case you went into panic or in case I lost my head and went out of control, because I wanted you, Stephanie, I wanted you like hell, but I wouldn't risk scaring you and so I made myself hold off, treat you carefully, when all the time you were letting that bald old man . . .'

His voice broke off in a guttural snarl. 'God! You made a fool of me!' The grey eyes swept over her, the hard mouth taut.

Stephanie was whiter than ever, her blue eyes very dark and enormous with shock and emotion. She put out a hand to him, her mouth trembling.

'Gerard, if you liked me then, don't do this to me now. Don't hurt my brother through me! I'll do anything not to hurt him.'

He took her hand, held it. Stared down at it oddly, as if he had never seen a hand before, turning it palm upwards as if he might be going to read her lifeline, her future, predict what else lay in store for her.

'Is this a proposition,' he asked in a low, husky voice.

Stiffening, she tried to pull her hand free, but he would not release it. He slid his fingers underneath hers, still holding her firmly, his eyes still fixed on her palm.

'I might be prepared to do a deal,' he murmured, and she gave a gasp of shock.

'What . . . what are you talking about?'

'You know what I'm talking about.' He slowly bent his head and Stephanie shivered with a terrifying mixture of excitement and horror; her mouth went dry, her skin turned icy and then burned.

Gerard's mouth touched her palm and and her eyes closed; she swayed, shuddering. It was the strangest kiss she had ever had in her life: his lips had a strangely deep heat, and suddenly she remembered a moment five years when they were dancing together at a party at the Burgesses' house and Gerard had taken her out into the garden to show her the Australian moon, copper-coloured, rising through mists in that echoing vault of a sky. There had been music from the house and a constant noise of insects, cicadas or crickets. It had been so hot; she had fanned herself with a fern branch and listened while he pointed out the stars, naming them. She had been breathless, enthralled, watching his handsome profile and that silken blond head, her heart beating so fast it made her giddy. And then Gerard had looked down at her and smiled, and he had kissed her hand the way he was doing now: slowly, with intense passion and a sensuality that turned her knees to water.

He lifted his head and their eyes met, and she came back to this moment, to the present—and the bitter knowledge that the way he had just kissed her hand had not been the same at all. Just now there had been an insulting quality to that kiss, something that had not been present that first time.

'I'll hold my tongue, Stephanie,' he said softly, watching her. 'On one condition.'

She didn't move, didn't ask what he meant—his grey eyes were eloquent enough, she knew what he was going to say before he said it, and her whole body went rigid with denial, with refusal, with hatred.

'I still want you,' he said, smiling.

Stephanie had never thought that a smile could hurt so much. He used it like a poniard, stabbing her, watching intently to see her bleed.

'Perhaps even more now,' he added, enjoying her helpless rejection, the look in the blue eyes. 'Ironic, really—I'd put you on a pedestal, I was just at the age when a very young, very innocent girl could get to me, really get to me. I wanted to strew rose-petals for you to walk on; I was head over heels in romantic dreams about you. My last madness, I suppose. I was thirty-two and I'd had all the fun of finding out about women; all that was over and I was thinking of settling down, getting married. When I was in my teens I chased the glamorous types: experienced women much older than myself. Most boys of eighteen are turned on by women who know what sex is all about, and I was no exception. I didn't even bother to look at girls of my own age; they bored me stiff. Innocence was something I wanted to shed as fast as I could. But by the time I'd met you I'd gone full circle. I was sick of women who were ready to jump into bed at one word from a man. I knew I would only marry a girl who'd never known any other man.'

'My God ...' Stephanie was still trembling, but anger was burning up inside her. 'Talk about double standards, you're a hypocrite, a total hypocrite—one law for you, another for women, is that it?'

He smiled drily. 'That's it. Maybe it is a double standard. It was what I felt then—I wanted ...' He broke off, his teeth biting down on his lower lip, and was silent for almost a minute, staring at her.

'Well, never mind. I've told you the deal I'm offering. It's up to you to decide whether to come away with me and leave your brother to carry on with his life here in peace—or to stay and take the consequences.'

She turned and walked away shakily towards the window. The town was coming to life; the sun glittered on the pale waves she could see between the buildings along the sea front. There was far more traffic now. She would have to leave soon or Robert and Gwen would wonder what on earth had happened to her, and she was in no state to face their questions.

She leaned on the windowsill, grateful for the support. 'You know this is blackmail, don't you?' she accused.

'Call it what you like, but make up your mind before tomorrow. Whatever happens, you won't be marrying Euan Cameron, get that through your head.' Gerard paused and she felt his eyes fixed on her back; they burned through the thin material of her blouse like a red-hot laser.

'Are you in love with him?' The grate of his voice made her nerves jangle.

'That's no business of yours!' she snapped, and for a moment there was silence in the room. A seagull flew past the window, sunlight striking the underside of the spread white wings, turning them to magical molten gold so that the bird had a new beauty. On any other day Stephanie would have been entranced by that; her spirits lifted, her mind illuminated by that glimpse of fleeting beauty. Today her eye dully followed the gull's flight while she tried to think.

What was she to do? Gerard was offering her a choice between her own happiness and Robert's, or was it even that simple? She wasn't going to be happy whatever choice she made. He was right about that. Euan wouldn't marry her now. She couldn't marry him even if he swore he didn't care about the scandal attached to her. Gerard Tenniel's arrival had made that much crystal clear to her. She should have known it without needing him to point it out, but she had been kidding herself, allowing herself to dream impossible dreams.

She would have to go away. How could she explain to Euan that she suddenly did not want to see him any more? Everyone expected them to get married; they were too close to make an abrupt separation possible without some explanation. Even if she tried to break off with him, Euan wouldn't let it go at that. He would demand to know what was behind her change of heart and he wasn't the type to be convinced by some glib fabrication. He was too shrewd, too tough-minded. No, she would have to leave town without a word. Euan would be hurt, he would try to find her. Robert would be baffled and upset too. All her friends would be stunned.

She would have to go, but she certainly wasn't leaving with Gerard. Did he really think that she would let herself be blackmailed into bed with him? She closed her eyes, sickness clawing at her. The very idea of giving herself to him, knowing he despised her, knowing that the price of his silence had been her body, made her feel unclean.

She turned slowly, her mind made up. 'I have until tomorrow, then?' she asked in a remote, cold voice.

He was watching her with narrowed eyes, the sunlight falling on his beautifully sculpted face. She remembered so vividly how his bone structure ran: the high, austere cheekbones and the strength of jaw and temples. She had often stared at him and been struck dumb with wonder by that combination of fair hair and lean vitality.

'What's going on inside that head, I wonder?' he asked, rubbing one thumb along his jaw, his expression thoughtful. 'I hope you aren't planning anything I wouldn't like. I wouldn't advise you to try skipping town without telling me.' His quick eyes caught the flicker of apprehension in her face and he gave a silky little sound. 'Aha! I see you were planning just that.' His smile was menacing. 'It wouldn't do you any good,

Stephanie. I'd feel that you'd broken our agreement and I'd be forced to tell the Camerons everything.'

'You really are a bastard, aren't you?' she whispered.

'I mean what I say—if that's being a bastard. We have a deal or we don't. If you don't keep your side of the bargain, why should I keep mine?'

'I don't see what you'll get out of this—I'll hate you, can't you see that?' she burst out, and he moved towards her, smiling.

'How do you think I felt about you five years ago when I discovered that the blue-eyed innocent I'd been treating with such reverence was just a little whore?'

The last word didn't quite leave his lips. In the middle of it she hit him; so hard that his head snapped back and a dark red stain came up in his cheek.

Only as she saw the livid flash of his eyes did she realise what she had done. Her palm stung, she watched him with fear, thinking for a moment that he was going to hit her back. The violence between them had a tangible quality; the air burned with it.

Then he swung away, his back to her, as if he couldn't trust himself if he faced her. She sensed that he was fighting to get control of himself; it was a minute before he turned round again and by then the dark stain on his cheek was beginning to fade.

The look in his eyes made her shrink. 'You shouldn't have done that, Stephanie,' he said very softly. 'I won't forget it.'

She hurriedly moved to the door, picking up her bag, in which she had stuffed her tracksuit and running shoes.

'I must go or Robert and Gwen will wonder ...'

'You have a car, don't you?'

She nodded, her hand on the door.

'Good. I came by train because I wanted to be certain of getting here early enough for the party and driving would have taken too long. We can use your car to go back to London, though.'

'My car? But . . .'

'Be here at nine tomorrow,' he interrupted, ignoring her angry protest.

She made one last attempt to make him be reasonable. 'You can't be serious about this. You can't mean it. It's crazy!'

He laughed. 'Crazy? Yes, perhaps. But I mean it, Stephanie, don't think for one second that I don't.'

She ran a shaky hand over her face, rubbing her eyes, as though she thought she was having a bad dream and would wake up any minute.

'Look, be reasonable, Gerard—I understand why you can't let me marry Euan. I was stupid to think I could; I don't want to hurt the Camerons by involving them in an old scandal. But to blackmail me like this! How can you do it? *Why* are you doing it?'

The grey eyes glittered, she saw his nostrils flare. 'You aren't that naïve!' He ran a finger lightly down her throat and she flinched as though he had hit her. 'Let's say I have an old obsession to satisfy—or an unpaid bill to collect. You used me ruthlessly as cover for your affair with Burgess . . .'

'No, that isn't true!'

He ignored her outcry. 'And in my turn I'm using you. That's fair, isn't it?'

Stephanie closed her eyes briefly, then gave a deep, painful sigh. He was crazy. He was out of his mind. But she was in his power and there was nothing she could do about it without hurting people she loved.

'I can't just walk out at a moment's notice, though. What about my job?'

'With unemployment as high as I gather it is here, they won't have any problem in getting a replacement at once.'

She tried another argument desperately. 'But my brother—what shall I tell him? You aren't thinking straight, Gerard. People don't pack up and leave home without a good reason. My brother is my landlord, too. What about my flat? All my things here? Robert is bound to ask questions, want to know where I'm going and why?'

'You'll think of something.' His smile was cynical, mocking. 'You're very inventive.'

'Damn you!' she whispered, staring at him. Why was he smiling as though she had paid him a compliment?

'Tell him you've fallen madly in love with me and we're going to live together,' he suggested, and she flushed darkly.

'He wouldn't believe me; he knows I'm not the type.'

'He obviously doesn't know you very well. Or does he know you better than I think? Tell him I'm rich and can give you the earth. That will convince him.'

She sighed wearily. 'Gerard, listen . . .' She put a hand on his arm and he glanced down at it, lids hooded. 'Gerard, tell me the truth—are you playing games with me? Is this some sort of prolonged teasing? Five years is such a long time. You can't have carried a grudge against me all those years. My God, I'd almost forgotten your name!'

She shouldn't have said that. The grey eyes held a

seething violence; his mouth hardened and tensed.

'Then you'll never forget it again! You have just one choice—so I'd advise you to be here precisely at nine o'clock tomorrow.'

He pulled open the door and she slowly walked out of the room, turning with another cry of protest: 'Gerard, I . . .'

He shut the door on her and she stared dumbly at the polished wooden panels. This could not be happening. He couldn't mean it. He was a barrister, for heaven's sake; he lived by the law, he understood it. He was supposed to uphold it. Yet he was cold-bloodedly blackmailing her into giving herself to him to buy his silence.

What if she went to the police? He would end up in prison. She began to walk slowly along the carpeted corridor towards the lifts.

He wouldn't, of course. What evidence did she have? Would the police believe her story? She was the one who had been mixed up in an unsavoury court case five years ago. If the police investigated her background they would soon uncover the details of the murder trial; the accusations against her, the reputation she had acquired during that trial.

Gerard was a well known, very successful, very respectable barrister.

Which of them would the police believe? If she did attempt to tell her story all she would achieve was that her secret would be known to the whole town, Robert would have to give up his job and move, Euan and his family would find themselves engulfed by scandal and she would carry the blame for all that.

When Stephanie emerged from the ground floor she was lucky enough to be swept out of the hotel in a tide of guests heading for a waiting coach. The desk clerk was too busy to notice her. She walked along the sea front to her car, staring at the sunlit tide pouring on to the sand. It was going to be a fine day; the sky was blue and the waves reflected that deep colour.

What in heaven's name was she going to tell Robert and Gwen? She couldn't discuss it with them face to face—she simply couldn't lie and then have to answer questions ... and there *would* be startled, worried questions!

It took her ten minutes to drive back and to her relief she realised that her brother and his wife weren't yet up. Their bedroom curtains were still closed. They would be sleeping late after last night.

Stephanie slipped into her own flat and sat down to think the problem out, but she could see no way round it. She would have to write Robert and Gwen a letter. Gerard was right—the only thing she could do was tell her brother that she had fallen in love and was going away with Gerard. Euan was going to be badly hurt. Her eyes clouded with tears. What on earth would he think of her? But however low his opinion after reading her letter, he would have thought far worse if he ever heard about the Burgess case and her involvement in it.

Was that going to overshadow her whole life? She had only just left school when her parents decided to take her out to Australia with them to visit her married sister who had been living there for four years. Stephanie had been over the moon. She hadn't been further than France until then and suddenly she was flying right the way round the world, stopping off at exotic and exciting places whose very names were like a string of flashing stones: Singapore, Bali,

Bangkok, Hong Kong. It was the trip of a lifetime and her parents knew it would never be repeated. They meant to stay in Australia for at least a year, possibly longer, but as they were on that side of the world it seemed silly to miss the chance of visiting other places which had only been names on a map until they had the opportunity of spending a few days at each.

Their travel agent had worked out a travelling schedule and booked hotels and flights. The Stuarts planned the trip for months ahead, arguing over where to stop off, how long to spend at each place. They couldn't leave until Stephanie had finished her summer exams and was free to go with them. Robert was going to be working through the summer; he had a temporary job in a holiday camp. He no longer lived at home by then: he had digs in a hostel near his London hospital, so the Stuarts didn't have to worry about him.

It wasn't until they finally reached Australia that it dawned on them that Stephanie's presence would create a problem for their daughter and son-in-law. Andrea was delighted to see her sister, who had been a little girl the last time they met, but her bungalow only had three bedrooms. She and her husband shared one with their youngest, the baby, Benny; the second room was fully occupied by Andrea's three-year-old twin girls, Ann and Philippa, and the third room was earmarked for the Stuart parents.

'You don't mind sleeping on the couch in the living-room, do you, Stevie?' Andrea asked uncertainly and, of course, Stephanie said she'd be perfectly comfortable doing that, but she could see that in the constricted space of the bungalow, which had only one big room apart from the three small bedrooms, it made life awkward for her sister to have her using the couch as a bed. Phil had to get up at the crack of dawn to go to work. If he forgot something he needed, left it in the living-room the night before, he had to tiptoe through the darkened room, stumbling over chairs, in search of whatever he wanted.

Stephanie didn't say anything to her parents; she simply made up her mind that she must get a job and somewhere else to live. She couldn't occupy the couch in the living-room for a whole year, but if she said she wanted to go back to England, her parents would feel they had to come too. They wouldn't like the idea of her living alone on the other side of the world from them.

She began reading the small ads in papers and almost at once found what she wanted—a job as a mother's help on a farm in Queensland, only fifty miles from Andrea's home. She would have her own room and full board and be earning a real salary for the firt time in her life. She showed it to her parents, who agreed that she could apply, and a few days later her brother-in-law drove her to the Burgess house for an interview with Mrs Burgess.

Stephanie had liked her at first. It was hard to believe that now, but she had soon come to realise that Mrs Burgess could put on an act which deceived almost everyone she met. She wasn't so much two-faced as a dual personality.

Stephanie was shown around the beautiful, luxuriously furnished house and grounds which stretched further than you could see from the upper-storey windows. She was bowled over by the beauty of the place. Mrs Burgess was delighted by the wide-eyed amazement, and she offered Stephanie the job.

There were two Burgess children, five-year-old Matt and seven-year-old Elnora. Even at that first meeting, Stephanie sensed something odd about them. They were quiet and well behaved, but seemed very nervous, especially with their mother. Stephanie had been naïve enough to decide that Mrs Burgess must be very strict with them.

On that first visit she did not meet Theo Burgess; his wife had said that he was away on business. She had made it clear that her husband was a wealthy man: he owned several large farms and a canning factory, and was a prominent member of local society.

Mrs Burgess was a very beautiful woman: in her late twenties, she managed to look far younger, her skin smooth and suntanned, her eyes the colour of jade, a cool green, her hair blonde and bleached almost white by hours of sunbathing every day. She dressed with flair; it was obvious that her husband gave her anything she wanted, for her slim wrists were loaded with bracelets, her fingers with rings that flashed as she talked.

Even at that first meeting, though, there were reservations in Stephanie's mind about her. Even Phil had commented, as he drove her back to his home, 'Did you ever see so much expensive junk on a woman? I'm surprised she could walk with all those stones weighing her down!'

'She was wearing a lot of jewellery,' Stephanie agreed doubtfully.

'A lot? Honey, she jingled with it! A lot of money and no taste. Well, who cares? So long as she treats you right she can wear the Taj Mahal on her head as far as I'm concerned.' He had grinned round at her, white teeth gleaming. Phil was an Australian of two

generations, although he was descended from English
settlers. It was while he was back in England in search
of his ancestors that he had met Andrea and fallen in
love. Andrea still had to be careful how much time she
spent in the sun at one time, but Phil soaked it up, his
skin had inherited tan from the day he was born,
Stephanie suspected. He had been brown and glowing
even in London after weeks away from his native
land.

'Are you sure you'll be okay there?' Andrea had
asked her that evening, looking anxious. 'Fifty miles
isn't far out here, but it may seem like it to you at first.
But if you need us, just pick up that phone and we'll
come and get you.'

Stephanie had been slightly nervous, of course, but
on her first day at Sweetwater she had met Theo
Burgess and been reassured by his gentleness and calm
manner. He was, as Gerard had unpleasantly pointed
out, old enough to be her father—a man just over
forty, inclined to be a little overweight, his hair
receding and turning grey.

He seemed slightly uneasy about Stephanie's age.
'You're younger than I'd expected, are you sure you
can cope? My children are in need of firm handling.'

'They seemed very well mannered, I'm sure I will
get on with them, and your wife is charming.'

She had expected him to smile at that, but she saw
anxiety in his pale eyes, which surprised and bothered
her. Why did he look at her like that?

He had sighed, giving a little shrug. 'Well, we'll see
how things go.'

Stephanie had been depressed by that interview in
one way. She realised that her job was far from secure.
But on the other hand she liked Mr Burgess: he had

been the unknown quantity involved in the job, or so she imagined! Having met him she now knew she had nothing to worry about from him; all Andrea's lectures about how to react if her boss tried to make a pass at her could be forgotten.

A week later she had met Gerard Tenniel at dinner. He was a remote cousin of Mrs Burgess, a young barrister spending a year in Australia as part of an exchange scheme. He was acting as a junior in a well-known set of chambers, going around the circuit with his senior counsel, learning how the Australian legal system worked and earning his keep by doing whatever work the head of chambers set aside for him, largely briefs which paid little and were just good experience.

That evening he hardly took his eyes off Stephanie and after dinner cornered her on the terrace where she was watching the stars and asked her out to dinner the next day.

Stephanie was barely eighteen; he scared and excited her. He was the most beautiful man she had ever seen: above his dark evening clothes his fair head gleamed like pale silk; his skin had acquired a golden tan, his grey eyes were mysterious and inviting. He turned her head, right from the start, and she didn't know how to talk to him—she just sat and listened, chin in hand, while Gerard talked. She had promised to write to her best friend at school who had gone on to university in Bristol, and her letters to Liz were soon full of nothing but Gerard. Liz obviously didn't believe the half of it. She bluntly said so, teasing Stephanie about her wild imagination, so Stephanie sent her photographs of herself and Gerard, swimming, dancing, sunbathing.

She was so wrapped up in Gerard that it was quite a
while before it dawned on her that Mrs Burgess no
longer liked her. Gradually she noticed other things—
that her employer's wife was changeable, erratic,
moody—one minute sunny and smiling, and the next
becoming violent or malicious or even both. Stephanie
slowly realised why Matt and Elnora were nervous of
their mother—they never knew where they were with
her. She hugged and kissed them one minute, calling
them her precious pets; the next she slapped them
viciously, once even drawing blood from a cut made
by one of her rings on Elnora's cheek.

Stephanie found herself watching them, trying
never to leave them alone with their mother. She only
went out with Gerard if they could go with her during
the day. At night she knew that their father would be
around so it was safe to see Gerard in the evenings.

Theo Burgess didn't confide in her at once. He was a
very discreet man, intelligent, cautious, self-con-
tained. It was after the incident when his wife made
Elnora's face bleed, that Theo first hinted that his wife
wasn't quite normal, and even then he tried to wrap it
up in muffling words, veil it, in case he frightened
Stephanie too much.

'My wife is highly strung and she has a quick
temper, it's better not to let the children see too much
of her, sometimes they get on her nerves and . . .' He
smiled uneasily. 'Well, you know how mothers can be
at certain times; a little edgy. You will be careful with
the children, Miss Stuart?'

Some afternoons he took time off work to swim with
his children and he and Stephanie played games with
them, throwing rubber rings from one to the other,
having a water-polo match in the pool with lilos for

horses and a big beach-ball they smacked with the flat
of their hands. They were noisy, uninhibited games;
they all behaved like children, splashing and shouting
and laughing, and very soon Theo was calling her
Stevie, the way the children did.

He was an utterly devoted father; he loved both
Matt and Elnora equally and had their love in return.
Seeing them when they were so happy together, when
Viola Burgess was absent, finally made Stephanie
realise that there was something very wrong with her
employer's wife.

Viola had maids to do the housework, of course, and
a cook to prepare meals—she entertained a good deal
and loved to drive around in her expensive foreign
imported car, tearing along at speeds that sent
Stephanie's heart into her mouth if she and the
children were also in the car. Matt would grip the seat,
white to his hairline. Elnora would turn green and
whisper to her, 'Stevie, I feel sick.' Viola Burgess
sometimes laughed and slowed down or parked to let
her little girl walk off the sickness. Sometimes,
though, she swore and put her foot down, accelerating,
making the car bump and roar until Elnora threw up,
and then Viola would turn round and start hitting her
hysterically while the child sobbed and shivered. If
Stephanie said a word, tried to intervene, Viola would
begin screaming at her, calling her names that
Stephanie had never been called before, using words
she had never heard spoken aloud, only seen written
on walls. She was aghast and unable to do anything
but back away.

The climax came on the morning after a party at a
neighbour's farm. Stephanie had danced with Gerard
for hours. She had been in another world. The

memory, the reflection of that intense happiness, was
in her face when Viola walked in on her the following
day and launched her attack.

'I don't want you running after Gerard Tenniel, do
you hear me? He isn't interested in a little schoolgirl
like you. He's sophisticated, a man of the world. You
just embarrass him, I could see he didn't know what to
do last night; he wanted to dance with me, but you
clung round his neck like a limpet. If I see you chasing
him again you'll be fired!'

Stephanie had made the mistake of protesting,
arguing with her. She had been appalled and terrified
by the outpourings she had to listen to after that.
Viola's face was shrill and hysterical. She had lost
control, and Stephanie had suddenly realised that
Viola was furiously jealous of her. Viola fancied
Gerard herself; she was very angry because instead of
pursuing her he had shown so much interest in her
children's nanny.

It was as if the beauty and gloss had been wiped out
from her face abruptly leaving another woman staring
at Stephanie, distorted, violent, dangerous. The
threats grew more and more shrill. 'You're not to see
him again! Gerard comes here to see me, not you.
Leave him alone, do you understand? Leave him
alone. Gerard's mine!'

When Stephanie just stared, aghast, Viola flew into
one of her manic rages and began hitting her. She tried
to get away and was knocked off her feet, sprawling
helplessly on the carpet. Viola kicked her in the ribs
and Stephanie gave a hoarse gasp of pain, but then the
door opened and Theo Burgess ran across the room,
white and horrified.

He pushed his wife away from the girl and knelt

down, putting his arm under her to lift her. 'My God, Stevie, are you hurt? What did she do to you? I'm so sorry, my dear, don't cry like that.' He brushed a shaking hand over her tumbled hair, stroking it. 'Don't, my little love. I won't let her near you again.' He kissed her forehead gently while Stephanie froze in shock at the tenderness in his voice. It hadn't occurred to her that Theo had become so fond of her. 'My poor little love, I should never have let her out, she's been getting worse lately, but I hoped . . .'

Stephanie interrupted him, a scream breaking from her throat as over his shoulder she saw Viola, completely mad, face unlike anything Stephanie had imagined in her worst nightmares, with a gun in her hand. It was Theo's gun which he kept locked in a drawer beside his bed in case of intruders in the night. God knew how Viola had got hold of it. She must have forced the lock.

Theo looked round and became rigid, and Viola laughed.

'Oh, yes, you're scared now, aren't you?' She waved the gun at them, laughing in that shrill, crazy way. 'So you're going to put me back in that madhouse—not on your life! I'm not going back there, never, do you hear? I'm not crazy, there's nothing wrong with me, you just want to get rid of me so that you can have her, that sly bitch—what's she got anyway? Gerard's after her, now you. She must be hot in bed to have you both on a string!'

'Viola, you're upset, now listen to me,' Theo said very carefully, beginning to get up.

'I'm sick of listening to you! Goodbye.'

For a second or two, Stephanie didn't believe it had happened. She was kneeling, staring, her ears deafened by the crash of the shots, and Theo was slumping over her and pinioning her body under his. Viola stalked over to them both, the gun still pointing, but now it was aimed at Stephanie's face and her finger was slowly squeezing the trigger while she laughed down at the girl's terrified face.

That was when Stephanie fainted, and woke up to find herself in the centre of a maelstrom.

CHAPTER FOUR

SHE couldn't hide inside her flat for ever, of course. An hour or so after she got back from the hotel, Robert tapped on her door. 'Are you up yet, Sleeping Beauty?' he called, teasing in his voice. He must have thought she hadn't been awake long, because he looked surprised when she opened her door fully dressed and wearing make-up. At least he hadn't heard her go out and return; he wouldn't guess how much had happened since he last saw her. She seemed to be a million miles from the girl who, only yesterday morning, had set off for work, never suspecting that in a very few hours her life was going to be blown apart for the second time.

'How's the head this morning?' Robert asked, eyeing her. 'You still look pale and you've got shopping bags under your eyes.'

Stephanie managed a smile. 'Oh, thanks, you're such a comfort. That makes me feel just great!'

'Come and have breakfast with us,' he invited. 'I'm a messenger from Gwen; she's making waffles, and there's your favourite maple syrup.'

'Lovely,' she said, following him to the sunlit kitchen, Gwen was in her oldest jeans and a pink tank top, a butcher's apron over her clothes, waiting with a jug of waffle mix for them to arrive. 'Right,' she said, pouring the batter into the hot waffle iron. 'This is Rob's, okay, Stevie? You're next.'

They never had time for enjoying breakfast during

the week. They all grabbed a cup of coffee and a slice of toast and ran. Sundays were a bit of a ritual. Gwen enjoyed cooking when she got the time, and surprised them with a variety of different breakfasts.

This was the last breakfast Stephanie would eat with them. The thought kept chiming in her head; it had a mournful sound. She was glad they didn't know. They were both very cheerful, arguing over who got the funny section from the Sunday paper, talking about planting a new lilac tree in the garden later that year, discussing the front-page headlines with indignation. It was an ordinary Sunday and she didn't want to ruin it even by a hint that anything was wrong.

Would Robert ever forgive her? He had been a wonderful brother: after she came back from Australia he had insisted she live with him, and as soon as he and Gwen bought this house they turned the spare rooms over their garage into a flat for her. She had sometimes wondered if Robert kept such a careful eye on her because he had some reservations about what had really happened five years ago. He'd never said anything, hinted that he doubted her story, but had he secretly wondered if she was suppressing anything? The trouble with mud is that if it hits you, it sticks, and enough mud had been thrown at Stephanie during Viola's trial. Her family had stoutly insisted on her complete innocence; the prosecution had built their case around the accused's long history of intermittent schizophrenia. From their point of view, Stephanie was simply irrelevant. Viola had become dangerously violent from time to time long before Stephanie arrived on the scene. It had been Viola and her defence team who had accused Stephanie of having an affair with Theo Burgess. Viola did not make the

mistake of mentioning her jealousy over Gerard—that
might have ruined her case. She had concentrated on
the lie about Stephanie and Theo and made it so
convincing that Stephanie almost came to believe it
herself.

On the day when she was giving evidence she had
been asked about what Theo had said as he knelt
beside her, holding her in his arms. She should have
lied; she tried not to answer. She stammered, flushed
and unhappy, but in the end she had to admit that
Theo had called her 'my little love'.

She could never forget the intake of breath in the
court, the way people exchanged looks. Viola's eyes
had glowed with triumph; catlike, malicious. Stephanie had betrayed herself, making Viola's case for her.

What could she have done? She had protested that
she had no idea why Theo had said it, there had never
been anything between them, Theo was just her
employer, but there was so much evidence from other
sources—of her and Theo playing in the pool with the
children, the hours they spent together while Viola
was out at parties or driving around in her fast car.
When witnesses stressed how unpleasant, how violent, Viola could be, they also admitted that Theo and
the children had been much happier after Stephanie
arrived. Somehow, it became far more believable that
Theo, badgered and unhappy with his wife, had
turned to the young girl who was managing to make
life easier for him. Stephanie had been convicted
without ever being charged, guilty at least of
contemplating adultery if not actually committing it.

Viola had been found guilty, but on grounds of
diminished responsibility, because of her schizophrenia, she was committed to the mental hospital

within the prison system. The two children were taken
to live with their aunt in Sydney. Stephanie fled for
England, where the case had not made headlines and
nobody recognised her.

She had not been on trial, but she had been found
guilty; conversation buzzed and people stared at her
wherever she went in Queensland. Everyone believed
that she had been Theo's lover; she couldn't even
defend herself because such rumour was a hydra-
headed monster. Nobody actually asked her directly.
She couldn't deny it; she could only flinch under the
curiosity and disapproval.

Gerard had swallowed the story, hook, line and
sinker—his silent contempt in that courtroom had
made Stephanie's ordeal that much more painful, and
when she went back to England she had hoped she
would never see him again.

'So, what are we going to do today?' Robert asked
her and Gwen, throwing down the Sunday paper he
had been reading.

'The washing,' said Gwen, and he made a face.

'Not this morning, Gwen. Can't it wait?'

'Will your shirts wait? Will your underpants? Or is
that an indelicate question?'

'You are putting my little sister off marriage,'
Robert said reprovingly. 'She'll think that's all there is
to it—waffles and underpants.'

'You said it, not me,' retorted Gwen, taking the
dirty plates into the kitchen and dumping then in the
dishwasher. The house was crammed with labour-
saving devices to save them both time, but somebody
had to load the washing machine and hang out the
washing, and it was usually Gwen or Stephanie.
Robert pleaded ignorance of such complicated ma-

chinery; to prove his point he once volunteered to do the wash and managed to turn Gwen's favourite white sweater bright pink by washing it with a pair of his maroon socks. Since then, Gwen hadn't let him near the washing machine, but Stephanie had the strong suspicion that there had been method in her dear brother's madness.

Stephanie got up. 'Euan may be coming round for me later, so why don't I stay here and do the washing and tidy up for you while you and Rob drive out to the country?' she suggested to Gwen, who gave her an uncertain, grateful look.

'Are you sure? It will take an hour or so, you know, Stevie. I can manage it.'

'Help me talk her into it,' Stephanie said to her brother, who laughed.

'Come on, Gwennie, grab your jacket and let's go before baby sister changes her mind. We're not on call, damn it. Let's see the world for a few hours.'

Gwen gave Stephanie a hug. 'You're an angel, thanks. I've put the washing in the basket. Shall I sort it out for you before I go?'

'I can read labels, thanks, and I don't wash maroon socks with people's new white sweaters.'

'Ouch!' said Robert, taking his wife's hand and dragging her away, still talking earnestly about whites and woollens and water temperatures.

When their car had gone Stephanie methodically began to do the washing; it helped to stop her thinking. She did some housework and then sat down to write letters. They were very hard to write. There was so much she wanted to say.

She took several hours over them and when they were in their envelopes she hid them in her handbag.

Euan drove up to the house at three in the afternoon. He was expected to have Sunday lunch at home with his mother; Stephanie never saw him for that meal.

He looked sharply at her as she opened the door. 'Hallo, how are you today?'

'I'm fine.' Her answer was automatic, but his searching stare made her uneasily aware that she didn't look so terrific.

'I think you should have spent the day in bed,' Euan thought aloud in a professional tone. 'It could be the start of 'flu; there's a lot of it going around town.' He looked past her. 'Where are Rob and Gwen.'

'Out. A drive in the country, lunch somewhere special.'

'That's what you need—a country drive,' decided Euan, and whisked her out to his car.

He talked as they drove, but Stephanie found it hard to concentrate on what he was saying and she didn't say much herself. The unexpected spring sunshine had brought out a crowd of other Sunday drivers; the roads were far from empty.

Suddenly Stephanie was alerted by hearing Gerard's name. She looked round at Euan, who was talking lightly.

'Odd chap, though. My mother was surprised to see him; she'd sent an invitation to his mother, but she hadn't expected Tenniel to turn up out of the blue. I suppose he was killing two birds with one stone—had business down here and dropped in on the party while he was in the neighbourhood.' Euan laughed shortly. 'My mother seems to think he's a ladykiller. That's what his mother claims, anyway. I suppose he's a good looking guy. What did you think of him, Stevie?'

She took a deep breath, the truth jamming up her mind. She simply wouldn't know where to start answering that. So she fell back on a dry generalisation.

'I distrust fair men.'

'Tall, dark and handsome for you?' Euan looked round at her, grinning. 'I'm not in the running, then? Why didn't you warn me? Is it too late to have my hair dyed?'

She managed a pretence of a smile. 'I like red hair; it's different.'

'They used to call me Foxy at school. That really got my goat.'

Stephanie felt a heavy sadness, looking at him secretly, realising with a bitter qualm how close they had become to being happy together. If Gerard Tenniel hadn't turned up at the party Euan might have proposed this weekend and she would have said yes, without a second's hesitation. She had been expecting it and there had been no doubt in her mind that she wanted to marry him.

Why had life played such a lousy trick on her a second time? Why did Gerard Tenniel have to be Euan's mother's godson?

They drove for some twenty miles along the coast, watching the sea dance and glitter as if the waves were silver scales on a million leaping fish. By the time they got back to Wyville it was dusk. They had a light supper in a seafood restaurant along the front; the place was crowded, it was a popular eating place. There was no privacy for them, but tonight Stephanie was relieved about that. She did not want to be alone with Euan now.

They had to park at the far end of the sea front, so

they walked slowly back there at about nine, Euan's arm around Stephanie's waist. Just before they reached the car they met Gerard Tenniel who was strolling along the front too, his hands in his pockets and his body lazily graceful.

'Hi, still here?' Euan asked, surprised.

'Yes. I leave tomorrow,' said Gerard, his eyes resting on the way in which Stephanie and Euan were entwined. He looked slowly upward and Stephanie defiantly met his gaze, refusing to be intimidated by the hard glint in those grey eyes. Let him stare. What could he do about it? This was her last time with Euan. The very last time.

'You remember Stephanie?' said Euan politely, oblivious of any tension in the atmosphere.

'Vividly,' Gerard drawled.

'We've just had a marvellous day out—drove right down the coast, came back, had a lobster supper—very indigestible and loaded with calories, but it was delicious, wasn't it, Stevie?'

'Don't you have to get up early tomorrow?' enquired Gerard with a little, malicious smile.

'Don't remind us—yes. Back to the labour camp at crack of dawn. You picked the right profession, Tenniel—all those bar dinners and expense-account lunches! Only a fool chooses to be a doctor.'

'You love it,' Stephanie said angrily, leaning on him. He was a wonderful man; she was going to miss him badly.

Mildly surprised, Euan looked down at her, smiling. 'So I do, darling, thanks for reminding me.' He glanced at his watch. 'We must rush now, Tenniel—nice to see you. Give my respects to your mother.'

'I will,' said Gerard, watching him unlock his car.

Stephanie stood there, waiting to get into the passenger seat, not allowing her eyes to stray towards Gerard, but she felt him watching her, was conscious of the secret reminder in his stare.

Euan opened the door for her and she slid with relief into her seat.

'See you,' said Gerard softly.

'Yes, have a good journey back tomorrow,' said Euan, blithely unaware of the hidden meaning in Gerard's light words.

They drove away, and Stephanie found herself shaking violently. Time was running out. Tomorrow would soon be here. And what was she going to do about Gerard Tenniel and his blackmail?

She left the house next morning at her usual time, but her car boot was packed with her cases and in her handbag she had the letters she had written. She posted them on the way to the hotel. Robert had already left, but Gwen was still on the night shift and would be sleeping late today. Stephanie looked up at the windows of the house, her face melancholy. She had been happy here.

Then she looked away and started the car. There was no point in sitting here brooding; she had learnt that five years ago. You didn't just lie there when fate knocked you off your feet! You made yourself get up, even if it took a long time, even if you had to crawl on your knees at first. It had taken her a long time to get over the murder and then the trial. Depression had been the worst part of the process of recovery; some days she felt as if she saw everything through a black filter. The world was dark for her, her food tasteless, her body lethargic. But she had got over that too, in

time, and come through to a sunlit plain here in
Wyville, with her job, her friends, her brother and his
wife, and Euan.

And Euan. She bit down on her lower lip; she
mustn't even think about Euan. It was going to hurt
whenever she did, and it was wise to avoid the
occasion of pain.

When she got to the hotel, there was no one on
reception except the night porter, who was sorting
through the day's post and whistling through his two
front teeth in a penetrating way.

'Hallo, sunshine,' he said, looking up as she walked
towards him. 'Who stole your smile?'

She pretended to laugh. 'I had a tiring weekend.'

'Why don't you marry the guy? He wouldn't keep
you up at night then.' The night porter grinned
delightedly at her blush.

'Is the boss down yet?' Stephanie asked huskily.

'Still eating his breakfast. Oh! I forgot—there was a
message for you from one of the guests.' He consulted
the pad beside the telephone. 'Mr Tenniel. He said
he'd like to see you the minute you came in.'

Stephanie nodded wearily. 'I'll go up and see him
now.'

'Is he a problem?' The porter watched her curiously.
'Want me to deal with it?'

She laughed, her eyes feverish. 'No, thanks, I'll see
to it myself.'

Gerard was fully dressed when he opened his door.
He gave her a cool nod, his eyes probing her pale face.
'Come in.'

When the door closed he gestured to his two pigskin
cases. 'I'm packed and ready to go. I saw the manager

last night, paid my bill and told him I was taking you
with me.'

Her eyes flew upwards to read his expression. 'What
did you say to him?'

'Don't look so tense! I told him I'd offered you a
new job in London.'

'What?'

'And I compensated him for the inconvenience of
having to find someone to take your place.'

'You had no right . . . you told him I was going away
with you?' Stephanie had gone white, her eyes
horrified. 'Why on earth did you do that? Can't you
see he'll tell my brother? This is a small town;
everyone knows everyone else. It will be common
gossip inside twenty-fours hours. Robert will know
where to find me and he'll come looking for me. My
God . . .'

'Did you intend to vanish from your brother's life
for ever?'

The dry question stopped her in her tracks, and she
stared at him in dumb misery. At last she whispered,
'What else can I do?'

His face reflected impatience, a dry sarcasm. 'What
an extremist you are, Stephanie!'

'You dare say that to me?' A rush of rage sent colour
surging through her face and her blue eyes flashed.
'You blackmailed me . . .'

He put a hand over her mouth. 'Do you want the
world to hear you? I thought you were afraid of people
finding out about your past?'

She was angry enough to bite and he snatched his
hand away, looking at the two small impressions on
his skin with lifted brows.

'I hope you're as passionate in bed as you are out of

it!' He caught her wrist as her hand swung up to hit
him. 'No, you don't—not twice, Stephanie. Try that
again and you'll wish you hadn't.' He yanked her
closer, ignoring her furious struggles. 'Now listen to
me—you're a grown woman, an adult, you have a
perfect right to live your life your way without
consulting your brother. He's not your keeper. If he
comes looking for you in London, we'll deal with that
without losing our heads.'

'We?' she spat out, infuriated by his calm assump-
tion of rights over her.

His eyes mocked her. 'That's right.' He lifted her
hand, his fingers still locked around her wrist. 'We're
chained together now,' he murmured, as though that
amused him. It did not amuse Stephanie, who pulled
helplessly against his strength, trying to free herself,
while Gerard watched her useless efforts with dry
indulgence.

She gave up at last, breathing thickly. 'You had no
right to speak to the manager on my behalf—I've
written to him, I said I would.'

'What excuse did you give?'

She looked away, very flushed. 'I didn't. I couldn't
bring myself to lie. I just told him I had to leave the job
at once, and I was very sorry for the short notice.'

'What did you tell your brother?'

'That's my business.'

'If he does come looking for you, it may well be
mine, so you'd better tell me now.'

Irritably she said, 'I told Robert that I'd realised
that I could never quite get away from what happened
in Australia and I didn't want to cause a lot of gossip
and scandal here, so I was going to London, where
nobody would even notice me. It's easier to avoid

gossip in a big city.'

He nodded, his fingers unlocking from her wrist, and she snatched her hand back, massaging the red mark he had left on her.

'You should have gone before you got involved with Cameron,' he said drily. 'What did you tell *him*?'

She turned away. 'Hadn't you better ring for the porter to take your cases down? We'd better go now before there are too many people about.'

'What did you tell Cameron?'

'That's my affair. Why don't you leave me alone? I'm leaving here, isn't that enough for you?' Her blue eyes burned with bitterness as she stared at him, and Gerard Tenniel considererd her expressionlessly, as if she was a specimen under a microscope.

'Not quite,' he said, then picked up the two pigskin cases. 'We won't bother the porter. Is there a way out of here so that he won't see us leaving together?'

'The back stairs,' she admitted with a sigh, and followed him into the corridor. 'Did you check that you hadn't left anything?'

He paused, frowning. 'Thanks for reminding me—my coat is on a chair over there.'

Stephanie walked over to get it and carried it over her arm as they made their way down the back stairs and out into an alley which led eventually to the car park. She was tense with nerves until they had put his cases into the back of the car and were driving away. At any minute she expected someone to call her name, come running after them, but nobody was about, the car park was empty.

She deliberately took a back route through the town to reach the motorway to London. With any luck they wouldn't pass anyone who might recognise her car or become curious about the man with her. It was still early in the morning and traffic was light on the minor roads. Concentrating on driving did something to ease her ragged nerves; she couldn't spare the energy to think about her own problems and found herself calming down gradually.

As they turned into the motorway and she fed into the faster moving traffic on the three-lane highway she caught the pale silk gleam of Gerard's hair as the wind whipped it sideways.

'Would you rather I drove?' he asked.

'No, I like driving,' Stephanie said, surprised. He hadn't been serious when he said he still wanted her, had he? In the first shock of that conversation yesterday morning she had been too upset to think clearly, but now in the gentle spring light she couldn't believe he had meant it. He had only been trying to frighten her enough to make her leave town. That was why he had come here the minute he had read that letter to his mother from Mrs Cameron. He had been determined to make sure she didn't marry Euan and risk involving the Camerons in an old scandal.

'Can you recommend a good hotel in London?' she asked. 'Not too expensive, I haven't got much money.'

He didn't answer and she looked round at him, searching his cool face with anxious eyes. 'I have to find somewhere to stay until I can get a place of my own,' she stammered.

'You know you'll be living with me.'

The succinct answer made her hands slip on the wheel; the car swerved violently and a vehicle coming up fast on her right only just missed hitting them. The blare of its horn made her jump; it swept past, the driver leaning forward to glare at her, mouthing angry comments on women drivers that she couldn't hear but lip-read without difficulty.

'For God's sake take the next exit off the motorway and pull up as soon as it's safe,' snapped Gerard angrily. 'I'm in no hurry to get killed. From now on, I'll do the driving.'

Stephanie was so disturbed that she obeyed, turning off the motorway and into a quiet country road where she stopped the car and sat there, trembling, her hands on the wheel while she fought for self-control.

'Get out,' Gerard said firmly.

'What did you mean? I'm not living with you,' she muttered.

'This is no place to discuss it. Wait until we get to London. And get out of that driving seat.'

She opened the door and got out, looking angrily at him as he strode round to take her place.

'You can't seriously think that I'd accept that invitation?'

He slid into the driving seat, buckling the seat-belt. 'It wasn't an invitation, it was an order.'

She bent to glare at him through the open window. 'You aren't giving me orders!'

'Get in the car!'

She walked round the other side of the car and got into the passenger seat, so angry she could hardly breathe.

'Do up your seat-belt. Are you hoping to get killed today?'

Her hands fumbled with the belt as she muttered, 'It wouldn't be a bad idea.'

Gerard swivelled in his seat and leaned over to push her hands out of the way, then deftly clipped her belt into place.

'You little coward,' he derided.

She looked up at him, hot and trembling with anger. 'I am not living with you!'

'I'm not letting you out of my sight until we're married,' he drawled, watching the shock of the words hit her as if it gave him great satisfaction.

CHAPTER FIVE

STEPHANIE sat in silence for most of the rest of the journey. Gerard occasionally threw her a brief, amused glance—which she ignored—but he didn't try to talk either. As they came closer to London, the traffic became so heavy that he needed all his attention for the road. Stephanie began to be relieved that he had taken over the wheel. London traffic was nerve-racking; until now she had only driven on the comparatively quiet roads around Wyville. She had a sinking feeling that she wasn't up to the cut-throat standards of city drivers, who wove in and out, used every spare inch of space, or shot out from nowhere forcing their way into the stream of traffic, apparently without turning a hair. She was stiff with tension just watching from the passenger seat, but Gerard seemed completely calm about it all.

The shock of his announcement about getting married had sent her into a frenzy. Her spluttered rage had only made him smile. 'No,' she had kept saying. 'You're crazy! I'd rather die!'

He had started the engine without a word and driven back on to the motorway. Stephanie had kept up a furious monologue for a few minutes until his cool silence had made it impossible for her to carry on, so she lapsed into sullen silence too. When they reached London she would make it crystal clear that here was where they parted. She was neither living with him, sleeping with him nor marrying him. She never wanted to set eyes on him again, in fact. She would drop him off at his house, find a small hotel somewhere not too close to the centre of London, and set about finding a job and somewhere permanent to live.

He hadn't meant it, of course. It was the most insane idea she had heard in her life, and Gerard Tenniel wasn't actually mad, although his idea of what was funny was perverted. That was all his sudden announcement had been—a stupid joke at her expense. Her rage had only amused him, that was why she had shut up in the end. Why let him get any fun out of her helpless fury?

She stared out of the window at the endless vista of roofs and television aerials clustering under a cloudy sky. The lovely spring weather they had been enjoying down in Wyville had avoided London, and she could understand why anyone in their right mind would prefer to stay away from the place.

Gerard shot her a quick look. 'We're here—this is London.'

'I know that,' she said coldly. Did he think she hadn't been here before? The houses were all too small, too close together, too grey. The air was thick with petrol fumes and city dust. There seemed no end to the gloomy streets, blackened yellow bricks and bumper-to-bumper cars. She thought of the cool, clean air she had left behind her, the open miles of sea, the green fields and white cliffs with the gulls skating overhead, and sighed.

'We should be home soon,' he murmured.

She didn't like the way he kept using the plural. 'Where do you live?' she asked, stressing 'you', and Gerard's eyes slid sideways to observe her with dry amusement, but something more—something she liked even less than the way he kept saying 'we'—an unmistakable glint of determination.

'Highgate. Ever heard of it?'

'Vaguely, I think. North London, isn't it?'

He nodded. 'Dick Whittington,' he added, peeling off into a new stream of traffic heading northwards across the city.

Stephanie looked round sharply. 'What?'

'Remember the apprentice boy who became Lord Mayor of London? He heard Bow bells from the top of Highgate Hill.'

'Do you have dreams of becoming Lord Mayor?' she mocked.

'I'm a lawyer, not a merchant.'

That was when a new idea flashed into her head and she sat up, watching him with triumph. There was one aspect he had forgotten.

'Isn't a lawyer just as much at risk from scandal as a doctor?'

Gerard didn't seem worried or taken aback. He drove with calm concentration, smiling.

'It doesn't do him any good to get mixed up in a scandal,' he agreed. 'But as long as he himself isn't involved . . .'

'But, professionally, I must be dynamite for you as much as for Euan!'

'Why?' he asked coolly, turning off the busy main road into a wide, tree-lined avenue which led up a steep hill. 'You were never charged with anything criminal. You were a witness in a murder trial five years ago. So what? If witnesses became immediate social pariahs our courts would be emptied overnight.'

Stephanie stared at him incredulously. They were

moving up the hill on either side of which stood large Edwardian houses; detached and set among spacious gardens. She didn't even spare them a glance.

'But . . . if it doesn't bother you,' she whispered, 'why did you insist that it would wreck Euan's life?'

Gerard turned the car suddenly and swung into a wide driveway, pulling up outside one of the Edwardian houses. He switched off the engine and leaned his arms on the steering wheel, his head swivelled to regard her almost compassionately.

'I'm not Euan Cameron and I don't have a mother like his. Do you really think she would let him marry you once she knew about your adultery with Theo Burgess?'

'I didn't . . .' Stephanie broke out, flushing. 'I told you . . .'

'His wife shot him over it. Can you see yourself convincing Mrs Cameron that you were innocent?'

She slackened in her seat, admitting to herself that he was right, damn him. When she didn't say anything, Gerard leaned over her and she tensed nervously, her eyes flicking to his face, but all he did was unfasten her seat-belt. 'Out you get!'

'Will you stop pushing me around?' she flared. He hadn't acted this way five years ago; he had been gentle and considerate. Now his high-handed manner annoyed her intensely.

He shrugged, getting out of his own seat to walk round the car. Stephanie saw her chance and slid over into the vacated driving seat, reaching for the ignition key.

It wasn't there. Gerard leaned in the other window, the key swinging from his finger. 'Looking for something?' His smile teased her briefly, then he was gone, and she sat rigidly, looking at the house. Ivy clambered over the walls and the building was solidly gracious, very suitable for an eminent barrister, no doubt, but it seemed very large.

Suddenly she realised that he had unlocked the car boot and was getting her cases out. She jumped out and ran to snatch up the case he had put on the tarmac of the drive, then threw it back into the boot. Gerard slapped her hand and withdrew the case again.

'You hit me!' she fumed incredulously. 'Who do you think you are? Give me back my car keys, leave my luggage alone!'

He slipped her car keys into his pocket, his smile lazy, picked up both of her cases and started to walk to the front door. She followed, shaky with rage. 'I'm talking to you! Don't you dare ignore me! Give my car keys back. You're not hijacking me. I'm going to a hotel.'

He put the cases down and Stephanie tensed, waiting for him to turn. She was surging with violence, she wanted to hit him even if it meant he would hit her back. It would let some of the tension out of her. But Gerard Tenniel didn't even look at her. He got a keyring out of his pocket and unlocked the front door, lifted the two pigskin cases into a spacious black and white tiled hall and then turned round and came towards Stephanie before she could back away. One minute she was looking at him angrily—the next she found herself over his shoulder in a fireman's lift, her legs kicking helplessly as he carried her into the house.

'Not quite the traditional way of carrying a bride over the threshold, but it will have to do for now,' he said coolly.

'Put me down,' she shrieked.

Gerard walked into an elegant drawing-room. She
had five seconds in which to take in the silk brocade of
curtains and upholstery, the cool green and white of
the décor, and then he dropped her from a great height
on to a couch.

She bounced, breathless at the surprise of it, then
burst out again. 'I could have hit my head on that
table—how dare you throw me around as if I was a
doll?'

'You asked me to put you down.' Gerard turned and
walked out. Stephanie scrambled up and looked round
the room. There was a piano taking up a great deal of
room, a polished mahogany grandfather clock, a white
and green carpet, and, through the open door, a view
of Gerard stacking her cases in the hall next to his
own.

She got to him just as he shut the front door and
turned. She collided with him at speed and his arms
went round her.

'Such flattering eagerness!' he murmured, and she
looked up to glare her fury at him, starting another
angry protest.

'I am not . . .'

She never got another syllable out. His mouth hit
hers with the force of a floodtide sweeping everything
before it. Her head was driven backwards, her body
bent helplessly, she could hardly stand and clutched at
his shoulders for support. Panic began to rise inside
her, she tried to struggle, but he was too strong for her.
She had to fight, she had to get away, she told herself,
writhing in the inexorable grip of his hands.

For the first time in her life she began to understand
what sexual drive really was; Gerard had unleashed it
on her and she was dazed and unable to control her

own response to it. Her eyes wouldn't stay open, her mind had become sluggish, reluctant to operate, as though the physical power Gerard had over her was also operating at another level, subduing her mind as well as her body. Her senses were busy, though, telling her a dozen things at once about what they were experiencing—the feverish insistence of his mouth, the sensual stroke of his hand up and down her spine, and then he had unzipped her dress and his hand was inside, exploring, travelling without hindrance. He pulled her dress down over her shoulders, lifting his head briefly, then began to kiss her neck, the pale skin above her breasts, her breasts themselves.

That was when Stephanie fought her way out of the sensual spell holding her. She dragged herself away from him, moaning. 'No, no! Stop it.'

Gerard straightened, his hands gripping her bare shoulders, and she stared up at him, aware of tumbled hair, a hotly flushed face.

'You look like a woman who's just made love,' he said, his mouth crooked with satisfaction. 'I used to wonder what you would look like if I kissed you like that, but I was always afraid to try.'

Stephanie suddenly felt a real fear. She hadn't been taking him seriously until now, she had thought he was playing games with her, that eventually he would take her to a hotel. It hadn't seemed possible that he could mean what he said, but the ruthless force of that kiss had changed everything. She looked into his grey eyes searchingly. What sort of man was he?

'Why?' she whispered dazedly.

His brows arched. 'Why? Why do I want you? Is that what you mean? That's a naïve question, isn't it, Stephanie?'

She closed her eyes, shuddering. 'Even if I don't want you?'

The hands tightened on her, hurting, and she winced. 'Five years ago, I fell in love with an illusion. Maybe I helped you to make a fool of me, I deceived myself, I wanted you to be some sort of dream, but even if I have to take some of the blame, you still used me, Stephanie.'

'No!' Her eyes opened, she looked urgently at him. 'I didn't, Gerard, please, believe me, I didn't!'

'You and Burgess.' He bit the name out as if he hated the taste of it.

'There was nothing between me and Theo!'

'Do you expect me to believe that?' He laughed harshly, shaking her. 'Listen to yourself! You call him Theo—your employer, old enough to be your father— but you use his first name, and don't tell me everyone did, because I don't remember you calling him Theo in public. You called him Mr Burgess then. The pair of you were very careful not to let anyone guess, but you knew him intimately, didn't you, Stephanie?'

She shook her head wildly. 'He never touched me. Never kissed me, never said a word you couldn't have heard—it was all lies!'

'Then why did she shoot him?'

'She was a schizophrenic—you know that! She was in a manic phase, liable to do anything, and Theo was in her way. She made up that story about him and me because it gave her an excuse for killing him. She thought she might get off if she invented a reason the jury would sympathise with.'

Gerard considered her coolly, with detachment. She was trembling passionately. He released her shoulders and walked away across the room. 'You need a drink.'

Stephanie stared after him, biting her lip. He hadn't listened, he didn't believe her.

'Brandy?' he asked with his back to her.

She didn't answer. She slowly walked over to the brocade-covered couch and sat down. The cool elegance of the drawing-room mocked her. She stared across it fixedly, seeing Viola Burgess as clearly as if she stood there now; her face distorted by jealous rage. If she told Gerard that Viola had been jealous over him, not over her husband, would he believe her? Why should he, when he didn't believe that she hadn't had an affair with Theo Burgess? It was obvious what he would think—that she was inventing Viola's interest in him to back up her protestations of innocence. He had made up his mind about her. Those cynical eyes would watch her with derision if she tried to tell him the whole truth. She hadn't told anyone about Viola's jealous outbursts over Gerard. Perhaps she should have done, but somehow she couldn't bear to repeat the other woman's words. She had felt sorry for Viola; the woman was sick and would pay a heavy price for what she had done. Stephanie hadn't realised then how heavy a price she herself might have to pay.

Gerard came back to her and sat down on the couch beside her, putting a glass of brandy to her lips. 'Drink it.'

She turned her dilated, distressed eyes on him slowly. 'You frighten me,' she whispered. The helpless inadequacy she had felt a few moments ago in the face of his insistent lovemaking had mirrored the way she felt when Viola hit her, screamed at her. Stephanie found violence terrifying, and she was alone here with a man whose emotions seemed to her as unpredictable as Viola's.

'I'm offering you brandy, not hemlock,' he drawled, his brows lifting. 'Why should you be frightened of a glass of brandy?'

'You know I didn't mean that, stop playing games with me!'

He fastened her fingers around the glass. 'Sit there quietly while I take your cases upstairs.'

'I'm not staying here!'

'We'll talk about that over lunch. I'm hungry— aren't you? We could go out or . . .'

'Go out,' she said hurriedly, too eagerly.

He gave her a mocking smile. 'On second thoughts, I think we'll eat here! You must be tired after your long journey. Wouldn't you like to come up to your bedroom and lie down?'

Stephanie threw the brandy at him.

He saw it coming and was quick enough to turn his face, but the spirit splashed his shirt and waistcoat. He straightened, producing a handkerchief and wiping the wet material without saying a word. Stephanie dropped the empty glass and shrank into a corner of the couch.

'Now I'll have to change out of these wet clothes,' he shrugged, his eyes sardonic. 'You'd better come up with me, I don't think I can trust you down here on your own. Who knows what you might get up to?'

Her lower lip bulged mutinously, and she tried to grip the arm of the couch, but Gerard took her by the waist and pulled her to her feet.

'Will you walk or shall I carry you?' he offered politely.

She walked. At the foot of the stairs he picked up several cases and carried them in her wake. Stephanie tried desperately to think of some way of making him see reason. Viola had been mentally unbalanced; surely Gerard couldn't be? His behaviour might be crazy, but he seemed sane enough apart from that.

He opened the door and carried her cases into the room beyond. 'This okay for you?' he asked, and she looked around her with pleasure. The room was furnished in cream and pink; it was very modern.

'It's beautiful. I love the décor of your house—did you get an interior designer to do it?'

'No, my mother was responsible for all that.'

'Your mother . . .' Stephanie wandered over to the windows and looked out into the large back garden; lawns and rose trees and ornamental shrubs, a number of trees just breaking into vivid new leaf. Although this was London, as her eyes rose to take in the immediate neighbourhood of the house she realised how many trees there were around here. All the houses had large gardens.

Staring out, she went on, 'Your mother's responsible for me being here, too. If she hadn't shown you that letter—why did she, anyway? Where is she? Where does she live? What if she comes here and finds me in the house?'

'My mother and father live in Essex, at Maldon.' Gerard began to unbutton his waistcoat and Stephanie looked round at him in tense alarm.

'What are you doing?'

'Getting undressed.' He slid out of his jacket and untied his tie.

Stephanie measured the distance between herself and the door. Could she get out of this room before he could stop her? She grimly recognised the improbability—he was too fast on his feet.

Gerard smiled politely. 'Sorry about this, but I don't

trust you,' he explained, backing while she stared,
wondering what he was going to do now. The next
second she knew. The door shut, a key turned in the
lock. She was alone, but she was a prisoner.

She ran to the door and banged on it with both fists.
'Let me out! Gerard! Do you hear me? Let me out!'

'Of course I hear you,' he said from the other side of
the door. 'I'd have to be deaf not to. Stop getting
hysterical. The bathroom door is on your right. Go
and have a shower, that will make you feel better.
When I've showered and changed I'll prepare lunch
and we can talk.'

She heard him walk away and stood with her ear to
the door, listening as he walked into some other room.
He hadn't sounded irrational just now, perhaps he was
still playing some elaborate and unfunny joke on her?
From time to time she caught an impression of
amusement: a gleam in his eye, a twist of his mouth, as
if he was secretly laughing at her.

There was a bolt on the door, so she decisively drew
it. She hoped he'd heard that. Turning away, she
surveyed the room again. The wallpaper was a
delicate cream printed with tiny pink roses, faintly
Victorian, Laura Ashley style. The bed was covered
with a heavy cream cotton and lace spread and a little
heap of heart-shaped cushions lay at the top of it. Each
cushion had a red silk ribbon carefully threaded
through the material from one side to the other. In the
centre where the criss-cross met there was a lovers'
knot; loops of red ribbon hanging. The whole room
had that Victorian feel; lampshades of pleated cream
and gold cotton, curtains printed with ears of wheat
and pink poppies, a soft, creamy carpet. Stephanie
wandered around, touching things, wishing she could

forget the reason why she was here, could stop being so
tense and uncertain and merely enjoy this pretty room.
She seemed to have been on edge for days. For weeks.
But it was less than forty-eight hours since Gerard
Tenniel had walked back into her life and started her
own private earthquake.

She opened the door into the little bathroom and
discovered that that had been given a country touch
too. Tiles in smooth cream alternated with an
occasional tile which carried a pink rose; the fittings
were all in pink and the carpet deep and luxurious, but
there was a glass trough along one wall which was
filled with plants and behind them a mirror. A mirror
on the opposite wall threw back that reflection of
green leaves, creating a shadowy greenhouse effect.

Stephanie opened the cabinet of the vanity unit and
found a wide array of toiletries—bubble baths, bath
oils, perfumed talc, soaps. She chose a bubble bath,
ran both taps copiously and poured the contents of the
glass bottle into the water, swishing with one hand
until the foam began to rise. While she watched it, she
wondered how many other women had used this little
suite of rooms.

They had been furnished with a woman in mind,
that was obvious. She had guessed that long before she
went into the bathroom, opened the cupboard and saw
all those very feminine toiletries. Even if there hadn't
been a selection of very expensive French perfume on
the shelves she would have known a woman had used
these rooms because she simply couldn't imagine
Gerard using any of those perfumed bath oils and
talcs. He carried around with him a very masculine
fragrance, fresh and cool, more pine than musk.

She slowly stripped off and got into the bath, lying

back with closed eyes. She had to relax somehow, take the edge of this terrible tension.

He had changed. Her mouth twisted angrily. Well, in five years who wouldn't? She had changed, too. She had been a wide-eyed adolescent just passing into womanhood when they first met. Gerard had knocked her for six, hadn't he? He had been unlike any other man she had ever met: glamorous, exciting, sophisticated. She had thought of him as a man of the world, and compared to her own gauche self that was just what he was. She tried to remember exactly how she had felt. Her stomach suddenly clenched in excitement and she knew she had felt that way then. She had been in love with him—why pretend she hadn't? Of course she hadn't known what love was really all about then, she hadn't been mature enough to recognise that those wild highs and melancholy lows were the swings and roundabouts of adolescent infatuation and not real love at all. It had been an unreal love, but it had hurt just the same: she had been uncertain and shy with him, frightened by her own emotions, yet in the grip of such a strong attraction that she had been provocative at times, flirting with him, almost inviting him to kiss her. A second later she would be running away, afraid that he might take her up on the invitation.

With hindsight she knew that it had been a typical first love; it should have been for a boy of her own age, someone as inexperienced as herself. She hadn't had a clue how to handle Gerard Tenniel. She hadn't even realised that he was the one controlling their relationship, he did all the handling. He hadn't been lying when he said that he had treated her with great care. Looking back, she realised now how cleverly he had handled the whole situation. She had been totally

unaware of the way he manipulated her, never coming
too close, never making her panic. She might well
have done if he had turned on the heat; she wouldn't
have known how to stop him if he tried to make love to
her—but he hadn't, had he? When he did kiss her it
had been a light, gentle kiss. She had been restless,
clinging, wanting more than that—but if he had
offered more she would have been scared witless.
Obviously he had sensed as much and kept the lid on
his own instincts.

A flush began to burn in her face. She sat up,
opening her eyes, sending a little wave of scented
bubbles upwards as her body shifted in the bath.

Had he been in love with her? Really in love? That
would explain the coldness, the glacial contempt she
had seen in his face in court. Had she hurt him?

Gerard had never seemed vulnerable; the idea of
him getting hurt was hard to accept, but if that was
what lay behind his attitude to her now she had to
make him see that Viola had been lying, that she
herself had never deceived him or meant to hurt him.

If they could only talk about it, stop this in-fighting,
these barbed exchanges, the threats and accusations,
then . . .

Stephanie climbed out of the bath, refusing to think
about what might happen after that.

She took one of the enormous fluffy bathsheets from
the airing cupboard behind the bath and wrapped
herself in it, staring at her flushed face in the mirrors.
The reflection of the plants crowded in around her,
making her look like someone in a jungle peering out,
and, oddly, that was just how she felt, trapped in heat
and darkness and trying to get out.

She was towelling herself when she heard the

bedroom door being unlocked. Gerard tapped as soon as he realised she had bolted it too.

'Lunch is on the table. A cold meal, I'm afraid—just salad and fruit.'

'I'll come down in five minutes,' she said through the bathroom door, holding her towel in place.

Perhaps if she was calm and matter-of-fact with him he would stop playing this nerve-racking game with her?

'Okay, but don't take too long. I'm ravenous!'

When he had gone back downstairs, she searched through her cases to find something to wear which would make her look cool and composed. She had a strong suspicion that for all his angry hostility, Gerard still thought of her as that eighteen-year-old whom he had manipulated for her own good. It was time he realised that she wasn't an uncertain girl any more— she was an adult woman.

She picked out a pair of white dungarees, a blue cotton top and a white gilet. When she had brushed her rich brown hair until it shone, added some pale pink lipstick and a touch of blue eyeshadow, she looked wryly at her reflection in the mirror.

It was one thing to look calm, quite another to feel it. Still, it helped to know that you gave the impression that you were sure of yourself.

She found Gerard in a sunny kitchen at the back of the house looking into the leafy garden. He glanced round as she came towards him, his brows arching as he took in her appearance.

'There you are. I was just going to pour the wine— white, I hope you approve.'

'Not for me, thank you. I don't drink wine in the

middle of the day, it makes me sleepy. I'll just have
some water.'

She sat down and watched him fill his own glass. He
gestured to the salad bowl.

'Help yourself.' He sat down and took a slice of roast
ham, then offered her the platter of cold meats.

'Thank you.' She took a thin slice of meat and a little
salad. 'Isn't this house rather large for a bachelor?' she
asked politely, as though they were strangers.

'Much too large,' he agreed, picking up his wine
glass.

'Why did you buy it, then?'

'I didn't. I inherited it from my uncle George. He
was a bachelor and was born in this house. He died
here, too.' Gerard looked at her quickly. 'I hope that
doesn't upset you.'

'Why should it? I didn't know him, and I suppose
most old houses have seen deaths as well as births.'

'My uncle was eccentric. He only left me the house
on condition that I was a bachelor at the time of his
death and remained unmarried for ten years.'

Stephanie's fork stopped halfway to her mouth.
'Goodness!'

Gerard grinned wickedly at her. 'Uncle George
hadn't thought it through very carefully. When he died
I was fifteen.'

She laughed. 'Oh. And not married.'

'No, I wasn't that precocious,' he agreed drily.

Stephanie glanced at him through her lashes, her
mouth curving in a faint smile. 'And I suppose the ten
years is up now?'

Gerard leaned over the table and kissed her nose.
'Thank you. I've never had a nicer compliment.'

A soft colour invaded her face and she looked down.

Before she could think of anything to say next there
was a loud ringing at the front door and Gerard
frowned.

'Who on earth can that be?' He threw down his
table napkin and stood up reluctantly. 'I'll get rid of
whoever it is.' He walked away and she stared after
him. For a second she had forgotten that they were
enemies. His eyes had smiled across the table, she had
smiled back, he had given her that light, teasing kiss
on the nose—and she hadn't remembered why she was
here, what he had done to her, what he planned to do.

She must have a mind like a sieve. How easy it was
to forget! And how some things refused to be
forgotten, clinging like limpets in the dark sea caverns
of the memory. She had never forgotten Gerard
Tenniel or anything that happened in Australia five
years ago. Those events, those people, had been
stamped indelibly on her mind.

Gerard's voice floated back to her from the hall.
'Julia! What on earth are you doing here?'

'Don't just stand there like an idiot, Gerry, take this
box from me, can't you see that I'm giving at the knees
under the weight of it?'

'Are you alone?'

'Of course I am. You're hardly very observant—or
are you seeing double these days? I knew you'd take to
drink sooner or later. All lawyers do, it's a professional
hazard. Well, get out of my way, why are you just
staring at me? I've come for lunch. Don't worry, I'll
get it myself.'

The voice had begun to move nearer as it talked; its
owner was obviously coming towards the kitchen and
Stephanie sat rigidly, wondering what she should do.
Sit there? Hide?

'If you're tired, Julia, go and sit down in the drawing-room—I'll bring you a drink and some sandwiches in five minutes.' Gerard sounded distinctly thrown.

'I wouldn't eat any sandwich you made, I shudder to think what it would taste like.' The kitchen door opened and a tall, *soignée* woman came in, only to stop and stare at Stephanie. 'Oh.' She looked round and said drily to Gerard, 'I see you have company. So that's why you hardly looked thrilled to see me!'

Stephanie stood up, flushing. Obviously, this woman was one of his girl-friends—she looked exactly the type Stephanie would have expected him to go around with. Her clothes were expensive and chic, in the latest fashion. She had silvery blonde hair which she wore in a chignon at the back of her head. Her features had a fine-boned distinction which wasn't easy to classify—not beauty but style was what struck you at first glance.

'Julia, this is Stephanie Stuart,' said Gerard, his mouth straight and impatient. 'Stephanie, this is my cousin, Julia.'

Julia looked thoughtfully at her, offering her hand. 'How do you do? So *you're* Stephanie?'

Gerard and Stephanie exchanged looks; their faces reflected an equal surprise, and Julia looked from one to the other of them, mocking amusement in her face.

'There's no point in beating about the bush—you're why I'm here.'

'What are you talking about?' Gerard demanded.

Julia sauntered over to sit down at the table. 'That salad looks good. Pour me a glass of Chablis, darling, while I fill my plate.' She picked up the salad servers and began heaping lettuce, cucumber, avocado and cress on to a clean plate.

Gerard picked up the bottle of wine and leaned over her, his face dark with rage. 'Don't be so bloody cryptic, Julia. What do you mean—Stephanie's why you're here?'

She picked up the small jug of mayonnaise. 'Is this fresh or from a jar?'

'From a jar,' snapped Gerard, so she put the jug down, wrinkling her nose.

'Lazy swine. You really ought to make it yourself; it tastes so much better.'

'Julia, my patience is wearing thin. Stop dragging this out.' He filled a glass with white wine and handed it to her. 'Why are you here?'

Julia looked mischievously at him, then at Stephanie. 'I had a phone call from your mother an hour ago. It appears that she'd just had an agitated phone call from someone called Robert Stuart.'

'Oh!' Stephanie broke out, her hand flying to her cheek.

Julia watched her, smiling. 'Your brother, I gather.'

Stephanie looked helplessly at Gerard, who asked his cousin, 'What did he want with Mother?'

'Your address, Gerry, dear.' Julia laughed at his expression. 'Your mother rang here, but there was no reply so she got in touch with me to ask if I knew if you were back yet. She was worried, Robert Stuart had breathed fire and brimstone on the phone and Aunt Louise had visions of him shooting you. It seems he said you'd taken his sister away with you. He made it sound positively immoral! What have you been up to, Gerry?'

CHAPTER SIX

STEPHANIE got to her feet, her face distraught. 'I must go—I can't stay here. What if Robert comes to London, tries to find me? He can't find me here, in your house!'

Gerard caught hold of her arm as she ran towards the door. 'Stop panicking. You've got to see him sooner or later, you said so yourself. He has no rights over you. If he does come, you can explain why you left and he'll have to accept your decision.'

She looked bitterly at him. 'I don't seem to be very good at explanations. You never believe a word I say. Why should Robert?'

'He's your brother and, in this case, you're telling the truth.'

'I've never lied to you!'

'Haven't you?' His mouth twisted.

Julia sat listening, her face intrigued and fascinated, calmly eating her lunch all the time as though she was watching television. Stephanie shot her a look, bit her lip. This wasn't the time and place for another of their angry exchanges, not in front of an audience.

'I don't want another argument with you!' she told Gerard, who seemed unimpressed by the assurance.

'Good, then just stop arguing.'

'Oh, why are you so maddening?' she wailed.

'He always is,' Julia intervened.

Gerard turned cold eyes on his cousin. 'Kindly refrain from interfering, we can do without your comments. I don't remember inviting you to lunch, but as you seem to have eaten most of the food now, would you mind leaving?'

'Charming,' said Julia, pushing away her plate and leaning back casually in her chair, quite obviously with no intention of leaving such an entertaining scene. 'I go to all the trouble of coming over here to warn you . . .'

'So that you could find out what was going on!' Gerard interrupted. 'You always were a nosy brat.'

Julia smoothed one stray hair, looking down her nose. 'Brat? Bite your tongue!'

'I can't understand how Robert found out so soon,' Stephanie muttered.

Julia looked at her, smiling. 'Oh, I can tell you that! Apparently he rang the hotel where you worked and they told him you'd gone off with Gerard.' Her bright, teasing eyes flickered to her cousin. 'I can see the headlines now—well-known lawyer arrested for kidnapping.'

'Oh, shut up, Julia!' Gerard snapped.

'Barrister,' corrected Stephanie.

'It does sound more distinguished, doesn't it?' Julia agreed.

Stephanie sighed. 'Oh, what bad luck that Robert rang the hotel—I didn't expect him to find out so soon. I wonder why he rang me? He can't possibly have got my letter so quickly. I only posted it at eight o'clock.'

'If it was a local letter,' said Julia, her face interested in the problem, 'it could have been delivered at midday.'

Stephanie made a wry face. 'I suppose that was it— I'd forgotten the second post. Isn't it typical that the one time when you don't want the post office to be super-efficient they take you by surprise?'

'Absolutely typical,' Julia agreed.

Stephanie decided she liked her. She gave her a thoughtful look. 'I suppose you couldn't recommend an inexpensive but respectable hotel where I could get a room for a few days?'

'You aren't leaving!' Gerard said sharply.

'If you need somewhere to stay tonight, I have a spare room in my flat,' Julia suggested.

'No!' said Gerard immediately, scowling.

'It's just a boxroom, but the bed is comfortable,' Julia said, ignoring him.

'Did you hear what I said?' Gerard almost snarled, grabbing Stephanie by the arm. 'You aren't going. Julia, kindly clear off—you're just confusing the issue.'

His threats didn't seem to bother Julia, and her cool smile made Stephanie feel braver.

'What exactly is the issue I'm supposed to be confusing?' Julia enquired, considering them both thoughtfully.

'There isn't one,' said Stephanie, pulling herself free of Gerard's grip. 'And I'd be very grateful if I could stay the night in your spare room.'

Gerard was distinctly grim-faced now. 'Have you forgotten why you came with me in the first place? That still holds, remember.'

A flicker of uncertainty passed through her face. 'You wouldn't do it,' she said huskily.

'What?' Julia asked intrigued.

'I don't bluff at poker,' Gerard said.

'Liar,' said Julia. 'You always cheated at cards.'

'Oh, for heaven's sake, Julia, will you shut up?'

Stephanie looked questioningly at his cousin. 'Julia, is he . . . unscrupulous?'

'As hell,' Julia said, grinning, then saw the way

Stephanie's face fell and frowned. Gerard gave a dry, triumphant smile.

'She isn't going with you, Julia, you know your way out.'

Julia sat down again, crossing her long slim legs. 'I'm staying. I think Stephanie needs a little female support in this male-dominated household.'

Gerard seethed, his mouth tight with fury. After a moment's consideration of them both, he said through his teeth, 'Out of the question, I'm afraid. There isn't a bedroom available.'

'You've got six of them up there! How many other people are staying?'

'Four of the rooms haven't been used for years: the beds are damp, haven't been aired since last summer.'

'A little damp won't hurt me.'

'You haven't any nightclothes with you. Why don't you go home, Julia?'

'You can borrow a nightie from me,' Stephanie offered.

'Thanks, I will,' said Julia, sauntering to the door. 'I'll go up and choose a room now.'

'You can get pneumonia, sleeping in damp beds!' Gerard threw after her, and she turned at the door to give him a sweet smile.

'I'll air the mattress in front of an electric fire if it seems damp.' She walked through the hall and began to go upstairs.

Stephanie moved to follow, but Gerard got between her and the door with a deft movement. He slammed the kitchen door and leant on it with folded arms.

'I don't want Julia here. Persuade her to leave.'

She met his insistent stare, shaking her head.

'Stephanie,' he said in a softer, coaxing voice, and suddenly he was much too close and she felt her

breathing impeded. The anger and tension had
vanished from his face and she found the intimate
gaze of those grey eyes disturbing. He had changed his
tack; what was he up to now? She didn't trust him, but
she couldn't quite cope with the way he was looking at
her, either. It made her feel as light-headed as it had
when she was eighteen.

'How are we going to get to know one another if we
aren't alone?' he asked, his hand lifting to touch her
cheek.

She stiffened under the tactile seduction, deeply
aware of the gentle brush of those fingertips over her
skin.

'That isn't the object though, is it?' she said huskily.
'You want to . . .' She broke off, biting her lip.

'Want to?' he prompted, a gleam of irony in his face
now.

'Sleep with me,' she finished, very flushed and no
longer able to meet his eyes.

'Do you know any better way of exploring the
opposite sex?'

Stephanie looked up angrily at the mockery in his
voice. 'I won't sleep with you!'

'Do you sleep with Cameron?' The question had the
speed and sharpness of a stiletto, and she tensed.

'No!'

He caught her chin, his fingers refusing to let her
escape. 'Look at me!'

She looked, defiance in her blue eyes. He leaned
very close, staring into them as if reading her mind in
them.

'Are you in love with him?'

Her eyes flickered, but she didn't answer.

'Are you?' he insisted.

'I don't know,' she admitted on a painful sigh. 'I

didn't have time to find out. Maybe I was, or maybe I
would have been. I like him more than anyone else; we
get on well. Euan's the sort of man most girls dream of
marrying. He's kind and thoughtful and . . .'

'Good husband material,' he finished for her as she
paused, and his mouth took on that mocking cynicism
again. 'How long had you known him?'

'A couple of years, but we only started dating less
than a year ago.' She knew Euan had been watching
her before he asked her out.

'Not love at first sight, then?'

'I don't believe in love at first sight.'

Gerard eyed her oddly, and she felt herself flushing
deeply. Her voice had a strangely melancholy sound; a
muted regret, as though she wished she did believe in
love at first sight. She had fallen for Gerard at first
sight, of course, but then that had all been illusory, a
wildfire which burnt along her veins for a while and
then died out, leaving her weary and disillusioned, no
longer willing to believe in any sudden, violent
emotion.

That was why she had believed in Euan's caution in
approaching her. At least she had been sure that he
hadn't rushed into it, that he didn't leap before he
looked. She could rely on Euan; he was calm and
dependable. She had understood that if Euan did
propose it would be because he was utterly certain that
she was the sort of wife he wanted.

'Have you ever been in love?' Gerard asked softly.

Stephanie froze, looking up helplessly into the dark-
pupilled grey eyes. They held some hypnotic attraction for her; she was afraid she might drown in their
depths. He wasn't comfortable, like Euan; he was far
from predictable or manageable. He was possessed of
some inner power she couldn't describe; a dynamic

energy she could feel even without touching him. She
saw it surging in his eyes and was drawn to it,
helplessly fascinated, like a moth fluttering towards
the brightness of a flame even though it knows it will
burn up, be utterly destroyed.

She must not let that happen to her; she mustn't let
him pull her over the edge. She closed her eyes
abruptly, shutting out the sight of his face.

'No,' she said, her voice raw. 'No, never.'

She heard him breathing, very close. His fingers slid
from her cheek to her throat and she shivered,
backing, until they no longer touched her.

'Never, Stephanie?' he asked, a thread of provocation in his voice, and she knew he was thinking about
himself, he was hinting that she might have been in
love with him once.

She opened her eyes, more in command of herself
now. 'I've thought I was once or twice, but it was a
mistake.'

Gerard was frowning now and the softness had
vanished from his voice. The sunlight gave his blond
hair a burnished look and under it his face was harshly
male, brooding eyes the colour of wintry skies, his
mouth with the tension of steel cord. Stephanie almost
relaxed; the danger had passed, she could resist his
male allure when he frowned like that. It was his
smile, his sensual gaze, that weakened her knees and
made her heart beat far too fast.

'I wish I knew what to make of you,' he muttered,
straightening. 'You're as elusive as a cat in the dark.
Every time I think I can see you and I reach out for
you, you slip though my fingers.'

They both heard Julia's footsteps on the stairs; she
was returning. Gerard walked towards the table and
began to clear it. Stephanie was still trembling

slightly, her nerves jangling from the last few minutes, but she went over to help him.

The door opened and Julia came in smiling. 'The rooms are perfectly aired,' she accused her cousin. 'I've picked one of the big back rooms, next to yours, Stephanie. If you have any nightmares during the night, you can yell for me.' She grinned and Stephanie smiled faintly.

'I will.'

'Or any intruders, of course,' murmured Julia, her eyes on Gerard.

He bared his teeth at her in a pretence of a smile. 'You think you're so funny!'

'How long are you staying in London, Stephanie?' asked Julia, taking no notice of his snarl.

'I was thinking of finding a job here.'

'What sort of job?'

'I've already offered you one,' Gerard snapped.

Julia regarded him curiously. 'In your chambers?'

He nodded. 'As receptionist—ours is leaving. Stephanie can start right away. She'll have to work with the present girl to learn the job.'

'What do you do, Julia?' Stephanie asked as she finished wiping the top of the table.

'Nothing,' Gerard said sarcastically.

'I'm in market research,' Julia said, giving him a pointed look. 'Gerard makes fun of my job but in fact I work very hard.'

'When you work!' he commented.

'All right, the hours are erratic and some days I haven't much to do, but when I'm involved in a project I work all the hours there are.' She went over to a cabinet. 'I feel like some coffee. Want some, Stephanie?'

'Make yourself at home by all means,' grunted

Gerard, going out and slamming the door behind him.

Julia turned, a bag of unground coffee-beans in her hand. 'Dear, dear, aren't we in a temper? Nothing quite as violent as the frustrated male, is there?' She produced a coffee-grinder and began to feed the beans into it.

Shyly, Stephanie said, 'It's very good of you to go to all this trouble for me. I'm very glad of the company.'

Julia finished grinding and emptied the coffee into the top of the percolator. 'Am I allowed to know what's going on? Or is it deadly secret?'

Stephanie hesitated; she didn't feel much like telling someone about her past.

Julia was just pushing the plug into the electric socket and switching on the percolator. 'Don't tell me if you'd rather not,' she murmured without looking round. 'As Gerard always says, I was born nosy. If you want to talk, I can be as discreet as you like, that's all.'

'Are you very close to Gerard?' Stephanie asked curiously. He had never mentioned his cousin to her, but then five years ago they had not done much talking about anything but themselves.

Julia looked round, face wry. 'Almost brother and sister, I suppose. My mother is his mother's twin and they're very close. Well, they're identical, actually, which probably explains why Gerard and I are so alike to look at. He's much older than me, of course.' She grinned. 'I hope you realise that.'

'It did occur to me,' said Stephanie with amusement.

'Ten years, actually. When I was born, he was a horrible knobbly-kneed schoolboy. He claims he used to push me in my pram. I know he used to swing me when I was a toddler, I remember that! My mother watched him like a hawk, afraid he'd push too hard and kill her precious infant. I'm an only child. A late thought on the part of my parents—my mother was thirty-two when I was born, and she claims she hated giving birth so much that she didn't want any more babies.'

'I have a sister and a brother, both older than me. I was an afterthought, too.'

The doorbell rang violently and Stephanie tensed, going pale. 'Robert!' she whispered, staring at Julia.

'It can't be, surely? I'm sure Aunt Louise said that he was coming from the West Country somewhere. He couldn't get here that fast.' Julia looked at her watch, then looked taken aback 'Good heavens, I've been here nearly two hours now, so if he rang Aunt Louise an hour before she rang me ...' She looked at Stephanie uneasily.

'It is him,' Stephanie said, moistening her lips. She didn't think she could face Robert at this moment. What on earth was she to say to him?

'We don't have to answer the door,' Julia suggested, but as she was speaking they both heard movements in the hall, then Gerard opening the front door. 'Too late,' said Julia, looking closely at Stephanie. 'I wish I knew what was going on ...'

'You bastard!' Robert's angry voice made them both jump. It was followed immediately by a crash and Stephanie gasped in horror. What was happening out there?

'That sounded like china,' Julia deduced. 'I bet it was that jardinière that Gerard payed a hundred pounds for last year.'

The front door slammed, but from the raised voices it was obvious that Robert was inside the house now. Gerard was talking curtly, but they couldn't hear what he said because Robert kept shouting over his voice.

'Do you want the police called in on this,' he
bellowed, and a moment later, 'Don't lie to me! My
sister wouldn't just vanish without a word to me unless
something was wrong.'

Stephanie went shakily to the kitchen door and
opened it. She had no option; she couldn't cower in
here while Robert broke up Gerard's home. The hall
was littered with earth and broken china.

Her brother was facing her; his eyes flashed past
Gerard and fixed on her. 'Stephanie! Are you all
right?'

Gerard glanced back over his shoulder; she got the
feeling that he had been holding her brother at bay,
making sure that he did not get past him and reach the
kitchen.

'I'm okay, Robert,' she said flatly, and walked
towards him with Julia in the doorway behind her,
watching intently. Stephanie caught a look of relief in
Robert's face as he noticed Julia, and flushed,
guessing what that expression meant. He was glad to
see another woman in the house. She could imagine
what he had been suspecting as he drove at some
dangerous speed to reach London as fast as possible.

'We'd better go in here,' said Gerard, walking into
the drawing-room.

Robert looked at him with dislike. 'I want to talk to
my sister alone.'

Stephanie gave Gerard a pleading look. 'Please,
leave me with my brother for a few minutes, would
you?'

Gerard visibly hesitated, his jaw rigid, then
shrugged and went out again. Robert stood in the
elegant, tranquil room and stared at his sister as if he
had never seen her before.

'What the hell is going on, Stephanie?'

She took a deep breath, wondering where to start. 'Can we sit down, Robert?' Her legs felt so strangely weak, she was afraid that if she didn't sit down she might faint.

He looked around as if only just realising where they were and then threw himself into a chair. Stephanie sat down too, her hands clasped in her lap to stop them shaking.

'Well?' Robert demanded.

'Did you get my letter?'

'Letter? No, what letter?'

'I sent you one, I posted it this morning on . . . on my way. Why did you ring the hotel if you hadn't had my letter?'

'Euan asked me to let you know that he was going away for a few days—he's been asked to go to Saudi to perform a heart operation on a sheikh. They couldn't fly the man over here and they claim they've got all the facilities Euan will need. The Director of their hospital was at medical school with old Bougham, our administrator, and . . . well, it was a typical old-school-tie deal. Euan was told to pack and leave at once, and he couldn't get hold of you at the hotel when he tried to ring. They said you weren't there and there was no answer at home, so he asked me to tell you he wouldn't be keeping his date with you.' Robert's eyes were blistering. 'The date you apparently had no intention of keeping, anyway.'

Stephanie bent her head, very pale. 'I wrote to him . . .'

'Oh, he got one of your letters too, did he?' Robert was scaldingly sarcastic. 'That will be something for him to look forward to reading when he gets back, won't it?'

She kept her eyes down, tears brushing her lashes.

'Robert, don't. I'm sorry . . .'

'Sorry? You vanish, without a word, with a man neither of us ever met before Saturday night and then say you're *sorry*?' Robert's breathing seemed very loud in the quiet room. 'I suppose I can make a good guess at why you went with that bastard—my God, he's a fast worker, I have to say that for him. You hardly saw him for two minutes, but he managed to talk you into going away with him.' He caught her restless movement and watched her in grim silence for a moment. 'Don't tell me you're in love with him—you can't be, not that fast, it isn't humanly possible.'

'I've met him before,' she whispered.

Robert bent forward. 'What?'

She repeated her words and Robert took a deep, audible breath. 'You've met him before? You didn't say so. Where? When?'

'Five years ago.'

Robert stiffened, staring. 'Five years. Did you say five. In Australia?'

Stephanie nodded, her hands tightly gripping, and Robert got out of his chair and came over to sit on the arm of hers, his hand gently cupping her head, turning her face up to him.

'What is this, Stephanie?'

The tears spilled then, and she turned her face into his arm and wept while Robert muttered uneasily and patted her heaving shoulders.

'It's okay, Stevie, don't cry. Come on, there's a good girl, just tell me what's going on. Oh, come on, Stevie—oh, hell!'

She buried her head against him, no longer crying but not wishing to see his face while she told him. She didn't start telling him for a minute because she couldn't find the right words, but Robert was shrewd.

Now that he knew that Gerard Tenniel had somehow known her in Australia five years ago, he began to put two and two together.

'Is that bastard blackmailing you?'

She sat up again, startled, turning a wide-eyed face up to him.

He scowled ferociously. 'So he is!'

'How did you guess?'

'Do you think I'm stupid?'

She laughed, her mouth trembling. 'No, Rob, I wouldn't say you were that. Of course, it isn't blackmail exactly—I mean, we aren't talking about money here.'

Robert still looked grim. 'What are we talking about? What is he blackmailing you for?'

She looked down, flushing.

'My God, I'll kill him,' gritted Robert. He sounded as if he couldn't breathe properly. 'The man's a lawyer, a barrister, for heaven's sake. And he actually blackmailed you into going away with him, moving in here with him.' He stopped abruptly and looked at her, embarrassed, uneasy. 'Stevie, you haven't . . .'

She looked blankly at him. 'Haven't what?'

Robert made a confused gesture with his hand. 'Well, you know.' He was pointing upward and Stephanie's bewildered gaze went up to the ceiling.

Then she caught on and turned a scalding crimson. 'No, I haven't! Robert! You don't think I'd let him talk me into bed—you didn't really think I'd be that stupid?'

'You let him talk you into coming away with him.'

'That was different. In a way, he was right.'

'Right? For God's sake, what the hell do you mean, right? Right to blackmail you?'

'Of course not, that's irrelevant in a way.'

'What is? The blackmail? Irrelevant to what? Stephanie, sometimes I don't think you're quite right in the head. This guy comes out of the blue and starts blackmailing you about something that happened years ago and you say it's irrelevant?'

'Look, just for a minute, leave the blackmail out of it . . .'

'How can I do that? The blackmail's the whole thing, that's what we're talking about!'

'No,' she said, getting up because she knew she would only make him listen and understand if he stopped thinking about her as his helpless little sister who had to be protected for her own good. Robert had something in common with Gerard Tenniel, although he wouldn't be too happy if she told him as much. So she stood there facing him, head up, chin defiant. 'Listen, Robert, just listen and let me explain, stop interrupting and shouting at me.'

Robert looked offended and furious. 'Shouting? Me? I'm not shouting at you! When have you ever heard me raise my voice to you?'

She turned and walked away across the drawing-room to the high bay windows, standing there staring out into the tree-lined avenue. The afternoon was wearing into dusk; blue shadows moved under the trees and birds gave poignant last-minute calls.

'Gerard made me realise something I suppose I hadn't wanted to admit—that I couldn't possibly marry Euan and risk the chance that one day someone else might come along and recognise me and resurrect the scandal about the Burgess murder trial. If Euan wasn't a doctor, if his family weren't the way they are, I could tell him the truth and it might not matter, but honestly, Rob, what do you think Mrs Cameron would say if she found out? It isn't just the murder, I wasn't to

blame for that—but everyone believed I was Theo
Burgess's mistress.'

'I didn't,' Robert said fiercely. 'Mum and Dad
didn't.'

Stephanie turned, her smile quivering. 'Thank you.
But even if I swore to Mrs Cameron that I was totally
innocent, do you think she'd want to have me as a
daughter-in-law?'

Robert stared back at her, his jaw clenched. She
read in his face the realisation that she was right, but
his equal determination not to admit as much, and
smiled wearily.

'That's why I went away with Gerard. I wanted to
go right away, make a quick break. It seemed simpler
than staying, explaining, talking about it. I didn't
want to go, I was happy with you and Gwen, I liked
my job and living in the town, it's a nice place, but you
know how people gossip—if it once got round that I'd
been mixed up in something unsavoury I'd never live
it down. I'd hate being stared at, whispered about.'

'Why should you be? Even if you were right and any
idea of marrying Euan wasn't on, there's no reason to
move away. You don't have to tell anybody anything.'

'What if they found out anyway? Gerard Tenniel
isn't the only person in the world who knows. It might
be a year, two years, even another five, before
someone else popped up who knew—but sooner or
later it might happen.' She paused, looking at him
gently. She loved Robert and she didn't want to hurt
him, but she had to point out the obvious, since he
hadn't yet seen it. 'And that might be very unfortunate
for you, Rob. The hospital board aren't exactly broad-
minded, are they? If you were involved in a scandal of
that sort, even as my brother, they wouldn't like it,
would they?'

She saw his face stiffen, his colour ebb. He stared
back at her for a long time without saying anything.

'That's why I can't stay. I don't want to do anything
to make life difficult for you and Gwen. You're happy
in Wyville, but from now on I wouldn't be because I'd
always be looking over my shoulder, waiting for
someone else to turn up, for everything to blow up in
my face, in our faces, Rob, because you would get just
as hurt as I would.'

He swallowed, shifting on the edge of the chair arm.
'We could move, find somewhere . . .'

'And go through the whole process again? Don't
you see, Rob, it wouldn't work? You and Gwen would
hate to live in a big city, but that's the only place where
you can be safe from this sort of gossip because with so
many other people around there simply isn't the same
curiosity. In a town like Wyville people love to talk
about each other and they're at least ten years behind
London in their attitudes. I love the town, you know I
do, but I know those people. They'd be shocked, they
would never feel the same about me again, and I'd
hate that.'

Robert got up and came over to her, put his arm
around her shoulders, patting her in that helpless way
because he didn't quite know how to express how he
felt.

'So what are you going to do?'

'Stay in London . . .'

He frowned, his eyes angry. 'Here? With Tenniel?'

Stephanie gave a wry smile, shaking her head. 'No,
of course not—I'm only staying here tonight and—
don't look like that!—his cousin Julia is staying here
too and has already told me that she'll be in the next
bedroom and if I need her I only have to shout.' She
smiled at him. 'I like her—she's offered to let me use

her spare room until I find somewhere of my own. I'll probably move on tomorrow morning.'

'But Tenniel did try to blackmail you? I could call the police and ...'

'And create an even bigger scandal?'

Robert seethed, frustration in his eyes. 'Why should he get away with such low-down, despicable ...'

'You broke his jardinière, you'll have to comfort yourself with that,' she said, laughing without real amusement.

'I wish I'd broken him,' Robert burst out, face red. He moved towards the door, as if bent on doing just that, and Stephanie went after him in alarm.

'No, Rob, don't!'

He was in the hall where they found Gerard lurking. Robert charged like a mad bull, his fist swinging. He had been a boxing champion at medical school and his fist connected before Gerard could get out of the way. Gerard went down in a thrashing sprawl, hitting his head on the bottom step of the stairs. Robert stood over him, fists clenched.

'Lay one finger on my sister and you'll have me to deal with, you bastard!' he growled, then swung round to look at Stephanie. 'Keep in touch, let me know where you are and what you're doing.'

'Yes,' she promised, watching Gerard with anxiety. He wasn't moving—had Robert really injured him? Julia came through the kitchen door, staring at her cousin's prone figure with dismay.

'Write!' Robert said. 'You'll write at least once a week, won't you?' He looked at his watch, his face hesitant, uneasy. 'I have to get back. I had a hell of a time getting someone to stand in for me and I swore I'd be there tonight. I swapped rotas with someone and I must get back to fill in for him.'

Julia had knelt down beside Gerard. 'Is he dead?' she asked, but although she looked faintly worried her tone wasn't serious.

'I wish he was,' said Robert over his shoulder on his way to the front door. 'When he comes to, tell him that I meant what I said—tell him to keep his hands off my sister!'

Stephanie followed him and Robert turned to kiss her cheek. 'I'm sorry,' she said huskily. 'Very sorry about all this. Give Gwen my love.'

'And Euan?' Robert asked brusquely. 'What am I to tell Euan?'

She looked away, sighing, shrugging. 'He'll get over me.' She looked back at her brother and saw that his eyes were angry.

'Poor Euan,' was all he said, though, and then he was gone and she slowly closed the door.

Gerard sat up, rubbing his jaw. 'Your brother has a fist like a steam-hammer!' He tentatively got to his feet. 'I hope that made him feel better. I thought I'd better let him win that round or he might have stayed all day.'

'He knocked you out cold!' Stephanie spat at him with venom.

He smiled, and she eyed him with doubt. Had he been faking the unconscious stillness? He was probably right; Robert had felt better after hitting him, but if Gerard had been acting, she would have to change her view of him. He was even more deceptive than she had suspected, but then he was a barrister, wasn't he? And she had heard that that profession demanded a considerable acting flair as well as a natural eloquence. She should have remembered that. This man was far from simple, far from easy to understand.

'He had a damned good try,' Gerard agreed coolly. 'I felt a certain sympathy, he was under stress.'

Stephanie stared, dumbfounded. 'Under stress? That must be the biggest understatement of the year!'

He grinned. 'Okay, he was beside himself with rage, is that more accurate? I'm no medic but I decided it would make him less likely to have a brainstorm if I let him hit me and didn't fight back.'

Julia looked amused. 'That's your story, and you're sticking to it, I suppose?'

Gerard grimaced, staring at his shattered jardinière with a rueful expression. Robert had managed to break both the graceful china flowerpot and the tall, matching stand. Among the earth and shreds of china lay a few green leaves, a scatter of pink flowers already limp and crushed.

'What a mess,' he said, and Stephanie felt the words were apt and described her whole situation.

'I'll clear it up in a minute,' offered Julia. 'But what about that coffee? I've kept it hot, bubbling on the hob. You look as if you need some, Stephanie. I know I do. All this drama makes life very draining.'

Stephanie began to laugh wildly, almost hysterically. Julia's calm, dry voice made everything suddenly very funny, but it was a joke on the wild side: black farce. All one could say was that laughing was better than crying.

CHAPTER SEVEN

STEPHANIE didn't think she would sleep that night. Leaving aside the succession of shocks which had hit her over the weekend, the breathtaking rush of events carrying her helplessly before them like a straw on a floodtide, she had never found it easy to sleep in a strange room for the first time. Even on holiday, she was usually wakeful on the first night in a hotel bedroom.

She and Julia had cooked the supper; a delicious paella made with frozen shrimps, shredded chicken and some chunks of garlic sausage added towards the end of the cooking time. Julia had found some turmeric in the larder and coloured the rice a delicate yellow; the spice gave the dish a faintly stronger tang, too. While they worked in the kitchen, talking, getting to know one another, Gerard was in his study, a thick brief spread in front of him, catching up on some of the work he had neglected over the past few days, he told Stephanie.

She went into the room several hours after he began work to tell him that the paella was ready. It was dark by then; he had drawn the deep red velvet curtains across the windows and was reading at his desk, a white angle-lamp fixed so that he could concentrate on the closely typed pages.

It was something of a shock to her to see that he was wearing spectacles, horn-rimmed reading glasses which he pushed down on his nose to study her. The grey eyes seemed abstracted, hardly recognising her.

'Hmm? Yes.'

'Supper's ready.'

He pulled off his spectacles and dropped them
casually on the desk. The bright lamplight glittered on
his blond hair and gave his eyes the sheen of steel.

'Oh, fine.' He ran his fingers over his eyes, as if he
was tired. Stephanie saw fine lines around his mouth
and upper cheekbones. The lamplight cruelly intensi-
fied that weariness; made him look older than usual.
He must be in his late thirties by now. Why hadn't he
married? It couldn't have been from lack of opportunity: he was far too good-looking and distinctly
eligible. He must be well off—this house would be
expensive to maintain.

'What is it?' he asked, getting up and stretching. He
was wearing a thin white silk shirt which was more or
less transparent; she saw the movement of his muscles
rippling under it, the faint brown of his skin. 'I'm
hungry,' he said, as if surprised.

'It's paella, and I'm not surprised you're hungry—
it's half past eight! I hope you won't get indigestion
from eating this late.'

Gerard had taken off his tie and opened his shirt
collar; she could see the strong line of his throat.

'Paella? Sounds good.' He turned and she quickly
looked away to stare round the room. The walls were
lined with books on polished mahogany shelves.

'Are these all law books?' she asked to distract him
from thinking about the way she had been watching
him.

'Some are, most aren't. I keep my reference books in
chambers, all but an essential few.' He watched her go
over to glance along the shelves. 'If you want
something to read in bed take what you like,' he
offered.

'Thanks, perhaps I will, later. But Julia's just serving supper, so . . .' She moved to the door and he followed, switching off his desk lamp.

That plunged the room into darkness, she collided with a chair she hadn't noticed and Gerard exclaimed impatiently.

'What have you done now?'

'Nothing,' she said, conscious of him beside her, a disturbing presence in the darkness. His body had a cool scent but there was a hint of musk under that, as though he had been working so intensely that he had perspired. For a second they both stood there, breathing audibly; then, in a rush of alarm, she reached out and groped for the door, pulled it open and almost stumbled out of the room.

Gerard followed, his eyes gleaming with mockery which she pretended not to notice. They ate the paella and drank a little white wine with it, had coffee, and then she and Julia stacked the dishwasher and tidied the kitchen before they went to watch television for an hour while Gerard went back to his study to work on his brief.

'Are you going to take this job Gerard has offered you?' asked Julia casually, and Stephanie shrugged.

'I might look for a job in another hotel.'

'It isn't as easy to find jobs in London as you might think. Unemployment's as tough here as anywhere else.'

Stephanie chewed her lower lip. 'I know, but . . .' She broke off. How could she tell Julia that she didn't trust Gerard and didn't want to work in his chambers?

'You could try it for a month, see how you got on,' Julia added, and Stephanie looked sharply at her.

'Oh, I've no axe to grind,' said Julia, laughing, reading her expression. 'If you hate the idea of

working with Gerard, tell him what to do with his job.
But you might find the work interesting and it's
probably better paid than the job you had in that hotel.
I've heard that hotel jobs aren't exactly highly paid.'

'Far from it,' Stephanie agreed, grimacing. 'But . . .'

'But what? You think Gerard might take advantage
of having you working for him?' Julia laughed
wickedly. 'Go on, I'm sure you can handle him. Don't
think I haven't had to cope with sexual hassle from
guys I've worked with—it happens all the time. They
have such simple minds. They look at my hair and
think: blonde girls are a pushover! Then they try it on.
It sometimes takes a few hard slaps before they realise
they're not on to a good thing, but you can get your
message over in the end.'

Stephanie had begun to laugh. Julia's light dismissal
of Gerard's menace as a little sexual hassle made her
feel a lot less tense. Perhaps she should take that job?
She probably wouldn't see much of him, anyway. He
would spend most of his time in court, he wouldn't be
in the office very much, and it might be rather
interesting to learn something about the law.

'The thing I liked best about working in the hotel
was meeting lots of different people,' she said. 'I took a
secretarial course, I can do shorthand and typing, but I
find it dull, just taking letters and filing—being in a
hotel reception was more varied.'

'I expect you'll meet quite a few people in Gerard's
chambers.' Julia gave her a teasing look. 'Criminals,
solicitors' clerks, policemen . . .'

Stephanie's smile froze. She had met enough
policemen and solicitors five years ago; she didn't
know if she cared to meet any more of them.

'I'm tired,' she said, getting up. 'I think I'll go to bed
now.'

Julia stared after her, looking puzzled. Stephanie said, 'Goodnight,' at the door, then added, 'say goodnight to Gerard for me, I won't disturb him while he's working.'

She went into her own room upstairs and found that a strong wind had got up during the evening. As she opened the door the curtains blew wildly about; she had left the window open and the room was full of cold air. Stephanie shut the door and ran over to close the window, too, shivering. It was bitterly cold in here now.

She went into the bathroom to change into her nightdress. Here it was far warmer. She brushed her hair, staring at herself in the mirror. How odd that she looked no different; she felt as if she had changed radically over the past three days. Three days! Was it so short a time since Gerard Tenniel had walked back into her life? Her blue eyes betrayed confused emotions: anger, uncertainty, a cloudy regret. When Euan got back from Saudi Arabia he would find out that she had gone.

He would miss her, she knew that, because she would miss him too. They had been close friends who might have been lovers—if Euan hadn't been the sort of man he was, by now no doubt they would have been, even if they hadn't talked of marriage. Euan was the product of his environment, a man very much in control of his life and himself, a disciplined man, a careful man, whose work was the breath of his being. He was a brilliant cardiologist; he worked precisely, and with a depth of knowledge and experience that would undoubtedly increase as he grew older. His career was more important to him than anything else in his life. He might miss her, but if she hadn't gone, if she had offered him the choice, she was convinced that, however reluctantly, he would eventually have chosen his career rather than her, if it meant wrecking his reputation. Euan was his mother's son; he disapproved of reckless behaviour, he despised immorality.

She turned away impatiently and decided she would think about all that some other time. If she didn't put Euan and all her problems out of her mind, she'd never sleep tonight.

Still brushing her hair, she wandered into the bedroom just as the outer door opened. Stephanie stiffened, changing colour, as she saw Gerard walk in. His gaze flashed across the room towards her, and only then did she remember that her nightress was almost transparent: a floating blue silk with a deep v-neck trimmed with white lace. In a certain light you could see right through the material to what was beneath it, and Gerard was staring as if he could do that now.

'What do you want?' she stammered, then wished she had chosen another way of putting the question. He was grinning in a way she found distinctly annoying. 'I mean, get out,' she added hastily.

'I brought you some books, as you forgot to come in and get some,' he said, walking over to drop the three volumes on her bedside table. 'I wasn't sure what you'd like, so I picked out a murder story, a biography and a straight novel, but there's a wide selection in my study, if you prefer to pick them yourself.'

She grabbed up a négligé which matched her nightie and quickly slid into it. Gerard watched. Stephanie wished he would look at something else; his gaze made her very nervous. She tied the wide blue silk belt decisively, and felt less vulnerable.

'Thank you.'

Without taking his eyes off her, he kicked the door shut, and Stephanie felt a jagged stab of alarm.

'I asked you to go,' she reminded him icily, stepping behind a chair and gripping the back of it with both hands. If he came a step nearer, she'd pick the chair up and hit him with it!

He sauntered over while she watched, ready to raise the chair, but Gerard had out-thought her. Before she could lift the chair an inch, he sat down on it.

Stephanie's jaw dropped. He leaned backwards, his head tilted so that he could look up at her, eyes glinting, pure provocation.

'You haven't told me your decision yet.'

'What?' She felt as if her mind was suddenly full of fog, she couldn't see straight, let alone think. Her hypnotised gaze wandered over his sleek fair hair, the brush of his gold-tipped lashes on his cheek, the riveting beauty of those hard cheekbones under his smooth skin. Only at the jawline did he betray a need to shave: the faintest roughness around his chin, a pale stubble that caught the light.

'Made up your mind yet?' he enquired.

'About what?' She stared at the warm curve of his mouth; firm, masculine, sexually intriguing, especially when it smiled the way it was doing now. She had a terrifying desire to lean over and kiss it. It was, she thought numbly, a little like emotional vertigo—one step too far and she might plummet to her doom.

His hand suddenly shot sideways, caught hold of her wrist and yanked abruptly. Stephanie gave a squawk of alarm as she lurched forward, but she didn't hit the floor as she had expected. At the last moment Gerard gave a deft twist and she fell into his lap.

'Don't you . . .' she burst out a second before his mouth closed over hers. She didn't want to shut her eyes, but somebody else seemed to be controlling her; it certainly wasn't her intention to let her lids droop, but they obviously had—or else someone had turned out the lights, because it was very dark, a velvety smothering darkness in which her senses rioted. His mouth was doing things to her that were positively immoral, and his hands led a busy life of their own without Stephanie feeling the energy to halt their restless explorations.

'I don't want this,' she mumbled against his coaxing lips, putting a languid hand on his shoulder to push him away.

He lifted his head obediently and looked at her through half-closed lids; the darkness in which she had been lost seemed to be in his eyes now, in those dilated black pupils, which gave back her own reflection, in soft focus, cloudy, shimmering.

'Don't you?' he murmured, mouth twisting.

'Certainly not,' she said, trying to retie her belt. When had he undone that?

'I don't think you know what you want,' he said, pulling the belt undone again.

'Stop that!' protested Stephanie, wishing that she didn't feel so weak and abandoned when his hand found its way to places where it shouldn't be.

She sat up and tried to get to her feet, but Gerard held her waist with both hands, his eyes fixed on the low, revealing neckline of her nightdress.

'Sooner or later, Stephanie,' he murmured, his voice a silky mixture of threat and promise, then leaned over and kissed her at the the deepest angle of the neckline, where her pale breasts rose out of white lace.

'Don't bet on it!' she snapped, angrily wrenching herself away and managing to stand up again. She was several feet away before Gerard knew anything about it.

'Now, please leave my room before I call Julia,' she said crossly, tying her belt for the third time.

He gave a yawn, smothered by his hand. 'I'm tired, anyway,' he said, as though apologising. 'It will have to keep.'

She would have thrown something at him if she had anything easily to hand, preferably something heavy and potentially lethal.

He sauntered back towards her and she backed, opening the door for him to go through.

Gerard paused. 'By the way, you can have the rest of the week off, but I'd like you to start work on Monday next.'

'I haven't decided yet.'

He shrugged. 'Make up your mind quickly. I'll have to fill the job almost at once.' About to go, he paused again. 'Oh, you do have secretarial skills as well?'

'As well as what?' she asked suspiciously, ready to take offence.

His eyes mocked. 'As well as being trained as a receptionist. What did you think I meant?'

Stephanie wouldn't admit what she had thought he meant. Instead, she said coldly that she was a fully trained secretary and could type and write shorthand at a rapid speed.

'Good. In an emergency we might have to call on your secretarial skills,' he said. 'Goodnight, Stephanie.'

She bolted the door behind him loudly and heard him laugh before he went across to his own room. How much of all that had Julia heard? she wondered as she climbed into bed and began to look at the books he had brought her. A fine bodyguard she was! Or was she in bed and asleep already?

Stephanie sat up for a while reading the murder story Gerard had brought her. It was after midnight before she put out her light and long after one before she finally slept.

She woke up in the morning to the smell of coffee and bacon floating up the stairs. Julia called a moment later. 'Want your breakfast in bed?'

Stephanie leapt out of bed and went to open the bedroom door. 'No, thanks, I'll come down in five minutes.'

'Any later than that and the food will have dried to a husk,' Julia told her, going back to the kitchen, and Stephanie flew into the bathroom, washed and dressed at record speed and took the stairs two at a time. It wasn't until she entered the kitchen that she discovered three things: it was raining, it was nearly ten in the morning, and Gerard had already left for work.

'Speedy must be your middle name,' said Julia, going to fish her plate of bacon and mushrooms from the electric hostess trolley. 'Careful, the plate's hot,' she warned, placing it before Stephanie.

'Thanks. It's very good of you to cook this for me. I'm sorry I overslept, but I couldn't get to sleep last night. How long have you been up?'

'Since eight. I'm an insomniac, I only ever get six hours at the maximum. I came down just as Gerard was leaving—he was out of the house by five to eight.'

Julia poured coffee for both of them and sat down, smiling. Stephanie said, 'Julia, you mentioned a spare room in your flat?'

Julia looked at her and nodded. 'If you want it, it's yours.'

'On a strictly business basis,' replied Stephanie

quickly. 'That is, I'd like to pay rent. I don't know if you meant a purely short term arrangement or something more permanent?'

'Up to you. I have shared my flat from time to time and I'm ready to let you have the room short or long-term, just as you like. We could see how we got on, couldn't we? We may be incompatible as flatmates. I once met a very nice Swedish girl when I was running a market campaign in Harrods. At first sight we hit it off like mad. She moved into the flat on a Monday and by the Saturday she'd seduced my boy-friend and broken my favourite LP. She had to go.'

Stephanie giggled. 'Which did you regret most?'

'Oh, the LP. It wasn't in production any more, I couldn't get another copy. I had a new boy-friend within the month.'

'Well, I'll try not to break anything and I promise I won't seduce your boy-friend.'

'He's not in London at the moment; he flew to Rio last week and won't be back for three months. He's a biologist and is out there to study the local flora and fauna.' Julia smiled. 'And I just hope the local fauna doesn't include the human variety! I haven't been very lucky with my men in the past. I never seem to meet the faithful sort.'

'Who does?' Stephanie said lightly. She might have thought of Euan, but somehow she didn't, she thought of Gerard and wondered how faithful he was and how many other women there had been in his life in the past five years. He hadn't married any of them, but that didn't prove anything. He didn't give the impression of being the type who broods alone over a broken heart. All that stuff about how he had felt about her was probably just moonshine, a fairy story he'd invented because five years ago she had bruised his male ego. Gerard Tenniel probably wasn't used to discovering that the woman he had his eye on apparently had her eye fixed elsewhere.

She must be very careful not to let him know how seriously she had been attracted to him, how hurt she had been when he dropped her like a hot brick.

He hadn't been hurt; he'd been insulted. He thought that she had been using him as a cover for an affair with an older man, a man he despised, whose only attraction for her would have had to be money. Gerard hadn't been jealous of Theo. She didn't believe it. He'd been personally offended, the blow to his ego all the more lasting because she hadn't preferred a younger or more attractive man. She did not accept that he had had any serious intentions towards her—how could he have been serious about a naïve eighteen-year-old who was too inexperienced and shy even to recognise a sexual invitation when she got it?

If he had genuinely cared for her, he wouldn't have believed the lies Viola told. He wouldn't have gone away, vanished from her life. He wouldn't have come back last weekend and ruthlessly blackmailed her into coming away with him. He wouldn't have come into her bedroom last night with the unhidden intention of seducing her if he could.

He was treating her with mocking cruelty, a derision she found hard to bear. Only a man driven by hostility would have come to Wyville determined to wreck her life, break up any possible chance of happiness with Euan, force her into flight.

That afternoon, she moved into Julia's flat in Chelsea. It was small: two bedrooms, a small sitting-room with a tiny kitchen area at one end of it, and a bathroom. The décor and furniture were modern and rather characterless; Julia said she had inherited them

from the previous tenant, and hadn't yet got round to
changing anything except to import a few personal
items—ornaments, a couple of pictures and some
books and records.

Julia wasn't working that week, she admitted
cheerfully. Some months she earned considerable
sums, other times she had to start budgeting tightly
until her next big payment came in. At the moment
she was solvent but couldn't afford to be extravagant,
so Stephanie's share of the rent would come in handy.

'As I said, I like to check out possible flatmates
carefully. You can make some costly mistakes. A
friend of mine let someone move in who moved out the
same day with half my friend's belongings.'

Stephanie suggested hesitantly, 'Would you like me
to get some references?'

Julia laughed. 'Oh, I'm quite good at reading
character now. I've met your brother, he seems very
respectable—even if he was rather short-tempered.'

Gerard rang that evening and Julia called Stephanie to the phone, her face quizzical. 'Guess who?' she
teased, holding out the telephone.

Stephanie flushed and took it reluctantly. 'Hallo?'

'How are you settling in?' asked Gerard, and the
sound of his voice had an odd effect on her
metabolism. Her body went into overdrive: heart
beating too fast, lungs like worn-out bellows, skin icy
one minute, feverish the next.

She tried to keep her cool. 'Very well, thank you,'
she said in a distant voice.

'Miss me?' he enquired.

Aware of Julia still in the same room, Stephanie
kept her remote tone. 'I've been very busy.'

He was quick and shrewd. 'Julia still there?'

'Yes.'

'Can she hear me?'

'Of course not.'

'Good,' he said, a thread of laughter in his voice.
'Why don't you come here for the evening? I'm much
more fun than Julia.'

'No, thank you,' she answered with dignity.

'You don't know what you're missing.'

'Yes, I do.'

His voice took on a relentless note. 'Do you, indeed?
Who demonstrated?'

Stephanie's face flushed hotly, even though he
couldn't see her and Julia couldn't hear him. 'That
wasn't what I meant.'

'Are you sure you haven't slept with Cameron?'

'No, I haven't,' she said angrily. 'I've got to go now,
goodbye.'

She hung up without waiting for him to say any
more, and Julia watched her thoughtfully as she
turned away from the phone.

'Gerard's okay, you know,' she said quietly. 'I've
known him all my life. He can be maddening, he's as
clever as a wagonload of monkeys, he's tough and
ambitious and damned good at his job, and he's okay.
If I was in trouble I'd bellow for him like a shot. You
can trust him, Stephanie.'

'Can I?' Stephanie wasn't so sure. Julia was his
cousin, after all. As close as brother and sister, hadn't
they said? Of course she would spring to his defence!
Gerard was obviously fond of her and had never given
her any reason to distrust him. Between Julia and
Gerard there was a vital element missing—the sexual
conflict which had bedevilled his relationship with
Stephanie from the beginning. Once sex enters into
any woman's friendship with a man it loads the dice.
A friendly game becomes a battle, each determined to

win. With any winner there has to be a loser, and
Stephanie's pride wouldn't let her admit the remotest
possibility of defeat at the hands of Gerard Tenniel.

He wanted to win too much. His ego was involved.
He wasn't fighting fair, he would use any methods,
take any advantage he could, but she wasn't going to
let him beat her.

Julia took her sightseeing next day, from the Tower of
London to Kew Gardens, by bus and by underground
train. They ate their lunch in the cafeteria at the
National Gallery, overlooking Trafalgar Square. The
salad was crisp and delicious, and after the meal they
crossed over into the square to feed the pigeons and
admire the lions and fountains.

Gerard rang again that evening; he sounded far
away. 'I'm in Brighton,' he told her. 'Had to come
down to see a client. The moon's full. My hotel looks
over the sea—you ought to see this moonlight; it
makes the sea seem quite unreal, all silver.'

Stephanie pulled back the curtain at the window
and looked out at the same moon; over London it had
a coppery glow, as though reflecting back the yellow
streetlamps, but it shone on both of them.

'What did you do today?' he asked, and listened
while she told him about Kew and the pigeons and
some buskers she had seen outside a theatre stage
door.

'You won't forget that you start work next Monday?' he prompted. 'Nine o'clock sharp. Julia will give
you the address. I won't see you until then. I've got a
heavy case starting tomorrow and I'll be in court for
the next few days, but with any luck it should be
wrapped up before Monday.'

'What sort of case is it?' she asked curiously.

'Quite simple. A burglary and G.B.H. My client's accused of breaking into a house and hitting the owner over the head with a torch.'

'Is he guilty?'

Gerard's voice was wry. 'My dear girl! You shouldn't ask me questions like that. I told you, I'm defending.' He paused, then asked, 'Heard from home? Your brother? Cameron?'

'No,' she said stiffly. 'I told you, I've been out all day, and anyway, Euan is probably still in Saudi Arabia.'

'If he does show up, you're not to talk to him,' Gerard said brusquely. 'Refer him to me, tell Julia to get rid of him, but don't you see him.'

She didn't even answer that. 'I must go,' she said instead. 'Goodnight, Gerard.'

It was only after she had hung up that it dawned on her that she hadn't said goodbye, her voice had implied that they would talk again soon, and she had called him Gerard, saying his name gently, almost intimately.

She pulled back the curtain again to look at that moon which was shining down on him, too, at the same time. Was he looking up at it, thinking about her?

A shiver ran down her spine. He was sneaking up on her; insidious as spring, inevitable as winter. If she didn't watch out she would find herself in his possession.

CHAPTER EIGHT

STEPHANIE began working in Gerard's chambers the following Monday morning. For some reason, she had imagined that he would work in a prestigious building, a beautifully furnished showplace for the talents of himself and his colleagues. She knew that he was successful and in most other professions success required display, advertisement.

Instead, she found herself going up the steps of an early nineteenth-century house with iron railings at pavement level surrounding the steps down into the basement. The house was in a terrace; it was narrow, three storeys high. The brick was blackened with age and city grime; the stone surrounds of the windows had cracked and become porous; the windows were divided into the original lozenges. It looked like something out of Dickens. Stephanie peered at the brass plate on the wall. Had she come to the wrong address?

'They're all dead,' said a voice behind her, and she jumped, swinging round.

The young man on the step below her grinned. 'Can I help you? I'm a clerk in the firm. Looking for someone?'

'Yes, I'm Stephanie Stuart, and I'm . . .'

'Our new receptionist! Right.' He joined her on the broad top step and pushed open the door into the narrow hall beyond. 'I was told to look out for you. We're upstairs, by the way.' He gestured and she led the way up the very narrow, badly lit stairs. All the

141

way the young man talked to her back.

'I'm Barry Tomkins, junior clerk, I work for the chief clerk, Mr Monday, you'll meet him in a minute. He arrives at nine eleven precisely.'

'Nine eleven?' Stephanie repeated, laughing.

'His train arrives at Kings Cross at five minutes to nine. He walks here, arrives just after ten past.' Barry grinned at her. 'Unless his train is late, which it is about twice a month.' He waved towards a door facing them at the top of the stairs. 'This way, Stephanie. We use first names, by the way, among the secretarial staff, I mean. The barristers are Mr, of course, all except Diana Kenge and she's Miss. Sorry, Ms.'

Stephanie walked into the office and found it empty except for a girl in a neat grey dress who was sitting on a step-ladder filing papers in large black box files. She squinted down at the new arrivals and said, 'Hallo, Barry. You're late!'

'Your watch is wrong again, Lulu.'

'Don't call me Lulu!' she snapped, glaring through her spectacles at him.

'Stephanie, this is Lulu,' said Barry, gesturing upwards. 'She's our senior secretary and thinks she runs the place.'

The dark-haired girl came down the step-ladder with Barry observing her slim legs with interest all the way. She was aware of it and flashed a cool look at him. 'Haven't you got anything to do?'

He saluted smartly. 'Yes, ma'am. Sorry, ma'am. You've got a run in your stockings, ma'am.'

He vanished before she could snap back at him and she turned back to study Stephanie, offering her hand. 'Hallo, I'm Imogen Barber. I'm afraid Joan hasn't arrived yet, but when she does eventually get here she'll explain what your job consists of. She should have typed up a clear description of what has to be done, I've reminded her countless times, but Joan isn't interested in anything but pop music, her boy-friend and having a good time.' Imogen gave Stephanie one of her cool smiles. 'That's why she's leaving.'

'She was fired?'

'Let's say we preferred her to resign. It is essential that clients are efficiently handled, briefs correctly despatched, messages accurately passed on—Joan found that hard. She was more often in the cloakroom than at her desk here; she got telephone messages scrambled, or forgot to pass them on and she lost vital letters.' Imogen consulted her watch. 'And she's late again. She's always late and she always leaves early unless I catch her going out of the door.' Imogen looked at Stephanie hard, as if trying to read her character in her face. 'I hope you're going to do this job rather better than Joan did.'

'I'll do my best.'

Imogen considered her with piercing, remorseless pale blue eyes. 'Then we must hope your best is good enough.'

Charming, thought Stephanie. So this girl worked for Gerard? She looked super-efficient, cold as an iceberg, but very attractive in a streamlined way. No doubt Gerard appreciated the efficiency. Did he find the icy good looks interesting, too?

The door opened and a distinguished man in his late forties walked into the room, nodding to Imogen, giving Stephanie a brief glance.

'Good morning, Mr Beaumont,' said Imogen, and when he had gone through a door on the far side of the cluttered reception area she told Stephanie, 'That was Mr Beaumont, he's our silk, specialises in civil law, very fat fees. The oldest counsel is Mr Allnew; you

won't see him for several days, he has a bad cold and
Diana's handling his brief for him. She usually
dogsbodies for the senior barristers. Mr Allnew is
sixty, talks of retiring all the time, but I doubt if he will
just yet. He dislikes work, can't stand the law, but he's
good. A number of solicitors won't have anyone else.
They trust him. He's reliable.'

'Except when he's got a cold?'

Imogen eyed her blankly. 'Is that a joke? I must get
back to my own office. My boss will want to dictate
some letters.' As she moved away the door opened
again and another girl came breathlessly through it,
halting as she saw Imogen.

'Late again,' said Imogen, as if more in sorrow than
anger. 'What's the point of saying anything to you?
This is your replacement, Stephanie Stuart. Try not to
teach her any of your bad habits while you train her.'

She vanished, and the new arrival made a furious
face at her back. 'Sarcastic cat! She's so perfect she
makes me sick.' She pulled off her coat and hung it on
a row of pegs behind the door, then smiled at
Stephanie. 'Welcome to Colditz. I'm Joan and, thank
God, I'm getting out of here, away from Lulu and her
sniping.'

'Why do you call her Lulu?'

'Oh, we had an American working here once, she
was working her way around the world and spent
three months in the office, while one of the other
secretaries was off having a baby. She came back
afterwards you see, so . . . well, anyway, this Yank
hated Imogen. It was mutual, Imogen was always
getting at her, and the day she left this girl said to
Imogen. "You know, you're really a Lulu, you're out of
your skull. No job's that important. One day the little
men in white coats will come for you, Lulu."' Joan

laughed gleefully. 'Imogen hated it! She went bright red. And we call her Lulu whenever we want to annoy her. Me and Barry and Celia, that is—Celia's another secretary, by the way.'

'The one with the baby? Doesn't she mind leaving it all day?'

'She hates it, but she hasn't any option—she isn't married.'

'Oh, I see.'

Joan looked quickly at her. 'She's very sensitive about it. It was tough on her; Celia's okay. I'd swap her for a dozen Imogens.'

The door opened and a very tall, thin, black-haired man came striding in with a frown as his eye fell on Joan and Stephanie. 'Gossiping again, Joan? I hope that post is sorted and despatched and the day's schedule pinned up on the wall?'

Joan gave a weak smile. 'I'm afraid I . . . I've been explaining the way we do things to Miss Stuart, the new receptionist, sir.'

The man stared at Stephanie, looked her up and down, his thin mouth tight. 'I'm the chief clerk, Mr Monday. I expect my letters to be on my desk when I arrive. Please remember that.' He looked back at Joan. 'Get a move on, then!'

After that, the morning was hectic. Stephanie had little time to notice much beyond the fact that people came and went at amazing speed; the door was always opening and shutting. Clients arrived with their solicitors to see counsel; junior clerks arrived with briefs under their arm, senior clerks arrived to have a talk with Mr Monday, uniformed messengers arrived with parcels and letters, the telephone rang, people shouted for them. Stephanie was on her feet all the time and seemed to be awash in a sea of paper. Joan was helplessly, hopelessly inefficient, that was clear to her immediately. She put things down and forgot where, she got flustered when people shouted, she muddled messages and was obviously bored stiff by the law and everything to do with it.

'What time do you want to go to lunch?' asked Joan at ten to twelve. 'I usually go at one. All the partners vanish then; things quieten down for several hours. They don't see anybody between one and three and often they don't get back from lunch until later than that. Of course, officially, we only get an hour, but the place is peaceful until three and if you're a few minutes late back . . . nobody notices. Except Imogen.'

'Perhaps I ought to go at twelve, if you're going at one? We shouldn't both go at the same time, should we?'

Joan shrugged. 'Please yourself.'

Stephanie left at twelve, intending to familiarise herself with the surrounding neighbourhood as well as snatch a quick light snack. She wasn't hungry; a sandwich or a salad would do.

As she walked away down the street she heard running footsteps and a voice called her name. She looked round to find Barry following her. 'Hi, wait for me. I'll show you the best place around here to eat. Cheapest, too. We all eat there.'

'I'm not very hungry, I was just going to have a sandwich.'

'You'll need more than that to keep you going all afternoon. It's a long day, you may not get away until six.' He put an arm round her to steer her round a corner. 'There's a little café just round here; we call it Luigi's, but the Luigi who ran it died years ago. The new guy answers to the same name, though.' Barry's eyes twinkled. 'You'll love his food.'

Stephanie abandoned her plan of exploring the district and resigned herself to lunch with Barry. He was entertaining and told her a great deal about the firm as they ate the set meal of the day—a shepherd's pie made with grated cheese on the top and served with two vegetables, carrots and brussels sprouts. It was a very cheap meal and Stephanie had to admit the food was good.

Barry was discontented when she insisted on returning to the office by one o'clock. 'Nobody minds if we take a little longer for lunch,' he protested.

'I only started today, I don't want to make a bad impression.'

He slid his arm around her waist as they approached the narrow terraced building. 'You've made a terrific impression on me!'

A car which was pulling away from the kerb slowed; a cold face observed them. Startled, Stephanie looked back into Gerard's narrowed eyes and flushed. Barry suddenly saw Gerard, too, and his hand dropped from her waist. The black limousine purred away and Barry grimaced at her.

'That was our Mr Tenniel, the devil incarnate when he's in one of his moods. I reckon him and Imogen are a couple of bookends; both of them have tongues like scorpions. It's wisest not to fall foul of either of them, but he's the most dangerous. I tease Imogen, but I wouldn't advise teasing Mr Tenniel.'

'I've no intention of teasing him,' Stephanie said coldly, going back to work.

The office was cool and quiet now. The windows were open; spring air circulated, sunshine showed her the small specks of dust floating in the air. Joan had gone to lunch and didn't hurry back. Stephanie cleared the desk and set about investigating the rows

of box files on the shelves. She was still confused about
her duties. Joan had been working there for months,
but she seemed even more confused than Stephanie.

Joan got back at half past two and at around three
the flow of people had begun to step up again. There
was no sign of either Mr Beaumont or Gerard, but
towards the end of the afternoon Diana Kenge came
back from court, still wearing her black gown, a parcel
of papers under her arm. She took no notice of
Stephanie, gave Joan a brief, impatient nod and
strode past. She had very short, pale hair and a faintly
spotty complexion. She didn't wear make-up and had
a myopic look, as well as a faintly worried, hunted
expression. Stephanie already knew that Diana was
the youngest member of the chambers, a harassed
junior doing all the jobs none of the seniors wanted to
do, the legal-aid jobs, the poorly paid jobs, the dull
cases with neither cash nor kudos to appeal to the
experienced barristers.

'Diana's all right, but a bit ratty when she's pushed,'
Joan told her. 'I like her better than any of the others.'

'She looked tired.'

'Probably is—they work her to death. Oh, I'll be
glad to get out of here!' Joan looked at her watch.
'Quarter to five.' She threw Stephanie a cunning look.
'If I left now I could get the early train and I might get
a seat, if I miss that and get the next one I have to
stand all the way to St Albans.'

'Is that where you live? It's a long way to come every
day.'

'Don't I know it! I'm dead by the time I get home.'
Joan gave her another hopeful smile. 'Would you
mind if . . .?'

'No, I can manage,' Stephanie said drily. 'Off you
go.'

'You're an angel!' smiled Joan, grabbing her coat and handbag and making for the door. 'See you tomorrow—worse luck!'

The door banged and the windows rattled. Imogen came out to see what all the noise was and stared at Stephanie accusingly.

'Where's Joan?' Her eye moved to the peg on which Joan's coat had hung. 'Oh, I see, gone early again. You shouldn't have let her, she knows perfectly well that she shouldn't leave before five-thirty and she was late this morning, so she ought to have worked late.'

Stephanie got up and walked over to the step-ladder to begin filing some case papers which Mr Beaumont had borrowed and wanted put back in their correct box.

Imogen stared up at her, frowning. 'I hope you understand that you can't leave before five-thirty.'

'I understand,' said Stephanie, looking at the dust on her hands. 'Does anybody clean this place? I get filthy just filing a letter. All these boxes are coated in years of dust!'

'That isn't our job. The cleaners come in after we've gone. And they aren't allowed to touch anything.'

'Or clean anything, apparently.' Stephanie climbed down. 'I must go and wash my hands again for about the twentieth time today. It's like working in a coalmine!'

Imogen looked faintly human. 'You could try leaving the cleaners a note asking them to do some dusting, but I'm not sure they'd take any notice. They're a law unto themselves.'

She left half an hour later, looking surprised to find Stephanie still working. 'You can leave at five-thirty,' she pointed out.

'I'll just finish filing these. The tray was crammed

with them and it makes the desk so untidy.'

'See you tomorrow,' said Imogen, smiling.

Stephanie had been working hard since she got back from lunch just to clear the long, wide desk of unnecessary debris. Joan's method of filing was to push everything into an enormous, metal wire tray. Stephanie felt she could almost judge how long some of the documents had been in the tray by the depth of dust between the layers. She couldn't work in a clutter. It made her feel confused, hampered, but although she had been working at full stretch, almost running on tiptoe all day, she already felt she was going to like this job. It was so interesting and varied, so lively. She wasn't sure how much she liked Imogen, but the other people she had met seemed pleasant, and something was happening all the time. She had lost count of the number of people she had met today.

She leaned back in her chair, massaging her back with a groan. Six o'clock. She must go before she noticed something else to do. She put on her coat, gave her pale, tired face a rueful look in her compact mirror, renewed her lipstick and hurried down the stairs.

The door at the bottom opened as she reached out for the door handle.

Startled, Stephanie found herself staring at Gerard in a wig and gown, his austerely modelled features chilling in that formal frame. She froze, suddenly whisked back five years, to the courtroom where she had last seen him looking like that; his eyes accusing, harsh, his mouth taut and contemptuous.

'You're still here,' he said. 'Good, I wanted to talk to you. Come back upstairs—I have to change.'

'I'm sorry, I must go, I . . .'

'Don't argue, Stephanie.' He took her arm between

biting fingers and marched her back up the stairs.
'How did you get on today? Finding your feet?'

'I suppose so.'

He shot her a sideways look and his face relented a
little. 'Don't sulk.'

'I'm tired, I've been here since nine this morning
and everyone else has gone.'

'I'm not asking you to do any more work.' He drew
her after him through the reception lobby along a
narrow corridor lined with doors that led to the
various offices of the barristers. Gerard pushed open
the final door; she followed him into a square, dimly
lit room containing little furniture but a desk, several
chairs and a wall lined with books.

Gerard discarded his gown and wig, then sat down
behind the desk in a black leather swivel chair,
waving her to a chair on the other side of it. He
considered her through the gloom. It was almost dark
outside; she wondered why he didn't put on the light.

'Do you think you're going to enjoy working here?'
He leaned back with his hands linked behind his fair
head, and she tried not to watch him.

'I hope so.' Stephanie was guarded, unwilling to
admit too much.

He put one polished black shoe on the desk and
swivelled lazily in his chair, his long body totally
relaxed. 'You had lunch with young Barry?' He made
Barry sound insignificant, his tone derisory. 'I
shouldn't encourage him; he's what Imogen calls a
liberty-taker. He needs to be kept firmly under
control.'

'I liked him,' Stephanie said defiantly, and saw a
steely flash in his eyes.

'If he starts putting his arm around your waist on
your first day, he'll be taking your clothes off by

Friday—or wouldn't you object to that?' The flinty
grate of his voice contradicted the lazy posture of his
body, and she sat up, startled, then became angry in
her turn.

'I can manage Barry. He's rather nice.' She looked
pointedly at her watch. 'I really must be going, I
promised Julia I'd be back by six-thirty.'

Gerard was frowning, but he leaned forward,
taking his foot off the desk. 'Did you come by car?'

'No, tube.'

'Very wise, parking is a nightmare around here. I
managed to get a free meter half an hour ago, I'll give
you a lift home.'

'I thought you'd been in court all afternoon.'

'I was. I should have said that I got an attendant
from the private car park where I leave my car to bring
it round here as soon as the rush hour slackened off.
You can usually find a meter in this street by then;
most people have left for home.'

Stephanie got up and Gerard rose too. 'It's very
kind of you to offer, but there's no need to go out of
your way for me.'

'No problem. Have dinner with me tonight.'

She had put a hand to the polished brass knob on his
door. His hand immediately covered hers and she
stiffened, warily becoming conscious that he was now
behind her, his body touching hers.

'I can't, I'm sorry,' she stammered. 'Julia said
something about cooking spaghetti tonight.'

'Julia won't mind if you ring and say you've got a
date. She can cook spaghetti another night.' He
moved closer, his shoulder warm against her. 'Have
dinner with me, Stephanie, I haven't seen you for
almost a week.' His voice was deep, low, intimate. It
sent a disturbed quiver through her whole body.

'It's getting dark in here,' she muttered.

'Are you scared of the dark?'

She felt the hair rise on the back of her neck, and couldn't answer.

'Or of me?' he murmured, his mouth almost touching the nape of her neck, his breathing warm on her skin. 'It's easier to let your senses do their work in the dark, Stephanie; they aren't distracted by visual signals, they pick up other give-aways like the fact that you're trembling, for instance.

'I'm not,' she said huskily, trying to snap out of the sensual trance which was making her immobile. All she had to do was open the door and walk away from him. Why wasn't she doing that? Why was she standing here like a zombie and, come to that, why was he kissing her neck and sliding his arm around her waist? Why was she letting him get away with it? He had called Barry a liberty-taker; beside him, Barry's behaviour paled into insignificance.

'I've got to go,' she said vaguely, shivering at the feel of his mouth on her neck.

'I've missed you,' he said right into her ear; his teeth gently nibbled her lobe, but it wasn't his teeth that were giving her cause to worry, it was where his hand had got to—angrily she felt her breasts rounding, growing taut, their nipples hard against the thin material of her blouse. 'I thought we might have dinner somewhere special,' he suggested, hardly making a ripple on the surface of her mind. All she could think about was the deep, sensual passion that had gripped her body; waves of desire kept sweeping up into her head, making her forcibly aware of what was going on in the rest of her. He must know. He must hear her rapid, erratic breathing, feel the heat radiating from her.

The telephone began to ring. Gerard swore, giving a start she felt, his body tensing.

'Who the hell is that?' He opened his door. 'Let's go now, I'm not here, I don't want to talk to anybody.'

Stephanie was too dazed to argue or think straight. He swept her out of the building, down the street and into his big black Daimler. She was still blinking in the glare of the yellow street lamps after the darkness of his office, and didn't notice at first that he had turned northwards instead of heading for the river and Chelsea.

When she did realise it, she sat up in the seat, frowning. 'Where are you taking me? I'm not coming to Highgate—please, let me out up here. I'll get the tube from the next station.'

He drove on, ignoring her, and her nerves jumped and leapt with tension.

'I'm serious, Gerard. I'm not going to your house.'

'I want to talk to you,' was all he drawled.

'We have nothing to say to each other.'

'Oh, but we have.'

'What, for instance?' If only he would slow down, halt at some traffic lights, she could jump out and escape.

'Tell me about Theo Burgess.'

Stephanie turned cold. After a silence she said flatly, 'There's nothing to tell. Why must you keep going back to that?'

'I hate unsolved mysteries,' he said with a bitter dryness. 'That's probably why I'm a lawyer. I like to sort out the facts, understand them. So—tell me about Theo Burgess. Was he in love with you?'

'No. I told you—no! There was nothing going on between us, he was my employer, nothing more.'

'Viola must have got the idea from somewhere. She

wouldn't have killed him if she hadn't believed it.'

'She was unbalanced, and anyway, it wasn't . . .' She broke off and Gerard looked sharply at her.

'Anyway, what?'

She looked uncertainly at him. Would he believe her? Or would he think she had made the story up to convince him of her innocence? She decided to risk it; she couldn't be worse off than she was now.

'It wasn't Theo she was jealous about.'

Gerard had jerked to a halt at a set of traffic lights which had turned amber. She could have jumped out then and got away, but she had forgotten her plan. She was too intent on convincing him of the truth.

He turned to watch her intently. 'Who was it, then?'

'You.'

His eyes hardened, became fixed, the pupils glazed and glittering with anger.

'What the hell are you talking about?'

'It's the truth,' she said wearily. He wasn't going to believe her; she might have known it. 'That day when she killed Theo, she'd found me alone and started screaming at me to stay away from you, she said she'd fire me if I didn't stop dating you. She began hitting me, I fell over, and that was when Mr Burgess came in and ran over to help me.' Her voice had a flat monotonous sound; she told him what Theo had said, Viola's reaction, the shots. 'I thought she was going to kill me, too, she turned the gun towards me and I passed out. That was the last thing I remembered, but she was lying when she said we quarrelled over Theo—we didn't, it was you.'

Gerard was driving away from the traffic lights when her voice trailed into silence. She looked uncertainly at his rigid profile; the jaw unyielding, the mouth cold and straight. She didn't need to hear his voice to know he was angry; rage vibrated around him.

'You don't believe me, do you?' she whispered. 'I don't know why I told you the truth. Oh, let me out. I want to get away from you. I've had enough!'

He swerved over and stopped dead, almost sending her through the windscreen. Stephanie opened the door and stumbled out, and was hardly on the pavement when the car screeched away.

CHAPTER NINE

A week later, Joan left and Stephanie began running the outer office on her own. She adapted easily to the new routine; the work wasn't difficult, merely exacting, and she was interested in the people she met and the cases the firm handled. It was a more demanding job than the one she had had in the hotel, yet it was so much more varied and challenging that the longer hours and constant activity during the day only registered in the sense that she was far more tired when she left in the evening than she had ever been in her previous job.

She liked the people she was working with; even Imogen was a little more unbending now that Joan wasn't there to irritate her. As Stephanie began to streamline the filing and tidy the muddle Joan had left behind her, the outer office began to look much neater. Mr Beaumont congratulated her during her second week there. He had the grand air of an actor-manager, his smile gracious. 'Keep up the good work, Stephanie, we rely on you girls to keep us working at full pitch.'

When he had left, Barry imitated him. 'Keep up the good work, Stephanie!' He swept back a lock of hair with one of Mr Beaumont's theatrical gestures, preening. Stephanie laughed and Barry grinned. 'Feel like a show tonight, darling? We could have supper afterwards.' He perched on the edge of her desk and she looked ruefully at him, hunting for a kind way of refusing. Barry was rather an idiot and he was much

157

too young for her, but she liked him and didn't want to
hurt his feelings.

'Get on with your work, Tomkins!' Gerard's voice
hit them like a wind from the frozen north, and Barry
jumped down and left in a hurry while Stephanie
began to type, her gaze fixed on the shorthand notes in
her pad. Gerard came over to stand behind her,
watching, making her even more nervous.

'Haven't you finished those notes yet?'

'Almost.'

'I thought I warned you against encouraging that
boy?'

'I wasn't.' She typed furiously, ignoring the mistakes she was making. She would have to go back and
retype them when he was gone.

He suddenly caught hold of her wrists, lifting her
hands from the keys and holding them up in the air,
flapping limply. 'Look at me when I'm talking to you!'

'You told me to hurry with these notes, sir,'
Stephanie reminded him angrily, and looked up. That
was a mistake; he was bending and she hadn't realised
how near he was. It gave her a shock, her pulses
skipped a beat, her colour changed passionately, and
Gerard took a deep, audible breath.

'Have dinner with me tonight,' he said huskily,
holding her nervous eyes.

She shook her head mutely. She couldn't trust her
voice.

'I have to see you,' he muttered, voice rough, his
reluctance to admit as much all too clear.

'What's the point? You never believe a word I say.
I've told you the truth, but you won't accept it.'

'I want to,' he said, his hands slackening their grip.
He turned her hands over and stared down at the pink
palms, one thumb gently touching each in an almost

absentminded caress. 'If what you told me was true, why didn't you tell the court five years ago? Why didn't you challenge Viola's evidence?'

She looked up, then, sighing. 'I didn't want to drag you into it. I knew I was innocent as far as Theo was concerned and I knew Viola had shot him and might have shot me—I didn't think her threats about you had anything to do with it, and I.didn't want to talk about it in front of a room full of strangers.'

'Even if it meant that your reputation was ruined?'

'I didn't realise it would be,' she whispered. 'It wasn't until I was in that court and saw your face, the way other people looked at me, that it dawned on me that I might not be on trial, but I'd been found guilty of something I hadn't done.'

He watched her intently, his brows heavy, but before he could say another word they heard someone coming up the stairs. Gerard let go of her and straightened.

'I'll pick you up at Julia's flat at eight,' he said, walking away.

When she got back to the flat that evening Julia was in the bath, singing. She broke off, mid-aria, to call, 'Hi, is that you?'

'What if I'd been a burglar?' asked Stephanie from outside the door, laughing.

'I'd have sat in this bath until it turned to ice,' Julia assured her. 'In to supper tonight? I'm going out with a fellow from the glassware firm I'm doing market research for—purely business, of course.'

'Of course,' Stephanie agreed, amused. Julia might miss her absent boy-friend, but she still managed to go out several times a week, always insisting that the dates were 'purely business'.

'Don't sound so dubious!' said Julia, laughing.

'Who, me?' Stephanie went into her own room and looked through her wardrobe for something to wear. She still hadn't made up her mind whether or not to go out to dinner with Gerard. It would probably mean another bitter argument, if she did. He had made up his mind about her and so far nothing she had said had been able to dissuade him. She didn't know why she bothered to try—he had pushed his way back into her life, but that didn't mean she had to care what he thought of her. Going out with him would only encourage him to believe he might seduce her, but he could think again. She had no intention of letting him talk her into his bed.

She heard Julia vacate the bathroom and went out, a towelling robe over her arm, to take a quick shower herself, before dressing. Julia paused as she was about to go into her bedroom and looked curious.

'You going out too?' Stephanie hadn't been out in the evening since she moved into the flat.

'Probably,' Stephanie said evasively, shutting the bathroom door before Julia could ask any more questions. They got on very well. Stephanie hadn't shared a flat with anyone before, but she found it easy to co-exist with Julia, who was good-tempered, easy-going and lively. All the same, she didn't want to talk to her about Gerard.

She ran the shower, stripped and stepped under the water, her eyes shut. Julia had told her a great deal about Gerard over the past few days, casual remarks at intervals about his family, his home, his background. It was obvious that Julia was fond of him; they teased each other and made fun of each other, but it was a sound relationship based on what seemed to be a healthy respect. Stephanie didn't want to say anything that might lead to a squabble between herself and Julia. If she so much as hinted that Gerard wasn't her idea of the perfect man, Julia might be offended. She seemed to have a romantic illusion about Gerard's interest in Stephanie.

As she stepped out of the shower, wrapping herself in her towelling robe, she heard the phone ringing. She opened the bathroom door and Julia called agitatedly. 'Answer that, will you? If it's for me, take a message. I'm trying to wriggle into a dress that seems to have shrunk. I'd swear I haven't gained an inch, but this damn thing won't slide over my hips.'

Stephanie smiled and walked into the small sitting-room. 'Hallo?' she asked, and had a slight shock as she heard her brother's voice.

'Stephanie?'

'Oh, hallo, Robert. How are you?' she said guardedly, wondering why he was ringing.

'I'm okay. How are you? Thanks for your letter. I'm glad the job's working out.'

'I'm enjoying it, it's very interesting. How's Gwen?'

'Fine.' Robert paused. 'Stephanie, Euan's back.'

'Oh.' Her hand tightened on the receiver.

'He's very angry. He wants to know where you are, he won't take no for an answer, Stevie.'

She bit her lip. 'You didn't tell him this address?'

'Not yet. I said I'd ask your permission first.'

Stephanie thought for a minute, frowning. 'Robert, couldn't you explain that I'd just decided it wouldn't work out between us? I really can't face him. There's no point.'

'Don't you think you owe it to him to talk to him face to face?'

'What can I say to him? You admitted yourself that his family would be horrified if they knew about the trial.'

'I suppose you're right,' Robert said uncertainly. 'But I'm sorry for Euan. Coming back from Saudi to find your letter waiting for him was a slap in the face.'

'I'm sorry, I wish there had been another way of dealing with it, I wish I hadn't had to do it like that, but I couldn't see anything else to do.' Stephanie was upset. Did Robert think she had acted without thinking? That she enjoyed hurting people? Didn't he realise that she had been hurt, too?

'I thought you were keen on Euan,' said Robert flatly.

She paled. 'I liked him very much.' She had almost been in love with Euan; in fact, she'd been pretty sure she was in love, but now she knew she hadn't been. She had never quite given herself to that relationship. Her early experience of love with Gerard had made her too wary to risk her deepest feelings without being totally certain the man was the right one. She hadn't wanted to get hurt again.

'He seems to have believed it was more serious than that,' said Robert with accusation in his voice.

Stephanie closed her eyes. 'I'm sorry.'

'Is that what I'm to tell him? That you're sorry but you just don't want to know any more?'

'Don't be angry, Rob,' she pleaded.

'Euan's a good friend of mine. What do you expect?' Robert breathed audibly for a second or two. 'Well, I'll try to make it easier on him, but it's just as well you've left here. Euan is angry enough to get violent.'

He hung up abruptly and Stephanie slowly replaced her phone, on the point of tears. She couldn't blame Robert for being angry; he must be having a difficult time with Euan. She couldn't blame Euan, either—he must have been thunderstruck when he got back and found her letter. They were both angry with her, and there was absolutely nothing she could say in her own defence except that she had been trying to protect them both from the consequences of her past.

The doorbell rang and she jumped. Julia gave a shriek from her room. 'Oh, no! Stevie—get that, will you? I'm in a tearing hurry to get out of here and I still haven't finished my make-up.'

Stephanie reluctantly opened the door, on the chain, so that the caller shouldn't see her in her short robe.

Gerard eyed her through the slit, his mouth ironic. 'Aren't you ready?'

She clutched the neck of her robe, shaking her head, keeping to one side of the partially opened door so that he could only see her face.

He studied it shrewdly, his face alert. 'What's the matter? Has something happened?'

'Nothing,' she said bitterly, her eyes diamond-bright with unshed tears. 'I feel as if I've been put through a wringer, that's all. My brother rang me. Euan's back and asking questions.' She broke off, starting to close the door. 'Oh, never mind—I'm really in no mood to go out to dinner, I'm sorry, Gerard.'

He had his foot in the door. 'Open up, Stephanie,' he said coolly. 'I'm not going away, so you might as well, or I'll keep ringing the bell and hammering on the door until you let me in.'

She looked at him in angry resignation. He meant it, he wouldn't hesitate to make a scene, force her to open the door.

'You're totally unscrupulous, aren't you?' she told him with dislike.

'Totally,' he agreed as she unhooked the chain. He was through the door a second later and she backed, only too aware of the fact that he had her at a disadvantage.

'I'm going to get dressed,' she said, not quite able to meet his eyes. They saw a damned sight too much; moving with the speed of lightning, from her damp hair, quivering mouth and pale throat down over her body to her bare legs and feet.

'Where's Julia?'

'Getting dressed herself, she's going out to dinner.' Stephanie could have kicked herself for telling him as she saw the gleam in his eye. She shouldn't have let him know she was going to be here alone all evening. She turned and hurried back to the shelter of her bedroom. At least she would be fully dressed next time she saw him.

She was brushing her hair when she heard Julia talking to him. 'Oh, you're here to collect Stevie, are you? I wondered who she had a date with.'

'Who else does she have dates with?' asked Gerard, and Julia laughed.

'Green eyes don't suit you, coz. And I don't tell tales. I like Stevie.'

Stephanie moved away from the door, her face a little more relaxed. She hadn't needed to hear Julia say she liked her, but she was glad she had. She liked Julia, too. She looked at herself in the mirror, wondering if the simple little white dress had been the right choice. It made her look demure, the neckline high and frilled in a sort of ruff, the sleeves long, billowing from the elbow to the cuff, the waist high, almost under her breasts, and the skirt straight and smoothly flowing over her hips. The only problem was that it also made her look younger, and she needed to impress Gerard with her self-assurance if she was to make him go away.

When she went back to the sitting-room she found

him alone. Stephanie looked around, frowning.
'Where's Julia?'

'She left to meet her date.' He was casually seated on
the couch, a glass of whisky in his hand. He had taken
off his dark overcoat and she could see that he was
wearing an elegant dark striped suit with a crisp white
shirt and maroon silk tie. His blond hair shone in the
lamplight, his eyes were thoughtful, speculative as
they roamed over her.

'You look charming,' he complimented. 'Sweet as
honey. Clothes can conceal a lot, can't they?'

'So can faces,' Stephanie said with bitterness.
'When I met Viola she seemed friendly and pleasant. I
never guessed that she was a manic depressive. People
are a lot more deceptive than clothes.'

He turned the glass in his hand, studying the amber
liquid as if he had never seen whisky before. 'That's
what I thought when I heard the rumours about you
and Theo Burgess. I was stunned. Do you think I
wanted to believe it? But think of the evidence—Viola
had shot her husband, killed him. The maid who ran
into the room when she heard the shots found Theo
lying on top of you. She thought Viola had shot both of
you at first. Viola swore she'd walked into the room to
find you in Theo's arms, she swore Theo had said he
was going to have her put away in a mental home so
that he could marry you. I heard all this from Viola,
but I heard it from the police and the servants too, and
it seemed to fit.'

'But you knew Viola wasn't normal! You knew she
had a history of mental illness.'

'That didn't make her a murderer. Her illness was
intermittent and even when she was in the manic
phase she'd never actually attacked anyone before.
She smashed furniture, windows—yes. But things

aren't people.' Gerard lifted the glass to his mouth and swallowed all the remaining whisky, then looked at her, his eyes darkened and glowing.

'And I was jealous. I was out of my mind with jealousy and disgust—the very thought of you with Theo Burgess made me sick. My judgement was warped by my own emotions.'

She sat down slowly, hardly daring to breathe. 'Are you saying that you believe me now?'

He put down the empty glass with a little click which made her nerves jump.

'Yes. I was never a hundred per cent sure even at the time, but I didn't get the chance to see you, talk about it.'

'You didn't try!'

'I did, in the beginning. I went to see your parents and they said you couldn't see anyone. The police knew I was working with the defence team. They didn't want your evidence to be influenced by anyone connected with Viola Burgess. I couldn't see you until the trial, and then in the witness box you admitted that Theo had called you his little love, and it seemed conclusive, it was such a damaging admission. There could only be one explanation—Theo must have been in love with you.'

'I'm sure he wasn't,' Stephanie broke out, flushing hotly. 'He never gave me a hint, not a look, not a word . . .'

'Perhaps he knew he didn't have a chance with you but that doesn't mean he wasn't in love with you. He was an unhappy, lonely man. You were young and pretty and he saw you every day. It would have been natural enough for him to be attracted to you.'

She lowered her eyes and couldn't think of anything

to say. It made her miserable to think of Theo. The
tragedy had brushed her life and darkened it for years;
it still affected her.

'What was all that about your brother ringing you?'
Gerard asked flatly.

'He wanted to tell me that Euan was back and
demanding to know where I was.' She sighed, a
wrenched sigh that made her slender body shudder.
'It's so unfair! I didn't do anything wrong. I was just in
the wrong place at the wrong time, quite innocently,
but because of that one tragic coincidence I can't seem
to escape from the past. I don't know what to do. I
asked Robert to tell Euan I was sorry but I couldn't see
him again. So Robert's angry with me. He can't deny
that there's no other way of dealing with the situation,
and his job might suffer if anyone found out about the
trial, but he still blames me, I know he does. Robert's
angry with me, Euan's angry with me—it simply isn't
fair!'

Gerard watched her intently. 'Are you in love with
Cameron?'

She didn't answer.

'Stephanie, are you? Tell me!'

'What difference does it make if I am?'

'I could see Cameron for you, explain, give him the
chance to choose.' His voice was cool and clear, almost
remote. It shocked her into looking up again
incredulously.

'I thought you were the one who said I ought to go
away? You blackmailed me into leaving him.'

'I shouldn't have done that,' he said as though it was
a purely academic question they were discussing.
'Whenever you come into a situation I stop thinking
rationally and make emotional decisions. When I saw
that letter from Mrs Cameron and realised that I'd

found you again, that you were apparently on the
point of marrying her son, I guessed at once that you
hadn't told him about the Burgess case. I've known the
Camerons for years—I know the sort of people they
are, and I couldn't imagine Margo Cameron being
happy about her son marrying a girl with a sordid
scandal in her background. So I told myself that it was
my duty to go down there and put a stop to any idea of
marriage between you and Cameron.' His mouth
twisted in self-distaste. 'Oh, I convinced myself that I
had the most impeccable reasons for smashing up your
love affair. I was full of self-righteous indignation
about you lying to the Camerons, hiding your past
from them, but of course the truth was that I was
jealous. I couldn't bear the idea of Cameron having
you.'

A pulse beat fiercely in her neck. 'But now you're
offering to bring us together again!'

'I want you to be sure what you want,' said Gerard
brusquely. 'When I first read that letter to my mother
and realised who it was about I had a rush of blood to
the head. After the trial I was too angry to want to see
you, but I didn't forget you. I kept thinking back over
everything and being puzzled and uncertain about the
whole story. One day I'd be sure Viola was telling the
truth, another time I'd remember your innocence and
I couldn't believe you would ever have had an affair
with Theo. That's what I meant about being bedevilled by emotion. I wasn't thinking with my head, I
was too bitter and jealous. I thought with my heart,
and that never works. Love is a violent emotion; it can
destroy, it can smash lives the way a hurricane
smashes a whole town. I shouldn't have let my feelings
dominate my thinking.'

'Whatever your reasons for interfering,' she said

slowly, 'you were right about Euan and his family. I
couldn't see him again without telling him the whole
story, and once he knows I don't think he would still
want me.'

'But with your family and myself to back your
version?'

'If I brought an archangel and several judges to
back me up, I don't think Mrs Cameron would want
me in her family, do you? I'd still have a slur on my
name.'

'Stephanie, if you love him . . .'

'I don't,' she said flatly. 'I told you that last time you
asked. My heart isn't broken because I won't see Euan
again. I'll miss him. I liked him, I was fond of him, I
might even have loved him enough to marry him one
day, but it wasn't the violent kind of love, not the kind
you were talking about. I didn't think with my heart
where Euan was concerned. I felt with my head, and I
wonder if that isn't just as bad?'

His mouth had a crooked humour and his eyes
smiled. 'You may be right.' He moved suddenly, along
the couch, his arm going around her. 'Stephanie . . .'

She got up. 'I thought we were going to dinner?'

Gerard stiffened, watching her, then shrugged and
got up too. 'Of course. I booked a table at the Caprice.'

'I'll just get my jacket,' she said, and went back into
her bedroom. The last thing she needed at the moment
was for Gerard to try to kiss her. She needed time to
think, or rather, to separate thought and emotion,
understand how she really felt.

She had been hiding things from herself right from
the first moment when she saw Gerard again outside
the hotel. The shock of that first sight of him should
have told her how much he still affected her, but she
hadn't wanted to believe it.

Until that day she had been thinking herself into a state of blissful deception, convincing herself that she could love Euan, marry him. She had built a new life for herself; it was calm and tranquil and safe, but she had blinded herself to the fact that it was built on sand. She hadn't simply omitted to tell Euan and his family about an unpleasant episode in her past; she had lied to herself when she pretended she had forgotten Gerard and no longer cared about him. You can't build a life on lies.

Seeing Gerard again had brought her phoney paradise into sharp, realistic focus, shown her the truth about herself. Her reaction to Gerard had been so intense and passionate, a chemical change that was physically violent. She had gone hot, then cold, she had been white and then flushed—her emotions had gone crazy. She had been off balance ever since. Compared to her calm and civilised relationship with Euan, that white-hot emotional drag towards Gerard had been little short of catastrophic. It had blown to smithereens her cosy self-deception.

But she didn't want Gerard to know all this—he might suspect how she felt, but while he wasn't certain he wouldn't really turn the heat on.

She wasn't going to run away from her feelings, but she had been invaded by a sense of panic in case Gerard rushed her. How could she think when her chemical reaction to his presence had such a disturbing effect on her mental processes? She wondered if Gerard even understood himself—she didn't understand him. She didn't know what he really wanted from her—a satisfaction he hadn't got five years ago? A delayed revenge for the frustration he had felt then? She didn't need to wonder if he wanted her; her feminine instincts had warned her about that from the

minute he had walked back into her life. She was five
years older and five years wiser, especially about men.
Gerard wanted her, but why?

Until she knew the answer to that, until she knew
whether *she* felt more than a violent physical desire for
him, she would have to try to keep him at a distance.

That wouldn't be easy, she accepted with a qualm of
nerves, as she rejoined him and Gerard's grey eyes
fixed a brilliant, triumphant gleam on her. She picked
up the excitement in him without any trouble, and her
body clenched. How was she going to deal with him in
this mood?

CHAPTER TEN

THAT dinner seemed to drag on endlessly. She had never been so on edge in her life, her senses piercingly aware of every move he made, every intonation in his voice, every passing expression in his eyes. They were seated on either side of a table, a few feet apart, but her heart did a nosedive every time their eyes met.

Gerard suddenly stretched out a hand holding the menu and blocked her view of her plate. 'What are you eating?'

Stephanie glanced down and could only see the menu. 'What are you talking about?' she hedged. 'Don't be silly!'

'Tell me what's on your plate,' he insisted, eyes mocking.

'I'm not playing one of your games.' She tried to remember what she had just swallowed. Fish. She was sure it had been fish, although her attention hadn't been on what she was putting into her mouth. It had all been riveted on Gerard; she might just as well have been eating sawdust.

'Fish,' she said coolly. 'I'm eating fish.'

He took the menu away and she hurriedly looked down. There was a médaillon of veal on her plate in a delicate creamy sauce. Gerard laughed softly and her cheeks burned.

'Well, I was thinking about something else,' she said crossly.

'I know, so was I,' he murmured, a glint in his eye. 'It was when I realised that I didn't have a clue what I

was eating that I looked across and saw the same
blank look on your face.'

'I wasn't really hungry,' she said with dignity. 'I
didn't want to have dinner out, but it seemed . . .' Her
voice faltered.

'Safer than staying in?' he finished for her with a
dry smile. 'I deduced as much. It's true that there are
fewer opportunities for making love in a restaurant
than there are in an empty flat.'

The waiter came to take their plates and overheard
that. He gave Gerard an interested look and an even
more interested glance at Stephanie, who looked
down, biting her inner lip.

'A dessert, madam?' asked the waiter.

'No, thank you,' she refused with vehemence.

'Coffee for both of us,' Gerard ordered, and they
didn't sit for long drinking it. Half an hour later they
were in Gerard's car driving back to her flat, and
neither of them had much to say. Stephanie knew
what he was thinking; the car was full of a tense
silence vibrating with feeling and when he pulled up
outside the flat she said hurriedly 'No need to get out.
Thank you for dinner. I'll see you tomorrow.'

He caught her arm as she turned to get out.
'Stephanie . . .'

She threw him an uneasy look over her shoulder, her
dark hair blown across her eyes by the night wind.
'Please, don't,' she said huskily. 'I'm too tired, I can't
take any more.'

She thought for a moment that he was going to
ignore what she said, ride roughshod over her plea to
be left alone, but although his brows drew together his
hand dropped, allowing her to get out of the car. She
began to walk quickly towards the building, hearing
the car engine flare into life again.

Just as she reached the front door a figure stepped out of the shadows and grabbed her, and Stephanie gave a cry of shock.

For a second she thought it was a stranger, a mugger, grabbing for her handbag, but then he moved and the light of the street lamp shone full on his face.

It was Euan. 'I've been waiting for over an hour,' he said roughly. 'Where have you been?'

She glanced over her shoulder and saw Gerard's car moving off. Her body sagged in a sort of relief. At least he wouldn't be present at what was bound to be a difficult interview, thank heavens she hadn't invited him in for coffee, or rather, allowed him to invite himself, which was probably what had been on his mind when he caught her arm just now.

She looked back at Euan with uneasy regret. 'You'd better come in—we can't talk on the doorstep.' She led the way and unlocked the front door of the flat. It was dark. Obviously Julia was still out at dinner, but she was bound to get back before too long and Stephanie didn't want her to find Euan in the flat.

She switched on the light and Euan followed her into the flat, closing the door behind himself.

'You haven't driven all that way this evening?' she asked as she switched on the light in the sitting-room.

'Yes, I left at seven-thirty and got here at almost nine-thirty, but there was no answer so I've been sitting in my car waiting for you ever since. I saw you drive up with your friend.' His voice flattened on the final word and she felt him watching her intently, although she didn't look in his direction.

'Please sit down,' she said huskily. 'Can I get you anything? A drink? Coffee?'

'I wouldn't say no to a whisky.' He took off his overcoat and laid it over a chair, then sat down, crossing his legs.

Stephanie hunted for the bottle of whisky Julia kept in a cupboard and poured a little into a glass. There was no soda, so she asked if Euan would like some water in it, but he shook his head.

She gave him the whisky and sat down nervously, not too close to him.

'How did you find me?' she queried.

'Your brother told me your address.'

Her eyes widened in anger and shock. Robert had promised he wouldn't tell Euan!

He swallowed a mouthful of whisky, watching her. 'Yes, I know you asked him not to tell me where you were—but I managed to persuade him otherwise.' His eyes had an impatient darkness in them. 'I practically had to choke it out of him. I told him if he didn't explain what was going on, I'd get a private detective to dig you out, I wasn't just accepting this meekly. So then he told me the whole story.'

Her eyes flew to his face in shock. 'The whole . . .'

Euan stared back at her gently, his face softening. 'The whole story, all about the trial, the murder, the accusations against you—my God, Stephanie, you must have a low opinion of me if you really thought I'd believe that you would have an affair with a man twice your age! I know you better than that and I'd hoped you knew me better.' He drank a little more whisky, then sat staring into the glass, his face sombre. 'I can understand why you wouldn't want it to become public knowledge, why you'd hate the thought of strangers talking about you, but why didn't you trust me, Stephanie? Didn't you feel you knew me well enough to confide in me instead of bolting like this?'

She looked down, shifting unhappily in the chair. 'I'm sorry if you're hurt, Euan. That was the last thing

I intended, but I couldn't stay. Not once I'd realised
that it wouldn't do. You may not believe that I had an
affair with Theo Burgess, but a lot of other people did
believe it, and if any of them turned up in town and
started spreading the story it would be very embarrassing for your family. Your mother wouldn't want to be
mixed up with someone like me.'

'Leave my mother out of it,' Euan said tersely. 'It's
my opinion that matters, not hers.'

'Is it?' she asked on a sigh. Didn't Euan realise how
much his family mattered to him?

'I want you to come back with me,' Euan said
firmly. 'You can't run from something like this. You
have to face it, you have to be brave, Stephanie.'

She smiled wryly. 'I'm sorry, Euan, it wouldn't
work. There's no point.'

'You don't need to worry about my mother. She'll
come round once she realises I'm serious about you. If
there's trouble, we'll face it together.'

He was so civilised, so reasonable, but in a way he
was blind to the truth about his family situation. He
was reacting now with awareness of what was the
proper thing to do; Stephanie had run away because
she feared public opinion in a very conservative little
community, and Euan's sense of justice wouldn't allow
her to suffer because of something she hadn't done. He
was prepared to fight for her, face his mother for her,
but he was ignoring the truth—that his family, his
mother, mattered more to him than she did. If she had
doubted that for a second she wouldn't have run away.
It was because Gerard had made her face that, that
she had left.

He put down his glass and came over to her chair,
sat down on the arm of it, and stroked her wind-ruffled
hair gently. 'I want you to marry me, Stephanie. I've

been meaning to ask you for a long time, but I'm asking you now. You must know how much you mean to me. I think we could be very happy together and . . .'

The doorbell rang violently and she jumped. Euan stopped in mid-flow, his hand stiffening on her hair.

'Who can that be at this hour?' He looked down at her as the bell continued to peal. Whoever was out there had left his thumb on the button. 'Is that the girl who shares your flat? She must have forgotten her key.'

Stephanie knew it wasn't Julia; she knew whose thumb was jammed down on the button. She didn't want to open the door to him, not while Euan was here. It would only mean trouble, and she was so sick of argument and fight and threats.

'Ignore it,' she said, very agitated.

Euan looked amazed. 'Ignore it? You can't do that.'

'It will go away.'

'Have you quarrelled with your flatmate already? But I thought this was her flat. You can't leave her on the doorstep, whatever she's done.'

'It isn't her, not Julia,' she said in confusion. 'Oh, take no notice, he'll give up in a minute.'

Euan stiffened. 'He?' He seized on the pronoun sharply, looking down at her. 'Stephanie, who's out there?'

Suddenly she knew that Robert had carefully omitted one vital part of the story. He hadn't told Euan about Gerard Tenniel's intervention, he hadn't mentioned that Gerard had brought her to London, that she had been in Gerard's house when Robert caught up with her the day she left town.

Why had Robert been so discreet? But she knew the answer to that, didn't she? Her brother hadn't wanted

Euan to be aware that she was mixed up with Gerard
Tenniel, but if Euan forced her to open the front door
now, he would soon realise what Robert had gone to
such pains to keep from him.

'Nobody,' she said, very flushed. The ringing hadn't
stopped; it was now augmented by some angry
hammering on the door. It sounded ominously as if
Gerard was trying to break into the flat.

'It sounds very much like a persistent somebody,'
said Euan, still staring at her. 'If you want me to get rid
of whoever it is, I'll be glad to deal with him for you.'
He got up and she shot to her feet, grabbing his hand.

'No Euan, don't go out there!'

'Why not?' he asked reasonably enough, his eyes
puzzled and beginning to be distinctly suspicious.
'Have you met someone else, Stephanie? Is that it?
Another man? Robert didn't warn me about that. Or
is this a neighbour who won't take no for an answer?
There must be a good reason why you don't want to
answer the door.'

She tried to think of one, her face distraught, but her
mind wasn't working fast enough. Euan walked away,
dragging her after him, her heels grinding into the
carpet at every step.

'Euan, please don't!' she wailed as he put a hand on
the latch, but she was too late. He had opened the door
and Gerard fell into the flat, taken by surprise. He
must have been trying to shoulder his way through the
door.

Euan looked staggered. Gerard didn't. Once he had
recovered his balance he said angrily 'If I hadn't
glanced into my driving mirror just before I got to the
corner, I wouldn't have seen him. I had to drive right
round the block before I could get back here, because
of this damned one-way system, and then I couldn't

find anywhere to park.'

'What are you doing here?' demanded Euan, having got his breath back.

'Snap,' Gerard said drily. 'I was just going to ask you the same question.'

'I didn't know you knew Stephanie!'

Gerard smiled; it was a deliberately provocative smile and it had the effect intended. Euan's face stiffened and reddened. He didn't have a belligerent nature, but he had a very male dislike of being laughed at and he vaguely realised that Gerard was making fun of him.

'Why were you ringing the bell like that at this hour?' he demanded, his hands screwing into fists.

'I wanted to come in,' said Gerard with silken mockery. He turned his eyes on Stephanie. 'Why didn't you open the door right away? What was going on?'

He had drawn Euan's attention back to her. Before she could answer him, Euan asked tersely: 'Why's he here? You only met him once, at our house, didn't you?' He paused, obviously thinking. 'Wait a minute—he said something about driving away and coming back—was that his car you drove up in? Had you been out with him tonight? Have you been seeing him since you came to London?' His usually calm expression had broken up in lines of anger and disbelief, he was looking at her in a way that distressed her.

'Do you suppose these are rhetorical questions?' Gerard asked her ironically. 'He doesn't stop long enough to give you a chance to answer, does he?'

Euan ignored him, his eyes on Stephanie's pale face. 'Did you come to London because of him? Am I to gather that Robert did *not* tell me the whole story?'

Gerard whistled softly. 'Oh, I see! Your brother decided to spill the beans!'

Euan swung round to glare at him. 'Does that mean you know all about this?' Apparently he read the answer in Gerard's cool eyes, because he turned back to Stephanie, looking even angrier. 'You told him, but you didn't tell me?' That seemed to stick in his throat, and she could understand why, her body wrenched by a deep sigh.

'Euan, I'm sorry, it isn't quite what you think.'

Gerard was smiling. 'A canny fellow, your brother—he was careful not to spill all the beans, obviously.' He was watching her face shrewdly, reading her reactions. 'If you've been having any hassle from him, let me deal with him,' he said quietly, touching her arm. 'You don't have to put up with any nonsense from him.'

Euan made a growling sound in his throat, poised on the balls of his feet as if about to hit Gerard.

'Oh, why did you come back?' Stephanie burst out to Gerard, her eyes angry. She felt like pushing both of them out of the flat, but she knew that that would merely postpone the inevitable. Euan was here and he had to have an answer, an explanation. It was Gerard who was the real problem, but she would deal with him when she felt up to it. She didn't feel up to it at the moment. 'Go away!' she almost snarled. 'I want to talk to Euan and I don't want you here!'

Gerard stared fixedly at her; the pupils of his eyes dilated until they were enormous, black, hard with anger.

Euan held the door open. 'You heard her.'

Gerard slowly turned and walked out and Euan let the door slam after him, before turning back to Stephanie with cold eyes.

'You don't need to tell me anything you don't want
me to know. Obviously, I made a stupid mistake. Your
brother should have been a little less discreet. I
thought this business of the trial was the only
problem; I didn't realise there was another man in
your life now.'

She could have explained the whole complicated
tangle, but she saw suddenly how much simpler it was
to let him go away believing she had left because she
had fallen in love with another man. It would make it
easier for Euan. He wouldn't need to wonder if he
ought to face a break with his family for her sake. She
wasn't in love with him, but he might have felt he had
to try to talk her into going back with him.

'I'm sorry, Euan,' she said.

'I had a wasted journey, didn't I?' He was looking at
her; disillusion in his eyes, as though he had never
really known her, and perhaps he hadn't. She had
never really known herself. The years since the trial
had been ostrich years, a period when she hid herself
from sight and refused to see what was happening
around her. She had been afraid to lift her head, but it
was time she did.

'I'm afraid you did. I told Robert that it would be
best just to let me slip away.' She looked quickly at
him. 'Euan, for Robert's sake, don't tell anyone, even
your mother—you haven't told your mother yet, have
you?'

'No,' he agreed flatly.

'His reputation is more important than mine. I
wouldn't want to jeopardise his career.'

'You won't. Everyone at the hospital thinks very
highly of Robert. I had no intention of spreading this
story, anyway, but you can have my word on it if you
need it.' Euan was on his dignity now; he had

withdrawn from her. She recognised the remoteness of
his face; that was how his mother looked. Euan was
very like his mother. Even if Gerard Tenniel had
never come along to break them apart, she saw
suddenly that she wouldn't have been happy with
Euan, because sooner or later she would have had to
tell him about the trial. You can't live with a lie for
ever. And when she did tell him he would have looked
at her the way he was looking at her now—as though
she was a disappointment to him. He might have been
kind and forgiving, but he wouldn't have trusted her
after that.

He'd said that he believed she was innocent, but
what was hidden in the very far reaches of his mind?
A doubt? He had jumped so quickly to the belief that
she was having an affair with Gerard now. Why
should he be so ready to believe that if he didn't
wonder how much truth there was in Viola Burgess's
accusations?

He opened the front door to go and she saw Gerard
leaning against the wall out there. He hadn't left; he
was waiting. Euan's eyes flashed to him and his mouth
indented distastefully.

Gerard came towards them at a stride. 'You aren't
taking her with you,' he said harshly. 'She's mine!'

'So I gather,' said Euan from a great height, his face
contemptuous as he glanced back at Stephanie.

Gerard didn't like the way he looked at her. He gave
a furious snarl, shoulders hunched, and hit Euan, who
ducked as he saw the punch coming. Gerard got him,
all the same, a glancing blow on the jaw that sent Euan
reeling backwards.

'No, Euan, don't hit him—your hands!' Stephanie
cried out with horror.

Euan gritted through his teeth, 'I had no intention

of risking an injury to my hands.' He turned and walked away and Gerard stared after him in disgust.

'He's a surgeon; his hands are vital to his work,' Stephanie accused angrily. 'How could you, Gerard?'

'He insulted you.'

'He was angry, can you blame him?'

She turned and walked back into her flat and Gerard came too. 'Oh, why don't you go home and give me some peace?' she implored, turning on him as she realised he was in the flat 'again.

'Is he coming back?' he merely asked.

She gave him a bitter stare. 'Well, what do *you* think?'

He considered her fixedly. 'Did you want him to go? Or have you realised you do care for him?'

'I'm sick of talking about it. Go home, Gerard.'

'Not until I know where I stand!'

'Where *you* stand? You were asking about Euan.'

'Now that you've seen him again, how do you feel about him?' he asked curtly, still watching her with that intent gaze.

Stephanie looked away. 'How dare you tell him that I'm yours? You must have known what he'd make of that, then you say he's insulting me because he assumed what I think you meant him to assume—that I've been sleeping with you!'

'That wasn't what I meant, and he had no right to assume anything of the kind.' Gerard moved nearer, his voice dropping, becoming husky. 'You belong to me, you have ever since the first day I saw you. I don't need to sleep with you to say that you're mine.' He stood there, watching her. Very flushed, her eyes lowered, she could hardly breathe and wished he would stop staring. 'You can feel it, too, can't you?' he murmured, even closer now.

'No,' she whispered.

'Liar.' He wasn't touching her, but he was so close that she could hear his breathing, the rapid beat of his heart.

She closed her eyes to shut out the sight of that insistent face. 'Oh, why don't you stop tormenting me?'

'You're the one doing the tormenting,' Gerard whispered, kissing her eyelids gently one after the other. His lips brushed like butterflies, making her lashes flicker, sending a tingling feeling through her nervous system.

'Julia will be home any second,' she protested, taking hold of his arms to push him away. He didn't so much as move an inch; it was like trying to push over the rock of Gibraltar.

'Julia never gets home this early when she goes dancing. She told me she was getting back at the crack of dawn.' Gerard was lightly sliding his lips down her face, making for her mouth.

'You shouldn't be here!' she wailed. She had refused to let him come in earlier because she had known this would happen; she had seen it in his eyes, felt it inside herself. All evening they had been looking at each other with rapt attention; all evening she had been on edge, weak with desire, and Gerard had known. His eyes had warned her that he knew. She turned her head away before he could kiss her and he kissed her ear instead, biting gently at her lobe.

'I want you so badly, Stephanie,' he muttered, burying his face against her throat. 'I love you. I fell head over heels the first time I saw you and because of my own jealous stupidity I've wasted five years of my life. Don't waste any more of our precious time, darling.'

She made a helpless little moaning noise, swaying against him. He wasn't being fair, he was rushing her before she had had time to think it out, to be sure what she felt.

'I'm not sure yet,' she told him, aware of his arm round her, his hands touching her, his mouth advancing stealthily towards her lips.

'Sure about what? Marrying me? Whether you love me?' He took hold of her chin and turned her face back towards him. His mouth took hers before she could evade it and she yielded, her arms going round his neck, her body giving in to him under the insistent pressure of a hand in the small of her back. She stopped resisting, trying to think, she was all feeling; a rush of fierce pleasure swamping everything else.

Gerard suddenly lifted her off the ground and carried her into the sitting-room. He sat down on the couch and she found herself lying across his lap. He was still kissing her and she could hardly breathe; the remorseless demand of his mouth left her limp, suffocated. When he finally lifted his head, she just lay there, her head on his shoulder, her body tumbled along the couch.

She forced her lids up and he was bending over her, watching her with a probing intensity.

'I love you,' he said again, his voice rough, and Stephanie could see that she had nowhere left to hide.

'Love me—or want me?' she asked huskily. 'You told me you wanted me, that day in the hotel, when you blackmailed me into coming away with you. You made it clear you wanted your revenge; you didn't mention love then. How do I know you mean it now? How do I know this isn't another form of blackmail, meant to persuade me to sleep with you?'

His mouth went crooked. 'I was too angry and

jealous that day to be ready to admit I was still in love
with you. I'd seen you with Cameron the night before,
remember? I was afraid you'd marry him if I didn't get
you away at once. I had to use sledgehammer methods,
but I was certain you didn't love him. I was so sure you
belonged to me. The minute I saw you, at the party, I
felt it again—a drag between us, an instant flare of
awareness. Don't tell me you didn't feel it, too,
Stephanie, because I wouldn't believe you. You
knew—I saw it in your eyes.'

She looked away, trembling. 'Is it love, though?
That need.'

She heard his breathing quicken. He kissed her
neck, mouth urgent, passionate. 'A need, darling, yes,
that's just what it is—all lovers need to show what they
feel, get that feeling back. When I first met you, you
were just a girl and I thought I loved you simply
because you were so inexperienced and innocent, but I
was wrong. I love you far more passionately now;
haven't you felt how much stronger it is, this feeling
between us? Every beat of my heart makes it stronger.'
He held her close to him, their bodies merging. 'Like
this,' he muttered into her hair. 'We belong like this,
darling, part of each other, for ever.'

He was right. She had known, from the minute she
saw him again, that he was the only man she had ever
loved and would ever love. Euan had become a
shadowy figure to her after that, although she had
tried to go on pretending for a while longer. It had
been no use; no other man could ever mean as much to
her. Gerard had been imprinted on her heart five
years ago when she was too young and plastic for that
deep seal ever to be removed.

She and Gerard belonged to each other. Even if she
hadn't said it aloud her body was telling him so now,

the heat of desire melting her flesh, burning through
her senses. His hands were aware of that, she heard
him breathing thickly, felt the heat in his face as his
cheek brushed hers.

'Darling,' he said again, and he was asking her to
admit it, to tell him. He was urgent because of the
waste of five years, urgent as she was, because they
needed to touch, to merge, to be one.

'I love you,' she said, and after that neither of them
said anything for a long time.

CIRCLE OF FATE

CIRCLE OF FATE

BY

CHARLOTTE LAMB

MILLS & BOON LIMITED
Eton House, 18–24 Paradise Road
Richmond, Surrey TW9 1SR

All the characters in this book have no existence outside the imagination of the Author, and have no relation whatsoever to anyone bearing the same name or names. They are not even distantly inspired by any individual known or unknown to the Author, and all the incidents are pure invention.

All rights reserved. The text of this publication or any part thereof may not be reproduced or transmitted in any form or by any means, electronic or mechanical, including photocopying, recording, storage in an information retrieval system, or otherwise, without the written permission of the publisher.

This book is sold subject to the condition that it shall not, by way of trade or otherwise, be lent, resold, hired out or otherwise circulated without the prior consent of the publisher in any form of binding or cover other than that in which it is published and without a similar condition including this condition being imposed on the subsequent purchaser.

First published in Great Britain 1987
by Mills & Boon Limited

© Charlotte Lamb 1987

Australian copyright 1987
Philippine copyright 1987
Reprinted 1987
This edition 1991

ISBN 0 263 77557 7

Set in Linotron Times 10.5 on 10.5 pt.
19–9110–48575

Made and printed in Great Britain

CHAPTER ONE

THE doorbell rang as Melanie was closing her case and she straightened, dark blue eyes surprised. Surely that couldn't be Ross already? He had said that he would pick her up at ten. A swift glance at her watch told her that it was barely eight-fifteen. She had just finished packing and hadn't even had breakfast yet.

'Melanie—it's Ross!' Her cousin's voice had a familiar dryness—Liz had been cool towards Ross from their first meeting, but then Liz wasn't the type to go overboard about anyone. It might be her nature, or the job she did, but for as long as Melanie could remember, Liz had kept most people, life itself, at a distance. No doubt a journalist had to keep a neutral stance and Melanie admired her cousin's control and poise; yet at the same time it troubled her.

'I'll be down in a second!' she called back, giving her reflection in the dressing-table mirror a hurried check. Her hair was ruffled; she picked up a brush and ran it over the straight, dark strands which floated to her shoulders. Ross was always immaculate; she felt she ought to look the same, not that he ever said anything about her occasional untidiness, but those calm grey eyes noticed everything. It was odd that Liz didn't like him, because Melanie felt that they had a good deal in common.

She ran downstairs, her heart speeding up as she

saw Ross in the hall, waiting for her, the sunlight streaming through the fanlight above the door touching his smooth fair hair, making it gleam. In spite of the sun, the autumn air was crisp, the wind biting. Ross was wearing an elegant dark cashmere coat over a grey suit. Melanie frowned as she noticed that—he wasn't dressed for a weekend in the country, surely?

'You're early—why are you wearing a suit?' she asked as she stood on tiptoe to kiss him.

His pale head bent to meet hers; his mouth fleetingly touched her lips, without passion, without much feeling of any kind, she thought, frowning.

'I'm sorry, Melanie. I can't make this trip to the Lakes. There's been an emergency in Bahrain and I have to fly out there today to deal with it.' His voice was deep, urgent; it was obvious that his mind was already elsewhere and he was in a hurry to deal with the problem of Melanie before rushing off to Bahrain. Yet again she was an interruption in his busy life and he was pushing her aside.

A flush of hurt and anger ran up her fine-boned face. 'Ross, you promised!'

'I know.' He frowned, his mouth impatient. His features had an incisive quality, even when he smiled. When he frowned, as he was doing now, she only saw coldness, remoteness, in the angularity of the cheekbones, the deep-set grey eyes, the harsh jawline and firm, restrained mouth.

'I wouldn't break our date if it weren't absolutely unavoidable,' he said, looking at her as if she were being unreasonable, and her flush deepened.

'It always is, though, isn't it? We're supposed to be getting married, yet I hardly ever see you. We talked this out last month and you promised me you'd take a weekend off and we'd go away, get away from the office and the phones and find somewhere peaceful to spend some time alone, and now this happens . . .' Melanie didn't find it easy to talk to him like that, her voice was shaking and she was trembling, but she was afraid that if she didn't tell him how she felt it would all build up inside her until something disastrous happened.

'Don't shout, Melanie,' he said in a quiet, cool voice, watching her from a distance even though he was merely a foot away. 'Do you want the whole house to hear you?'

She bit down on her inner lip. Liz had gone back into the dining-room and closed the door before Melanie came downstairs. The family were eating breakfast in there, voices lively as usual, laughing over something Teddy was reading aloud from the newspaper. Her uncle Teddy enjoyed making people laugh; he was a natural clown, physically comic with his short, stout figure and bald head, his saucer-like brown eyes.

'Look,' Ross said, 'this crisis on the site isn't something I can shelve or let anyone else handle. There's too much at stake. I have to deal with it myself, or, believe me, I'd send Martin or Gregory. When I get back, we'll fix something, we'll have a long talk.'

There was a new outburst of laughter from the dining-room, and Melanie winced. They all sounded so cheerful, it jarred. A short time ago she had been cheerful, too, imagining that she would soon be driving away with Ross and able to spend time alone with him at last. There was so much about him she didn't know, so much she had to ask. Sometimes she was frightened because she knew so little about him.

'Ross,' she said huskily, 'our wedding day gets closer all the time and I don't feel I know you well enough. We can't go on like this—I hardly seem to see you.'

He looked at his watch, frowning. 'Melanie, I haven't got time for this discussion, I'm sorry. We'll talk when I get back.'

'You keep saying that, but it never seems to happen!' she said. He didn't seem to understand how she felt. He had so much more self-assurance than she did; he had asked her to marry him within a few weeks of meeting her. Maybe she should have said no, but, swept off her feet by his blind rush, she had said yes, completely dazzled. Since then it seemed to her that she had hardly seen him, and she was getting very nervous about the whole situation.

'I'm sorry,' he said again, with impatience. 'I wish I could get out of this Bahrain trip, but I can't. I'd love to be with you this weekend, but I have a company to run and sooner or later you'll have to understand the way my life works. You say you want to get to know me better. Start with that.' He turned and walked away without a backward glance.

He was opening the door as she suddenly came after him, her eyes pleading. 'Ross, why don't I come with you? We could at least talk on the plane; it's a long flight to Bahrain, isn't it?'

He looked round, his mouth taut and wry. 'It sounds wonderful, but it isn't practical, I'm afraid— I have a mass of papers to read before I get there. I wouldn't have time to talk, even if you came.'

He strode away, a tall man, moving with determination, and she watched, her dark blue eyes bright with anxiety and pain, the autumn wind whipping her black hair backwards over her shoulders. As he slid into the back seat of the white Rolls she realised that he wasn't travelling

alone. His secretary was in the car, too. Melanie
stared at the older woman's profile, averted from
her as Brenda Upfield read the pink pages of the
Financial Times she held. She should have known
that Brenda would be going, too. It wouldn't have
worked if Melanie had insisted on making the
Bahrain trip; she and Ross would never have been
alone.

She shut the door and leaned on it, fighting an
outbreak of tears. She couldn't let the family see
her crying. She ran a trembling hand over her
eyes; her lashes were damp. Thank heavens she
wasn't wearing mascara, there would be no
betraying streaks to tell the family what had
happened.

It was five minutes before she felt calm enough
to join them. When she opened the door they were
all talking at once, which wasn't unusual. Breakfasts
in this house were often sheer chaos.

This morning, though, she got the impression
that their chatter and laughter wasn't quite genuine.
They were acting. How much of what was being
said in the hall had they overheard?

Aunt Dolly immediately poured her some coffee.
'Your kipper's still hot, dear, come and eat it. I'll
make some fresh toast.' She was over fifty, not
that you'd guess it if you didn't already know,
because Dorothy Nesbitt had always looked years
younger than her real age. She was exactly the
same weight and shape as she had been when
Edward Nesbitt first met her, so Uncle Teddy
insisted. It was impossible to get out of them a
true account of which had first acquired the
nicknames by which they had now been known for
years. Nobody else remembered. They had been
Dolly and Teddy throughout their married life and
old snapshots of Aunt Dolly showed her as a girl

with the same curly blonde hair and round baby blue eyes, the dimples in her cheeks, the sunny smile. She hadn't aged the way Teddy had—he had once had auburn hair, he claimed. Now it was a grey fringe at the back of his bald head, no sign of red in the few straggling hairs.

Their son, Will, had red hair, so perhaps it was true. Lanky and cheerful, his mop of orange fuzz was his most memorable feature. Will's face wasn't handsome, it wasn't even comic, like his father's. He had a lugubrious face, in fact, but a far from mournful nature.

As Melanie sat down in her usual chair, next to him, he gave her a gentle smile. 'You look fabulous in that sweater. Blue's your colour, you ought to wear it more often.'

He was trying to make her feel better. She gave him a smile that tried hard to be steady. 'It's my sailing sweater, I've decided. Perfect for sailing, don't you think?' Then she bent her head to eat the kipper which had been kept hot under a plate. It was perfectly cooked, of course, the smoky tang exactly right and the flesh melting off the bones. Aunt Dolly was a very good cook and up to tackling anything from a boiled egg to a cordon bleu meal.

'Toast coming up.' Will passed the white bone china toast-rack while Uncle Teddy poured her a cup of tea, and Liz pushed the white bone china dish of marmalade towards her. It was the usual concerted family effort to make her feel happy; Melanie loved them for it and was angry with herself for feeling at the same time a prickling impatience, not with them, but with fate. She sometimes got so tired of being an object of pity; that was the last thing she wanted at this moment. She felt like saying to them: stop feeling sorry for me, stop being so kind, but how could she? It would hurt their feelings, and she didn't want to do that.

The family team-work had begun when she was thirteen and her parents were killed in a car crash, which left Melanie seriously injured. For six months she had been in and out of hospitals. Her father had been Uncle Teddy's brother. From the minute she was conscious of what was going on around her, after the accident, Uncle Teddy and Aunt Dolly had been at her bedside to reassure her. She had a home with them, they loved and wanted her, everything was going to be all right, they said. Will and Liz welcomed her with open arms. This house was Victorian, large, shabby, with many rooms. When Melanie got out of hospital and came here to live, she found that they had moved every stick of furniture from her old bedroom at home and had a bedroom redecorated for her. Her dolls sat on the bed in which she had always slept, her books were arranged on a shelf, her clothes hung in the same wardrobe. It was sensitive and thoughtful, and she didn't cry until she was alone and they couldn't see.

They wanted so much to help her. Their own lives revolved around that thought. They treated her like precious china and Melanie began to wish that Will would shove her the way he did his sister, that Liz would be sarcastic with her the way she was with Will, that Aunt Dolly would sternly tell her to tidy her room the way she did both her children or Uncle Teddy scowl over her school report and say, 'This isn't good enough!' as he always did to Will, who was more or less the same age.

How could Melanie tell them that their unremitting tenderness towards her made her feel like a

victim of tragedy all day? She couldn't forget the
way her parents died because the family were so
terrified of hurting or upsetting her. She was
constantly reminded of the crash.

Gradually, of course, life had become normal,
but today Melanie was bleakly aware that they
were sorry for her again. The very fact that they
hadn't asked any questions or made any comments
told her that they had guessed what Ross had
come to tell her, and were busy trying to comfort
and pet her.

'Look at that time,' Uncle Teddy said, getting
up with a last gulp of tea. 'I'd better rush. Want a
lift, Will?'

'Thanks, Dad. Will you have time to help me
with my bike this weekend? It's still in pieces in
the garage.'

'Why did you take it apart if you didn't know
how to put it together again?' Uncle Teddy said
drily but without heat as he kissed his wife on the
top of her silvery blonde head.

Will leapt up; a gawky young man, he plunged
about like a nervous horse, his body never quite
under his control. 'I thought it would be simple
enough,' he explained defensively.

His father grinned. 'Famous last words.' He
came round to kiss Melanie's head. 'Have a good
day, sweetheart.'

'Hey, why don't we go to the pictures tonight?'
suggested Will. 'There's a great film on this week.
Want to see it, Liz? You like horror movies. You
should, you belong in one.' He skipped out of the
way as his sister threw a punch at him. 'Missed
me. Yah, yah.' He slammed out of the room after
his father, laughing noisily.

'I'm glad he isn't riding that terrible motor-cycle
at the moment. I wish it would stay in pieces.

Every time he goes out on it my heart is in my mouth.' Aunt Dolly began clearing the table and Melanie and Liz got up to help her.

'What are you going to do today?' Liz asked a few minutes later as Melanie was going upstairs to her room.

'I'm going to the Lake District,' Melanie said calmly, and felt Liz do a double take.

'Oh.' Liz stood on the bottom step, staring after her, mouth rounded in surprise. She bore no resemblance to any of the rest of the family. Tall, slim, with sleek brown hair and brown eyes, Liz had a face which kept its secrets: calm, smooth-skinned, even-featured. You could rarely tell what Liz was thinking. Even her flashes of sarcasm were carefully controlled. She never exercised them on Melanie.

In her bedroom Melanie lifted her suitcase down and went to the wardrobe to get her anorak. As she knew, it often rained in the Lake District, and it was wisest to be prepared for bad weather, especially in the autumn.

Liz loomed in the doorway. 'I'm in the mood for a little sailing, myself,' she said casually, but not quite casually enough. Melanie heard the thought behind the words and gave a short sigh.

'I'd rather be on my own, Liz, if you don't mind.' She wished Liz hadn't made the oblique offer because she didn't want to offend her. It was kind and thoughtful, but company was the last thing she wanted.

'It isn't a good idea to sail alone,' Liz pointed out gently enough. 'You know the weather can come up suddenly and Ullswater can be pretty rough.'

'I won't take any risks.' Melanie threw her anorak over her arm and picked up her case. She was warmly dressed in the blue sweater and dark blue cord trousers. She was slightly built, a girl who resented her own look of fragility because she didn't feel fragile inside; she wanted to claim an independence and self-sufficiency those around her seemed reluctant to admit. Her outward look betrayed her; those large haunting blue eyes, the long fine black hair, the pale skin and finely shaped features. Inside, she felt much tougher than that. She didn't want to lean or cling, she didn't want to be protected, she had had too much of it in the past, she didn't want Ross to treat her as a plaything, a doll, to be picked up and put down when he hadn't anything more important on his mind.

'It would be fun,' Liz said, faintly wistfully. 'We haven't been to Ullswater for a month.'

The family kept a small sailing boat moored there, had done for years. They lived on the outskirts of Carlisle, only half an hour's drive away, and throughout their teens had spent most of their summers on the lake, sailing, swimming, walking.

'Next time,' Melanie said, almost desperately. She turned and looked at her cousin frankly. 'Liz, please—I have to get away on my own. I have to think.'

Liz shrugged, a mixture of anxiety and wry understanding in her watchful eyes. She was three years older than Melanie, and had always been just that little bit ahead of her. Liz, of all the family, would be most likely to understand Melanie's need to be alone and think, because Liz wasn't given to confidences either. Cool, sophisticated, very sure of herself, she wasn't easy to get to know.

'Don't brood over Ross Ellis. It's time you

realised that he puts his job before everything else,' Liz suddenly broke out. 'He's never going to have time for you. Men don't change, Melanie. Don't hope he will.'

Melanie didn't answer. She walked past her cousin out of the room and down the stairs. Her case wasn't heavy; she had packed very little. She wouldn't need much for a weekend's sailing—denims and shirts and sweaters, one pretty dress for evenings, a change of underclothes.

'You'll be staying at the pub, as usual?' asked Liz, following.

Melanie nodded. 'Say goodbye to Aunt Dolly for me. I'd better be on my way.' She didn't want to go through a session of questions and parried answers with her aunt too.

Her car was old and temperamental. She was terrified that it wouldn't start; on cold mornings it often didn't. She had a routine of taking out the sparking plugs and heating them to get the engine going but she didn't want to be delayed this morning because it would give Aunt Dolly a chance to get at her.

She prayed silently as she pulled out the choke then turned the ignition key. One outraged splutter, then the engine reluctantly fired and she drove off just as Aunt Dolly appeared in the doorway, distraught and flustered in her flowered pinny, waving a delaying arm, her mouth open in a wail of dismay. Melanie waved back without stopping.

It was a Saturday morning; the roads crowded with traffic. People going weekend shopping, people heading for the lakes or the sea. Melanie got on to the motorway and was able to put on more speed. Her old Ford couldn't safely do more than fifty or sixty miles an hour, but even so she was cresting the hill above Ullswater in no time at all, her eyes delightedly absorbing the landscape. The sky was a stormy blue, rainwashed but full of light; the green hills seemed to float in that brilliance like a mirage, reminiscent of a Tolkien illustration. Watery sunlight struck across Ullswater, the rippling surface of the lake shimmering.

The family always stayed at a lakeside pub owned by people they had known for years. Melanie turned into the crowded little car-park and saw just one space left, over by the wall. It wasn't easy to get into, which was probably why it was still vacant. She moved forward a little to get into position to reverse carefully into it, only to have her engine stall. Muttering under her breath, Melanie tried to get the car started again. While she was busy doing that a sleek red sports-car shot into the car-park, moved behind her and neatly slotted into the space she had been going to take. Melanie was too angry to admire the skill of the driver who performed the manoeuvre swiftly and without hesitation. Turning red with fury, she stumbled out of her car and went across to tell him what she thought of him.

He was just climbing out on the far side near the wall, his black hair blown around by the wind. He glanced over his shoulder at her as he bent to lock his car. His profile had a rakish elegance; sharp cheekbones, a long, arrogant nose, a rugged jawline. It was a very memorable face; hardly handsome yet stamped with a strong personality.

'You've taken my space!' Melanie accused.

'I didn't see a name on it,' he said with breathtaking insolence, straightening to stare at her. Seeing him full-face, she realised that it wasn't the jagged lines of his features that made the most impression, it was his wild black eyes. She'd never seen such amazing eyes before, and stared at him for almost a minute in surprise.

It wasn't until he was walking past her that she came to her senses. 'I was just going to park there!' she told him angrily.

He paused beside her, looking amused. 'How was I to know that? Your engine was switched off.'

'It wasn't switched off—it had stalled!'

One brow rose crookedly. 'Oh, was that it? Well, I'm sorry, but I saw an empty space and I got into it. That's the way it is around here. Parking is at a premium. If you see a space you don't wait around, you grab it. You may find somewhere further along the lake if you hurry.'

He turned on his heel and vanished into the pub and Melanie stared after him, bristling. He didn't even care! But there was nothing she could do about it now. She would have to take his advice and go and find somewhere else to park once she had checked into the reception desk and left her suitcase. She drove over to the side of the pub and parked there while she carried her case inside the little lobby. The owner was sitting behind the desk, going over some paperwork and operating the small switchboard.

'Hallo, Fred,' Melanie said, putting down her case, and he looked up, his thin face breaking into a grin.

'Melanie. Hi. I hope you've brought some better weather with you. It's been raining on and off since early morning.' He peered past her. 'Where's your fiancé?'

'He couldn't make it,' she said, hoping she didn't sound too uneasy about that. 'He'll have to come next time.'

'Okay. You'll just be wanting one room, then.'

'I'm sorry, Fred. If you can't let the other one, of course we'll pay for it.'

'Don't worry your head about that—we'll let it! We're turning people away all the time. We get busier every year. Sign in and I'll give you your key.' He pushed a card over to her and she quickly signed her name and address.

'Fred, I couldn't find anywhere to park,' she began, taking the key he held out.

'Give me your car keys and I'll put the car round the back, but don't tell anyone or they'll all want to do the same.' He winked at her. Fred Hill was in his early sixties, grey-haired, fit, with wind-tanned skin and a relaxed manner. He'd once told her that he had worked in a factory in Birmingham for thirty years until he had an accident and had to retire early. He'd invested his life savings in this little pub beside Ullswater. His wife, June, did the cooking and saw to the bedrooms. Fred managed the books and entertained the bar guests. The eight bedrooms were always full, and so was the bar. June's cooking was good. Fred's cheerful smile brought people back again and again. They often wished that Fred had had his accident years sooner; they were happier than they had ever been in their lives.

'Thank you, Fred,' Melanie said, relieved and grateful, and handed him her car keys before she went up to her room. June had put her in the one she always had; a room with a bay window and a view over the lake. It was comfortably but shabbily furnished; an old, faded red Axminster carpet on the squeaky floor-boards, well-washed chintz curtains at the windows, solid Victorian furniture which was always highly polished. There were none of the delights of modern hotels; no television, no telephone in the room, the bathroom was poky and only just held a shower cubicle and lavatory, a tiny wash-basin. But the bed was more than comfortable, the mattress was stuffed with feathers, and sleeping in it was like sinking into a snow drift. The quilt was massive, a faded pink satin. There was no central heating in the pub yet; in winter these rooms were like wind tunnels and the air smelt of damp. You needed a thick quilt. Whatever the season, Melanie always slept well here, especially after she'd been out on the lake or climbing in the hills all day. Fresh air, exercise, good food, made her ready for bed by nine o'clock each night.

She unpacked and changed into her old sailing denims. Before she went downstairs she stood by the window looking over the lake—the water sparkled, the pine trees across the water gave a mysterious edging to the horizon, dark, battlemented. Autumnal colours touched everywhere else; the birches and elms rustled golden leaves and every breath of wind brought new leaves blowing along the water's edge.

Ross would be on his way to Bahrein now. If he loved her, he'd be here. What was she going to do?

She closed her eyes, fighting with new tears, and turned away, refusing to think about it yet. She needed the solace of the silence on the water before she could think without crying.

She ran downstairs and June met her in the lobby, giving her a comfortable hug. 'Hallo, ducks, how are you? Where's your lover boy, then? Not coming, Fred said. Business! You shouldn't let him get away with that, lovey. If they're at it before you're married, they're devils after the knot's tied.'

Melanie forced a smile. 'You know what men are like, June!' she said gaily. 'Anything special for

lunch today? I thought I'd have a snack before I
went out in the boat.'

'Come in the bar and have some of my shepherd's
pie. I've put a cheese topping on it today. One of
my better efforts, if I say so myself.' June bustled
ahead, plump, gaudily blonde with an easy smile
and a genuinely kind heart behind it. Her natural
colouring was brunette—you could see the dark
roots because she dyed her hair herself—but
somehow being blonde suited her far more, it
matched her cheerful personality. All the regulars
at the pub loved June; she was an instinctive home-
maker and enjoyed looking after people.

As Melanie climbed on to a bar stool she saw
the man who had snatched her parking space. He
was sitting at a table in the corner with a tall red-
head in a smart dress. They both looked out of
place, for different reasons. This wasn't a 'smart'
pub. It was down-to-earth and lively but the jet set
didn't congregate around here, and the red-head
looked pretty jet set to Melanie. The studs in her
ears were real emeralds and she was distinctly
wearing a Cartier watch.

Her companion wasn't as easy to place. He had
been wearing a sheepskin jacket which he had
thrown over a chair. Now Melanie could see that
his denims were as old as her own and his sweater
was hand-knitted Fair Isle. He was wearing trainers
on his feet—no doubt he had been or was about to
go sailing, but not with the expensive lady sitting
next to him. Her high heels were delicate enough
to be hand-made.

'Here you are, ducks. Get that inside you and
you'll be fit for anything!' June placed an oval dish
of cheese-topped shepherd's pie in front of her.
'Now, what'll you have to drink with it?'

'Let me buy you a drink,' said a voice behind Melanie. 'A small apology.'

'What's that when it's at home? Don't think we've got any,' said June and gave one of her roars of laughter at her own joke. 'Now then, Jamie Knox, what've you been up to? Melanie's a friend of mine. I won't have you upsetting her.'

'He stole my parking place,' Melanie said without looking at him as he slid on to the stool next to her. She remembered his striking face without needing to see it.

'Typical,' June said, leaning her elbows on the counter to enjoy the discussion. 'Watch out that's all he steals—he's a devil with the ladies, aren't you, Jamie?'

'If Fred hadn't seen you first, I'd never stray from your side, June,' he said lightly, and June chuckled.

'Flatterer. Come on, Melanie, what about some champagne on Jamie? Make him pay for his piracy.'

'I'll just have a Perrier, thanks.'

'Don't let him off lightly; that's a mistake with guys like Jamie Knox!'

'I'll need all my wits about me while I'm sailing,' Melanie said coolly, turning her head to meet his dark gaze. June moved away, shrugging, to get the drink, and Jamie Knox smiled into Melanie's wary eyes. He needn't waste that charm on her, she thought, staring back.

'Crewing for someone?' he asked and she shook her head, the sleek dark strands of her hair floating sideways and flicking against his arm. He was sitting far too close for comfort. Melanie found something about him disturbing. She tried to shift away without being too obvious about it. She didn't want him to know the effect he had on her. Those dark eyes were far too aware and cynical.

'I'm going out alone, today,' she told him reluctantly.

His brows shot up. 'What in? A rowboat?'

She stiffened, her colour high. 'Don't be so insulting!'

He grimaced. 'It was, wasn't it? Okay, I apologise—but you look far too ritzy to be the sailing type. Do you really know what you're doing in a boat? What are you going out in? Have you sailed it before?'

'Literally dozens of times—and alone as well as with help,' Melanie said crisply, and he considered her thoughtfully.

'If you want a crew . . .'

'I don't,' she said, before he could offer, trying to sound polite. 'I want to be on my own, thanks.' To make it quite clear to him that she wasn't interested in him, she put up her left hand to brush back her hair and saw his eyes narrow as he noticed her ring. It was hard to miss—Ross had given her an enormous, square-cut sapphire ringed with smaller diamonds. When her hand moved, the stones blazed.

'What about you and your lady-friend, Jamie? Want anything else?' June asked, putting the glass of mineral water in front of Melanie.

'No, I came over to pay the bill,' he said. June told him how much he owed her and he paid, then slid down off the stool and said quietly to Melanie, 'Watch the weather this afternoon; it's very changeable out there.'

Then he was gone and Melanie concentrated on her meal. There was far too much in the oval dish; she apologised to June as she left half of it. 'It's gorgeous, but I can't quite manage all of it, sorry, June.'

'Never mind, ducks. I make my meals man-sized, so I don't expect you to eat all that. Want a coffee?'

'No, I think I'll get out on the water while the sun's out. See you tonight.'

She walked down to the mooring-space in front of the pub, her long black hair whipped around by the strong wind. Good sailing weather, she thought, looking up at the blue sky. Clouds scudded across, driven by that wind, but they weren't rainclouds now. The afternoon was set fair.

As she sailed out from the shore she caught a glimpse of the red sports-car racing along the lakeside road. Ullswater wasn't as swamped with traffic as Windermere, which in the summer was impossible. You couldn't park, or drive faster than a snail's pace, anywhere around Windermere.

She hoped Jamie Knox wasn't staying at the pub too. It wasn't often that Melanie met someone she positively disliked, but she had been left with a far from favourable impression of that man.

The light lasted until well after seven that evening and Melanie stayed out, her body going through the automatic routine of sailing the boat while her mind ran blindly through mazes of doubt and uncertainty about Ross. It all came back to one question—did he love her? If he didn't, why had he proposed? If he did, why did she see so little of him, and when they were together, why did she always feel so strained? When he kissed her it was like being kissed by a stranger, which was what Ross was to her, despite the glitter of his ring on her finger. Was he too old for her? Did he feel that he was? He was thirty-six, Melanie just twenty-two.

Fourteen years, she thought, her heart uneasy. Fourteen years *is* a long time. What do I know about those years of his life? He tells me nothing, and when I try to ask he kisses me to silence me, but making love can't solve everything; and that brought her back to the original problem—did he love her?

That evening she went to bed early after a light snack of salad and an omelette and slept heavily until her alarm clock went off at six-thirty. She had arranged with June to take a packed lunch with her that day. When she got downstairs for breakfast the small morning-room was crowded. Everyone who came here was intent on spending the day in the open air; some were going sailing, others, like Melanie, meant to head for the hills and walk.

There was a faint ground mist as she set out, but the weather forecast had been encouraging. During the morning the mist cleared and the sun came out. At noon Melanie was high above Ullswater on the mountainside. She had climbed up through an oakwood's shadowy glades out into the sunlight on the steep flanks of the mountain, over shifting, jagged stone and short rough grass, pushing herself onwards with an angry need to tire her body and stop her mind working.

She was beginning to be hungry, though, so she stopped, took off her anorak and threw herself down on a patch of coarse tall grass; the purple dancing heads of couch-grass dominating it. Her legs ached and she was out of breath. She unpacked her rucksack and found that June had given her a large slice of cold game pie, a tossed salad in an airtight plastic box, an apple and a flask of coffee. Melanie ate her picnic staring down at the distant gleam of blue water, the ribbon of road, the toy houses and cars around the lake.

When she had finished eating she felt heavy and sleepy. The sun was hot, the grass comfortable.

She only meant to lie down for half an hour before beginning the climb downwards, but she must have been more exhausted than she realised.

The next thing she knew was when a shrill chattering call very close to her woke her. She opened her eyes in time to see a slate-blue merlin chasing downwind with prey in its talons. Melanie was surprised that it came so close to her until she realised that it hadn't seen her. Sitting up in alarm, she realised that mist had come stealing down the mountain while she slept. The lake was no longer visible. The sky was enveloped in damp grey.

Shivering, she got up and put on her anorak, slipped her arms through the straps of her rucksack and began to pick her way carefully downwards. She could still see a few yards ahead of her and so long as she kept going down she must reach the lake in the end, she told herself, but the mist kept getting thicker and the loose stones were slippery and wet now. Her feet kept sliding from under her. She was reduced to moving very slowly, checking each foothold before she risked it, and the longer it took her the less she could see.

Thank heavens she had told June exactly where she was heading! At least her whereabouts would be known if she had to stay put up here. If the mist got much thicker she knew she wouldn't dare risk the descent. The mountains could be treacherous in weather like this. One false step and she could go plunging down to her death.

She had no sooner thought that than her foot skidded on a shifting stone and she felt herself sliding. She clung on to some coarse grass but it couldn't hold her weight. The fall was short, luckily. She found herself sprawling in a narrow gulley. She banged her head but otherwise seemed okay, until she tried to get up. Then she discovered that she had hurt one ankle. Putting any weight on it was painful. She sat down and examined it anxiously; not broken, but already puffing up. She had sprained it, she suspected. This would make her climb downwards even more difficult and dangerous.

It might be wiser to stay where she was until the mist lifted. The sides of the gulley were some protection from the cold. Her anorak was warm, her sweater helped too, and she had a flask of coffee which she had barely touched. June had packed far too much food, as usual. Melanie had been stranded on the hills before now. She knew the drill. Keep warm and take no risks. Sighing, she settled herself more comfortably. She might be in for a long wait—Lakeland weather was unpredictable, this mist might dissolve at any minute, but on the other hand it could set in for hours.

She looked at her watch and was amazed to realise that it was gone four. She must have slept for several hours! Pulling up her hood, she drank a little more coffee; it was still hot and circulated nicely in her chilling body. The mist was very cold, she felt it dewing her lashes as she curled closer to the side of the gulley.

It was some time later that a new sound made her sit up, ears pricked. The sound came again, the rattle of a stone under someone's foot, and then the rough sound of breathing.

Melanie clambered to her feet, wincing as she remembered her swollen ankle. 'Hi!' she called. 'Hi!'

The sounds grew louder, she saw a shape through the mist—a tall, dark shape which materialised as that of a man in a green anorak, the hood hiding his face until he came closer and bent to stare at her.

'There you are,' he said conversationally. 'Not very sensible of you to stay up here with the mist coming down, was it?'

Melanie's heart sank as she recognised Jamie Knox's dry voice. It would be him!

CHAPTER TWO

SHE sank back, her face a battleground, half
grateful to see him, half wishing it had been
someone else. 'Have you been climbing, too?'

'No, I was having lunch at the pub when the
weather warning came at the end of the news.
June said she was worried because you were
climbing alone.' He dropped lightly into the gulley
beside her; she saw drops of mist on his dark hair.
'We took a look through binoculars and thought
we saw you right up near the summit, but you
weren't moving. June got into a panic, thought you
might have hurt yourself, but then we saw you get
up and start coming down so I decided to come up
and meet you just in case the weather worsened.
Just as well I did, isn't it?'

He was still breathing rapidly; he must have
climbed fast if he had had lunch at the pub. 'That
was very good of you,' she said unevenly. 'I fell
asleep, you see.'

'Good God!' he said impatiently, his mouth hard.
'You ought to know better! Falling asleep on the
fells—were you trying to get yourself killed? You
know how the weather changes around here!'

She bit her inner lip, tempted to snap back, but
knowing he was right. It had been very stupid of
her to fall asleep, and there was enormous relief in
having another human being around in this cold
mist.

'It wasn't very bright of me,' she admitted

28

reluctantly. 'And when I woke up and saw the mist I had to hurry and I slipped and hurt my ankle.' It was best to get the worst out right away, then he could tell her what he thought of her and get it over with.

He gave her one look, charged with feelings she deserved, then knelt down. 'Let me see.' His hands were gentle but she still flinched at the pain of their probing. 'Only sprained,' he said quite soothingly. 'Can you stand on it?'

'Barely.' She had had to unlace her climbing-boot, anyway, which made it dangerous to walk far on these steep slopes.

He stood up and looked away from her, his brow furrowed, as he thought about the situation. 'God knows how long this mist will hang around, and it can be very cold at night up here. We ought to get inside if we can. There's an old shepherd's hut about a quarter of a mile from here on a lower level—if we could reach that we'd be out of the weather. Do you think you could make it if I helped you?'

Melanie tensed her muscles. 'I can try.'

She felt him watching her. 'June says you're used to hill-walking, you know what you're doing, but I'd never have guessed.'

Very flushed, she ignored that. 'I vaguely remember that hut. If we're going to make it before it gets dark, we'd better start now.'

'Let me fix that boot of yours before we move off.' He knelt down again and managed to tie the laces without putting pressure on her swollen foot. 'If you need to lean on me, don't hesitate,' he told her curtly, as they set off.

There was a distinct track running horizontally towards the hut, which was often used by climbers in bad weather. It was easier going than the descent

on loose stone, but before they got there it began
to rain; thin, driving rain that soaked through her
clothes within minutes. Shivering, she paused to
wipe her face—she could hardly see a foot ahead
now.

Jamie paused, too, looking at her in impatient
concern. 'Can you go on? It isn't far now. The
sooner we're out of this the better.'

She nodded, her teeth chattering, and Jamie slid
an arm around her waist. The track was just wide
enough for both of them now but the relentless
rain made every step difficult, and just before they
got to the hut Melanie stumbled and fell headlong
before Jamie could save her.

He lifted her to her feet, his hands under her
arms. She leaned on him like a spent swimmer,
gasping and shuddering, blood running down her
temples where she had grazed her face in the fall,
and heard Jamie mutter impatiently, then he
hoisted her over his shoulder and carried her the
last few yards. She was too weary to argue or fight
him. She had never been so tired in her life.

The door creaked as he pushed it open, then
they were inside and he kicked the door shut, put
her down and produced a torch whose light showed
her a bare, stone-floored interior. The hut was
primitive, intended only as a shelter from the
weather, and it held no furniture. Cobwebs hung
dustily from corners, the one window was grimy,
straw littered the floor and a set of stone steps led
up into a hayloft at one side of the room. Melanie's
eyes focused on the wall which held a blackened
stone hearth.

'I'll light a fire,' Jamie Knox said, walking away,
his torchlight making circles on the floor.

'What with?' Melanie couldn't see any kindling
material. She was so cold her body shuddered

violently, and she had to lean on the rough stone wall. Local stone, she thought, the same material that had traditionally been used for building drystone walls.

Jamie was up in the hayloft, his feet scuffling in straw. 'They keep a pile of logs up here for these emergencies.' He came down a moment later with his arms full of logs.

'You've been here before,' she said, drawn forward by the idea of a fire. He had knelt down by the hearth and was carefully making a pyramid of straw. and pine-cones with logs as the main structure. 'Can I do anything? Get some more logs?' she asked.

'Once I've got this started you can watch it while I bring some bedding down for us,' he said, producing a lighter. Hypnotised, she watched the flame and inhaled the scent of burning resin as the pine-cones blazed up. There was something so primitive about fire; both dangerous and reassuring. Out of control it could kill, but contained within the smoke-blackened chimney it cast a spell, the warmth of it very comforting.

Jamie was crouching down to blow gently upwards; the dry logs caught the flame with a sudden crackle, a fiery tongue licking upwards. 'I'll get the bedding now,' he said, turning to face her on his knees. That was when she realised what he had said the first time, and she reacted with alarm as the firelight flickered, showing her the carved hollows of his face.

Melanie stiffened. 'Bedding?' she repeated guardedly, and his black eyes flashed at her.

'We're going to be here all night, from the look of it out there. I'm not prepared to risk trying to get down in that mist and rain, even if you are.' He got to his feet and she backed, suddenly afraid.

Until then she hadn't really thought about their isolation, but now she was very conscious of it.

He watched her, his features mysterious and sinister in the leaping firelight. Black hair, black eyes, a wilful cast of face—he wasn't the companion she would have picked for a night on the mountain.

'We should be comfortable enough on straw,' he said drily and moved away, taking the torch with him but leaving her in the comforting glow of the firelight. She sat down near it, crouched inside her wet anorak, which began to steam gently. She ought to take it off but she was still cold.

Jamie came back with armfuls of straw and a couple of old sacks. 'These will make useful covers,' he said, laying them down within a safe distance of the fire. 'You'd better take your anorak off or you'll be going down with pneumonia.'

She unzipped the anorak and pulled it off. Her sweater was damp but the rain hadn't actually soaked it, she decided.

'The sweater too,' Jamie Knox said tersely.

'It's okay!'

He took one long stride and caught her shoulder, his hand moving along the sweater. 'As I thought— it's damp, the rain soaked right through your anorak, didn't it? Get it off! You aren't sitting around in damp clothes all night.'

She pulled free, her dark blue eyes stormy. 'I'm not sitting around naked, either. I haven't got anything on underneath it.'

His mouth went crooked with impatient amusement. 'You crazy female! Don't you even know what to wear for a day on the fells?' He unzipped his own anorak, which had, she saw, a warm waterproof lining, stripped off his sweater and then pulled off the cotton shirt he wore under that. Melanie watched, backing, her eyes alarmed.

'What are you doing?'

He threw her the shirt. 'No need to get excited. I'm not about to make a pass. Take off your sweater and jeans and put this on. You're so small and skinny it should come to your knees.' He put his sweater on again and turned to attend to the fire, talking without looking at her. 'Hurry up. I'm not watching, and if you could see yourself you wouldn't be so scared I might make a pass at you. You're covered in mud, your hair's like wet string; you are a very bedraggled object, Miss Nesbitt. My male instincts aren't going to run amok at the sight of you, naked or otherwise.'

She hurriedly took off her sweater and jeans and slid into his shirt. It was still warm from his body and carried his scent; male, faintly musky. It clung to her and she smoothed it down, feeling odd about wearing his clothes.

'Now put my anorak on,' he said, 'Mine's more weatherproof than yours; the rain didn't penetrate it.' A shower of sparks flew up as he put another log on the fire, which was burning nicely now.

'Are you sure you'll be warm enough?' Melanie said hesitantly.

He gave her a dry smile. 'Quite sure.' He began rummaging in his rucksack and produced some thin twine. 'I'm going to stretch this across the chimney breast; it will make a nice drying-line for your clothes.'

'You think of everything, don't you?' she said with faint hostility.

'I try, Miss Nesbitt.' The black head turned, he grinned at her, wicked charm in his face. 'To tell you the truth, the nails are there—I'm not the first person to have the idea. I told you, this place is often used by climbers caught out by the weather.'

She looked in her own rucksack. 'I have some

hot coffee left,' she offered. She unscrewed the top, grimacing. 'Well, warm coffee, anyway.' She poured some and held it out to him and he came over to her and sat down beside her, taking the plastic cup, sipping the coffee.

'Thanks, this is very welcome. What else have you got in there?'

'Biscuits and an orange and a little slab of cheese.'

He smiled, his eyes crinkling. 'Then we shan't starve, shall we? I brought Kendal mintcake, a couple of apples and a flask of tea.' He finished the coffee and held out the cup. 'Now you have some—it will make you feel more human, believe me. I feel better already.'

She managed an answering smile and poured herself half a cup. Holding it between her palms to let the warmth percolate her skin, she glanced at him apologetically. 'I'm sorry to have got you into this. It isn't going to be very comfortable, is it?'

'Not exactly,' he agreed without resentment. He had very long black lashes, she noticed, and his skin was smooth and tanned over those sharp cheekbones. 'June told me that your fiancé was supposed to be coming, but backed out—did you have a row with him?'

'No, I did not,' she denied, scowling. 'Why should you think . . .'

'Pure guesswork! You were obviously angry when you arrived—and it wasn't just because I'd taken your parking space. You over-reacted about that. I could see you were in a mood to bite the first person who gave you an excuse. You were mad with the guy in your life—so with typical female logic, you decided to go off alone and take risks just to show him!' He got up and began to arrange her jeans and sweater on his taut washing-line above the fire.

'That's not true!' Melanie said angrily. There was, of course, enough truth in his speculation to make her furious with him. She and Ross hadn't had a quarrel, but only because Ross hadn't stayed long enough and she hadn't had a chance to lose her temper. Ross rarely gave her any opportunity to let him see how she felt, in fact. The pent-up frustration made her look at Jamie Knox with smouldering eyes. She might not be able to confront Ross, but Jamie Knox was just a few feet away and she could tell him just what she thought of him.

'Your guesswork is light-years off course, and pretty insulting, too. I made a stupid mistake, but I'm not a complete fool. If I was angry with my fiancé, I'd tell him, I wouldn't punish him by trying to kill myself. You know nothing about me so don't dream up fantasies to explain what I do.' Anger made her voice shake and he leaned on the chimney breast, listening with derision in his eyes.

'Did I hit a button?'

Her flush became red-hot. He had, of course, damn him. She tightened her lips, not daring to risk a reply to that.

After a pause during which she heard the rain beating against the dirty window and the crackle of the fire, Jamie Knox asked conversationally, 'What do you do for a living, by the way?'

'I work in an estate office,' she said curtly, staring at the smoke and flare of the fire.

'In Carlisle?'

She gave him a surprised look. 'Yes. You seem to be very well informed about me.'

'June told me,' he said, his mouth amused again, and she knew June well enough to understand

why. June loved talking about her guests; she
was a compulsive news-gatherer and passed on
everything she learned to everyone else she talked
to.

'What do you do and where do you live?' she
asked pointedly, because why should he know so
much about her when she knew almost nothing
about him?

'I've got a cottage half a mile from the pub,' he
said, and her eyes widened.

'You live here all the year round?'

He nodded, producing a slab of mintcake and
breaking off a piece, which he offered her.

'Thank you.' She took it and nibbled it. 'And
what's your job?'

'At the moment, I haven't got one.' He got up
and threw another handful of pine-cones on the
fire. Their aromatic scent reached her nostrils and
she leaned forward to inhale it with pleasure as she
answered him.

'Were you made redundant?' Her voice was
sympathetic now; it had happened to several people
she knew. Unemployment was very high in this
part of the country, even more so in the big urban
centres within a few hours' drive of the Lake
District, of course. He had a very expensive car,
presumably he had had a good job. He must have
had a shock when he lost it.

'More or less.' His voice was dry. 'Don't look so
sorry for me—I'll get another one. No need to pass
round the hat just yet.'

She smiled at him, her dark blue eyes gentle. 'It
must be very worrying, though. I'd hate the
uncertainty.'

He considered her, his head to one side. 'Yes, I
suppose you would. You look very highly strung—

it must be those fine bones of yours. You seem fragile, as though you snap under pressure.'

Her chin went up; his voice held what she thought to be a note of dismissal. 'I'm not fragile and I don't snap under pressure!'

'You're snapping now!' His mouth was crooked and she sat back, biting her lip.

'You're a very irritating man, Mr Knox.' Turning away, she looked in her rucksack for a comb and began to drag it through her damp, tangled hair, crossly aware that he was watching her.

'I wish I could wash my face,' she said, wondering how she looked, although what difference did it make? She wasn't trying to attract him, she didn't care what he thought.

'Why not? I'll fetch you some water, although it will be very cold.' He got to his feet and she stared at him in surprise.

'Water? Where from?'

'There's a rain barrel right outside the door. Don't you notice anything? You weren't in the Girl Guides, were you? When you're in strange terrain, it pays to keep your eyes open.'

'You try keeping your eyes open when someone's carrying you over his shoulder!'

'I'd like to see the guy who tried,' Jamie Knox said, laughing. 'Can I borrow my anorak for a second?' She took it off and he slid into it and headed for the door. As he opened it, a gust of wind blew in, bringing rain, and Melanie shivered, crouching closer to the fire. He was back a moment later, carrying a rather rusty old bucket.

Melanie washed hurriedly, conscious of his stare, and dried her face on a handkerchief.

'You'd better put my anorak on again,' he said softly. 'My shirt seems to be rather transparent in firelight.'

She glanced down hurriedly, her cheeks burning as she saw the way the thin material of his shirt clung to her body, outlining the dark circles of her nipples. He must be able to see every inch of her, as if she were naked. Melanie put out a hand blindly as he took off his anorak. She couldn't look at him. She fumbled her way hurriedly into the garment and zipped it up with shaky fingers.

Jamie washed his own face and dried it, while Melanie stared fixedly at the fire. They were alone here; she knew nothing about him. What if he suddenly grabbed her? She would have no chance of fighting him off. She eyed him secretly through lowered lashes. The black hair was plastered to his skull by rain, showing her the powerful contours of a face which disturbed her. She couldn't begin to guess what he was thinking.

'It's raining hard out there,' he said. 'By the way, there's a pretty primitive outhouse at the back, if you need it.'

Her flush deepened. 'Can I borrow your torch?'

'You'll need it,' he said, handing it to her as she got up. 'By the time you get back, your sweater should be quite dry. You'll feel more human when you can get dressed again.'

She avoided catching his eye, but she was relieved by the remark. Had he meant her to be relieved? Did he realise that she was alarmed by being alone with him here?

She limped round the hut, her head bent against the cold, driving rain, the faint circles of light from the torch showing her where she was going, the wind howling on the fells. She came back a few moments later, drenched and with chattering teeth. The outhouse had been even more primitive than her worst imaginings, and more than that, she had seen something with a tail in there.

'There are rats in it!' she said, bursting back into the hut and slamming the door after her, to drip her way back to the fire.

'Probably,' he said coolly, watching her take off his sodden anorak. Melanie pulled her sweater off the line and hastily put it on, her head averted. Her jeans were dry, too; once she was fully dressed her nerves stopped jumping every time he moved. As she sat down, huddling next to the fire, he produced a leather flask and handed it to her.

'What's this?' she asked.

'Brandy, just what we need to put some warmth back into us!'

She shook her head. 'Thanks, but I don't like brandy.'

'You don't have to like it. Swallow some, it will do you good. Your hair's soaked again; a pity neither of us thought of bringing a towel.'

'Isn't it?' she muttered sarcastically. 'Next time I get lost I'll remember to bring one.'

'That isn't so funny, Miss Nesbitt,' he said with dry amusement. 'I've only known you a short time, but I get the feeling you're prone to get lost.'

Melanie frowned, pointlessly rubbing her handkerchief over her hair in an attempt to dry it a little. She wasn't sure what he meant but she didn't like the way he had said it.

He moved, and she grew tense again. 'Stop arguing and drink some of this brandy,' he said, holding the flask to her mouth. 'You don't want to get pneumonia, do you?'

'You bully,' she said with animosity. He smelt of rain and woodsmoke, his face inches from her own. She glanced through her lashes at his brown cheek; the hooded dark eyes watched her from hiding, their gleam unnerving. A pulse of panic beat in her throat. To hide that, she reluctantly swallowed some brandy with a shudder. It went to her head; she felt almost dizzy.

'Feel better now?' Was he laughing at her or was that crooked little smile meant to help her relax?

She stared into the fire, watching the blue and orange tongues of flame curling round the wood. Jamie Knox drank a little brandy, sitting next to her, his knees bent up and his chin resting on them.

'What are you seeing in the fire?' he asked casually a moment later. 'Pictures? I remember doing that when I was small. At Christmas we used to roast chestnuts in the ashes; they tasted smoky and burnt, but that was part of the fun.'

'We did, too,' Melanie said, smiling. 'On a shovel—I liked hearing the chestnuts burst open. We made toast in front of the fire, too.'

'Instant nostalgia, a fireside, isn't it?' he murmured. He began to tell her about Christmases he had spent abroad, often in hot countries, and how much he had missed the traditions and even the cold wintry weather of home. He had travelled a great deal, presumably because his job took him all over the world. He talked casually but gave her vivid word pictures of places he had seen; Melanie was fascinated. Was he a journalist, she wondered?

'I haven't really travelled at all,' she admitted ruefully. 'Just a couple of holidays abroad—one year we went to Spain, and spent two whole weeks just lying on the beach. Last year we went to Italy and did some sightseeing in Rome and Naples. That was a coach tour, I found it rather exhausting. We only stopped in any place for two or three days. I got coach-sick.'

'We?' he queried, watching her intently.

'My family—we all went together.' She turned

her head and their eyes met; Melanie felt that odd quiver of panic again, although there was no real threat in his gaze. Hurriedly, she asked, 'Do you come from a big family?'

'No,' he said. 'Where's your fiancé this weekend?'

Her fine-boned, expressive face quivered with feeling at the abrupt question, and he stared at her, his eyes narrowed.

'Bahrain,' she said huskily. 'He travels a good deal, too.'

'Doing what? Business?'

'Yes,' she said.

'What sort of work does he do?'

'You ask a lot of questions,' Melanie said shortly, reluctant to talk about Ross.

'We must pass the time somehow,' he said, smiling mockingly. 'Of course, there are alternatives, but if you're in love with another man, I suppose you wouldn't be interested?'

Melanie turned her head towards the fire again, staring into the flames with fixed gaze but intensely aware of his every movement, every breath he took.

'Don't,' she said in a very low voice.

'Don't what?' He sounded amused still; she didn't find it at all funny.

'Flirt. This is difficult enough without you making it even harder.'

There was silence, then he laughed shortly. 'You're right, of course. I apologise. The trouble is, Miss Nesbitt, you're a very attractive girl and this is a very intimate situation we're in—I'd have to be superhuman not to . . . well, let's just say that your fiancé must be crazy. What's his name, by the way? As we're always talking about him, I might as well know who I'm talking about.'

'I don't want to talk about my private life at all,' she said. 'But his name is Ross.'

'Surname?'

'No, that's his first name. Ross Ellis, if you insist.'

There was another silence. She looked around, sensing something odd in the air, and saw his eyes narrowed, hard and black.

'Ellis? The Ellis who runs the big construction company?'

Slowly, she nodded, wondering what he was thinking. The humour had vanished from his face, no doubt because he had been impressed by hearing that she was engaged to one of the most important men in the north-west. Ross had inherited a construction firm which until that time had been a purely local company in this area. Ross had built it into a worldwide company in just fifteen years. He was a man of dynamic energies. Whenever she was upset because she never saw enough of him, she reminded herself that Ross was in the habit of giving his entire attention to his firm. He simply hadn't realised yet that she needed him, too. If he would only stay still long enough to listen to her, she might make him understand that. He must love her, or why would he ask her to marry him?

'I'd heard he had got engaged,' Jamie Knox said slowly.

That didn't surprise her. The announcement had caused quite a bit of local interest. Ross was a big local employer; naturally people took an interest in everything he did. Melanie had been rather nervous when she had to be interviewed by reporters, but Ross had been there too and he had smoothed over her hesitations and stammered answers.

'Do you want anything to eat? A biscuit? An orange?' Jamie asked and she shook her head.

'June packed a huge lunch for me—oh, they must be worried by now, wondering where we are!'

'I told them that if I found you, I'd bring you here. With binoculars they'll be able to see the light in the window and guess that we got here safely.'

She gave him a daunted look. 'You really do think of everything, don't you?' There was something very disturbing about that.

'If I can,' he said with an oddly wry smile. 'Sometimes things happen that you couldn't possibly foresee—but that apart, I try to anticipate what I may meet before I set out. If we haven't started down at first light, June and Fred will call the mountain rescue people, but they'll wait until then. Nothing could be done in the dark, anyway, not with this rain and wind. They couldn't even get a helicopter up here to take a look around.'

Melanie was beginning to feel very sleepy; the brandy, no doubt. She lay on her side, the straw was comfortable enough, she was warm and dry and very tired. Her lids grew heavier and heavier. Through them, half-closed, she secretly watched Jamie Knox gazing into the fire, as unblinking as a cat, his knees up, his chin on them, his rakish profile all that she could see of his face. She wondered about him. He was rather secretive for a man who asked so many questions. Her lids drooped. She couldn't keep them open any longer and she slid into sleep.

She woke when something touched her cheek. Her lids stirred, she drowsily opened her eyes and looked up straight into Jamie Knox's face. Still locked in half-sleep, Melanie stared at him as if she had never seen him before, bewildered by his presence in her dream, but then her heart began to beat faster and faster, she went cold and then hot, with shock and memory. In a flash she remembered where she was and who he was, and then she felt a stab of fear as he bent closer.

'Wake up, Sleeping Beauty,' he murmured, smiling, his mouth inches away.

She knew he was going to kiss her. For a second her muscles stiffened; then his lips touched her mouth, warm flesh, softly persuasive, and Melanie jack-knifed upwards, pushing him away.

He went without resistance and got to his feet. 'Obviously, it works with a vengeance,' he said, puzzling her. 'I wonder if the original Sleeping Beauty slapped her prince?' He moved away without waiting for her reply. 'Time to start down, Miss Nesbitt. It's almost light and the rain has stopped. It is going to be a beautiful morning.'

Melanie sat there for a moment, breathing hard. The hut was filling with pale grey light, and the fire was out. She shivered in the chill of the stone walls and the early morning, and felt strangely depressed.

CHAPTER THREE

'OF course, you mustn't drive a car until the swelling has quite gone down, it wouldn't be safe,' said the doctor as he finished binding her ankle, and Melanie forced a smile, nodding. She hadn't thought of that aspect of her accident. She would have to ring the family and ask one of them to drive over to pick her up, and that would mean telling them the whole story. She didn't look forward to doing that.

When the doctor had left, hurrying to get on with the rest of his round, June considered her unhappy face and patted her shoulder.

'Don't look so down, lovey. I tell you what, Fred was going into Carlisle some day this week to pick up some things I want from the Lanes. Wonderful new shopping centre, I wish it was nearer here. Whenever I go to Carlisle I head straight for it. Anyway, I'll get him to go today, he can drop you off at home and do my shopping at the same time, then you can pick up your car any time you like. We'll look after it for you; it will be safe in our car-park.'

'Thank you,' Melanie said gratefully, but when Fred came into the kitchen he had Jamie Knox with him and the two men had already hatched another scheme.

'Jamie's going to drive you home, Melanie,' Fred told her. 'And I'll drive over to Carlisle this afternoon, after the bar shuts, to do June's shopping

45

and pick Jamie up afterwards. You don't want to
leave your car sitting around in our car-park for
days, do you?'

Melanie said flatly that she didn't. 'Thank you,
Fred. You're very thoughtful.'

'It was Jamie's idea,' Fred said generously, as if
he needed to tell her that.

She turned a tight smile towards Jamie Knox.
'Thank you.' She didn't want him driving her
home, she didn't want her family to see him, to
ask questions, to be curious about what had
happened between them. She knew that last night
had been totally innocent, and of course her uncle
and aunt would believe her when she told them
that nothing had happened, but something about
Jamie Knox's bright, amused eyes and cynical smile
made her feel absurdly guilty, as if she were lying.
Yet she didn't quite dare to refuse his offer because
that might make Fred and June curious, and so far
they hadn't raised any eyebrows or looked askance
over the explanation of how Melanie and Jamie
had spent the night in the shepherd's hut. Such
things happened all the time in this district; people
were always getting lost in the hills or trapped by
bad weather. The important thing was that they
had got safely back, that was all that June and
Fred cared about, and no doubt Uncle Teddy and
Aunt Dolly would feel the same, but Melanie
would still rather not let the family meet Jamie
Knox.

Meeting his gaze, she was certain he could read
her mind and was amused by everything she wasn't
saying.

June helped her pack and Fred carried her case
down to her car. She got hugs from both of them
and messages for the family, then Jamie Knox
started the car and shot out of the car-park.

Melanie was aggrieved to see that he could get more speed out of her old car than she ever had.

'It might be faster by mule,' he observed as he followed the winding road beside the lake. Maddeningly, the weather today was gorgeous; the sky clear, the sun bright, the hills a sharp outline on the horizon.

'You're doing forty miles an hour. What more do you want?' she muttered, settling reluctantly into the passenger seat next to him. 'I don't believe in driving too fast, anyway, especially not on these roads.'

He looked sideways through his lashes at her. 'Did you ring your family and tell them what had happened?'

The heat in her face was answer enough and her silence underlined it.

'He whistled softly. 'Going to?'

'I'll tell them whatever suits me,' she said defiantly.

'You've got to explain that bandaged ankle somehow!'

'Anyone can have an accident walking the fells!'

'Do June and Fred know that our night on the bare mountain is a deadly secret?'

'Oh, be quiet!' she wailed, because of course she couldn't ask Fred and June to lie for her and sooner or later the whole story would come out.

'June tells me your parents are dead and you live with an aunt and uncle,' Jamie informed her, undeterred.

Furiously she snapped, 'Did they forget to mention my two cousins and the cat?'

'Cats didn't come into the conversation,' Jamie murmured. 'There was some talk of a Liz and a Will who both like to sail. How do your family get on with your fiancé?'

Melanie averted her face, staring out at the russet colours of oak and elm, the scarlet of rose hips and haw berries in the hedges. Autumn was in its early days, there were still lingering signs of summer here and there—a few last roses, rich green grass in pastures.

'Very well, thank you,' she said stiffly. What was he implying now? 'What job did you say you did? You aren't a policeman, by any chance? Or a tax inspector? You seem very fond of asking questions about things that have nothing to do with you.'

'I'm interested—any reason why I shouldn't be?'

She turned, her dark blue eyes very wide and startled. 'In what?'

He turned his head and their eyes met and her heart skipped a beat. 'In you,' he said softly, watching the betraying colour run up to her hairline.

Melanie hurriedly looked away again and kept her head turned as she answered huskily. 'I asked you not to do that . . .'

'Do what?' he teased, turning off to get on to the motorway.

'Flirt. You knew I meant that! It may be just a game to you, but I don't play that sort of game, Mr Knox. I'm engaged and I love my fiancé so please stop talking to me like that.'

They were beginning to put on more speed; it made her nervous to find herself in the fast lane, passing cars which would normally pass her, but Jamie Knox was coaxing a surprising power out of her old vehicle. She hoped he wasn't wrecking the engine for ever.

He seemed to have nothing to say in response to her and they drove in silence for a while, until he asked suddenly, 'How old were you when your parents died?'

'Thirteen,' she said, reluctantly, because she was beginning to feel that every scrap of information he wheedled out of her was a hostage to fortune and might be used against her at some future time. Talking to Jamie Knox was like being under X-ray—Melanie felt mentally naked, her innermost thoughts and feelings observed and speculated upon. She didn't like it, especially as she didn't quite trust the man. It was more than distrust now, though; she was half afraid of him.

'Thirteen? I see,' he drawled, and she made the mistake of looking round at him, her blue eyes apprehensive. It was dangerous to ask, she knew that, but she couldn't resist the nag of curiosity.

'What do you see?'

'Losing your father in your early teens must have had a traumatic effect,' he murmured coolly. 'And Ross Ellis no doubt makes a great father figure.'

She went rigid with anger. 'Don't try that cheap psychology jargon on me, Mr Knox—it won't work. We don't know enough about each other for you to have a clue what makes me tick. We're practically strangers.'

'Are we?' he asked drily, apparently untouched by the ice in her voice.

'We only met this weekend and . . .'

'Time is relative. How long have you known Ross Ellis?'

'Mind your own business.' Her throat was hot with resentment and helpless fury. 'Please don't keep needling me, Mr Knox. Just concentrate on your driving. I don't want to talk any more. You've given me a headache.'

He laughed. 'That tired old female excuse! I'm ashamed of you.' But he lapsed into silence as she asked and it wasn't long before they were on the

outskirts of Carlisle. Melanie broke their silence to
tell him how to get to her home. With any luck,
nobody would be in because at this time of day
Aunt Dolly was often out shopping. She had a set
routine; had coffee in the pedestrian precinct and
then enjoyed a walk round the Lanes, the new
shopping centre which brought so many people to
Carlisle from the surrounding area. Sometimes
Aunt Dolly met a friend for a snack lunch before
coming home.

Jamie pulled up outside the old, white-painted
gate and sat forward, his hands resting on the
wheel, to stare up at the ramshackle Victorian
house. It had been built in 1832, by a prosperous
Carlisle corn merchant with a large family and
several servants. There were seven bedrooms, a
huge and draughty drawing-room, a panelled dining-
room and a muddle of other rooms downstairs,
often oddly shaped and very eccentric in design. It
was hardly convenient or modern but it had a
certain style and character and the Nesbitts loved
it, even Aunt Dolly, who had to do most of the
housework, except at weekends when Liz and
Melanie helped her. As Aunt Dolly always said,
'You can tell the man who had this house built
expected someone else to keep it tidy. All very
well for him—all those servants! How much easier
life was in those days.'

'Except for the servants,' Liz usually said in her
dry way, and Aunt Dolly would laugh and say that
Liz was so down to earth, not at all romantic.

'A very handsome house,' Jamie Knox murmured,
his eyes flicking over it from the delicate fanlight
above the door to the little gables in the roof. The
shabby stucco had a creamy glow in the sunlight;
the house looked loved and contented, the small
garden in the front was rich with dahlias and

chrysanthemums; golden amber, rust, dark blood-red. A spiky cluster of Michaelmas daisies bloomed near the wall, their petals visited by bees and butterflies on this surprisingly summery morning, so that the air was full of a busy hum, a flutter of wings.

'Thank you for driving me back here,' Melanie said stiltedly. 'And for . . . for everything you did.' She felt ungrateful—he had, after all, gone to a lot of trouble for her and she hadn't really thanked him properly. She would have been more fervent in her thanks with almost any other man, but Jamie Knox had made it difficult for her to be too nice to him. He might misread friendliness. He seemed to misread most things.

He got out and came round to help her down, his hand under her elbow. 'I'll see you to the door then come back for your case,' he said, urging her towards the gate.

'I can manage. The case can stay in the car for the moment,' she said firmly, and glanced up the road. 'If you walk to the top of this road you'll get a bus straight into the centre of town. They're very frequent and it isn't far.'

He didn't relinquish her arm, indeed his fingers tightened on it.

'Got your door key?' he enquired, somehow managing to make her keep walking through the gate and up the path with its black and white Victorian tiles, laid in a symmetrical diamond pattern. A few had been cracked over the years, and some were missing altogether, but the path had a certain style, like the house, which Melanie loved.

He was still being kind; she didn't like to dismiss him too peremptorily, so she produced her key and he took it and inserted it into the door.

The door was reluctant to open; it needed oiling but none of them ever remembered until the matter became crucial, and the heavy rain over the weekend had obviously warped the timbers further, because when Jamie pushed it politely the door didn't budge and he had to let go of Melanie to use his full strength on it.

At his shove, the door fell open with a protesting creak and Jamie tumbled into the house leaving Melanie outside, which was why Liz, seeing a complete stranger crashing through the front door, leapt down the last two stairs and faced him with one of her father's walking sticks grabbed up from the hallstand.

'Who are you?' she asked firmly. 'And what are you doing?'

Melanie hobbled into the hall at that instant and her cousin's voice halted.

'Melly? What's wrong with your foot?' Trust Liz to be so sharp-eyed and observant, thought Melanie, hurriedly smiling at her.

'I had a tumble when I was climbing, it's nothing much, just a slight sprain.'

Liz slowly slid the walking-stick back into the hallstand, her eyes moving to Jamie Knox enquiringly.

'I drove her back because she couldn't drive with one ankle out of operation,' he said lightly, smiling. 'My name's Knox, Jamie Knox. You must be Liz—I've heard a lot about you.'

Liz's eyebrows arched. 'Really? All of it good, I hope.' She glanced at her cousin with interest. 'You *have* had a busy weekend.'

Melanie's cheeks stung with hot colour and she looked away. It was bad luck finding Liz at home.

'Why aren't you at work?' she asked, wishing Liz hadn't seen Jamie Knox—or that Jamie Knox hadn't met her cousin, she wasn't sure which was the more worrying.

'I've taken a day off,' Liz said. Melanie should have remembered the complicated rota system by which Liz worked four days one week, five the next; a shift system made even more complex by the addition of paid annual holidays which Liz could taken *en bloc* or piecemeal thoughout the year. 'I'm working on the economics article I'm supposed to have ready by Wednesday,' Liz added. 'I can work better at home—no interruptions.' She paused, grimaced. 'Usually,' she said, her eyes smiling as she glanced at Jamie Knox.

'Did we interrupt?' he chimed in immediately. 'Sorry about that, but it must be nearly lunchtime—weren't you going to eat?'

Liz looked amused. 'I suppose I was, sometime, I think my mother left me some cold roast lamb and a salad—she's having lunch with a friend in town. I expect there'll be enough for three.'

Aghast, Melanie said, 'Oh, Mr Knox isn't . . .'

'Thanks, I'd love to stay for lunch,' he overrode her.

She turned angry eyes up to him. 'You've got to meet Fred in Carlisle, don't forget.'

'Not until five o'clock—that was the time we arranged, to give Fred time to get here and do June's shopping.'

Liz listened with interest, watching them both, her cool face alert and attentive.

'You know Fred and June? How are they? I haven't seen them for weeks.'

'Oh, they're fine—wonderful, aren't they?' Jamie put his shoulder to the front door and forced it shut. 'These hinges need oiling, you know—have you got an oilcan? I'll do it for you now. It's a mistake to let these little problems drag on; you have to deal with them as soon as they come up.'

Liz looked amused. 'How very forceful. Yes, there must be an oilcan in Dad's toolshed. Come and get it. He never throws anything away, even if he has no intention of using it.'

They walked away along the hall and Melanie followed grimly. Her heart had sunk as she recognised that Jamie Knox had no intention of going. He had shamelessly angled for that invitation to lunch—what was so surprising was that Liz had offered it in response to his blatant hint. It wasn't like her; she was usually rather cool with strangers and particularly strange men.

Liz looked over her shoulder. 'You're limping badly. Why don't you use one of Dad's walking-sticks, Melanie?'

Jamie turned and recrossed the hall rapidly and came back with one of the sticks which he offered to Melanie with both hands, his smile mocking.

She was tempted to hit him over the head with it, but controlled herself. 'Thank you,' she said through her teeth, and perhaps her iciness was a mistake because she felt Liz watching her curiously. Liz scented a story; her news nose was twitching. The last thing Melanie wanted to do was arouse Liz's curiosity.

She had hoped to skate lightly over the explanation of what had happened last night, but it was obvious that she wasn't going to be able to do that with Jamie around, deliberately stirring up curiosity. Liz only had to take one look at him to guess that a night spent alone with Jamie Knox was unlikely to be incident-free.

'Were you staying at the pub, too?' asked Liz as they all went into the large, sunlit kitchen.

'No,' Jamie said. 'I live nearby—I've got a cottage beside the lake.'

Liz gave him an envious look. 'Oh, lucky you! I've always dreamt of having one. It must be heavenly, being able to look out across Ullswater every morning. Is your cottage old?'

'Eighteenth century, typical local architecture— very simple and solidly built of stone. When I bought it the previous owner assured me that Dorothy Wordsworth had once called in there to ask for a glass of water when she was on one of those long walks they used to take, but I expect he'd invented the story to help sell the place.'

Liz laughed. 'A lovely thought, though. I've always preferred her to good old brother William. He's a little too pompous for my taste.'

'Oh, you're one of those people who prefer to think Dorothy wrote the poems and William just borrowed her ideas?' Jamie was drily mocking and Liz made a face at him.

'I didn't say that.' They went out through the back door into the garden. 'The toolshed is over there,' Melanie heard Liz say.

Sitting down on one of the shabby old horsehair chairs, Melanie listened grimly to their fading voices. They were talking in a lively, friendly way as if they had know each other for years. Liz liked him. That was bad news. Jamie Knox was mischievous; who knew what he might say to Liz? Melanie wanted him gone, out of her life at once and for ever. He disturbed her peace of mind.

When they returned Jamie had an oilcan in one hand, a rag in the other. He went into the hall to deal with the front door while Liz laid the lunch on the table.

'Does your ankle hurt much?' she asked Melanie. 'You'd better take the rest of the week off work.'

'A sprained ankle won't stop me sitting behind my desk and doing what I always do,' Melanie said flatly.

Liz shrugged. 'Up to you.' She put the platter of cold lamb in the centre of the table. 'Where did you find *him*? He's quite something, isn't he?'

'Is he?' Melanie asked coldly.

Her cousin eyed her. 'You know he is! I couldn't quite make out how he happened to be the one who brought you back home. How did you meet him?'

'He was in the pub,' evaded Melanie.

'And drove all this way for a total stranger! How admirable.' Liz was given to sarcasm; Melanie ignored it. 'I suppose he does know you're engaged?' asked Liz.

'Of course!' Melanie said tersely.

'Of course,' Liz echoed with dry amusement. 'You wouldn't flirt with other men, would you? You're too devoted to Ross Ellis, although heaven only knows why you should be. You seem to see little enough of the man. Half the time he's abroad, and when he's back in the UK he never seems to have time for you.'

'Liz!' Melanie said harshly, going pale. 'Don't say things like that, it isn't true. Ross is just very busy, but if he didn't love me he wouldn't have asked me to marry him.'

Lis sighed, looking contrite. 'I'm sorry, Melly, I didn't mean to upset you, don't look like that—it's just that sometimes I get angry with you for being such a doormat. You let Ross walk all over you; you shouldn't, you know. Men don't respect you for it. If you stood up for yourself, Ross wouldn't be so casual with you.'

Melanie heard Jamie Knox's footsteps in the hall and hurriedly stumbled to her feet, her face drawn.

'I don't think I'll have any lunch. I'm not hungry.' She hoped Jamie hadn't heard their argument. She didn't want him to know any more about her than he already did. 'I'll go up to my room and take a rest,' she said as he came whistling into the kitchen.

'The door's moving freely again,' he told Liz cheerfully, but at the same time shot Melanie a probing stare sideways.

Thanks,' Liz said absently, watching her cousin too. 'Melanie, do have a little lunch, the lamb's very good.' Her smooth-skinned face held apology, appeal. 'You can take a rest after the meal,' she coaxed, touching Melanie's arm gently.

'No, really, I don't want anything to eat,' Melanie said. She turned to go, then halted. 'Oh, thank you, Mr Knox, for everything.'

'My pleasure,' he said drily.

She forced a smile. 'You're very kind. Well, goodbye.'

'Oh, not goodbye,' he mocked. 'We're going to see each other again.'

Her dark blue eyes held startled anxiety and he smiled into them with maddening amusement.

'After all,' he added, 'you obviously visit Ullswater frequently, and I'm there all the time.'

Melanie retreated, limping up the stairs into her bedroom. She hated tension and that was what she felt whenever she was near Jamie Knox. He seemed to know the effect he had on her and enjoy causing it.

She lay down on her bed and closed her eyes, but she knew she wouldn't sleep. She had slept well enough last night and, anyway, her mind was working overtime, worrying about what Jamie Knox was saying to Liz downstairs. How much had he told Liz? He seemed to like her cousin and Liz obviously liked him; she had said as much. Jamie

Knox was Liz's type, after all—sophisticated, sure of himself, experienced. He wasn't Melanie's type, though. She simply couldn't cope with him.

It must have been an hour later that she heard the front door bang and then the sound of a car driving off. Melanie swung off the bed and got to the window in time to see Liz's car vanishing round the corner. Liz must be driving Jamie Knox into the city to meet Fred.

Liz still hadn't got back by the time Aunt Dolly let herself into the house. Melanie was in the kitchen drinking some tea, watching the clock and wondering where Liz had got to and if she was still with Jamie.

'Hello, pet,' Aunt Dolly said, dumping her loaded shopping-bags on a chair with a sigh of relief. 'Had a good weekend? Very naughty of you to go off on your own like that. Liz could have gone with you. I was just going to suggest it when I heard you drive off.' She patted her silvery hair in front of the mirror over the mantelpiece. 'Was the weather fine?'

'Some of the time.' Melanie took a deep breath and said in a rush, 'But while I was climbing in the fells it turned misty and I had to spend the night in an old hut.'

Aunt Dolly swung, mouth wide. 'Melanie! All on your own?'

'No, there was someone else—June and Fred sent a friend of theirs up to look for me and guide me, so I had company.'

'A friend of theirs? Who was that? Anyone I know?' Aunt Dolly wasn't yet alarmed. She might have been if she had known in advance that Melanie was going to be stranded in a hut all night with a stranger, but as Melanie was here, safe, telling her about it, she wasn't as horrified as she might have been.

'I don't think so,' Melanie said vaguely. 'And I hurt my ankle—it's only a sprain, though, nothing serious, I'll be able to go to work tomorrow.'

Aunt Dolly exclaimed again. 'Have you seen a doctor?'

'Yes, he said it was a simple sprain. He bound it for me.'

'Let me see,' Aunt Dolly said, and gazed at the bandaged ankle, shaking her head. 'There! If you'd taken Liz you wouldn't have done that. It isn't sensible to go climbing on your own, you should have learnt that by now. How lucky that June and Fred knew where you were. I hope you thanked them for being so thoughtful. Where was this place where you took shelter? It couldn't have been very comfortable. Really, Melanie, you were silly, weren't you?'

It hadn't been quite as much of an ordeal as Melanie had feared, telling the family, and she was able to go through it again when Uncle Teddy came in with Will, but that time she had Aunt Dolly to help her out, adding a chorus of comment and explanation which took some of the tension out of Melanie herself. She could sit back and let Aunt Dolly tell the story, with a few frills and some embroidery. Aunt Dolly enjoyed telling people anecdotes; she had forgiven Melanie for running such a risk by now and almost seemed to have been there herself. She made it very dramatic—a daring mountain rescue. She had one detail wrong, of course. She had the impression that Jamie Knox was Fred's age, an old hand in the Lake District, a weather-beaten hill-climber old enough to be Melanie's father.

Melanie did not disillusion her. She didn't say

anything when Aunt Dolly looked at the clock and said, 'Liz must have gone out on newspaper business, after all. I suppose that tyrant of a news editor rang her up and bullied her into working tonight. Really, it's disgraceful the hours they want her to work.'

Melanie's dark blue eyes watched the regular movements of the clock hands. Liz had been gone now for three hours. What was she doing all this time, and was she doing it with Jamie Knox?

She went to bed early that night; Liz still hadn't put in an appearance. When Melanie got up for breakfast she found Will at the table eating egg and bacon as if he hadn't eaten for days. He gave her a grin, saying cheerfully that Liz had left a note on the kitchen table asking not to be woken up as she had got in late.

'I knew she had; she woke me up at some unearthly hour—two in the morning, I'd swear it was,' Will said, taking a slice of toast and spreading it with marmalade. 'She cleaned her teeth so noisily I had nightmares about it. Wonder what she got up to last night and who with? Who's the latest victim of her fatal charm? I don't know what guys see in her, I really don't. I've seen prettier heads on a pint of beer.'

'Don't be rude about your sister,' said Aunt Dolly, removing the toast from him firmly and putting it near Melanie. 'Now, Melly, you're to eat something this morning. I don't hold with you going off to work with nothing inside you.'

Melanie forced down a cup of coffee and a slice of toast before rushing off to work. She did most of the paperwork in the estate office. The firm handled several private estates as well as selling houses, offices and shops. The work was varied enough to keep her interested and the pay was quite good by local standards. There wasn't that much choice in the area and Melanie disliked the idea of working in a large office where she would specialise in typing letters or spend all day filing. In the smaller office she had more responsibility, did a wide range of jobs, and also met quite a few people every day.

Her boss was already in the office, checking an inventory. Looking up, he said at once, 'Melanie, you're limping.'

His son, Andrew, grinned. 'Old eagle-eye misses nothing. Did you fall or were you pushed, Mel?'

When she explained, George Ramsden shook his head at her. 'How many times have I warned you young people about fell-walking? It's dangerous to do it alone.' He had a strong Northumbrian accent and a face that looked as if it had been hacked out of local stone, but that belied his character. He was a very kind man.

'It won't stop me doing my work,' Melanie said, sitting down at her desk, and George Ramsden patted her shoulder with one raw-knuckled hand, smiling at her.

'Good lass. I'm off to the auction rooms. Old Hamish will have stuck the wrong labels on everything if I'm not there to stop him.'

When he had left, Andrew made some coffee and sat talking to Melanie until a customer came into the shop. She was the first in a long line; it was a very busy morning. Melanie hardly had time to think about anything but work, for which she was grateful. Just before she went to lunch, the phone rang. 'Oh, damn,' she said, but picked it up reluctantly. It was Ross.

'Where are you?' she asked huskily; he sounded very far away.

'Still in Bahrain. I've no idea when I'll get back.

Did you have a good weekend? I'm sorry I couldn't be with you, but you understand, don't you?'

'Yes, I suppose so,' she said uncertainly, and his voice came distantly.

'What? I can't hear you.'

'I only said I understand. This is a very bad line.'

'Melanie?' His voice was a whisper at the end of a tunnel. 'I can't hear you. There's no point in talking on a line like this. Can you hear me? I'm ringing off. See you when I get back.'

She replaced the phone slowly, remembering the first time she had ever heard his voice. He had rung to enquire about a building site in which he was interested. Melanie had been impressed by his deep, cool voice. For some reason it had made her nervous; she had stammered. It was a week or two before she actually met Ross in person and she had known the instant he walked into the office that it was the man she had talked to on the phone. His features matched the confidence of that voice. So often a face was disappointing after you had heard a nice voice on the phone, but not with Ross. He was even more than she had imagined.

He had asked her to have dinner with him that first day, and after that she had been caught up in a whirlwind. Ross was so busy; he had to snatch time for himself. Dinners, lunches, drives in the country—all hurriedly arranged, all too brief. When he asked her to marry him, she was feverish with disbelief and excitement, she hadn't even stopped to think, she had just said, 'Yes, oh, yes, Ross.'

Where had that feeling gone? It was all such a short time ago. She had been in love with him, hadn't she? She still was, wasn't she? But her head was full of question marks about the way Ross felt and, if she were honest, about the way she felt herself. And how would she ever find any answers if Ross was never here and had no time to talk to her? If he loved her, wouldn't he find the time? she thought, and then, again the questions surged into her head and found no answer.

She paused in the pedestrian precinct to look at a dress in a shop window, working out if she could afford to buy it. The colour was so pretty, a warm turquoise. She always looked good in blue.

'It'll suit you,' a voice said behind her, and she saw the wavering reflection of Jamie Knox in the shop window with a shock of surprise that made her pulses leap and flare.

'Oh, hallo,' she said reluctantly.

'Buy it,' he urged, but she shook her head and began to limp away. He kept in step. 'How's the foot?'

'Still painful.' She halted at the door of a small restaurant where she often ate. 'Well, I'm going to have some lunch, excuse me.'

'What a coincidence,' he said, and her heart sank. 'This is where I was heading, too.' He took her arm and steered her across the crowded room. There was only one table free and she couldn't think of a polite excuse for refusing to share it with him. As she sat down she looked at him through her lashes, suspicion in her blue eyes. Had he really been coming in here?

'Hallo, Jamie,' said the waitress, coming over with a broad grin. She never smiled at Melanie like that. 'We've got your favourite on, today— hotpot. Good, too. I had it myself.' She handed Melanie the menu with a nod of curiosity and Melanie ran a hurried eye down the list.

'I'll have soup and the chicken salad,' she said.

'Have the hotpot,' Jamie said, taking the menu from her. 'We'll both have soup and hotpot, Ethel.'

Melanie angrily opened her mouth to protest, but the waitress was already moving away and Jamie grinned mockingly at her.

'Their idea of a salad is two lettuce leaves and a wrinkled tomato. You'll be much better off with hotpot. My grandmother used to make it for me when I was small. She lived in Carlisle, we used to come and stay with her for Christmas, my mother, my sister and I, and she made us the best hotpot you've ever tasted. I don't know what she put into it, but I've never tasted one as good since.'

'She's dead?'

He looked at her with a wry smile, nodding. 'Years ago. She was eighty when she died; she'd had a good life, but I miss her. She was a wonderful old darling. One minute she was a tartar—if you'd done something she disapproved of! The next she was giving you a cuddle and everything was forgotten. She always said you should never let the sun go down on your anger, but she thought children needed discipline, especially when they had no father around to make sure they were kept in line.'

The waitress brought their soup, a Northumbrian broth made with barley. As they began to eat, Melanie asked, 'Your father was dead?'

He laughed, breaking off a piece of the crusty roll which had been brought with the soup. 'Not dead, no, but he was never there. He was in the merchant navy. Half the time he was on the other side of the world.'

Melanie's eyes widened. She watched him curiously. 'That must have been lonely for your mother, never having her husband there.'

Jamie looked up, shrugging. 'If it was, she never showed it to us. We had a wonderful childhood. When Dad was home it was always exciting, he brought us presents from all over the world and took us out, and then he'd go back to join his ship and things would be normal gain. Mum wrote to him several times a week, and read us bits from his letters, about where he was and what he'd seen. I had the best stamp collection in my class.'

'But he didn't get home for Christmas?'

'Rarely,' he agreed. 'That's why we always came to stay with Granny Carlisle. Mum thought we ought to have a family Christmas. Our other grandparents lived in London, my father's parents. Mum didn't get on too well with them. We didn't see much of them.'

Melanie finished her soup and watched his bent, dark head. It sounded a very interesting childhood. Did he take after his father? She wondered if he had gone to sea or had his father's long absences turned him against that idea?

Hesitantly, she asked, 'You said you hadn't got a job at the moment.' He might be sensitive about it; she wasn't sure how he would react to questioning.

He looked up, his face suddenly taut, the dark eyes hard. 'No,' he said through tight lips.

'You didn't go to sea, like your father?'

His face softened a little. 'I rather fancied the idea when I was small, but I got interested in other things and went to college instead. To my mother's great relief.' He grinned at her. 'She hadn't said a word, but I could tell she was heaving sighs of relief.'

Melanie laughed. 'She sounds great. Where does she live now?'

'She and Dad have retired. They live in Ullswater, just down the road from me.' His eyes held affectionate amusement. 'Keeping an eye on me and what I get up to even now!'

The hotpot arrived and Melanie had to admit that it was good; the lamb tender, falling apart as you touched it with your knife, the vegetables perfectly cooked and the flavour delicious. Jamie gave her a quizzical look, lifting one brow. 'Well?'

'You were right, it's marvellous,' she said.

'I'm always right,' he told her with maddening amusement.

Melanie gave him a look but didn't rise to the bait; she concentrated on the meal instead. When the waitress removed their plates and suggested a dessert, Melanie refused politely and just had coffee, and Jamie did the same. The hotpot had been far more filling than the lunch Melanie usually ate.

Jamie walked back with her to her office, talking about the fine autumn weather most of the way. She wanted to ask him if he and Liz had spent the evening together yesterday, but she was afraid that he would misinterpret her interest and imagine that she was jealous. He was conceited enough to jump to a conclusion like that. It wasn't true, of course. She didn't care who he went out with, but she was surprised at Liz.

'Why were you in Carlisle today?' she asked instead, and he made a wry face.

'I had to see my dentist—a half yearly check up. I hate dentists, don't you? Even when it is only a routine check I dread going.'

'You come all the way from Ullswater to see a dentist here?' she asked in disbelief, her face becoming suspicious. Did he expect her to believe that?

He considered her expression with dry mockery. 'He's been my dentist for years. I used to work here and he was the nearest good dentist. I've never got around to changing to someone else.'

She was about to ask him where he had worked, but as they reached the estate agency they walked straight into Andrew Ramsden who greeted Melanie urgently. 'Oh, great, you're back—I've got to go out to Penrith to see someone, can you hold the fort until I get back?'

'Of course,' Melanie said and Andrew handed her the keys to the office before rushing off. Melanie unlocked the doors again, gave Jamie a polite smile and said, 'Well, goodbye. I enjoyed the hotpot.'

She half expected him to linger, but he didn't, he nodded and walked away without a backward look. She watched him go with a strange feeling, biting her lip. She hoped she would never see him again, and at the same time that thought made her oddly depressed.

CHAPTER FOUR

THE following Friday was Will's birthday. He was twenty-three, although, as Uncle Teddy said, it was very hard to believe. Will still acted and moved like a teenager, either crashing about noisily or laughing like a hyena over nothing. Sometimes he didn't eat for hours without seeming to notice, but then he would come in at midnight and demolish every particle of food in the fridge or the larder. Bottles of milk vanished; cheese, cold meat, bread, fruit, all ready to eat and all gone next morning, so that his mother would survey her depleted resources and wail. 'Will's been at it again.' There was never any doubt as to the culprit; who else could eat so much at such an hour? Aunt Dolly knew without asking that Liz and Melanie were on a diet because they always were, and even if hunger came over them in the middle of the night they wouldn't eat everything that wasn't nailed down. Only Will would gorge like that.

But as today was his birthday his mother looked mournfully at her empty fridge and only said, 'I must go shopping.' She had cooked Will his favourite breakfast and he had departed for work with his father. 'Where's my list?' Aunt Dolly asked herself, looking about. 'I wish I hadn't said he could have this party, he's getting too old for birthday parties and his friends are so noisy. You will be here to keep an eye on them, won't you, girls?'

'Don't worry, you won't get back to find the police here investigating an orgy,' Liz said, laughing.

Flustered, Aunt Dolly said, 'Well, you never know—some of Will's friends seem very nice, but did you see that girl he brought round the other day—her hair was green and purple, and she had shiny orange marks on her face, like a Red Indian.'

'Tracy Simmons? She works at the Town Hall,' said Melanie, and Aunt Dolly looked incredulous.

'Well, whatever do they think there?'

'Not much,' Liz said drily.

Aunt Dolly began hunting for her shopping-list, muttering to herself. 'Where did I put it? I had it just now. Oh, look at that, how silly, I was holding it all the time, with my gloves. Melanie, come along, aren't I giving you a lift to work?'

Aunt Dolly and Uncle Teddy were going away for the weekend to the Lake District, so that they need not get involved with Will's party, and Melanie was secretly afraid that they might run into Jamie Knox. There was no hope that they wouldn't now hear June and Fred's version of how she came to be marooned for the night, but so long as they didn't meet Jamie that might not alarm them. One look at him, though, and Aunt Dolly would get agitated. The habit of worrying about Melanie was too ingrained with her.

Friday was always a busy day in Carlisle. People drove in from the surrounding countryside to shop, adding to the tourists who came to see the town, often staying overnight so that they could visit Hadrian's Wall. Of course, they were usually taken to Housesteads, the most spectacular of the forts on the wall, where they could park their coach beside the road in a walled car-park, have a cup of coffee and buy souvenirs and postcards before visiting the small museum. The more energetic could then make the climb uphill to the fort itself, to stand on the summit, buffeted by winds, staring entranced at the incredible views on each side of the wall, the misty green countryside falling away in a sheer drop into echoing vistas.

While they were in Carlisle itself they had a choice of either visiting the many shops or taking in the cathedral. Melanie often had lunch there; it was a short walk from her office and the salads were beautifully prepared and inexpensive. Of course, that meant that the Buttery was always crowded with housewives, children, friends of the cathedral, but the profits from the little restaurant went to help maintain the cathedral structure. Built of red stone—she always felt it had a baleful look at sunset—it wasn't the most elegant of architecture. Begun in the twelfth century, it was a strange mixture of periods. Melanie preferred the original style; there was something so beautiful about the massive columns and Norman arches; their strength had a confident simplicity. The cathedral was far lovelier inside than out.

She was glad to be kept busy that Friday; it stopped her thinking too much, wondering if Ross was flying home, if he would soon ring her, if she would see him today, tomorrow—soon.

Will's party didn't begin until eight and for several hours before that they were all busy getting the ground floor of the house ready for invasion, clearing out most of the furniture, arranging chairs and cushions on the floor, collecting tapes and records, laying out the cold buffet in the kitchen. Aunt Dolly had cooked most of it well in advance— the spread was amazing, cold quiches, sausage rolls, vol-au-vents, pizzas they would have to re-heat, bowls of salad covered by cling-film, open fruit tarts and gateaux. She had cooked the sort of food she knew Will loved, but had done it in embarrassing abundance.

'She expects a plague of locusts,' Liz said, considering it all.

'Yum yum,' said Will, taking a sausage roll, and putting it into his mouth before his sister could stop him.

'Don't do that again,' Liz said, slapping his hand. 'Go and check that we've got enough glasses.'

'Done it. I've got my priorities right,' he said smugly.

The doorbell went and Liz groaned. 'Oh, no, they haven't started arriving already!'

Will looked at his watch. 'Nearly eight, not that early.' He danced off to open the front door while Melanie took off her apron and checked her appearance in the mirror over the fireplace. She had dressed for the occasion in what most of Will's friends would be wearing—smooth-fitting trousers and a casual top. Melanie's trousers were dark red velvet, her top cut quite low, sleeveless, glittering with black sequins. She had brushed her lids with a violet shadow that deepened the colour of her dark blue eyes, and her lipstick was a warm musk rose.

'I love that top,' Liz said, appearing in the mirror just behind her and assessing her own appearance coolly. 'You're lucky having such dramatic colouring; bold shades suit you.'

'You look pretty startling yourself,' Melanie teased her. Liz was normally very elegant but tonight she too had dressed not to look out of place among a crowd of Will's friends. Although the males at the party would be in their early twenties, they tended to bring much younger girls.

In her vivid poppy-splashed white shirt and tight green cords, Liz wasn't going to melt into the crowd.

Laughing, Liz said, 'I feel middle-aged faced with girls like Tracy Simmons. Do you realise, she's almost nine years younger than me? That's almost a generation. I look at her and ask myself— did I ever look that young?'

'No,' Melanie said, laughing back at her. 'You were horribly advanced for your age at eighteen. I was scared stiff of you.'

'You weren't?' Liz looked aghast.

'I was—you drawled everything you said and kept raising your eyebrows and smiling sardonically.'

'Oh, my Noel Coward phase,' Liz accepted resignedly. 'I must have been a horror.'

'I remember Aunt Dolly staring at your fingernails when you came in and waved them around—do you remember? You'd painted them black and your lipstick was a sort of mud colour. Poor Aunt Dolly, she was so horrified.'

'Not at all, it made life more exciting for her! She lived in a perpetual turmoil, never knowing what I'd be up to next. Think how much fun she must have had.'

Melanie laughed and behind them someone else laughed too, freezing the laughter on Melanie's face. She stared with stricken incredulity into the mirror, seeing Jamie Knox's face reflected there, dark, amused, unforgettable.

Liz turned, her smile welcoming. 'You're early— good. I'm so glad you could come.'

She had invited him? thought Melanie dazedly, watching them both in the mirror. They looked well together, she had thought so the morning Jamie drove her back here and he met Liz. They were talking as if they were old friends, casually at ease.

'Just as I drove up a vanload of kids arrived, too. Will is showing them where to park, but any minute now the balloon goes up. I hope you're prepared—boiling oil on the battlements and guard-dogs on the food? They looked a formidable collection to me.'

Liz laughed. 'Oh, I'm sure you can handle them—that's why I asked you. You're chucker-out-in-chief if things get rough, so look tough and sound dangerous.'

His black brows arched. 'Don't I always?'

'Now you come to mention it . . .' Liz said and at that minute Will yelled from the hall.

'Liz, where can they put their coats?'

'Well, here we go,' Liz said, vanishing.

The noise in the hall made it sound as if a riot had just broken out. Jamie pushed the door shut, his eyes on Melanie's back. She was still staring into the mirror fixedly, one hand restlessly tidying her immaculate black hair. She was afraid to turn round; that would mean admitting he was there, and Melanie wished he wasn't. Why had Liz invited him? Why wouldn't he get out of her life and stay out?

'How's the ankle?' It was a perfectly innocent question on the face of it, but it summoned up memories she preferred to forget and she felt her face burn.

'Much better, thank you,' she managed stiltedly.

He took a step towards her and she turned in agitation, stupidly afraid of having him too near her. She couldn't understand why she felt this instinctive alarm every time she saw him. He constituted a threat of a kind she had never felt before with anyone. Was she imagining the silent challenge he sent out? Perhaps her imagination was working overtime; her mind becoming feverish? Liz didn't seem to find him any problem. Perhaps it's just me? Melanie thought. I could be dreaming up conflicts which don't exist except in my own head.

'Ellis back yet?' He managed to make that question stiletto-sharp.

'Any time,' she muttered, angrily on the defensive.

'But he isn't going to come tonight? To the party, I mean?'

'I don't think he'll be back in time for that.' She was nervously twisting a lock of hair around her finger; it gave her something to do with her shaky hands.

'You don't seem to see much of him,' Jamie said, his mouth wry.

'Ross is a very busy man.'

'You're very understanding.' The sarcasm made her flinch and Jamie watched her nervous, restless fingers. His hand shot out and suddenly trapped them, pulling them down from her hair. 'Stop doing that. You're making me as edgy as you are.'

'I'm not edgy!' she lied, panic-stricken by his touch. His hand was cool and strong, and he was standing far too close.

'Aren't you?' His tone was almost angry now. He laid the fingertips of his free hand on her throat. 'No?' Under his touch she felt the savage beating of a pulse and was shocked by it. What was happening to her?

This was how he had been that night in the mist and rain; this was how she had felt every time he turned that dark stare towards her. It wasn't just her imagination, she wasn't losing her mind—Jamie Knox threatened her, his physical presence was overwhelming her at this instant, his touch was more than she could bear.

'Let go of me,' she said hoarsely, jerking backwards, and without a word he released her and turned away, pushing his hands into the back pockets of his black cord pants.

Melanie shot out of the room, but she took with her an indelible picture of his lean, prowling figure in the black pants and black sweater. Without a syllable he managed to set up echoes in her head. She fought her way through the cheerful throng in the sitting-room and began to help Will pour drinks for everyone, she smiled and answered when someone spoke to her, but she was in that other room, with Jamie Knox, vibrating with the anger coming out of him and confused by her own feelings about him.

She saw him with Liz some time later, circulating hot slices of pizza and trays of sausage rolls. Melanie stayed firmly behind the makeshift bar they had set up. She didn't drink anything but orange juice herself; she wanted to keep her head clear.

Liz drifted over with her tray and offered it to her. 'Better eat something while there's something to eat. You're going to need the blood sugar. Thank heavens this house is detached. If we had neighbours they'd be calling the police by now.' She had to use her voice on full volume to be heard above the music. Some of the guests were dancing now, others just sitting on the floor and talking, while some were wandering from group to group so that Melanie had long ago lost count of how many people were actually here.

Will had put the lights on dim; the room was shadowy and very stuffy.

'They've used up all the oxygen,' Liz said when Melanie mentioned that. 'At least there hasn't been any trouble.'

She spoke too soon. Half an hour later Melanie went to the front door when the bell rang and was almost knocked over by a crowd of gatecrashers who surged past her before she could check their identities.

Will was on his way out of the kitchen and said sharply, 'Hey, who are you? You weren't invited.'

Melanie reeled back against the stairs and took cover there as a fight broke out between the newcomers and Will's friends. As soon as Jamie realised what was happening he charged into the scrum and began hurling gatecrashers out of the front door by the scruff of their necks. Will and his friends followed suit. For a few minutes the hall was a heaving mass of struggling bodies, then the front door slammed and Jamie leaned on it, breathing thickly. Laughing like idiots, Will and the other boys went back to the party.

Melanie stole back downstairs, looking at Jamie's flushed face anxiously. 'Your cheek is bleeding. You'd better let me put a plaster on it.'

He straightened, a hand touching his cheekbone where a bruise was beginning to show. 'That certainly livened things up, didn't it?' He seemed unconcerned about the cut just below his cheekbone, but he followed Melanie into the kitchen and leaned against the draining-board while she got some boiled water from the kettle and some cotton-wool and gently began to clean the cut.

'Tell me if it hurts,' she said absently, her eyes fixed on his cheek.

'It hurts,' he said oddly, and her eyes lifted to meet his. 'That's better, you're always so reluctant to look at me.'

'Don't start that again!' Melanie muttered, concentrating on the cut, which was still bleeding. It was quite deep; perhaps he ought to have some stitches in it. It looked as if someone's ring had caught him—a heavy signet ring, perhaps?

'I make you nervous, don't I?' he said, as though that idea pleased him. 'You get very agitated when I'm around, that's why you won't look at me—while I'm looking at you, that is! I felt you watching me while Liz and I were handing round food a while back, but the minute I looked at you, you started staring somewhere else.'

She pretended not to have heard that. 'I think I ought to put some disinfectant on that cut, and it really should be seen professionally, it's very deep. You could go along to the casualty department at the hospital and see if it needs some stitches.'

'No,' he said coolly. 'It will be okay.'

'I'll get some disinfectant, then,' Melanie said, but before she took her hand away his hand covered it, held it there, against his cheek. At the same time his other hand went round her waist, pulling her closer.

Melanie had no chance to push him away before Liz came hurtling into the room. 'That fight has given them a new appetite—they want more food and . . .' Her voice stopped short as she saw them.

Melanie broke free and rushed past her, scarlet to her hairline. She couldn't face going back into the party. She ran upstairs to her bedroom. What must Liz have thought? Why did she have to come into the kitchen just then? Another minute and Melanie would have pulled away from him and there would have been nothing to see.

She closed the door, but didn't put the light on—she couldn't face the light, for the moment. Standing in the quiet darkness, she covered her face with her hands. Her skin was so hot. A strange mixture of emotions burned inside her. Why didn't he leave her alone?

She hadn't encouraged him. She had made it plain that she didn't want him to touch her. Was he like this with every girl he met? Was this how he was with Liz?

She forced her palms into her aching eyes—her head was throbbing with a sick headache. What sort of man was he, anyway? He ignored the fact that she was engaged to someone else—didn't he think it mattered? The anger grew inside her; all the words she never managed to get out when he was there were bubbling inside her head now. She despised him and he must despise her, of course, or he wouldn't ignore her protests and keep flirting with her.

Or did he think that secretly she wanted him to touch her? Her hands fell from her stricken face and she stared at the lamplit window of the room, all the colour and heat leaving her cheeks. Was that what he thought?

And on the heels of that came another, even more painful idea—was he right? She didn't even want to consider it, but once it had crept into her mind she couldn't push it out again. Did she secretly want Jamie Knox to kiss her? Hadn't she been on edge ever since she first saw him? She knew she had been very aware of him tonight from the minute he arrived; she had watched him whenever he wasn't looking her way, she couldn't deny it. When he was in the same room all her senses seemed involved with him; her ears picked up every nuance of his voice, her eyes kept finding him even when she tried not to look in that direction, her body temperature changed dramatically if he came too close, her skin intensely sensitive to his lightest touch.

She swallowed, frowning. She barely knew the man, why did he have this effect on her? What she did know about him she didn't like—of course she wasn't attracted to him! It was a crazy idea. He made her nervous, that was all. He wouldn't take no for an answer and she was kept on tenterhooks worrying about what he might do next. Jamie Knox was an infuriating man.

There was a tap on her door. Tense as a coiled spring, she turned to stare as the door opened.

'Melanie?' It was only Liz, she realised, slackening in relief. Her cousin peered across the dark room at her. 'What are you doing up here in the dark? Are you okay? Have you got a headache?'

'No, I'm fine,' Melanie said and Liz came right into the room.

'I came up to warn you that some of those gatecrashers are still hanging about outside. We've rung the police and they're sending a car round, so there's no need to worry, but we may have some more trouble before the police get here. If you hear a lot of noise, ignore it.'

'What are they doing?' Melanie asked anxiously.

'Nothing, at the moment—it's what they might do that worries us.' Liz grinned reassuringly. 'I thought I'd better warn you, in case it gets rough out there. The police are on their way, so no cause to panic.' She turned to go and Melanie said huskily, 'Liz, wait!'

Her cousin came back. 'Yes?'

'Just now, in the kitchen . . . it didn't mean anything. Don't take it the wrong way.'

Liz gave her a long, wry stare. 'I'm not taking it any way at all. It's no business of mine if you fancy Jamie Knox.'

'Of course I don't!' Melanie said shakily, her face hot. 'I'm engaged to Ross, Liz, I wouldn't play around with other men!'

'Ross Ellis is engaged to you, too, but I doubt if he's as scrupulous as you are,' Liz said with sudden irritation.

Melanie was taken aback. 'Ross wouldn't . . .'
she began and Liz interrupted.

'Wouldn't he?'

'You don't know him,' Melanie said, staring at
her cousin in bewilderment. Suddenly everyone
was behaving oddly, she didn't understand what
was happening. Liz had never cared for Ross much,
but Melanie hadn't expected her to talk about him
with dry ice in her voice, or to hint that Ross
wasn't faithful to her.

'It's you who don't know him,' Liz snapped.

'What are you talking about? Ross doesn't make
passes . . .'

'He made one at me!'

Melanie turned to stone on the spot. The light
from the open door showed her Liz's face, an
angry flush on it. Liz bit down on her lower lip as
she stared back, then ran her hands through her
hair violently as if wanting to tear it out by the
roots. 'Oh, hell!'

Melanie stared at her, trying to speak; she
couldn't. Her lips seemed numb, as if she had just
had novocaine; her tongue hung heavily in her
mouth. Liz groaned, staring at her.

'Melly, I'm sorry, it slipped out. I lost my
temper. I didn't mean to tell you, I never meant to
breathe a word about it, but I got so angry hearing
you talk as if he was . . . you don't have to feel
guilty if you did fancy Jamie Knox, don't be so
blind. That's half your trouble: you're blind about
people, you shouldn't be let out on your own.'

Melanie found her voice—or a voice, anyway,
because she didn't recognise it as her own. It was
very high and shaky.

'Ross made a pass at you? When?'

Liz looked uneasy, confused. 'Look, I'm drunk,

I think, forget it, Melly. As you just said, it didn't mean anything—just another party . . .'

'What happened?' Melanie stared insistently at her. 'Tell me the rest, Liz, you can't just leave it now.'

'I wish to God I hadn't lost my temper,' Liz muttered. 'I could bite my tongue out. Melly, don't look at me like that—I didn't want to hurt you, that was the last thing I wanted to do—why do you think I never told you before? It was months ago, anyway. It only happened once and as I said, it was a party, and maybe Ross was drunk. I know I was pretty euphoric, high as a kite until . . . well, anyway, nothing much happened, a kiss, that's all. Don't make a big deal of it, he never tried again.'

'What party?' Melanie asked flatly.

Liz sighed. 'That one his secretary gave when she moved into her new flat, remember? What's her name?'

'Brenda.'

'Yes, Brenda. She showed us her tiny roof garden, you came out there too, remember that? Then the rest of you went back in to dance and I stayed out there—there was a moon, the most amazing colour, almost orange.' Liz broke off, swallowing, her face averted. 'Ross came back to ask if I wanted a drink and I said look at that moon, did you ever see anything like it?' Liz shrugged. 'And then he kissed me.' She looked almost wildly at Melanie. 'Look, I didn't invite it, don't think I did a thing to make him think I wanted him to—you could have knocked me down with a feather. It was the last thing I expected and I told him never to try that again. I pushed him away and went back inside and I've hardly said three words to him since. That was all there was to it, and maybe parties bring out the beast in men!'

She tried to smile at Melanie, but her heart wasn't in it, and her smile withered as it was born.

Melanie turned her eyes away and stared over her cousin's head at the blurred orange glow of the street-lamp outside the window. She could hear voices outside. Were the gatecrashers regrouping for a new assault? It didn't seem to matter, she no longer cared about anything.

'Liz, go downstairs,' she said vaguely.

'Melly, don't take it so hard, for God's sake. I can't bear to see you look like that! It probably didn't mean a thing. A moment's aberration; men do have them—an impulse at a party when he'd had a few drinks. It's all my fault for telling you. I honestly didn't mean to, although I suppose you won't believe that now. It was months ago, Melly, after all, and he didn't do it again.' She stopped talking and watched Melanie's averted face. 'Are you listening?'

'I don't want to,' Melanie said, her jaws tight. 'I need to be alone, to think.'

'I can't leave you like this, Melly!'

'It's okay, I'm not breaking up.' Melanie tried to laugh but it came out so hoarsely that Liz groaned.

'Oh, hell. You look as if you are, you make me feel so guilty.' She took another deep breath and broke out with anger in her voice: 'You hear that? *I* feel guilty! Why should I be the one to feel like that? I didn't do anything. I didn't want him to, but then how do you ever know what's going on inside yourself? Maybe I was sending out vibes, maybe he thought . . .'

Melanie's eyes widened in surprise and sudden irony. So Liz felt that, too? Wasn't that what she had been saying to herself about Jamie Knox a few minutes ago? She had begun to wonder if she was secretly inviting, provoking him, if it was as much her own fault. Did women always feel guilty? Was guilt an instinctive female reaction in these situations—however innocent you thought you were, at first, did every woman sooner or later start to feel the nag of guilt?

Will called from the hall. 'Liz!'

They both jumped and before either of them moved Will's voice came again, from the stairs. 'Liz, Melanie—are you up there?'

'I'd better go,' Liz said. 'You stay here, then. I'll be back later.'

She hurried out, closing the door behind her, and Melanie sat on the edge of the bed feeling cold and tired. This had been quite an evening for shocks; they had come one after the other and she felt as if she were on a crazy switchback ride. The whole world looked strange to her; it was spinning and dipping around her. She felt she had to get up, stand on her feet, make everything seem normal again, grab at the familiar.

She walked carefully to the window to look out at the street. She had forgotten the gatecrashers. When she stared down, she saw them, by the gate, a dark cluster of thicker shadows just out of the circle of lamplight. Melanie saw them—and they saw Melanie. One of them had something in his hand. He raised his arm and threw; before she could duck out of the way something hit the glass with a violent crash.

CHAPTER FIVE

MELANIE screamed, covering her face with her hands in self-defence as jagged splinters of glass sprayed in all directions. There was a deafening confusion of sounds outside; people shouting, doors and windows opening as the people in other houses looked out to investigate the noise, the high-pitched siren of a police car coming nearer with a screech of tyres and the race of an engine, the thud of running feet as the gatecrashers dispersed, the slam of car doors as policemen jumped out when their vehicle braked to a halt followed at once by the noise of their heavy pounding pursuit.

When someone's arms went round her Melanie jumped about six feet in the air in shock.

'Are you hurt?' Jamie's voice was deep and rough; anger in it as well as concern. 'Melanie, let me see your face—did any glass hit you?' Still holding her with one arm he forced her hands down, turning her white face upwards. He had turned the light on in the room as he entered. She blinked, lashes quivering, in the vicious light, as he studied her. Melanie felt like a mole caught in a searchlight, and would have hidden her face again if Jamie's fingers hadn't ruthlessly controlled it.

'I don't see any blood,' he said to himself as his dark eyes flicked over her.

'I don't think any glass hit me,' Melanie said, feeling like hiding her face against him but refusing to give in to any such impulse. He might look comfortingly solid and protective, but she knew what any weak clinging would lead to, so she lifted her chin and tried to move away.

'Oh, yes, it did! Your hair's full of it.' Jamie's mouth was tight and harsh as he began picking fragments out of her hair, dropping them on her dressing-table where they glittered dangerously in the light.

Melanie didn't want to look at his hard-boned features so she stared at the broken window behind him. The night air came in; scented with chrysanthemums and rain. She heard the sudden swish of it on the pavements. This was city rain, washing the dust from the streets and gurgling in the gutters, but it still reminded her of the night they had spent together on the mist-shrouded hillside.

To dispel that memory, she said, 'Aunt Dolly is going to go crazy. Her worst nightmares come true! This is the last party Will is going to have for a long time.'

'It was hardly Will's fault. He didn't even know any of those little thugs by sight, nor did any of the boys. I made a point of asking them. No doubt the gang outside was prowling around and spotted a party going on and decided to muscle in for some free drink.' He brushed a palm over her crown slowly. 'I think I found it all, but you'd better wash your hair before you go to bed, in case I missed some.'

He had released her and she quickly stepped back, relieved to get away from him. 'Thank you,' she said stiffly.

'I expect the police will want to talk to you about what happened.'

Startled, she frowned. 'What can I tell them?'

'You were in here—you saw them, did you? You saw who threw the stone?'

He hadn't needed to ask what had done the damage because it lay on the carpet among the glass. She looked down at it.

'It's from Uncle Teddy's rockery,' she said flatly. 'I hope they didn't trample all his favourite plants.' She looked up at Jamie, her mouth rueful. 'I didn't actually see anything—I couldn't identify anyone, I mean. They were just dark shapes. They threw the stone deliberately, though.'

'At you?' he asked as if he knew the answer, as if it made him very angry.

She sighed, nodding. 'I suppose so. I looked down at them—maybe they thought I was laughing at them or something.'

'And maybe they're just mindless hooligans,' Jamie said thickly, his cheeks dark red with anger. 'They could have killed you. Or maimed or blinded you. Don't you realise how lucky you were? When I heard the crash and heard you scream I went cold. All the way upstairs I was wondering just what I'd see when I got in here.'

Liz came running up the stairs and burst into the room, her gaze hunting out her cousin and staring. 'Melly, are you okay? I was in the kitchen, I didn't hear anything until Will came in and said your window had been broken.'

'I'm fine. Have the police caught anyone?'

Liz shook her head. 'What a mess,' she said, looking at the glass littering the floor. 'That will have to be boarded up until we can get a glazier tomorrow.'

'I'll see to that,' Jamie told them. 'You go downstairs and wait in case the police want to interview you, Melanie. Liz, get her a stiff brandy and a cup of sweet tea.'

'I don't want . . .' she began.

'Don't argue!' Jamie instructed tersely.

Liz laughed. 'Come on, Melly, the man's in a temper, can't you see that? Never argue with a man in a temper. It's like crossing a field with an angry bull in it.'

Melanie went, talking to herself. 'I don't see why he should hand out orders as if he were God, or something. I don't have to jump when he says jump. Who does he think he is?'

'Talking to yourself is the first sign,' Liz told her.

'Of what?'

'Madness or love or both,' Liz said with her customary dryness.

'Yes, they're much the same thing, aren't they?' Melanie said fiercely. 'Anyone who falls in love ought to be put in a strait-jacket for their own protection until they fall out of it.'

It wasn't until she caught the stricken look Liz gave her that it dawned on Melanie how her cousin had taken that remark. Liz thought she was talking about Ross, about what Liz had told her!

Melanie paused on the stairs, touching Liz on the arm. 'That wasn't aimed at you! I didn't mean anything, I was talking wildly. It was all such a shock, this has been an eventful evening.' She laughed unsteadily. 'See how calm I am? I can even make understatements, not my usual style. Oh, Liz, for the moment let's just forget what you told me about Ross. Please?' She needed time to think, weigh up what she had learnt, and then she must talk to Ross himself before she really decided what to do, but she didn't want Liz going around looking like a wet weekend because she thought she had hurt Melanie. It would make life much easier if Liz was able to be natural again.

Her cousin looked sideways at her, oddly, frowning. 'Okay,' she said in a low, flat voice.

Melanie was deeply fond of her cousin. She knew that Liz was fond of her, too. They had never competed for their men, there had never been any jealousy between them. Liz might squabble with Will and Will might resent his sister's seniority and call her bossy and superior, with a tongue like viper, but Liz always went out of her way to be kind to Melanie. It was part of that family habit, perhaps. But it was also a genuine personal affection, and Melanie was quite certain that Liz hadn't wanted to hurt her, hadn't planned, deliberately, to tell her what Ross had done. Some women might do that—but not Liz. Some women might have set out to flirt with Ross—but not Liz. Melanie wasn't angry with her cousin, nor did she blame her for what had happened. She was stunned and in a bleak mood, but she had already absolved Liz from all blame.

The police arrived a few moments later. There wasn't much that Melanie could tell them, nor were any of the other guests much help. When the police left the party broke up. People seemed eager to get away, their party spirit had been dampened. Nobody had been hurt, but the window incident had been a shock to them—their gaiety had been shattered with the glass.

Liz and Melanie shut the door on the last one and turned back into the house just as Will and Jamie came from the garden with a sheet of plywood which they had tracked down in Uncle Teddy's toolshed.

'Make some coffee,' pleaded Will as he followed Jamie up the stairs, gripping his end of the wood. 'It won't take us long to board up your window, Melanie. I'm afraid the carpet is a bit wet—the wind's blown rain all over the floor, but it will dry out when the central heating gets to work on it.'

'I could do with some coffee before we tackle the tidying up,' said Liz, yawning.

'While you make the coffee, I'll start the washing up,' offered Melanie. Upstairs they heard banging. The men were fixing the board into the window.

'Mum will never get over this,' Liz said, setting out four mugs. 'Let's hope we'll be able to persuade a glazier to work on a Saturday. They're almost as hard to get as plumbers. If things look normal on Sunday night, Mum won't be nearly as frantic as she would be if she saw the mess the house is in now.'

'I expect Jamie will find a glazier,' Melanie said vaguely and then felt herself flushing, caught the quick glance Liz gave her. Hectically, she stammered, 'Well, he's that sort of man, isn't he? He always gets his own way, he makes things work for him.' That was what worried her about him— Mr Omniscient, All-Powerful Knox. Half the time she found herself doing what he told her to do, even if she started out by being determined not to fall into line.

She concentrated on filling the dishwasher with every item of china she could pack into it. Liz went off with a tray and came back with a few dozen glasses on it, then the coffee was ready and a moment later Will came down looking tired and gloomy.

'I'll never live this down. A fine birthday party this was! And now we've got all the clearing up to do!'

'Come and drink your coffee,' said Liz.

'Take it up to bed with you, Will,' Melanie urged. 'We'll tidy up before we come upstairs—no need for you to help. It can be a special birthday

present for you. How's that?' She smiled at him
coaxingly and Will looked uncertain, picking up his
mug of coffee.

'I can't leave you two to do all the work . . .'

'I'll give them a hand,' Jamie said from the
door. 'Off you go, Will. We'll manage very well
without you.'

'I just bet you will!' Relaxing, Will grinned at
him. 'Thanks for all your help tonight. You're not
going to try to drive back to Ullswater at this
hour, are you? Why not stay here? We can find
you a bed, can't we, Liz?'

She turned from piling dirty plates on the
draining-board, her brows shooting up. 'I'm not
sure I like the way you phrased that!'

Jamie laughed and she grinned at him.

'If you don't mind sleeping in an attic . . .'

'Just love it,' Jamie said. 'I can sleep on a
clothes line if I'm tired—an attic will be luxury,'

Will ambled to the door, his skin very white
against the flame of his hair. He flapped a hand
towards them. 'Night, everybody.'

'Goodnight, Will,' they said, watching his depar-
ture with sympathy. Poor Will. He couldn't be
looking forward to what his parents had to say
when they got home.

'I'll start washing glasses,' Melanie said, filling
the sink with warm water. Liz went off with her
tray to find some more and Jamie found another
tray and followed her. Melanie stood at the sink,
methodically washing the glass, her eyes abstracted
as she thought about Ross.

In a sense, what Liz had told her was irrelevant
to the real trouble between Melanie and Ross. She
couldn't even guess why Ross had suddenly made a
pass at Liz—from the beginning, the two of them
had been distantly antagonistic, and Liz might be

right when she said that it had been an impulse, that Ross had been drinking at a party and finding himself out there under the stars with an attractive woman had kissed her without thinking. It probably meant no more than that. It didn't mean that Ross was promiscuous, made passes at every woman he met. That simply wasn't in character.

And that was the core of the problem—Ross's character. Because once she'd thought that, she had come up against the question—what was his character? What did she really know about him?

When he came into the estate agency that first time, he had chatted her up, whisked her off to have lunch. It hadn't been what Liz would no doubt call a pass—Ross hadn't touched her with so much as a finger. He had watched her, smiled at her, asked her about herself, and she had never felt sexually threatened or thought that he was flirting with her.

Her busy hands stilled in the water; she stared at nothing, her face fixed and pale. When had he ever made her feel that he was deeply attracted to her? She couldn't remember a flare of real passion between them. He had proposed so soon after they met, though. She had been dumbstruck, staring back at him incredulously. He was asking her to marry him! And he meant it! Ross had smiled, taking her hands. 'Will you, Melanie? I want you to be my wife.'

The moment was sharp and clear in her mind. She closed her eyes, face bewildered. She didn't understand. If Ross didn't love her, why had he asked her to marry him? And if he did love her, why was there this distance between them? Why wouldn't he let her come any closer? She knew little more about him now than she had that first time they met, and whenever she tried to reach him Ross seemed to her to slam a door in her face.

There was a jangle of glass behind her. Jamie had come back with a loaded tray which he set down on the kitchen table. Melanie hurriedly got back to her washing up without looking round at him.

'Where's your vacuum cleaner?' he asked. 'I've picked up the glasses and plates in that room, but the carpet is going to need some work—it's littered with ash and peanuts.'

Melanie dried her hands and turned reluctantly. 'I'll do it.'

'I know how to use a vacuum cleaner,' Jamie told her with impatience. 'Where is it?'

She went over to the cupboard in which Aunt Dolly kept it but as she got it out, Jamie reached for it, his fingers touching hers, and Melanie jumped as if she had had an electric shock.

Jamie's voice was rough with anger. 'Don't do that! I'm a little tired of having you behave as though I was some sort of threat to you!'

She stared downwards, her neck bent, the black hair smoothly flowing against her cheek and shoulder and her lids hiding her eyes from him. He *was* some sort of threat to her, but she didn't want to admit it, even to herself.

'I realise you're upset, but don't take it out on me,' he said fiercely, when she didn't answer.

Melanie looked up, then, startled, her blue eyes wide and troubled. 'What are you talking about? Upset?' Her stare searched his hard-boned face and then she gave a little sigh. 'Oh, the stone through my window, you mean? Yes, it was . . .'

'No,' Jamie said through his teeth. 'I meant what Liz told you, before that happened.'

An icy whiteness filled her face. Appalled, she

whispered, 'Liz told . . . she told *you*?' For the second time that evening, Liz had stunned her. It was unbelievable that her cousin could have told Jamie Knox something so private, so embarrassing. Melanie felt as if the room dipped and swayed around her. She didn't understand anything tonight. She didn't understand anyone. If Liz had told a stranger what she had taken so long to tell Melanie herself, then Melanie did not know Liz any better than she knew Ross.

Jamie pushed his hands into his pockets, his tough body tensely poised. 'She needed to talk to someone. She was going quietly crazy. The first time I came here, when I brought you home, Liz and I had dinner and talked—maybe it was the wine or maybe Liz just couldn't keep it to herself any longer, but it came out.'

'She had no right,' Melanie burst out shakily. 'No right to tell you anything. It has nothing to do with you.' She hated the thought that he knew that her fiancé had made a pass at her cousin. How could Liz do it? How could she have told Jamie Knox a story like that?

'That hardly matters,' he said tersely, brushing her anger aside. 'The question is—what are you going to do about it?'

'You don't really think I'll discuss it with you, do you?' she muttered, turning away. He kept forcing himself into her life, trying to impose his views, his wishes, on her. The man was a menace, but he wasn't getting his own way this time. She wouldn't even let him mention it. She didn't want to know what he thought she should do, which was what he was obviously about to tell her. He could keep his opinions to himself. 'It's none of your damned business,' she broke out, shaking with anger.

He grabbed her shoulders, his fingers digging into her flesh, and forced her round towards him again.

'You aren't just going to bury it, forget she ever told you?'

'Let go of me!'

'You make me angry,' he said, as if he needed to tell her. 'It's as clear as daylight that your engagement is a farce.'

'You know nothing about it!'

'Don't I?' His mouth was hard and contemptuous and his dark eyes raked her face, making her flinch. 'It was obvious to me when we first met— you were upset because he'd gone off on business instead of keeping his promise to spend the weekend in the Lakes. No, you didn't say anything, but you didn't have to.'

'Oh, you can read my mind, I suppose?' she said bitterly, hating the way he stared at her.

'Yes, that's exactly it. I read your mind,' he said in an anger that matched hers. 'There's something else about Ross Ellis that you don't know, too.'

'I don't want to hear!' she said, struggling to get away. She had had enough for one night. She wanted no more shocks; she couldn't cope with any more revelations.

'Oh, I can see that!' he told her with a savage smile. 'But you're going to listen.'

'No, let go, stop it!' She hated the contempt she read in that strong face. What right did he have to despise her? What did he know about how she felt, what she thought? The only person who could see inside her heart was her, and even she didn't yet know exactly what she was going to do.

'You prefer to live in a fool's paradise than to face up to the truth?' he sneered angrily. 'It's so much cosier, isn't it? Ross Ellis is rich and important and all your friends will envy you when you're his wife. You'll have wardrobes of gorgeous clothes—a mink coat, Melanie? I'm sure you'd like a mink, girls usually do, don't they? Never mind the husband, look at the mink he'll give you? Isn't that what really matters to you? Oh, and Ross Ellis could give you one. Several, no doubt. He can give you most things money can buy. A grand house, a flashy car of your own, holidays in the South of France—or would you prefer Florida? Well, it doesn't matter, that's a minor detail. Wherever the jet set goes, you can go too—if you marry him. If you can stand being the discreet façade hiding a very empty private life, because you aren't in love with him, don't kid yourself you are, and he isn't in love with you, either.'

'Stop it, stop it,' she said frantically.

'Not until you've heard the truth! You won't be happy with him, you stupid girl. Can't you see that? His money won't help you to be happy.'

'I'm not interested in his money,' she spat out, trembling with an anger she couldn't control. She had never been interested in Ross's wealth, or his power in the business world; she had never looked past Ross himself to all the things which came with him. If he had been as rich as Croesus but unattractive to her, she wouldn't have seen him again, and she bitterly resented the accusations Jamie had just made.

Jamie's mouth twisted. 'No? Who are you trying to convince? Me? Or yourself?'

The top of her head seemed about to blow off. 'You?' she threw back at him hoarsely. 'You? I don't give a damn what you think, Mr Knox!'

Dark red rose in his face, his hands tightened on her slim shoulders until she winced.

'What on earth's going on?' said another voice from the doorway.

Melanie looked around and saw Liz staring at them with startled eyes.

'Haven't we had enough drama for one night?' Liz said, trying to laugh.

Melanie didn't smile back, she turned angry eyes on her cousin. 'You told him. You told him about Ross. How could you?' Her voice rose word by word, trembling with rage. 'Why not get a megaphone and tell the whole street? Print it in your damned paper, tell the world, why don't you? Liz, how could you?'

Liz seemed, for once, lost for words. She had flushed and her eyes moved to Jamie Knox's face, as if asking why he had told Melanie how indiscreet she had been. If Melanie had wondered if Jamie was telling the truth about hearing the story from Liz, she stopped wondering as she saw the look they exchanged. They didn't say a word, but their eyes talked, and watching that made Melanie angrier than ever.

'I'll never forgive you,' she told her cousin. 'Never.' She felt Jamie's grip on her slacken, and pulled away without so much as a look at him. Walking across the kitchen she passed Liz with one bitter glance, went through the hall, up the stairs to bed. Liz and Jamie could finish the clearing up. They could have one of their cosy, confidential chats while they did it, really let their hair down.

It was so unlike Liz. She had never been one for idle gossip and she didn't let just anybody into her confidence, but then if she had fallen in love with Jamie Knox he wouldn't be just anyone to her, would he? For Liz to open up with him like that, he had to be very special to her, and that meant it had to be serious, because Melanie couldn't remember the last time Liz had ever taken a man very seriously. Her relationships tended to be brittle, passing—men found her attractive but the type of men who fell for Liz were often shy and insecure which meant that Liz couldn't go for them, or they were sophisticated and often shallow which she certainly wasn't. Sophisticated, yes. Shallow, never. Liz wanted a very special man—not that she had told Melanie as much, but it was pretty obvious. The man Liz settled for would have to be someone as cool and aware as herself, yet inwardly as caring and capable of love.

The description didn't fit Jamie Knox, she thought coldly, as she undressed with shaky fingers and slid into bed. She didn't see him being capable of love. All evening he had flirted with her, hadn't he? Right under Liz's nose, too, although Liz hadn't seemed too worried by seeing them together, which was another puzzling feature of the whole evening.

The wind rattled the plywood boarding on her window, keeping her awake. She lay in the darkness, wishing she could stop her mind working. Will and Jamie had swept up all the glass and disposed of it. Her room looked spotless again, although the carpet was slightly damp where the rain had blown into the room. The only evidence of what had happened was the boarded window, and if they managed to get a glazier that, too, would have gone by the time Aunt Dolly and Uncle Teddy got back.

It wouldn't be as easy for her to erase all traces of the violence which had happened inside her tonight, though.

CHAPTER SIX

SHE slept very deeply, and very late into the morning woke up at the click of her door opening. Drowsily her lids lifted and she turned her dark head on the pillow, still half asleep.

When she saw Jamie she came awake in a hurry, clutching the sheet up to her chin. 'Get out of here! What do you think you're doing?'

'The glazier's downstairs,' he interrupted tersely. Melanie drew breath. 'Oh.'

'Can you get up and dress quickly? I didn't expect him so soon or I'd have woken you earlier. I'm just going to make some coffee if you'd like to come down as soon as you're ready.'

The door closed and she stared at it, biting her lip, remembering everything that had happened last night, all the unpleasant, unjust things he had said to her. She hated him.

There was no point in lying there giving way to a brooding sense of the unfairness of fate for having brought Jamie Knox into her life, though, so she threw back the covers and swung out of bed, yawning. It was only then that she looked at the clock and saw that it was almost eleven o'clock in the morning.

On her way to the bathroom she saw that both Will and Liz had their doors shut; the sound of their slow breathing came through the wood very audibly. They were still asleep. They wouldn't stay that way once the glazier got to work, though.

A quick shower helped Melanie to come fully awake. Returning to her room in her brief terry robe, she met Jamie on the landing, his face thunderous.

'How much longer are you going to be? I've had to make the guy some breakfast now, or he'd have left without doing the job.'

'I'll be five minutes,' she said, trying not to notice the way his eyes explored the deep plunge between the lapels of her robe, the bare damp legs below the hem of it.

Jamie held up his wrist, tapping his watch. 'Five minutes—I'm timing you.'

'Oh, get lost,' Melanie said, furious, and dived back into her room, but she dressed rapidly in the first thing that came to hand—snug-fitting white denims and a sky-blue cotton top with a demure, scooped neckline. Her mirror showed her a neat reflection. She stared at it grimly. She looked like a schoolgirl. Well, why not? At least that might make Jamie Knox keep his distance, so she tied her black hair into two curling bunches, with blue satin bows, to complete the image. Let him come a foot too close today and she would hit him with something.

When she got down to the kitchen Jamie looked pointedly at his watch. 'Seven minutes precisely,' he said, but Melanie pretended not to have heard that.

A grey-haired workman in well-washed blue dungarees sat at the kitchen table finishing bacon, egg and toast. Picking up a cup of increadibly strong tea, he nodded to her. 'Sorry to get you out of bed in a hurry, miss, but I'm a bit pushed for time.'

Melanie smiled at him. 'That's okay, I'm glad to

see you—we're very keen to get the window done
before my uncle and aunt get back.'

'So I heard. I don't know what these kids are
coming to—chucking stones through windows
because they were thrown out of a party. As if I
didn't have enough to do, and this a Saturday too.'
The workman drained his cup, got up and picked
up his bag of tools. 'Well, I'll go up and get to
work, if you'll show me the way, Mr Knox.'

Melanie cleared the table and made herself some
toast and a boiled egg. She was eating it when
Jamie came back.

'You may be interested to hear that our glazier
thought you were still at school,' he drawled, sitting
down at the table too and stretching his long legs
with a sigh. 'It's the hairstyle, makes you look
about fifteen.'

Melanie drank some coffee, her eyes lowered.
How much longer was he going to stay? Why
didn't he go home now?

'But then that was the idea, wasn't it? They call
it regression—a deliberate retreat into childhood.
Makes it easier to ignore problems the patient
can't face.' Jamie paused, as if waiting for her to
defend herself, but she went on ignoring him.

'At a guess I'd say that that's why you went for
Ross Ellis, too,' he went on, when he saw she
wasn't rising to his bait. 'Does he realise he's just
your security blanket, I wonder?'

Melanie blazed into open rage at that, her dark
blue eyes hating him. 'Why don't you leave me
alone?'

He linked his hands behind his head, lying back
in the chair in an attitude of casual mockery. 'Why,
Melanie? Am I actually getting through to you, is
that what worries you?'

'Don't kid yourself,' she spat, glaring. 'I'm sick

of being a target for your bullets, that's all. So why don't you get back into that showy car of yours and go home? Go away, stay away.'

'You're losing your temper,' he taunted softly. 'You don't want to do that, Melanie, do you? Any sort of real emotion threatens that dream world you've gone to such trouble to build up. If you actually started to think about how you really *feel* you might not be able to go through with marrying Ellis, and that would never do, would it? All that cosy security gone! What might happen to you then?'

Melanie got stumblingly to her feet, trembling with fury, but before she had thrown something at Jamie or hit him or screamed, the doorbell went sharply and she regained control of herself enough to walk past Jamie down the hall to the front door.

When she saw Ross standing there she stared blankly at him for a second, almost shocked by the sight of him. He was casually dressed today; pale grey trousers, a fine slate-coloured cashmere sweater, over which he wore a blue leather jacket. Even in such casual clothes he managed to look very elegant and stylish.

'Ross! You're back, then—I'd been waiting for you to ring.'

'I came, instead.' He kissed her lightly and offered her a large gold, ribbon-tied box. 'I bought you some real Turkish Delight in a bazaar in Bahrain.'

'Oh, how nice,' Melanie said, hoping Jamie wouldn't come out into the hall. She was appalled by the prospect of a meeting between the two men, but how could she get out of it? 'Come into the drawing-room,' she stammered, wondering if Jamie had heard them talking.

Ross was observing her childish hairstyle and

clean-scrubbed face with faint surprise. 'You look very sweet today.'

'Thank you,' she said uneasily, afraid of actually hustling him out of the hall but still hoping to avert a meeting with Jamie. 'Did you have a successful trip, Ross?'

'I managed to pull the chestnuts out of the fire,' he said. 'Did you go to the Lakes? I'm sorry I couldn't make it, Melanie, but I hope you went and enjoyed yourself.'

She steered him into the drawing-room, hoping it was now reasonably tidy. Darting a look around it she saw with relief that Jamie and Liz must have spent some time on restoring it to normal. Nothing now seemed out of place.

'Yes, I went, and did some sailing and climbing,' she admitted, as the glazier began hammering upstairs. Ross lifted his eyes to the ceiling, his expression quizzical.

'What's going on in your bedroom? I saw one of your windows was broken.' He listened smilingly as Melanie began to tell him about Will's birthday party.

'And I forgot all about it! I'm sorry, my mind was otherwise occupied. I'd meant to get him a present—never mind, I'll remember to get him something tomorrow.' Then he smiled. 'It must have been a good party if windows got broken, though.'

She told him what had happened and he frowned, asking quickly, 'You weren't hurt?'

'No, just shaken.'

'And Liz?'

'She didn't even realise it had happened until Will told her.'

The sunlight streaming in through the high windows showed her the pale gold of his hair and, for the first time, a faint silvering of the immaculate strands. Perhaps it was because Ross was looking tired; his week of intensive negotiations in Bahrain had taken its toll. He looked older, faintly weary.

'Was your trip exhausting, Ross?' she asked gently, and he shrugged.

'The heat sapped my energy, I could never live in a climate like that. Even with air-conditioning in my hotel I found myself having to take cool showers several times a day, and when you were out on the site itself, you had a problem with the flies and sand and dirt. My throat was so dry all the time that I had a sore throat within two days. It was a useful exercise to go out there myself because I had a better idea why the men were causing so much trouble. Once I could see it from their angle, I knew how to solve the problem.'

'When did you actually get back?'

'Yesterday, but I had to see the other directors and explain what arrangments I'd made and by then it was too late to get in touch with you.'

They were talking like strangers, Melanie thought bleakly, as she nodded. That was what they were, though, wasn't it? Ross never really took her into his confidence, he didn't treat her as an equal, talk about what was worrying him, ask her advice or help. How did he think about her? Or didn't he think about her at all, apart from remembering to buy her a box of sweets before returning from this business trip?

Well, they had to talk and soon, because it couldn't go on like this—Jamie Knox was right, although she would die rather than admit as much to him. This wasn't the time or the place, however. At any minute Jamie might wander in and overhear them.

'I thought we might have lunch out somewhere,'

Ross murmured. 'Or have you made other arrangements?'

So polite, she thought, looking at him wryly. In his presence she found it even more incredible that he had made a pass at Liz, or that he was in the habit of making passes at any women. When she heard Liz telling that story she had believed it because she couldn't remember Liz lying to her before, but now, looking at Ross, her belief faltered and fragmented. There was something so out of character about the thought of Ross behaving like that. It didn't add up. Yet Liz simply didn't lie, so he must have made a pass at her. Had he been drunk? She hadn't noticed that, and she remembered vaguely that he had taken her home after that party. She was sure he had been sober; in fact, he'd been rather quiet and withdrawn for most of the evening. Melanie's bewilderment only deepened further the more she tried to work out the truth, tried to make sense of the puzzle. The pieces didn't fit together, which could only mean that there was a piece of the jigsaw missing.

Jamie Knox might mock her and say that she didn't know Ross at all and didn't understand him, but Jamie Knox was wrong in one sense—she understood what she knew about Ross, she couldn't believe he was the sort of man Liz and Jamie seemed to think he was and her own judgment of people wasn't as blinkered as Jamie imagined. It was Jamie who was looking at Ross from the wrong angle, not her.

'Lunch would be very nice,' she said slowly, and Ross looked at his watch.

'Good, and there's plenty of time for you to change.'

That was his only reference, gently indulgent, to

her neat schoolgirl appearance, and Melanie grimaced.

'Yes, I won't be very long. Do sit down, Ross. Would you like some coffee while you wait?'

'That would be very welcome,' he said in his calm, tired voice, taking off his leather jacket and folding it neatly over the back of a chair before he sat down on the couch.

Jamie was in the kitchen drinking black coffee, but if Melanie had hoped that he hadn't realised who had arrived she soon found she was wrong.

'He timed his arrival nicely,' he said, leaning against the draining-board, his mug in one hand, watching Melanie start to make a pot of coffee for Ross. 'Were his ears burning? I'm ready to bet you didn't tell him we'd been talking about him when he arrived.'

She hunted for a cup and saucer from Aunt Dolly's best coffee-service, a silver wedding anniversary present from Liz to her parents several years ago. Aunt Dolly rarely used the pretty bone china with its silver stripe and faint pink rosebuds. She liked to look at it in her china cabinet but was afraid it might get broken if it was actually used.

'It's madness, you know that, don't you?' Jamie said as she set out the silver tray. 'His money won't make you happy, Melanie. It's all an illusion. Wake up before it's too late.'

She filled the cream-jug and the silver sugar-bowl which matched the tray, still ignoring Jamie.

'Nothing but the best for Ross Ellis,' Jamie murmured with dry impatience a moment later. 'Can't you see that you'll be stifled by the way he lives? Look at you now—if you were making that coffee for me you'd make instant coffee in a mug and hand it to me. But for him it has to be all the frills. He expects it and he gets it, doesn't he?

That's not the life you're used to. Oh, no doubt
you find it exciting, moving in that world for the
first time, but when the novelty wears off and you
realise you've married a man you don't love, who
doesn't love you, all the glitter and frills in this
world won't help you, Melanie.'

'Who the hell do you think you are?' Melanie
erupted, turning on him at last with a flushed and
agitated face. 'You hardly know me. You can't
guess whether I love Ross or not.'

'You don't,' he stated with cool certainty.

'Don't say that!' Melanie seethed, dying to hit
him with something. 'You know nothing about it.'

'I saw the two of you together just now in the
hall. I saw the way he kissed you. It wasn't exactly
earth-shattering, was it? You didn't run into each
other's arms. In fact, you sounded like a couple of
bored strangers making polite conversation.' He
imitated her, his eyes mocking. 'Did you have a
successful trip, Ross?' His mouth twisted derisively.
'As for him, I should think he makes more show of
being pleased to see his dog.' He imitated Ross's
calm, quiet voice. 'You look very sweet.' Jamie's
face was scornful. 'Sweet! My God!'

The coffee was beginning to bubble against the
glass dome. Melanie felt rather like that, too; fury
was boiling inside her and she was tempted to
explode in Jamie's face, but she was afraid of what
that might precipitate, she had a distinct suspicion
that Jamie was determined to provoke some
reaction out of her and that she wouldn't enjoy
whatever he planned to do next.

'All men aren't like you,' she said instead,
keeping her rage suppressed but making her voice
icily contemptuous.

He flicked a glance at her through his lashes. 'So
you've noticed that, at last.'

She was disturbed by the gleam in those dark eyes. 'It wasn't meant as a compliment!' she denied.

'All the same, it is one,' mocked Jamie, his smile maddeningly self-satisfied. 'And for the record, the last word I'd apply to you is sweet . . . you're about as sweet as poison ivy. Every time I'm anywhere near you I get some dangerous symptoms.'

The coffee was ready; Melanie darted to switch it off, averting her flushed face from him. 'Thanks,' she bit out, putting the coffee-pot on the tray. 'I'm very flattered.'

He laughed as she walked to the door. 'But you'll notice that I keep coming back,' he said softly.

She didn't look round or admit she had heard that. Her throat was hot and dry and she felt strangely miserable. What did he mean by that? Or was it just empty words? Jamie Knox flirted easily with every girl he met, he had taken Liz out to dinner the first time he came here and Liz was by no means an easy pick-up. She had pretty high standards where men were concerned; she didn't fall for any man who looked twice at her.

She carried the tray into the drawing-room and poured Ross a cup of coffee. He was leaning back in the chair, his eyes closed, when she came into the room and opened them slowly to smile at her in that tired way.

'Everyone else out?' he asked casually.

'Liz and Will aren't up yet, but I expect the glazier has woken them by now. He's making quite a noise, isn't he?' The man was chipping all the broken glass out of the frame now.

Leaving Ross sipping his coffee, Melanie went up to her bedroom. The glazier turned his head and grinned. 'I'll be quite a time yet, miss, I'm afraid.'

'That's all right—I'm going out, anyway.' Melanie collected some clothes and went into the bathroom to change. A few moments later someone rattled the doorhandle.

'I'm in here—I'll be out in five minutes,' called Melanie.

'Melly? You pest,' Liz said with a yawn. 'My head is hammering.'

'That's the glazier in my room,' Melanie said, smiling, as she eyed her reflection in the bathroom mirror. She had put on a turquoise shift dress, pure silk, very simple and smooth-fitting. She began lightly brushing her hair into its customary soft style, curved inward around her face, framing it elegantly.

'Glazier? He got here quickly.' Liz pattered away, yawning again.

Melanie did her make-up without haste, using very little because her skin looked better without too much. Her mirror now showed her a very different image—cool, slender and composed, a girl who had herself and her life very much under control. She considered the reflection wryly; it was a lie, of course, an illusion she had conjured up with cosmetics and clothes, but knowing that she gave that impression would make it easier for her to talk to Ross.

She didn't yet know how to introduce the subject; she would have to play it by ear, wait for the right moment. Jamie Knox might imagine that he had prodded her into looking twice at her engagement, but he was wrong. The morning she drove off to the Lakes alone she had been poised on the edge of realising she had made a mistake; Jamie's interference had only accelerated a process which had begun before he met her.

Her blue eyes flashed as she remembered Jamie's insulting suggestion that she was marrying Ross for his money. He'd made her very angry when he said that, but she could brush the insult aside because she knew it wasn't true. Ross's money meant nothing to her. It wasn't as simple, though, to shrug off the accusation that she was clinging to Ross for emotional security, and she frowned at her reflection as if her eyes betrayed something disastrous.

Ross was a strong man, comfortingly assured. She had found a kind of peace with him at first; had it been a false peace? Much as she loved her uncle and aunt, and both her cousins, she had never felt she belonged with them in quite the way she had with her parents. It wasn't easy to put into words, or even think about; it was more a matter of instinct and intuition than logic. Looking back to her childhood she saw it as a golden warmth, like a summer day: confident, stable. Yes, secure— Jamie was right, damn him. However hard Aunt Dolly and Uncle Teddy tried, they could never take the place of her parents. There was always that something missing, indefinable but unforgotten. When Ross asked her to marry him that special feeling of belonging had seemed to shimmer ahead like a mirage in a desert and she had eagerly run to find it.

Perhaps she would, some day—but not with Ross, and she had come to see that long before Jamie Knox started making his derisive comments. She might have faced the truth sooner if she didn't feel a tremor of regret every time she thought of saying goodbye to that hope of love and security in a family again. Was that what people meant when they talked of falling in love with love? The state of being in love was so wonderful it was easy to deceive yourself.

She grimaced, turning away. The longer she left Ross alone the more chance there was of Jamie talking to him, saying something that might precipitate a crisis Melanie wasn't ready to face yet.

She came down the stairs just in time to see Liz in her old rose-pink velvet housecoat wandering across the hall. Liz paused at the open door of the drawing-room, glancing into the room.

Melanie saw her face in profile; saw the smooth skin tighten over Liz's cheekbones, a hot wave of colour flow up to her hairline.

It was rare for Liz to look so shaken; it wasn't easy to throw her off balance, but Melanie saw it happen now, and paused on the stairs, her mind working like lightning, putting two and two together with a rapidity that shook her as deeply as Liz was visibly shaken.

'Oh, hallo,' Liz said in an abrupt, deep voice.

Melanie couldn't see Ross but she knew that Liz was speaking to him.

'Hallo,' Ross said, and the sound of his voice made Melanie's eyes widen.

There was a strange little silence, then Liz said huskily, 'Does Melanie know you're here?'

'Yes,' he said, his voice becoming brusque.

'Oh, well . . .' Liz backed. Melanie saw her hand catch hold of the wall; the skin was stretched tautly over the white knuckles. 'Well, she won't be long,' Liz said. 'Excuse me.'

Melanie felt horribly out of place, she would have backed out of sight if she could have done so without drawing attention to her presence, but Liz didn't look up or notice her. She walked unsteadily towards the kitchen, the door opened and closed and Melanie stared at it fixedly.

How could I be so blind for so long? she thought.

CHAPTER SEVEN

THE shock of her new suspicions absorbed so much
of her attention that she let Ross put her into the
passenger seat of his Rolls, slide in beside her
behind the driving wheel and turn south out of
Carlisle heading for Kendal without Melanie
noticing the direction he had taken, or being aware
of anything much except her own thoughts.

Her immediate reaction was to think that Liz
had, after all, lied to her, but it slowly dawned on
her that Liz hadn't lied so much as suppressed her
own side of the story. Liz hadn't wanted to admit
she was attracted to Ross; and why should she? It
was a complication that Liz felt had nothing to do
with the matter. Melanie knew her cousin well
enough, and had noticed enough of her manner
whenever Ross was around to be certain that Liz
had not given him a hint how she felt. Far from it,
Liz had frozen when she saw him. She must have
gone to great lengths to make sure that Ross never
suspected her real feelings, because Melanie had
been totally deceived. She had been sure that Liz
disliked Ross, and she thought Ross had believed
that, too.

When Ross, nevertheless, made a pass at her,
Liz would have been doubly shaken—on her own
behalf as well as on Melanie's. Her mind must
have been in turmoil, wondering if she had betrayed
her feelings, terrified of admitting them, filled with
guilt. Hadn't she said as much? She had skated

over the reasons for her sense of guilt, but Melanie vividly recalled her cousin's face. Liz had been more upset than angry—Melanie should have guessed at once that her cousin was withholding something for Liz had been far too distressed for it to be mere sympathy for Melanie.

Melanie had only a hazy memory of that party which had been so traumatic for Liz. For her it had been just another night, one she had more or less forgotten almost at once. Wasn't it odd how one event could seem so different from other angles?

'I thought we'd eat by the river in Kendal, that restaurant we've been to before,' Ross said abruptly.

Looking round with a start, she said, 'Oh, yes, I remember—that will be nice. The place with the lovely view of the river?' He had taken her there several times. The restaurant was on the upper floor, its bar looked down over the river so that one could drink and watch the current flowing darkly under an old bridge.

'The food is good, too,' Ross said with a brief smile before switching his gaze to the motorway ahead. What was he thinking? Were their thoughts running on the same theme? She suspected that they were.

Why had he ever asked her to marry him? An impulse decision? They had met so casually, but Ross must have realised at once that he had bowled her off her feet. She had only been out with boys of her own age until then, and Ross was used to dating far more sophisticated women. Had it been Melanie's wide-eyed and dazzled gaze that had given him the idea of marrying her? Had he only proposed after he had begun to think she was in love with him?

A flush crept up her cheeks as it dawned on her

that she, herself, might have unknowingly brought about the proposal which had been such a surprise at the time. They had both been under a flattering spell, of course; she had been amazed at interest from a man like Ross and he, in turn, had been touched by her shy reactions to him.

But he hadn't met Liz until after he proposed, had he? Up to that time, their dates had been on neutral ground, like the restaurant to which he was taking her now. When had he begun to realise how he felt about Liz? Was it an instant attraction? Or did it grow gradually?

Looking slowly back over the months, Melanie felt sure that Ross had finally understood his own feelings on the night of Brenda's party. It was after that that his attitude had changed, that he began to be distant and suddenly far too busy to see her.

Or was she deluding herself? Had something been going on between Liz and Ross all these months?

She looked sharply at him, searching his features—no, she couldn't believe that, about either of them.

Ross sensed her gaze and turned his head. 'Sorry to be abstracted,' he said politely. 'I've got something on my mind.'

Melanie watched him, stiffening. 'Would it help to talk about it?'

The calm façade of his face seemed to crack; she caught a glimpse of confused emotions in his eyes, on his parted mouth. She took an expectant breath—one of them had to make the first move to unravel the tangle into which their lives had been scrambled. Was that what he was thinking? Was he going to say something at last?'

But he looked away with a deep sigh. 'No, I don't think so.'

Melanie bit her lip. The day he left for Bahrain she had told him that she simply didn't feel she knew him well enough to marry him. She had left out some of what she wanted to say; her uncertainty had been too vague, too indefinable—a muddled suspicion that she wasn't really in love with him? Or just an instinctive awareness that they were both making a mistake? She hadn't seen him again until today, they still hadn't talked frankly, yet she felt, oddly, that she had begun to learn a lot more about him in his absence, and she felt a distinct prickle of pity for him.

It surprised her because pity wasn't an emotion she had ever expected to feel for Ross, he wasn't a man one would imagine ever needing it, but, watching his tense profile, compassion was what she did feel. Ross was trapped and unhappy. Did he suspect how Liz felt about him? Or did he think that his feelings were not returned? Liz had been so angry when she talked about Ross that Melanie was sure that Liz didn't realise that Ross was seriously attracted to her; she had put his pass down to something very different. She had been hurt, humiliated, distressed by that moment on the roof garden of Brenda's flat. It had made her think that Ross was promiscuous and a flirt, without scruples, and Liz had hardened towards him after that. Melanie had picked up anger and pain in her voice when she stood in the doorway of the drawing-room looking at Ross. Poor Liz, she thought, frowning.

Suddenly it occurred to her that she might be in a better position to understand Liz and Ross than they could yet understand themselves—or each other.

It was a weird sort of irony. She was the third point of their triangle; from her angle she could see them clearly now, she was convinced of that. Each of them might imagine they could see her, but they simply didn't see each other. They were both too busy hiding how they felt, and in assuming those disguises they not only hid from each other, they no longer saw her, at all; they saw the image of her they had invented.

She watched Ross through lowered lashes, face thoughtful. He thought she was in love with him, didn't he? He was afraid of hurting her by telling her the truth. And Liz's feelings were even more complex because she would never take Melanie's man away from her knowingly, yet at the same time she had got the impression that Ross was a worthless flirt and not good enough for her cousin.

No wonder she was in such a state after she told me about the pass he had made at her! Again she thought: poor Liz!

The sun gleamed on the fells, glinted on the slates of Kendal as they approached the town. Ross seemed to have nothing to say, brooding in silence as he began looking for a parking place close to the riverside restaurant.

They were the first customers to arrive; the restaurant had just opened and the place was empty. They were able to get a good table by the window in the bar and the waiter immediately brought them menus and asked what they would like to drink. Melanie ordered a Snowball; Ross asked for Scotch on the rocks.

'I didn't touch a drink while I was in Bahrain,' he said, grimacing. 'It's quite a relief to get back home. I'm only just beginning to get the taste of sand out of my mouth.'

Considering him, she noticed the sunburn flush on his nose and cheeks. 'You caught the sun.'

'Unavoidably,' he murmured. 'The minute you

get off the plane it beats on your head like a gong. How was the weather in the Lakes?'

'Changeable.' She met his eyes. 'Ross, before you went to Bahrain I tried to talk to you about our engagement . . .'

'I remember,' he said, his face wary.

'Can we talk about it now?'

He looked away from her at the sunlit, flowing river. 'You said something about not feeling you knew me well enough to marry me.'

'Yes.'

His face was expressionless. What was he thinking? She had a spasm of impatience with him—was he going to let her do all the work? Couldn't he see how difficult it was for her to break their engagement without giving a reason? Or did he believe that she had a reason in his own behaviour, the distance he had put between them over the last few months? Ross wasn't the type to find it easy to pretend, to act a part he no longer felt. If he regretted asking her to marry him yet couldn't bring himself to admit as much, he might be sitting there now hoping that she would do all the difficult work for him. She couldn't decide whether that was cowardice or kindness; whatever it was, it made it hard for her.

'We got engaged so fast,' she said. 'We hardly knew each other.'

The waiter appeared again and she bit down on her inner lip. Ross didn't betray any impatience by so much as a flicker. He glanced at her politely.

'Ready to order?'

Melanie ordered a simple meal—iced melon and salmon mayonnaise. Ross had the melon, too, and then a rare steak. He ordered a wine he knew she liked and the waiter took the menus and vanished. Some more guests were arriving, local businessmen in sober suits who paused to inspect the cold buffet table in the centre of the room before clustering around the bar to order drinks. The restaurant was filling up, and she would have to talk in a lower voice unless she wanted to be overheard.

Ross drank some of his Scotch, then said, 'What do you want to do about it?'

For a second Melanie didn't realise what he meant, she looked at him blankly, then flushed. 'Oh . . . well . . . don't you think we should put off any talk of marriage, Ross? I mean . . .' Her mind was suddenly confused, she didn't know what she had meant.

'Postpone our marriage, you mean?' Ross suggested evenly, watching her.

How could you ask a man you were two months away from marrying if he really loved you? It wouldn't be so hard if she knew for certain that his answer would be no. That would make it all simple. But what if he looked her in the eye and said that of course he loved her. What did she do then?

When she didn't answer, Ross said in the same calm voice, 'Of course we can, if that is what you want. There's no rush. Take all the time you need to think it over.'

She picked up her glass and drank some of the yellow foamy drink, trying to work out how to answer. She hadn't intended a postponement; she had meant to give him back his ring and end their engagement altogether, but Ross had made that impossible.

A bewildered qualm hit her—had she read the situation wrongly? Had she jumped to crazy conclusions about how he and Liz felt? Was Ross still serious about wanting to marry her, after all?

She turned and watched the shadows under the

bridge; sleek and dark in motion, the water surged into them until she couldn't see it any more.

Anxiety tightened her stomach. Whatever Ross really felt, she knew that she did not love him. The certainty was as cold as lead inside her. The dazzled excitement of her first weeks of knowing him had faded, long ago. She wasn't in love with him but she liked him too much to risk hurting him if she was wrong about how he felt.

The waiter came over, smiling. 'Your table is ready when you are, sir.'

'Are we ready?' Ross asked her politely.

She nodded, getting up, and they followed the man across the restaurant towards a table for two by the window on the far side. Suddenly Melanie heard Ross draw a thick breath, stiffening. Puzzled, she glanced up at him. He was staring towards the door, a dark wash of colour flowing up his face.

Melanie followed his stare and her own nerves jumped as she saw Liz walking towards them with Jamie Knox.

'What the hell is Knox doing with Liz?' Ross muttered.

Melanie's dark blue eyes widened until her skin stretched painfully. Ross must have heard her gasp because he looked down at her, frowning.

'You know him?' she said incredulously. Jamie hadn't mentioned ever meeting Ross.

'We've met,' Ross said curtly. 'How do you and Liz come to know him?'

Before she could answer the other two were in earshot and Ross shot them a hard stare.

Liz looked sleekly elegant in a burnt-orange jersey dress which Melanie had never seen her wear before, it must be new.

Summoning a smile, Melanie said, 'Hallo, fancy seeing you here!'

'It's a small world,' Liz said coolly, but the brown eyes that met Melanie's held a glint of defiance. Was it pure coincidence that she and Jamie had turned up? Yet how could they possibly have known that Ross would bring her here? And why should they follow them, anyway?

'You look very chic—I haven't seen that dress before,' said Melanie, her eyes questioning.

Liz gave a wry little grin. 'That's because it's new—I only bought it this morning, and Jamie decided it deserved to go somewhere special.'

The two men were eyeing each other without any pretence of cordiality.

Ross nodded curtly. 'Knox!'

Jamie's smile held cold mockery. 'Ellis.' His tone deliberately mimicked Ross.

Melanie stared pointedly at Jamie—why hadn't he told her that he actually knew Ross? They had talked enough about him, heaven knew, so why had Jamie been so secretive?

He slid a sideways look at her, his dark eyes glinting, as if her astonishment and annoyance amused him. He had changed, too; he was wearing a crisp red and white striped shirt and a dark red silk tie. His suit was dark grey and made him seem taller, but it couldn't tame the wildness of those black eyes and the thick black hair. Even in these civilised and formal surroundings Jamie Knox carried an air of danger with him like private oxygen.

The waiter hovered politely, Ross glanced at him then said, 'I'm afraid we have to go—our table's ready.'

'See you later,' Jamie said drily, not to him, but to Melanie, who looked back at him without warmth. When she got a chance she was going to make him explain why he hadn't told her he knew Ross.

She sat down at the table, the waiter deftly laid her napkin across her lap with a faintly theatrical gesture, and a moment later the melon arrived and she and Ross began to eat.

'How long have you known Knox?' he asked her, his fair head bent. She looked uneasily at him.

'Oh, not long. I met him at Ullswater.'

He looked up. 'Last weekend?'

She nodded and ate some more of the cool, greeny-yellow melon; the refreshing taste did little to calm her overheated nerves. She hadn't looked towards the bar but she was aware of Liz and Jamie in there, drinking champagne—she had heard the little explosion of the cork coming out, Liz laughing. What were they celebrating? she wondered edgily.

Ross was frowning. 'And Liz? When did she meet him?'

'The same weekend.' Melanie wondered if she ought to tell him now that she had spent a night marooned in an isolated hut on the fells with Jamie Knox. Somehow she couldn't; if it had seemed fraught with difficulties at first, such a confession now would be ten times harder, because Ross very obviously did not like Jamie, and the feeling was clearly mutual. Jamie did not like him.

Ross looked towards the bar. 'He's a fast worker.' It was said with cold anger and Melanie followed his gaze. Jamie faced her, a glass of champagne in his hand. He raised it mockingly, smiling, and Melanie looked away.

'Yes, isn't he?' she said. Ross didn't know how fast or how unscrupulous.

Ross shot her a probing look. 'What do you know about him?'

Startled, she shook her head. 'Nothing much—he lives at Ullswater, he has a red sports-car and at the moment he hasn't got a job.'

Ross smiled tightly. 'Because I sacked him,' he said and Melanie almost choked on her melon. Coughing, she reached for her glass of white wine and drank a little. When she could speak again she asked, 'What did you say?'

'He used to work for me,' Ross repeated. 'He's a brilliant engineer, I certainly couldn't fault his work, but we didn't see eye to eye about certain things, so he had to go.'

Staring at him, Melanie asked, 'What didn't you see eye to eye about?'

Ross frowned. 'We were offered a huge contract by a certain country. Knox felt we shouldn't sign it; he disliked the government in question. He was entitled to his opinion, that wasn't why I sacked him—but he went too far, he tried to drum up support among members of my board, sent each of them a letter giving his views in rather lurid language. There was a good deal of trouble and several directors came out in his support. I couldn't sign the contract while the board was split like that, but before I could talk them round it got to the ears of the other people; they were very offended and withdrew the contract altogether.' He finished his melon and flung down his table napkin with an angry gesture. 'Knox cost the company millions of pounds. When his contract came up for renewal at the end of the year, I didn't take it up.'

'He didn't tell us anything about that,' Melanie said slowly. Or had he told Liz? They seemed to have become very confidential in a very short time. Liz had told him that Ross had made a pass at her.

Had she told Jamie because he had just told her why Ross had fired him?

'You don't surprise me. Knox is mischievous and irresponsible.'

Melanie stared at Ross, her dark blue eyes sombre. When she realised that he and Jamie knew each other, she had thought at first that Jamie hadn't told her because he was being mischievous, but his reason for silence had been rather more worrying. Jamie had a grudge against Ross; bitterly disliked him. He had wilfully misled her—why? Had he planned to use her as some sort of weapon in a revenge on Ross?

The waiter removed their plates and began to serve their main course, so for a while they hardly said anything.

Melanie ate her cold salmon and creamy mayonnaise without really tasting either; she left just under half of the meal, pushing the food around her plate idly, her mind angrily busy.

Once when she looked up she found Ross watching Liz and Jamie being shown to their table on the other side of the room. Ross looked grim, his grey eyes shadowed.

Melanie wished she could be sure what she was seeing—she no longer felt able to guess at anybody's motives, anybody's real feelings. There was no solid ground under her feet. Her ears beat with hypertension and her mind kept dissolving into endless, unanswered questions.

It seemed that Ross had some questions of his own. Leaning forward he asked abruptly, 'You didn't say how you came to meet Knox at Ullswater.'

Melanie hesitated, but she was so sick of hiding things, keeping back the full truth.

'I went fell climbing while I was there and got

trapped in heavy mist. He came to find me. We couldn't get down again, you couldn't see a yard ahead, so we had to spend the night in a hut up there.'

Ross sat there staring. 'Alone?'

She swallowed, nodding.

Ross held her eyes, his face hard. 'I see.'

'I doubt if I'd have found it on my own,' Melanie stammered. 'The hut, I mean. I vaguely knew there was one but in that mist . . . and I'd hurt my ankle, I could only hobble. He was a real survival expert; I was very grateful for his help. He made a fire and found straw to sleep on and he . . .' Her voice trailed off. 'He may not actually have saved my life. I don't think it was ever in danger. But all the same, I was very glad he was there.' Even to please and placate Ross she wasn't going to lie about that. Whatever Jamie's reasons for coming to find her—and she strongly suspected them now—she had to be grateful for what he had done for her.

'Of course,' Ross said, but those cool grey eyes asked other questions which she certainly couldn't answer, because even to admit she knew what was in his mind would be some sort of admission. Not of guilt, necesssarily, but of awareness. Jamie hadn't tried to make love to her that night. She could look Ross in the eye and tell him so truthfully. But something serious had happened while they were alone in the mist and rain, and that she could not talk to Ross about. Jamie Knox had got under her skin; he was there now, needling, infuriating, tormenting, driving her crazy.

Ross looked down, his brows level, then looked up again. 'Were your aunt and uncle worried?' The question was casual but his eyes were far from casual, and she couldn't meet them.

'They only heard about it when I got back safely.'

'And how did they react to the news that you'd spent a night alone with Knox?' Ross murmured, pushing his own reactions on to Aunt Dolly and Uncle Teddy.

She forced a smile; at least that made it easier for her to answer.

'Oh, they didn't get over-excited. They know me; I'm not stupid.'

'I wouldn't have thought Liz was stupid, either.' Ross said, glowering across the room at that other table. Jamie and Liz were just getting lobster Thermidor and were laughing like a couple of children. The sight of their enjoyment didn't seem to delight Ross, and it didn't do much for Melanie either. She felt stupidly excluded, shut out, watching them through a window. A glance at Ross made her supect that he felt the same.

'Ross,' she said.

He didn't take his eyes from the other two. 'Mmm?'

'We're not in love, are we?' she said gently.

That caught his attention, his head swung and he stared at her fixedly, turning dark red. 'What?'

Melanie gave him a wry, melancholy little smile. 'It was a mistake, wasn't it, for both of us?'

Ross swallowed, his throat moving convulsively, but he seemed struck dumb. She held his eyes, reading relief in them. The barrier that had hidden his real thoughts and feelings from her for months had gone. Ross watched her nod, still smiling.

'You should have said something. We might have gone ahead and got married and then we'd be in a mess,' she said.

Ross gave a sudden deep laugh, his hand moving over the table to take hers and hold it tightly.

'Melanie . . . what can I say?'

'Try the truth. I'd welcome it,' Melanie told him softly.

The flush on his face increased. 'I didn't want to hurt you, Melanie.'

'I know and I'm not. It dawned on me too, gradually.'

'Why didn't *you* say something long ago?'

'I'm a slow thinker,' she said, and he laughed.

'I don't believe it.' Then he stopped laughing and looked hard at her. 'You mean it? You really aren't hurt? I was afraid . . .'

'That you'd have to marry me, after all?' she teased. 'No, Ross, you can breathe again.'

He still looked concerned, uncertain, watching her intently. 'You aren't just saying this because you think . . . because you suspect I . . .'

'I'm saying it because I mean it, Ross. I'm very fond of you. I like you very much but I'm not in love with you. For a while I thought I was.'

'Yes, *I* thought *I* was!' he said quickly. 'You're so sweet and easy to love, Melanie. You're a very gentle person—maybe that's why I thought you were the wife I wanted. I'm not gentle. I'm afraid I'm far from gentle. In my world that's the last quality that's needed. I'm successful because I'm naturally tough. I've had to be. Throw me against a brick wall and I'd bounce.' He laughed shortly. 'Someone said that to me once, and he didn't mean it as a compliment.' He looked at her, grimacing.

'Jamie Knox?' she guessed, from his expression.

'Bull's eye. Jamie Knox.' Ross's upper lip curled angrily.

'I shouldn't let his remarks sting,' Melanie said in hidden irony at her own expense. She had let Jamie Knox's words sting her far too often; never again. 'He's not worth bothering about,' she added, and Ross shrugged.

'He had something that time, though. 'I've had to fight to get to the top of my business and I'd begun to feel it was time to relax, enjoy myself more, build some sort of private life for myself. I met you and you seemed purpose-built for me— exactly the sort of girl I'd had in mind.'

She looked startled and a little shocked, and Ross noticed that and gave her an apologetic smile.

'I know. It sounds like computerised dating, but I didn't stop to take a good look at how I was acting. I've got so used to seeing something I want, something I've had in mind, a big contract or a firm that might be useful to me, and just moving in on it fast and buying it up before anyone else can get to it first. That's business today, Melanie. You can't play gentlemanly games. You have to grab. So . . .'

'You grabbed me?'

'I'm sorry.'

'And then you realised you didn't want me after all?' She was glad she had realised she wasn't in love with him before she actually started to hear all this. If she had been emotionally involved it would have hurt to hear herself talked about with this ruthless neutrality, as a piece of property he had thought valuable but now no longer wanted.

Ross looked disturbed. 'I *have* hurt you. That was the last thing I wanted to do, I've really tried not to let you guess.'

'That was foolish. What sort of marriage would it have been? Hell for both of us. This way we part friends and one day we'll both be glad we came to our senses in time.'

He still held her hand. He look down at it and

only then did she realise it was the hand that bore his ring.

'Keep that, please, will you?' he said and she shook her head, horrified.

'Oh, no I couldn't—it's far too valuable, but I won't give it back here, we don't want people staring.'

'No, we don't,' he said, his eyes flicking briefly across the room and back to her again. He let go of her hand and leaned back in his chair, sighing heavily.

'My God, I feel tired. This sort of scene uses up more energy than a day on the Bahrain site. Melanie, Melanie, will you hit me if I say thank you?' His eyes held a wry smile.

'For letting you off the hook?' she teased. 'It's a relief, isn't it? Like letting go of a heavy weight.'

'For you, too?' He seemed tentative, surprised. They were actually talking to each other openly and easily without any more hesitation or wariness.

'I feel pounds lighter,' she said, laughing.

The waiter appeared and asked if they would like dessert but neither of them wanted anything else to eat. They had coffee and sat smiling at each other like happy idiots because there was no longer any need to watch every word they said; they could just be themselves at last and Melanie felt quite euphoric.

She hadn't breathed a word to Ross about Liz, hadn't asked him any questions or made any hints. Ross was entitled to his privacy. She wouldn't want to talk about Jamie Knox; not, of course, that she was emotionally involved with him, unless you counted wanting to hit him next time she saw him. She distrusted and disliked him but she would not want Ross to know just how passionate her dislike was, or Jamie, either, come to that. He might misinterpret it.

Jamie Knox was an easy man to hate. On that, she and Ross would be agreed, but she kept her silence.

When they got up to leave Jamie and Liz were at the coffee and brandy stage. Melanie fixed a billiant smile and waved to them from the door. They waved back, smiling too. She hoped Liz knew what she was doing. Playing with fire was a lethal game and Jamie Knox was a dangerous playmate. The minute the door had closed on her, she felt her smile wither and bitter aching start up inside her.

Ross gave her an anxious look as he slid her into the front seat of the Rolls. 'Are you okay?'

'Fine,' she said hurriedly. She was just fine—but breaking an engagement had its melancholy side even when it was an amicable arrangement, and she felt bleak and lonely as they drove back.

CHAPTER EIGHT

MELANIE was in bed but wide awake when Liz got home. Lying in the darkness, her mind frantically busy, Melanie heard Liz pause by her door and hurriedly shut her eyes in case her cousin looked into the room. She couldn't face talking to Liz at that moment. After a second or two, Liz tiptoed away and Melanie leaned on her elbow to look at the clock beside her bed. It was gone midnight. They couldn't have been in the restaurant until that hour! Where *had* they been?

She was in a strange frame of mind herself; seesawing between relief at having escaped from a marriage she had increasingly come to see as a potential disaster, and restless anguish over Jamie Knox.

He had consistently lied to her, by omission, right from the moment they met—what she guessed of his reasons made her bitterly angry and unhappy. He had been using her to get at Ross, hadn't he? Was that what he was doing with Liz now? Had he, too, guessed that Ross was attracted to Liz and far more serious about her than he had been about Melanie?

She should have picked up the vibrations between Ross and her cousin far earlier, but it hadn't even entered her head until Liz gave her that first clue by telling her how Ross had behaved at his secretary's party. Her unconscious had picked up some of the things Liz wasn't telling her, but she hadn't realised that for a time. It wasn't until she heard Liz and Ross speak to each other in that stiff, tense way that the truth clicked inside her head, and the whole picture flashed into focus.

Turning over, she shut her eyes tight, trying to get to sleep, but her mind wouldn't co-operate, it couldn't let go of consciousness. It had too much to process, to work out. It had been an eventful day, but then ever since she met Jamie Knox every day had been an eventful day. He was a catalyst; he caused crisis everywhere he went. What Ross had told her about him hadn't surprised her, once she thought about it. She could imagine Jamie Knox forcing his views on the board of directors, hammering away at them to get his own way, and she could imagine how furious Ross had been. He was possessive about his company; far more passionate about that than he had ever been about her. Jamie couldn't have hit him harder any other way—but had he been trying? Flirting with her, dating Liz—in his own way, Jamie was every bit as ruthless as Ross.

Thinking back over everything Jamie had said to her, she saw that he had been trying to turn her against Ross. He had wanted to see her engagement broken off.

She pushed her palms into her eyes to ease the ache behind them. She wouldn't think about him; he was beneath contempt. What sort of man would set out to wreck someone's life like that? His baffling behaviour was so much clearer, now. First chasing her, then Liz—oh, yes, she understood him now.

What had he said about Liz? 'She was going quietly crazy, she had to talk to someone . . .'

Liz had opened out to him because she needed to talk and Jamie had been only too happy to listen—Liz couldn't have guessed how happy! She had been handing him a weapon to use on Ross. Bitterness twisted Melanie's mouth. No doubt Jamie had been surprised when he met her and heard that Ross was going to marry her. She wasn't the type of woman he would have expected Ross to choose, and he had been right. Ross had for once made a mistake, moved too fast, leapt before he looked, and soon regretted it. Jamie had taken one look at Melanie and must have know that she was out of Ross's league, their relationship would never last. He hadn't been content to watch it founder; he had wanted to cause the wreck himself.

Then Liz had confided in him—and he had realised at once that she was far more Ross's type. Melanie had always been subconsciously aware of that, herself; her cousin's coolness towards Ross had puzzled her from the start. If she hadn't been blinded by her own feelings for Ross she would have paired them off in her mind. Once the first clue got to her, she had rapidly seen the truth.

Jamie Knox had caught on faster than she had, of course. She lay in the darkness, brooding on the tortuous complexity of that mind of his. He was clever, she had to give him that—but he had no scruples. He might be taking an interest in Liz now that he realised Ross was attracted to her, but he hadn't given up with Melanie. That might have puzzled her if she hadn't guessed that he was still applying his brand of pressure in the hope of getting her to break off her engagement.

He wanted to do Ross as much damage as he could, and he didn't care how he did it. Once he knew she had broken with Ross, he wouldn't bother with her any more.

Behind her closed lids danced a flickering series of pictures from earlier that evening—Liz and

Jamie drinking champagne, smiling at each other, talking intimately. How much of that had been acting—how much had been real? Was Liz more *his* type, too? It was probable, she thought grimly. Ross and Jamie Knox were hardly similar, yet they were both sophisticated and intelligent. Jamie might be using Liz, yet he might still enjoy being with her too.

How did Liz feel about him? Melanie's head was beginning to ache. She massaged it crossly with impatient fingers. She didn't find it hard to believe that Liz might fancy Jamie; he had the sort of instant sex appeal which was hard to define but even harder to resist. Melanie felt bleak as she remembered the way they had smiled at each other. It had all seemed so simple when she suddenly guessed that Ross and Liz were attracted to each other. In a flash she had imagined herself solving their problems by giving Ross his ring back, setting him free to go to Liz.

Like all simple plans, it was too good to be true. Ross was free but how did Liz really feel? Melanie had always been fond of her cousin, but she couldn't claim to have understood Liz or known much of what was going on in her head. Liz kept her secrets too well; she wasn't given to indiscretions.

If Liz and Jamie *had* begun an affair, that would complete Jamie's revenge plan, though, wouldn't it? He would have had a part in ending Ross's engagement and he would at the same time walk off with the girl Ross really wanted.

'Damn him,' Melanie whispered to the ceiling. She wished she could think of some equally cunning way of undermining Jamie Knox, but her mind wasn't as complex, she didn't have the Borgia touch he had. She might want to hit back at him, but she would never be able to go through with it.

It wasn't until she was drifting off to sleep that she realised that she had forgotten to give Ross his ring back, after all. She thought hazily about posting it to him, but it was so valuable—what if it got lost in the post? No, she must hang on to it until she saw him again, but first she must break the news to the family. Aunt Dolly was going to be very aggrieved; she had been eagerly looking forward to Melanie's wedding day.

Aunt Dolly and Uncle Teddy got back late on Sunday afternoon. They walked into a spotless house. Melanie had spent most of the morning in an orgy of spring-cleaning which made sure that there was no trace of the party left. She waited until her aunt and uncle had had a cup of tea before she broke the news about the gratecrashers and the broken window.

Aunt Dolly made choking noises, putting down her cup.

Uncle Teddy said: 'They did *what*?' but didn't wait for an answer. 'Did you call the police? Vandals, that's what they are, vandals. Did the police catch any of them?'

'We've had the window replaced,' Melanie said placatingly. 'But the police didn't catch anybody, I'm afraid.'

Her uncle stamped off to view the scene of the crime for himself, muttering ferociously. Aunt Dolly half rose to go too, but sank back.

'Never again. No more parties. I knew something would go wrong, it always does. Where's Will? Taken himself out of the way, I suppose? Afraid to face us?'

Melanie gave her a weak smile; Aunt Dolly

knew her son. Will had gone off on his motor-bike early that morning.

'Where's Liz?' Aunt Dolly asked and Melanie looked away, afraid for some reason of what her eyes might betray.

'She's out, too.' Liz had gone before Melanie came down—Will said Jamie Knox had come for her in his fast red sports-car.

Uncle Teddy came down, grim-faced. 'It was a mistake to go away and leave them to it,' he said. 'Never again.' His wife nodded, her lips tight, in total agreement with him.

Melanie saw that in their over-excited state it would be a serious error of judgment to tell them her other startling news. Aunt Dolly had had enough shocks for one day. The revelation that Melanie's engagement was over would have to wait until tomorrow night when they would have had a chance to get over the story of Will's party.

'Where's Liz?' asked Aunt Dolly again later, and Melanie said that she didn't know. She decided not to mention Jamie Knox; she wasn't sure she could talk about him without sounding bitter.

'Is she playing chicken, too?' Uncle Teddy asked wryly. 'Did they leave you to break the news, Melanie? Isn't that just like them?'

Melanie didn't tell them that Liz had other things on her mind and had probably forgotten all about her brother's party. They would soon find out. It looked as if Jamie Knox was going to become a semi-permanent landmark in their lives.

She went to bed early that evening. Liz and Will hadn't come home. When Melanie came down to breakfast next day she found her aunt and uncle giving Will a bad time. He was sulkily eating cornflakes and trying not to listen, a difficult feat when Aunt Dolly was in such operatic voice. She

had a lot to say on the subject of parties, drinking,
window-breaking, fighting and anything else that
occurred to her and was on her banned list.

Will was glad to get to work, and bolted as soon
as he had finished eating, leaving his mother
triumphantly in possession of the field.

Melanie had a tiring and difficult day in the
office. She had a pile of typing to get through and
the phone kept ringing; clients came in a steady
stream, wanting details of houses up for sale or
asking her to send someone out to give them an
estimate for their own home, and she seemed to be
running from the moment she arrived at work until
the stroke of five-thirty when she could at last shut
the front office. George Ramsden and his son were
back from a lengthy inspection of an estate possibly
coming up for auction by the time she was putting
on her jacket to go home.

'I've left some notes on your desk, Mr Ramsden.
I think Mrs Silvester has definitely decided to buy
the Market Square property. I said you'd ring her.
There were quite a few calls and several new
clients with houses to sell, but I've left a list.'

Mr Ramsden patted her shoulder. 'Thanks,
Melanie. Off you go and you can take the morning
off tomorrow. Andrew and I will be here all day,
and I owe you some time off.' He preferred to
give her the occasional morning off rather than pay
her overtime. Melanie smiled wryly, nodding.

'Thank you.' Ever since she had locked the outer
door she had been working intensely to finish the
typing she hadn't done during the day. It was now
six-thirty and she had been at work since a quarter
to nine. Sometimes she thought she had picked the
wrong job, but on the other hand Mr Ramsden
was a kind and likeable man, even if he expected
you to work very long hours. At least she had a

job, she thought, walking towards her parked car.
These days that wasn't something you took for
granted.

She unlocked her car and got behind the wheel,
her shoulders wearily slumped. A bath, a hot meal
and bed were high on her agenda for the evening.
She switched on the ignition and frowned. There
wasn't a flicker from the engine. She tried again;
still nothing.

It was five minutes before she admitted that her
car was as dead as a doornail. She got out again,
slamming the door. At this hour there was no
point in ringing the garage—they would have gone
home long ago. She would have to leave her car
here and get a taxi home.

As she locked the car door she heard the soft
purr of an engine and glanced sideways. A red
sports-car was slowing beside her.

Jamie leaned out, raising one brow. 'Having
trouble?'

Melanie was tempted to ignore him but it seemed
childish so she said curtly, 'My car won't start.'

He drew in to the kerb and braked, getting out,
long legs followed by a muscled body and windblown
black hair. She felt a tremor of resentment at his
height; he dwarfed her. If she ever did try to hit
him she would have to aim for his knees.

'Shall I have a look?'

It was a frail hope but she was so tired, she
couldn't be bothered to turn down any offer of
help, even from a man she loathed and detested.
Saving her face seemed, at that instant, less
essential than saving her energy.

She slid back behind the wheel, grateful for the
chance to sit down, while Jamie vanished under
the car bonnet, poking and prying into the engine
entrails. Melanie didn't have much hope that he

would get it started but he seemed confident that
he knew what he was doing. He was an engineer,
she thought, presumably he understood engines of
most kinds. All the same, she wasn't surprised
when he re-appeared with a faint smear of oil
across his cheek, slammed down the car bonnet
and came to her window, shaking his head.

'Not a chance of starting her, I'm afraid. You'll
have to have it towed away in the morning.' He
opened the door, standing back. 'Come on, I'll
drive you home.'

Melanie got out wearily, re-locked the door and
gave him a stiff smile. 'Thank you, but I'll take a
taxi.'

She began to walk away; he caught her arm.
'Don't be absurd. Why waste money on a taxi?'

Melanie's temper flared out of control. 'Because
I'd rather waste money than have you drive me
home!' She wrenched herself away and began
walking again, half expecting him to follow her
and mentally preparing her iciest brush-off if he
did.

She heard his car burst into life but he didn't
drive away; he kerb-crawled, leaning out.

'Get in, Melanie.'

She averted her face, quickening her pace. He
cruised along beside her, talking. 'Stop making a
fool of yourself. This is ridiculous, get in!'

'I don't want to talk to you, go away,' she said,
reaching the corner where she hoped to get a taxi.

What she had not anticipated was an interested
audience of teenage boys in jeans and bomber
jackets, standing outside a nearby café, smoking
and idly watching life go by. They all stared at
Melanie and her pursuing red sports-car. Their
wolf whistles and catcalls made her face burn, she
couldn't just stand there under that barrage, so she

crossed the road to get away and Jamie did a U-
turn in the road, slewing to a sudden stop in front
of her before she got to the other kerb.

Melanie gave up. He leaned over and opened
the passenger door and she got into the car,
ignoring the crude comments from the other side
of the road. Jamie accelerated away a second later.

'We made their day,' he said drily.

'You did, you mean! Why did you follow me
like that?' She was quivering with temper.

'I've been waiting for you,' he drawled and she
did a double-take, staring incredulously at him.

'Waiting for me?'

'For over an hour,' he expanded. 'You work
long hours—I hope they pay you well.'

'Why?' she asked huskily.

'If you work this hard you deserve to be paid
well,' he returned, but she knew he had understood
what she meant because his hard mouth betrayed
amusement.

'Oh, stop playing games!' she muttered.

'I haven't started yet,' Jamie mocked.

She counted to ten before she answered that
time. 'Why were you waiting for me?'

He halted at traffic lights and put his car into
neutral before reaching across her to pick up her
left hand. Startled, she watched him stare at the
glitter of Ross's engagement ring.

'So you're still wearing it!' He dropped her hand,
his face hostile.

'That's right, I am,' she said resentfully. She
didn't see why she should tell him that she had, in
fact, broken off her engagement. That was what he
wanted to hear, of course, but he wasn't hearing it
from her. He would find out sooner or later, he
could do his gloating then, and with any luck she
wouldn't have to watch him do it.

'After what Liz told you?' he asked contemptuously.

'What right do you think you have to discuss my private life with Liz?' she burst out angrily. 'Or with me, come to that? I don't want to talk about Ross.'

'You prefer to shut your eyes to the sort of guy he is, and cling to the thought of all that lovely money, do you?'

She took a sharp, painful breath, turning pale at the insult. She couldn't sit in this car to listen to this—she fumbled with the door handle, intending to get out, but the light turned green at that second and Jamie put on a burst of speed as he moved off, giving her a derisive look.

'You're not getting away from me until you've heard what I have to say!'

She sank back into her seat, fighting to hold on to her temper.

'Did you even talk to him about it?' Jamie asked.

She wouldn't answer; she threw back a question of her own. 'Was it mere coincidence that you and Liz turned up at that restaurant the other day?'

'No,' he admitted calmly. 'I knew it was one of his favourite haunts, that's why I picked it.' He gave her a wry look. 'And it wasn't a coincidence that your car didn't start just now, either.'

Melanie's mouth rounded in a gasp. 'You . . .?'

'Fixed it,' he said with apparent complacency. 'I wanted to talk to you and I had a strong feeling I wouldn't get anywhere if I rang you and asked you out.'

'You put my car out of action?' It hadn't even entered her head that that might explain his sudden appearance at such an opportune moment. Surprise gave way to anger. 'It would serve you right if I rang the police, and I may well do it, too,' she said furiously. 'Who do you think you are? Meddling with everything like that . . . following me and Ross about, flirting with Liz, spiking my car . . . no wonder Ross sacked you, you must have been a thorn in everybody's flesh.' That reminded her and, working herself up into a towering rage, she demanded, 'And why didn't you tell me that you used to work for Ross and that he'd fired you?'

His dark eyes flicked sideways. 'I didn't want to confuse the issue.'

'You mean that you didn't want me to know that you had a grudge against Ross!'

'It did occur to me that you might misinterpret the news,' he admitted coolly.

'Oh, I haven't misinterpreted it,' Melanie snapped. 'I get the picture only too clearly—you've been trying to use me to get back at Ross. That's why you're so eager for me to break off my engagement. You don't care what you have to do, or how low you have to stoop, so long as you get your revenge! All those cheap gibes about me . . . implying that I'm mercenary and that the only reason I got engaged to Ross was because of his money!'

Jamie braked suddenly and she almost went through the windscreen, her body flung forwards violently.

Turning towards her, he asked harshly, 'Are you in love with him? Are you? Be honest, Melanie— look me in the eye and tell me you're in love with him and I'll shut up and go away.'

CHAPTER NINE

MELANIE was filled with a sense of angry hurt. There hadn't been so much as a flicker of regret or apology in his face. He had simply brushed aside her accusations without even trying to deny them. He didn't care what she thought. All he wanted—all he had ever wanted—was to come between her and Ross. That was all she had meant to him from the day they first met—a weapon to use in his war against the man who had sacked him.

'I . . . I'm not g-going to tell you anything,' she said, stammering in helpless rage, her face white and tense. 'I don't want to talk to you. Take me home.'

'Not until you've faced up to the truth,' he said grimly.

'Then I'll walk!'

She swivelled to get out of the car; he caught her shoulder in a grip that made her flinch and flung her round to face him again, leaning over her with those hard dark eyes fixed on her in a hostile stare.

'You're making a bad mistake, Melanie. This dream world you've built for yourself is going to crumble one day, and when it does you're going to find yourself trapped in a painful mess.'

'That's my affair, not yours!'

'He's no more in love with you than you are with him,' Jamie went on brusquely.

'Oh, why won't you shut up?' she wailed like a

142

child, but the emotions she felt were far from
childhood, far from anything she had ever known
before—a painful mixture of feelings which like
some roughly shaken cocktail seemed to be
exploding in her body. How was it possible to
dislike someone and feel an intense physical
attraction all at once? Close to him in the car, she
felt her senses work violently. Her cooler mind
couldn't stop the process.

'You know I'm telling the truth,' Jamie said, his
mouth twisting. 'That's why you're so desperate to
stop me.'

'Let me go, you're hurting me!' she said, trying
to break his hold.

'At least that's a genuine feeling,' he said. 'If
I'm hurting you, and you can feel it, that should
tell you something about the way you really feel
about Ross Ellis. You're alive now; you know I'm
holding you. When you're with him you look like
someone sleep-walking, and I'm afraid you're going
to sleep-walk into marriage with him and right
over a precipice.'

Trembling, she said, 'Ross and I understand each
other—we don't need you to act as go-between.'

'Don't be such an obstinate little fool,' he broke
out, shaking her. 'I want . . .'

'I know what you want!' she interrupted angrily,
and then there was a charged silence while they
stared at each other, and Melanie began to feel a
peculiar languor; her throat seemed hot and dry,
she couldn't breathe properly.

'Do you?' Jamie asked softly, holding her eyes.
His head swooped, caught her mouth, the pressure
sending her head back against the seat of his car.
Melanie fought against a dizziness which made her
want to shut her eyes; the feel of his mouth had a
sensual warmth that sent slow waves of pleasure

through her body. She couldn't think clearly, couldn't keep her mouth closed in spite of her struggle to do so, and her lips parted, yielding and heated.

Jamie wasn't holding her shoulders any more. His hands had travelled, begun exploring; she felt them moving over her body and a harsh groan broke from her. She tried to shake her head, push him away, but his mouth insisted and with that provocative invitation constantly tempting her, her struggles died away and Jamie took her wrists and placed her arms around his neck.

'Kiss me,' he whispered, his lips moving on hers.

Her mind drowned; her body consented, their mouths clinging and the tremors of wild need making her shake from head to foot. Ross had never kissed her like that, never aroused the dormant instincts she was only just discovering existed deep inside her.

Jamie lifted his head a few moments later, breathing thickly. Melanie's fingers were in his thick black hair, her bruised mouth aching as his lips left it, her body quivering passionately, arched against him.

Drowsily, her lids quivered, lifted, the dark blue eyes looked at him in glazed confusion.

'Now tell me you've ever kissed him like that,' he said, staring at her without a smile, and the words were like a slap in the face.

There had been something dreamlike about the caresses they had just exchanged; she had let herself slip helplessly into a fantasy and the awakening was painful. Her face burned in shame and realisation.

She couldn't get out a syllable; her throat was clogged with the dryness of ashes.

'That's why you've got to break off your

engagement,' Jamie said harshly, watching her like an enemy. 'You couldn't kiss me like that if you loved him any more than he would have tried to kiss Liz if he had been in love with you.'

He had been proving his point in a brutal fashion. What did he care if he left her feeling shame and self-contempt?

She sat up, tidying her ruffled hair with shaking hands, turning her flushed face away, hiding the brightness of tears welling up behind her lids.

'Take me home,' she said hoarsely.

Staring intently, Jamie made a rough sound of disgust. 'You mean you still refuse to face the truth? What does it take to get through to you? Don't you understand . . .'

'I understand that you hate Ross and you're trying to use me to get back at him, but it won't work. I'm not being used as a weapon. Just stay away from me in future. I never want to see you again. I don't like you and I don't trust you, so stay out of my life.' Her voice had risen with each word; high and shaky, it was close to tears. With a wild gasp she threw the last words at him, 'Take me home, for God's sake!'

He swung round in his seat, started the ignition and shot away; his profile had frozen into glowering silence. Sitting next to him was like sitting under the very core of a thunderstorm before it breaks—there was no lightning flash, no crash of thunder, but darkness and threat concentrated far too close at hand.

He pulled up outside her home and she stumbled out of the car without saying a word. Jamie only waited for her to slam the door; the next minute he was racing away with a roar of exhaust.

Melanie walked slowly into the house and heard her aunt and Liz talking in the kitchen. She didn't

go in to see them, she went straight up to her
room and shut the door on herself quickly before
anyone could see her face. She stood listening to
the over-rapid thudding of her heart, shivering as if
in an icy wind. Jamie had proved his point, even if
she hadn't admitted it to him, and she was bleakly
facing up to the truth, even if it wasn't the truth he
had wanted her to face. She was in love with him;
she must have been falling in love ever since she
first met him. She hadn't wanted to admit it, but
just now, in his arms, her reluctant mind had
finally caught up with her senses.

It was chemistry, she told herself angrily. That
was all it was: mere chemistry. She didn't like
Jamie Knox, he was unscrupulous, prepared to use
people—the way she responded to him had nothing
to do with real love.

'Melanie?' The tap on her door made her jump.
She hurriedly dragged a smile into her face before
answering Liz.

'Yes?' She wished she could confide in Liz, but
she knew she couldn't. She had to lock it all away,
never tell anyone. She could only cope with it if
she pretended it hadn't happened. After all, it
might be another stupid mistake, she might fall out
of love as suddenly as she had fallen into it.

'Can I come in?' Liz asked.

'Of course,' Melanie said, hurriedly looking in
the mirror and appalled by her own reflection. She
was so flushed; she looked hectic. She smoothed
down her ruffled hair, and saw the gleam of Ross's
ring on her hand. Taking it off she laid it on the
dressing-table.

The door opened, Liz came in, smiling. 'Why
didn't you come and say you were home? I thought
I heard you running upstairs.' Her eyes widened as
she saw the discarded ring.

'I'm just coming down,' Melanie said, moving towards the door.

'You've left your ring on the dressing-table.'

Melanie met her cousin's eyes. 'I know.'

Liz turned pale, her lips parting but no sound emerging.

'The engagement's off,' Melanie said.

'Oh, no,' Liz said on a gasp. 'Melanie, you didn't break it off because of what I told you? I'll hate myself. You've got to forget what I said; it didn't mean anything, he didn't do it again. He was drunk.'

'I'm glad you told me. It made it all much easier.' Melanie saw that her cousin wasn't convinced by that. Liz looked almost anguished, her eyes guilty and distressed. Smiling at her, Melanie said, 'You don't understand—Ross and I talked frankly, for the first time and we both admitted we weren't in love, it had all been a mistake.'

Liz looked bleakly at her, wincing. 'Did he tell you that? That he didn't love you? Oh, God, Melly, I'm so sorry, I blame myself . . .'

'You aren't listening properly,' Melanie said, smiling at her. 'I don't love him, either, Liz, and stop looking at me in that guilty way. You did me a favour, honestly. If it wasn't for you I might have married him. I wasn't in love with him at all.'

'You must have been when you got engaged!' Liz sounded incredulous.

'He turned my head,' Melanie said wryly. 'I'd never met anyone like him; he's glamorous and sophisticated and I felt like Cinderella, but it was all a fantasy—a fairy tale. I didn't really know Ross. Jamie Knox said something to me that put it in a nutshell—he said I was sleep-walking, and that's exactly what I was doing. I was going around with my eyes wide open, but I was dreaming. Now I've woken up, and I can see what a mistake I would have made.'

Liz sat down abruptly on the chair behind her. 'You sound very sure,' she said slowly.

'I am,' Melanie said, curling up on the carpet beside her, knees up and her chin resting on them. 'What you told me about Ross making a pass at you didn't actually start the process in my mind, Liz—it was the flashpoint, if you like. I'd been worried about Ross and myself for ages. I never seemed to get to know him any better. I saw so little of him. He seemed to be reluctant to talk to me. Even when we did go out it was always somewhere public—a restaurant for dinner, the theatre, a cinema. I was slow to work it out, but it dawned on me that Ross was keeping me at a distance.'

Liz still looked worried. 'He hurt you . . .'

'No, Liz, he didn't because he couldn't,' Melanie said firmly. 'I was worried, not hurt. After all, we were supposed to get married soon and I was facing up to the prospect of being tied to a man I hardly knew. How could I be in love with him if I couldn't even guess what he was thinking? I tried to tell him; I wanted to talk it out before he went to Bahrain, but Ross was just as evasive then. Of course, he was worried, too, although I didn't realise it. He knew he'd made a mistake but he was too scared of hurting me to tell me so. It was stupid of him, and if we had got married it would all have been much worse. Sooner or later, we'd have had to face up to it.'

Liz was beginning to relax, her face smoothing out into its usual calm. 'Divorce *is* much messier than a broken engagement,' she said drily.

'And far more expensive,' Melanie agreed, laughing.

Liz sobered a moment later. 'When did you tell Ross?'

'We talked it over frankly at lunch in Kendal on Saturday.'

Liz stared. 'On Saturday? But you didn't give him back his ring?'

'It seemed a little public to do it there and then. I meant to give it back in the car later, but it slipped my mind.'

Liz watched her thoughtfully. 'You both seemed very cheerful. It never entered my head that you were discussing breaking your engagement. Whenever I looked over, you were both smiling.'

'We were euphoric with relief,' Melanie said gaily. 'I'm not sure how Ross felt, but I felt like someone breaking out of prison. Do you realise— marriage is a life-sentence?'

Liz laughed. 'You're sure Ross feels the same? I mean, you did ask if he . . .'

'I asked point-blank—we had both been skirting the issue for too long. Ross isn't in love with me any more than I am with him.' She looked steadily at her cousin. 'Stop worrying. I know what I'm doing.'

Liz sighed. 'Jamie said neither of you was in love!'

Melanie's smile vanished. 'Jamie Knox,' she said through her teeth. 'That's something else I want to talk to you about. Did you know he once worked for Ross, and that Ross fired him?'

Liz nodded. 'Yes, he told me that first evening when he brought you home from Ullswater.'

'Did he? And did he tell you that he hates Ross like poison and is looking for a way of getting back at him?' Melanie was pink with anger at the very thought of Jamie Knox. 'Don't trust him, Liz; he'll use you if he can.'

Liz eyed her thoughtfully. 'You don't like him?'

'Do you?'

They stared at each other, their eyes guarded. Melanie couldn't tell what her cousin was thinking and she tried to keep all expression out of her own face.

Aunt Dolly called from the bottom of the stairs, making them both jump. 'Liz? Melanie? Where are you both? The dinner's on the table—aren't you coming down?'

Liz got up. 'Coming,' she called back, then gave Melanie a crooked little grin. 'She sent me to fetch you; it went right out of my head.'

When they went down, Aunt Dolly gave Liz an impatient look. 'Where on earth did you get to? I sent you to look for Melanie, not sit up there gossiping with her!'

Melanie intervened. 'I was telling Liz something . . .'

'Couldn't it wait? Now, come on, sit down and eat this food before it gets cold!'

Uncle Teddy winked at the two girls behind his wife's back. 'Hurry up before she starts on the speech about slaving over a hot stove,' he advised, and Aunt Dolly turned on him too, her blue eyes indignant.

'When I've cooked food, I want it to be eaten— I don't want it sitting about getting cold.'

'It isn't,' Uncle Teddy said, handing Melanie the tureen of vegetables. 'Sit down, Dolly, and stop getting agitated.'

Aunt Dolly subsided into her chair and Will mumbled something about the fried chicken being delicious and he was starving. His mother told him he was always starving, it simply wasn't fair the way he ate so much without putting on an ounce. Will protested, Uncle Teddy teased him, and in the ensuing family discussion it was some time before Aunt Dolly's normally sharp eyes noticed that Melanie was no longer wearing her ring.

It wasn't until Melanie helped her to collect the plates, in fact, that Aunt Dolly noticed her bare finger and gave a startled gasp.

'Melanie! Your ring!'

Melanie flushed slightly, conscious of the others watching her. Aunt Dolly didn't give her a chance to explain. She said in agitation, 'You haven't lost it? Did you take it off to wash? And it's so valuable . . . you shouldn't be careless about anything so valuable, Melanie. I wouldn't have a night's peace if it was mine, I'd always be scared of losing it.'

'Mum,' Liz said gently and her mother's head turned at the note of Liz's voice. 'Melanie has something to tell you.'

It was far harder than it had been when she amazed them all by breaking the news that she was going to marry Ross Ellis. That had been a moment of sparkle and excitement; a champagne day. Melanie could see now how deluded she had been by the sheer surprise of getting engaged to Ross. She had walked into a fairy tale, now she was walking out again. She felt nothing but relief, but she had a shrewd idea that Aunt Dolly wasn't going to be so happy.

She was quite correct; no sooner had she got the words out than Aunt Dolly dropped the plates she was clutching.

'Not going to marry him? What on earth do you mean, not going to marry him?'

Uncle Teddy watched his niece anxiously. 'If you've quarrelled with Ross, I'm sure that . . .'

'It isn't a quarrel, Uncle Teddy, you don't understand.'

'People don't just break off an engagement out of the blue, pet. Something must have happened.'

'We both realised it was a mistake, we don't want to get married,' she said, smiling at him. 'It isn't a disaster, Uncle. We've come to our senses, not lost them.'

'I'm not surprised,' Will said suddenly. 'I never thought he was Melly's type.'

Aunt Dolly turned on him crossly. 'What would you know about it?'

'Are you sure about this, Melanie?' Uncle Teddy asked, and she nodded.

Will had got a dustpan and brush and was on his knees sweeping up the broken plates. 'There's plenty more fish in the sea,' he said airily. 'You'll soon hook someone else.'

'Will Nesbitt, be quiet!' Aunt Dolly snapped, very flushed. 'What on earth are we going to do about the wedding arrangements? The vicar, the hall we booked . . . thank heavens we hadn't got around to having the dress made. And we'll have to tell the rest of the family, all our friends.'

'If Melanie doesn't love the man, there's no point in crying over spilt milk,' Uncle Teddy said. 'Better to find out before the wedding than afterwards.'

Aunt Dolly looked gloomy. 'I suppose so.'

'Don't worry, Mum, Melanie's not going to stay single for long,' said Will. 'I know plenty of guys who'd jump at a chance to date her.'

'Melanie can do better for herself than date one of the bike freaks you go around with,' said Liz drily.

Her brother bared his teeth at her. 'Just because

you're too old for any of the guys . . .' Liz laughed scornfully.

Aunt Dolly sighed. 'As long as you're happy, Melly, that's all I want. I suppose it wasn't meant to be, I did think he was a little old for you but I like him; Ross is a man I respect. I'm sorry it didn't work out for you two.'

'Pin your hopes on Will,' Liz said teasingly.

'Who'd marry Will?' Aunt Dolly retorted. 'Who in her right mind, that is?'

'You'd be surprised how many girls chase me,' Will said, very offended.

'Surprised?' mocked Liz. 'We'd be amazed!'

'A guy in black leathers, riding a high-powered bike, is a big sex-symbol, you know,' Will snarled, and they all laughed.

'Come and help me serve the rice pudding, sex-symbol,' Aunt Dolly said indulgently, and Will was glad to follow her into the kitchen, away from the teasing of his sister.

The weather descended into rainy autumn the following day. The skies were livid, grey clouds clustered, the leaves blew along the gutters, sodden and decaying. People hurried along the pavements, heads bent. Melanie sat at her desk, watching the rain trickling down the windows, listening to the moan of the wind. The weather matched her mood. She didn't know why she felt so depressed; she told herself it was the rain, but she knew she lied.

She tried to get in touch with Ross to arrange to give him back his ring, but he was away again, on business, and Brenda off-handedly said she had no idea when he would be back. Melanie wondered if he had told his secretary that the engagement was over. Brenda had never liked her, Melanie didn't mention anything personal. She just left a message, asking Ross to ring her.

All the rest of the week was the same—the rain was unceasing, there was a chill in the air, the trees lashed backwards and forwards in the wind. Melanie concentrated on her work, went home and watched TV or read until she went to bed, and got up each day feeling grey and melancholy.

On Sunday, though, the weather changed. Autumn vanished and the air was soft and warm, and the sun shone with a poignant fragility which lit the russet leaves and gave a hazy blue shadow to distance.

Over breakfast, Uncle Teddy said wistfully, 'We may not get another day like this until the spring—why don't we all go to the Lakes for the day? A family outing, like the old days? We haven't all been there for ages.'

Will and Liz agreed that it would be fun and Aunt Dolly started planning a picnic lunch to pack for them all, but Melanie hesitated, afraid of running into Jamie at Ullswater. She glanced at Liz secretly, frowning. Was Liz seeing him? She never mentioned him, but then Liz had always been secretive. Melanie felt a sharp little niggle of pain in her chest and bit her lip. She didn't want to find herself face to face with Jamie; it would hurt too much. She didn't want to have to watch him with Liz; that hurt, too. She wasn't jealous of Liz, she was too fond of her cousin—if Liz was happy she was glad, but it hurt, all the same.

'Do you mind if I don't come? I'm expecting a phone call and I'd rather just have a lazy day at home,' she said.

They tried to talk her into it, but she was gently obstinate and in the end they accepted it and went without her. Melanie felt the silence in the house settle like fine dust on her; her spirits sank. They had all looked so cheerful; she envied them. Would

Liz call on Jamie at his cottage, introduce him to her parents?

How wrong she had been about love, how blind when she thought the glamour and excitement of dating Ross meant that she was in love with him. She had believed that falling in love meant a dazzle of light, a sky full of fireworks, each brighter than the one before. The truth was that love was no fun; it was an ache, a deep throb of need, a longing.

She put her hands over her face, shuddering. All week she had been thinking about Jamie; he was never out of her mind. She must stop thinking about him, or she'd go crazy.

She went into the bathroom and began washing her hair, then wrapped it in a towel, turban-fashion, and sat on the edge of the bath while she painted her toenails a delicate pearly pink. Her concentration on this task was broken by a sound she heard downstairs. She froze, head lifted, listening intently, then became quite sure that her ears weren't playing tricks—there was someone downstairs, moving about very softly and furtively.

CHAPTER TEN

MELANIE crept to the bathroom door and opened it carefully, ready to jump back into the room if anyone was within view. She stood there for a second, listening. Was that a stair creaking? Or just her imagination? Her skin was chilly with nerves; she wasn't really certain she had heard anything. This was an old house, full of strange sounds, especially at night or when you were alone in it and instinctively listening to every tiny noise. When there were other people around, it never occurred to you to notice the creaks and rustles.

A minute later she jumped about ten feet in the air, gasping in shock, as a man in black appeared on the landing.

Melanie was back in the bathroom in a flash, but as she began slamming the door she did a double-take of recognition and pulled the door open again.

'You!'

Jamie Knox considered her drily. 'Sorry, did I startle you?'

She clutched the neck of her dressing-gown with a shaky hand, glaring at him with eyes still dilated from the shock of her first glimpse of him.

'Of course you startled me!' she snapped. 'I thought you were a burglar.' He was wearing black jeans and a black sweater with a smooth-fitting turtle neck. He had walked softly because he was wearing grey soft-soled trainers on his feet; it was surprising that she had heard anything at all.

'Sorry,' he said without any apparent regret and she scowled.

'How did you get in, anyway?'

'Through the kitchen door. You really shouldn't leave doors unlocked,' he said lazily, his eyes half hooded by those heavy lids as he studied her. Melanie felt he took too personal an interest in the way her dressing-gown clung to her warm body. She walked past him, bristling, and went downstairs.

'You had no right to walk in here,' she threw over her shoulder.

'Lucky it was only me,' Jamie said coolly. 'Anyone could have got in.'

'So I see,' she said with hostility, turning to face him at the bottom of the stairs. 'That still doesn't explain why you came in and started prowling about.'

'I rang the doorbell, but there was no response, so I went round the back of the house to see if you were in the garden.' He seemed quite unabashed, which made Melanie angrier.

'It would serve you right if I'd called the police when I heard odd noises downstairs!'

He grinned. 'Perhaps it will teach you to take more care in future.'

Her hands clenched at her sides. She felt like hitting him, but he made her too nervous to risk it.

'If you were looking for Liz, she's out,' she told him curtly.

His brows rose. 'All day?'

'Yes, all day.' Melanie felt a roughness in her throat as she watched him. She wasn't jealous, she told herself, she wasn't going to be jealous of Liz, she wouldn't let herself feel like that. What was she going to do if Liz married him, though? She couldn't bear it if they were living near here, if she had to see them together all the time. She would have to go away. It might be cowardice but how else could you deal with a situation like that?

'I see,' he murmured, and his dark gaze wandered over her from her turbaned head to her bare feet. It made her intensely self-conscious when his gaze lingered on her deep-lapelled dressing-gown. She put a hand up to drag her lapels together, to hide the warm curve of her bare breasts from him, and Jamie's eyes fixed on her fingers.

'You aren't wearing your engagement ring.'

She felt her flush deepening. 'I took it off to have a bath,' she evaded. It was stupid to lie but she resented the satisfaction she had heard in his voice. He wanted her to break her engagement to Ross but he didn't care about her feelings.

She saw his brows lift, his eyes harden. 'Seeing him today?'

'No,' she said, then wished she had told another lie. She ought to make him believe she was still seeing Ross.

'Where have your family gone?'

'Ullswater, to sail,' she said.

'You didn't want to go? I thought you loved sailing.'

'I do, but I felt like a quiet day.' She didn't meet his eyes; she didn't want him to guess that she had been afraid of running into him if she visited Ullswater.

'It's perfect sailing weather—a gentle wind and lots of cool sunshine.' Jamie wandered away down the hall and Melanie followed him, frowning.

'Now where do you think you're going?'

'Why don't we have some coffee? I've had a long drive and I'm dying for some coffee.' He calmly began filling the kettle while she watched him, helpless with fury.

'Make yourself at home, won't you?'

The sarcasm was water off a duck's back. He put the kettle on and began to get out two mugs and a jar of instant coffee powder. It was typical of him to do as he pleased without asking permission. Argument with him would be a waste of time and energy.

He turned his head to grin, sunlight striking off the smooth tan of his skin. She felt her heart thud with a crash that sent her nerves jumping, and her mouth went dry.

'I like this house. I gather your uncle and aunt have lived here since they were married.'

She nodded, sitting down abruptly because her knees were giving under her.

'I like old houses,' Jamie said, spooning coffee into the mugs. 'They have more personality than new ones.'

'Your cottage is old, isn't it?' she managed huskily, watching him switch off the kettle and begin to pour the boiling water into the mugs. His body had a vibrant elegance which riveted her stare. At each movement she saw the muscles in his long back flex and relax under the clinging cashmere sweater. His clothes were always good. How was he managing now that he had lost his job? From what Ross had said, she realised Jamie must have earned a considerable sum. Had he saved a lot of it?

'Yes, it's Georgian—but without the frills of the big Georgian houses. Mine is a workman's cottage, but it was built to last. Very solid walls. Almost no foundations, of course, which has meant that I've had trouble with creeping damp, but I've dealt with that problem.' He began to talk about building techniques with the expertise of someone who had studied them, and she listened as she drank her coffee. 'I once thought of being an architect,' Jamie

said. 'I enjoy building things, but my personal bent
was more towards larger projects—that's why I
became a civil engineer. I enjoy seeing a road run
where it never ran before, watching a bridge go up
over a river. If the underdeveloped countries are to
trade successfully, they need better communication,
more roads, more bridges. That's the aspect of my
work I enjoy the most.'

'Why did you quarrel with Ross over this contract
with a foreign government?'

He studied her coolly, his eyes narrowed. 'I
didn't like their politics or their reason for offering
us the job. I told Ellis my opinion and he told me
to mind my own business—company policy was his
province. I didn't agree with him. He might be the
boss, but that didn't mean the rest of us had no
right to an opinion on how the company was run.
So I canvassed the rest of the board openly. Ellis
was furious, of course.'

'The contract *was* worth a lot of money,' Melanie
said, and he grimaced.

'You think that that's all that matters?'

'I think it could hurt the whole firm if Ross only
took work from people he approved of,' she said
hesitantly.

Jamie gave her a wry smile. 'Maybe, but a lot of
people in the firm agreed with me, including quite
a few on the board. I think that that was one
reason Ellis dismissed me. He resented the fact
that I'd swung a lot of people over to my point of
view. He likes to keep the reins firmly in his own
hands. He doesn't like interference in his decisions.
So I had to go.' His eyes glinted. 'I got quite a
handsome settlement—he was afraid I'd sue him
and the publicity of the case could harm the firm,
so he gave me a golden handshake.'

Her eyes widened. 'Is that why you're in no hurry to find another job?'

'Partly. I've been working very hard for some years, I felt I was entitled to some time off before I started looking for new employment.'

'Won't you find it hard, though? I mean, if Ross gives you a bad reference?'

'I'm pretty well known in my own field. I've already had several approaches, but I'm not ready to make up my mind yet.'

'Would it mean working abroad again?' she asked, finishing her coffee and putting down the mug. If he married Liz, it would make it easier to bear if they lived abroad; Melanie wouldn't have to keep up an act all the time.

'That's the question,' he said, his face wry. 'I wouldn't want to, if it could be avoided. I've had enough wandering. When I was younger I had the travel-bug badly, I couldn't wait to get on a plane for new places. I must be getting old.' He grinned at her. 'How about you? Do you like travelling?'

'Not much,' she admitted. 'I'm happy living here—where else would you find such breathtaking scenery? This part of England is so rich in history, too—Hadrian's Wall, for instance. We used to take a picnic up there in the summertime and walk along the wall until we found somewhere peaceful where we could eat our lunch and look at the view. My father . . .' She broke off, her eyes lowered, and was silent for a second, until she went on huskily, 'He was very interested in Roman history.'

'It must have been a traumatic shock, when he and your mother were killed,' Jamie said gently and she nodded without looking at him. 'Liz said that you were badly injured yourself, in the crash.'

'I was ill for ages. I hated hospital. I've hated

the sight of white coats and the smell of disinfectant ever since.'

There was a silence, then she forced herself to look up and smile brightly.

'I was lucky to have Uncle Teddy and Aunt Dolly there—not to mention Liz and Will.'

'You're very fond of them. You'd miss them if you had to move away, wouldn't you?' Jamie said oddly, and she wondered if he was realising how much she would miss Liz if he married her cousin and took her abroad.

Flatly, she agreed. 'In many ways, they're closer than a real brother and sister. Liz and Will squabble with each other far more than they ever did with me. We're all very close.'

'That must be comforting,' Jamie said gently, watching her with warmth in his dark eyes. She felt a sharp pain inside her chest. He shouldn't smile at her like that; it wasn't fair. It hurt.

She got up suddenly. 'I have a lot to do today, I'm afraid—why don't you go back to Ullswater and find Liz?'

He got to his feet more slowly, his brows dark above his watchful eyes.

'Melanie . . .' he began and she was disturbed by the note in his voice. Turning, she began to hurry towards the door, but his hand caught her shoulder and spun her to face him. The way he looked at her made her pulses go crazy; she almost hated him for making her feel like that. He knew what he was doing; it was intentional, all part of his plan to get his own back on Ross.

'You must go,' she said thickly, shivering.

'You don't want me to go,' Jamie said in a low, deep voice, his other hand caressing her flushed cheek. If she had her eyes closed she would recognise the feel of his fingers on her skin, she thought dazedly, trying to back away from the incitement of that gentle touch.

'How can you?' she asked bitterly, turning her head to avoid his searching mouth. 'No, don't. I don't want you to kiss me.'

'Yes, you do,' he whispered against her cheek, that insistent mouth moving closer while she struggled to break away.

'You came here deliberately,' she accused. 'I wouldn't be surprised to find out that you knew I was alone—did you see Liz and the others at Ullswater? Did you guess I was here by myself?'

'Yes,' he said shamelessly, kissing her neck, and she might have guessed from the start if she hadn't been so taken aback to see him.

'What sort of man are you?' she asked angrily, throwing back her head to look at him with hatred, and that was a mistake because it gave Jamie the chance he had been waiting for.

His mouth hit hers a second later, and temptation caught her by the throat, her own desire overwhelming her common sense. His kiss weakened her resistance; she felt herself kissing him back, her body trembling violently. Chemistry, that's all it is, she told herself, but her senses drowned that cold little voice. She had her eyes shut, her head was thrown back, the towel tumbling off and her damp hair cascading down her back. Jamie pulled her even closer; one hand slid inside her dressing-gown and caressed her bare breasts. Her skin burnt, the intimacy of the touch driving her crazy.

Did it matter why he was making love to her? she thought wildly. What did anything matter, except that she needed to have him kiss her, needed to be in his arms, closer and closer in this drowning sweetness?

A second later the shrill of the telephone made

her jump. Jamie started, too, lifting his head and staring at her with glazed eyes, as if he had been as far away as Melanie while they kissed.

'Ignore it,' he said, as she began to pull free. He tried to kiss her again but she broke away and almost ran to the phone, her legs shaky.

'Hallo?' she asked huskily, holding the receiver in trembling fingers.

'Melanie, is that you?'

'Ross,' she said, shock in her voice and across the hall her eyes met Jamie's. He was scowling, his body tense, his hand raking back his dishevelled hair.

Melanie swallowed in dismay at the folly she had almost committed—Jamie had just been using her, he didn't have any real feeling for her. He just wanted revenge on Ross, and of course it mattered why he had tried to make love to her. She must have been insane even to consider letting him kiss her.

Ross was talking brusquely in her ear; she barely heard what he said. He had got her message but he wouldn't be back for some time. What did she want? Was it urgent?

'It doesn't matter, Ross,' she said. 'I'll see you when you get back, ring me the minute you do.'

She hung up and Jamie came towards her, his face hard. He opened the door without a word. The slam of it made her nerves flicker violently.

She ran upstairs and flung herself on her bed, weeping passionately. It was a long time before she was able to reach some sort of calmness, and it was the stoicism of despair by then. She had to face the fact that she was deeply in love with a man who had no scruples and no heart. For a time today as they talked she had liked him very much, but he had fooled her again. He was so easy to like and so dangerous to trust.

Never again, she thought, as she dressed and blow-dried her hair into shape. She would never let him get to her again.

When she saw Liz later that evening, she discovered that Jamie had gone back to Ullswater and that Liz and Will had had drinks with him at the pub, then the whole family had gone along to meet his parents at their home. Melanie felt a stab of jealousy at this news. He must be serious about Liz, or why would he take her to meet his parents? she thought miserably.

'I liked them,' Liz said. 'His father's a darling—very like Jamie. He was a sailor, did you know? They have a boat, bigger than ours. They seem very happy together. Their house is charming; small but delightfully furnished.'

Melanie forced a smile. 'Is it Georgian, too?'

She half listened as Liz talked about the Knox family, half fought an inner sense of grief because she hadn't met his parents, hadn't seen his home.

Damn Jamie Knox, she thought, how can he live with himself, acting the way he does? Doesn't it occur to him that I might tell Liz about the pass he made at me today? Or is he so sure of her that he thinks he could talk his way out of any accusation? But then he knows us so well now, he probably guesses that I couldn't tell Liz, any more than she wanted to tell me about the night Ross kissed her. I couldn't deliberately hurt Liz, any more than she could deliberately try to hurt me. I'm silenced by my affection for Liz, and Jamie Knox knows it.

'What a pity you weren't with us,' Aunt Dolly said. 'Jamie's parents were so disappointed; they were hoping to meet you.'

Melanie looked at her in disbelief and surprise.

She couldn't believe that Jamie's parents had even heard of her, but then Aunt Dolly's love for them all had always blinded her.

She was glad to get back to work on Monday morning; keeping busy was the best way of keeping her mind off Jamie Knox. As the week went by, she was surprised not to hear from Ross. He seemed to have been away a long time. She rang his office and Brenda was icily off-hand. Ross was still away; no doubt if he wanted to speak to Melanie he would have given her a call. As he hadn't, Brenda could only say that she had passed on Melanie's message, the rest was up to Ross himself. Flushed, Melanie rang off.

The following Friday Melanie was alone in the office when the bell fixed above the street door jangled. Melanie thought that it would be Mr Ramsden back from lunch with his bank manager. She looked up, smiling.

The smile died as she recognised Jamie Knox. She didn't move from her desk, her body rigid as she stared at him with hostility. He let his gaze drift over her, his brows arched as he took in the simple blue sweater, the pleated white skirt and all the other details of her appearance—she was made to feel that he had even noticed that her nose was shiny and her lips had only a faint trace of pale pink lipstick. The way she looked hadn't bothered her until that moment. She was a working girl; not a fashion model.

Now, though, faced with Jamie Knox in a casually elegant dark suit, crisp shirt, silk tie, she ground her teeth impotently under that derisory stare.

He tapped peremptorily on the counter. 'Miss!'

Melanie began to type again, ignoring him.

'Excuse me, miss,' he said, leaning over the

counter, a lock of thick black hair falling over his eyes. He looked like an Old English sheepdog after a heavy night, she though viciously. Aloud, she said, 'Leave me alone and go away.'

'You know you don't want me to do that,' he purred, and she hit the keys with punishing precision. God knows what I'm typing, she thought. I certainly don't, but I will not . . . will not! look at him again.

'I'm interested in a property you're advertising,' he said in a silky tone which made her face hot and her temper flare.

'I'm too busy to deal with you, clear off,' she said furiously.

'Miss Nesbitt!' Mr Ramsden's horrified voice made her go crimson to her hairline. She looked round, dumb with shock. She might have expected him to use the back door after lunch with his bank manager. That always made him feel depressed and furtive. But why did he have to arrive just in time to hear her flinging insults at Jamie Knox?

She hung her head, unable to meet her boss's aghast stare. What on earth could she say in her own defence? It was fate. She was doomed. Every time she set eyes on Jamie Knox she could expect disaster.

'I'll talk to you later,' Mr Ramsden threatened before turning to Jamie Knox, his smile placatory.

'Please accept my apologies—I simply don't know what's wrong with young people today. Unforgivable, quite unforgivable. I can promise you, she won't get away with it.'

Melanie flashed a dart of rage at Jamie Knox through her lowered lashes. His mouth was crooked with triumphant mockery. He thought it was funny, did he? She was tempted to get up and throw her typewriter at him, but she suppressed the impulse. She had enough trouble as it was.

'How can I help you?' asked Mr Ramsden, bending over the counter with a smile. 'Mr . . .?'

Jamie ignored the polite query. 'I'm looking for a four-bedroomed house close to Carlisle; detached, with a good garden and a garage. Have you got anything of the sort on your books?'

Mr Ramsden beamed. Whatever a client wanted, he was always sure he could produce exactly what was required.

'Certainly, certainly. We have a very wide selection of properties and I'm sure we can find you what you're looking for. Please, come into the inner office, Mr . . .?'

Jamie had witheld his name the first time he was asked but now he said, 'Knox. James Knox, Mr Ramsden. It is Mr Ramsden?'

'It is indeed.' Mr Ramsden lifted the counter and Jamie strolled through the gap. He deliberately leaned on Melanie's desk while he observed her rigid countenance. She typed like a thing possessed, her eyes fixed on the paper, refusing to admit she knew he was there although she could see the brown hand out of the corner of her eye; the long fingers splayed on her desk, the crisp white cuff of his shirt half concealing his wiry wrist. An odd little shiver ran down her spine as she looked; a sharp stab of awareness piercing her ribs.

She hurriedly stopped glancing that way, riveting her eyes on what she was typing, but behind her half-lowered lids she still saw his tanned skin, the faint blue of the veins in his wrist, the individual shape of those long, cool fingers. Her mouth was dry; he had touched her with those fingers, her skin burned at the memory.

'This way, Mr Knox,' her boss said, opening the

door into the inner office. 'Please, take a chair, I'll be with you in a minute.' He closed the door and turned round, glaring, hissing at her in a tone calculated not to be heard on the other side of the door, 'Melanie, what on earth possessed you? I'd think you were drunk if I didn't know you better. I can only think you're tired. Maybe I've been over-working you. I'll be charitable and say that that explains it, but if it ever happens again . . .'

'It won't,' she said hurriedly, very pink. 'I'm sorry, Mr Ramsden, but I thought he was just a time-waster, I didn't believe he really wanted to buy a house here.'

Mr Ramsden frowned. 'Why on earth should you think that? Has he been in before? I don't remember the name.'

'No, I . . . he . . . it was a mistake,' she said, flustered. 'I'm sorry, mistaken identity, I thought he was someone else.'

Mr Ramsden considered her soberly. 'All the same, even if he had been a time-waster you shouldn't have spoken to him like that. How many times do I have to tell you? However much of a nuisance someone is, be polite at all times, even if you feel like throwing something at him.'

'Yes, Mr Ramsden,' she said with meek eyes lowered. 'I'm sorry.'

'So I should think. We might have lost a valuable client. Now, look out all the details of suitable houses for me and bring them in to us in a minute. I'll give him a drink and fill out the form in the meantime.' Mr Ramsden looked at his watch. 'I've got an appointment at four-thirty, so there won't be time for me to show him any houses today, but he can study the details of anything you find in the files and I'll make appointments for him to view

those he wants to see. Tomorrow will do, I don't
suppose he's in a tearing hurry.'

He went into the other room, and Melanie began
pulling out details of every detached or four-
bedroomed house they had on their books. As
always, she included several houses which fitted
neither description. People were so unpredictable;
they came in with a list of requirements, then
chose something completely different, which had
taken their fancy.

Was Jamie serious about wanting to buy a house?
Or was he playing one of his games? He had
seemed so happy with his little cottage on
Ullswater—why should he want to buy a large
house near Carlisle?

Unless, she thought, pausing with a bleak look
on her face, unless he was thinking of getting
married?

She bit her lip, then angrily gathered up all the
sheets she had pulled from the filing cabinet and
took them into the other office. Jamie sat on the
other side of Mr Ramsden's desk, lounging in a
negligent pose, his jacket unbuttoned and a glass
of whisky in his hand. His black hair gleamed in
sunlight and he followed Melanie's movements out
of the corner of his eye as she walked over to the
desk.

She refused to look at him. It was inexplicable
how she managed to notice so much, all the same.
He had crossed his legs, one polished shoe swung
idly. She kept her eyes down as she placed the
pages on the blotter in front of Mr Ramsden and
withdrew at his nod.

She got on with her work, trying not to catch the
deep calm tones of Jamie's voice in the other
room. It must have been half an hour later when

the door opened and Mr Ramsden re-appeared, looking harassed.

'Melanie, Mr Knox insists on viewing Steynsforth House this afternoon,' he said grimly. 'Apparently his time is limited and he's in a rush to find a house.' He gave her a shrug. 'You were way off course about the time-wasting; that is a man in a hurry and he certainly doesn't mean to let the grass grow under his feet. I can't take him there, I've got more urgent business as I told you—you'll have to show him round.'

Melanie's heart plummeted. 'Me? I can't.' She caught Mr Ramsden's impatient eyes and stammered, 'I'm not very good at taking people round the houses, you know that. Why can't the owners show him round?'

'Because the house is empty,' Mr Ramsden snapped. 'Old Aggie Steynsforth died a year ago, the house is only just out of probate and the new owner lives in Spain and doesn't want to waste any more time selling the house. If we can sell it to this client I'll be very relieved. The owner promised me a bonus if the house was sold within the next month and I never thought I'd collect it. It's in bad need of repair and the garden's a jungle. But try to talk him into it.' He bent a stern eye on her. 'And be very, very polite. Do you understand, Melanie?'

Melanie nodded, biting her lip. 'Yes, Mr Ramsden.'

'Your job could well depend on it,' he threatened.

'Yes, Mr Ramsden,' she repeated, keeping her smouldering eyes lowered. If Jamie Knox was playing games and had no intention of buying a house she would kill him, but until she was sure what he was up to she could not take the risk of saying or doing anything that Mr Ramsden could disapprove of. Jamie wouldn't hesitate to give her boss a lurid description of her behaviour if she stepped out of line again.

No doubt he was laughing like mad behind that polite smile he wore as he came forward to meet her. He had her trapped; she was going to have to smile at him and talk with honeyed courtesy. That didn't mean she had to like it. Or him.

'We'll take my car,' Jamie said softly, his dark eyes glittering with mockery.

'Certainly, sir,' Melanie said sweetly, collecting her handbag and jacket. Jamie held the door open for her. She briefly raised her eyes to him as she said, 'Thank you, Mr Knox,' in the same saccharine tone. Her stare said something very different; her blue eyes hated him and Jamie Knox laughed. Melanie walked into the street, teeth gritted. How dare he laugh at her?

CHAPTER ELEVEN

SHE sat next to him in the sports-car in offended silence. Jamie didn't appear to notice. He whistled softly as he drove, the wind raking back his hair and his profile amused. Melanie didn't have to give him directions; Mr Ramsden had done that. She had seen Steynsforth House from the outside many times; it was a solid Victorian house set in walled grounds which had become overgrown, so that one caught glimpses of the faded cream of stucco through tangled branches of trees and bushes. The rhododenrons had grown so high and spread so far that they had become a thick hedge.

Jamie parked on the drive and they walked through rustling leaves to the front door. Jamie paused, looking around at the almost bare branches, the tall, leaf-littered lawns which hadn't been mowed for months by the look of them, the grassy paths and weedy flowerbeds.

'Melancholy, isn't it?'

He shrugged as she unlocked the door, without replying. 'How long has it been empty?'

'A year.'

The hall was dusty and gloomy; the light filtering through those thick-set trees had a greenish hue. Melanie felt like someone walking on the bottom of the sea.

'These panels are original,' she said, reading from the sheet of details she had got from the file.

'Oak. The hall is fifteen foot by twelve, a very spacious . . .'

'I know all that, I read it,' Jamie said, taking the sheet from her and pushing it into his pocket.

Melanie bristled. 'Do you want to see the rest of the house? Or have you seen enough?'

'I haven't seen anything yet,' he said, walking past her into a large, square room. The furniture had been sold at auction and had fetched quite a good price because it was largely early nineteenth-century stuff and in good condition. Jamie looked up at the stuccoed ceiling with its swags of flowers and geometric designs, then at the pale blue walls. Every step he took made the bare floorboards creak. The house had that strange echo you always find in empty houses. Bushes tapped at the windows, swaying in the autumn wind. Melanie shivered, aware of the silence and isolation and oppressed by them.

Jamie went out and explored the rest of the ground floor. She followed him at a distance, waiting for him to tire of whatever game he was playing. He couldn't seriously intend to buy this house, not now that he had seen it. There was a faint smell of damp in every room; the floorboards were uneven and, she strongly suspected, might have dry rot. You would have to spend money to make it habitable, and there were far too many rooms for a normal-sized family, let alone a single man.

'This will all have to come out,' he said in the kitchen, wrinkling his nose at the ancient stove, the old-fashioned cupboards and dresser. 'It's quite a sizeable room, though. Polly will like that.'

Melanie's heart stopped. He was opening a cupboard, taking out a tin of mustard that looked as if it had been there since the start of the century.

'Polly?' she asked huskily. He had never mentioned the name before—was this Polly the girl he really intended to marry? Melanie had never liked the name Polly; she imagined this unknown girl with bitter dislike. Beautiful, no doubt. She would be, wouldn't she? If Jamie preferred her to someone as sleekly elegant as Liz, Polly had to be someone very special. Or did she have money? Jamie had seemed so convinced that Melanie only wanted to marry Ross for his money—was that why he was planning to marry this Polly?

'My sister,' he said casually, walking out.

Melanie shut her eyes. She felt faintly sick. His sister! Polly was his sister.

She ran after him. 'Are you looking for a house for your sister?'

'And her husband and three children,' Jamie said, grinning down at her. 'They've been living in Nigeria for four years—David's an architect, he's been working on government projects out there, but his contract is finished and he and Polly are coming home for good, so they want a big house that David can take to pieces and put back together again.' He put a foot on the bottom stair, his hand gripping the carved newel post. 'David plans to work from home in future. He's setting up his own firm and this house has plenty of room for an office. He'll have great fun redesigning it to suit their needs—typical architect, can never leave a house alone.' He gave her a brief look. 'He used to work for Ross Ellis, too.'

Melanie watched him turn away and start to climb the stairs. 'Was he fired, too?'

'No, he quit to take up this job in Nigeria,' Jamie said without looking back. 'He and Ellis got on quite well, actually. David is very easy-going; he did what he was told and never argued. Just the sort of employee Ellis likes.'

'Ross can't be as bad as you pretend—he's built up that firm in a very short time and he employs hundreds of people who wouldn't have a job if it weren't for him!' Flushed, Melanie followed him and he threw her a sardonic look.

'Still defending him? I thought you'd finally seen sense and broken off your engagement.'

She stood completely still on the landing, hearing him walk across a bedroom, his footsteps echoing in the empty house. So he did know. Liz had presumably told him.

He re-appeared and stood looking at her, his hands on his hips and hostility in his dark eyes. 'But perhaps you regret it?' he mocked icily. 'Hankering for all that cosy security, are you?'

'I'm getting sick of listening to remarks like that,' she said angrily. 'I'm not putting up with any more insults from you. I'll wait outside in the car. When you've seen the rest of the house, let me know and I'll come and lock up.'

She turned to go back downstairs, but found him barring her way; a dark impatience in his face.

'Oh, no, you don't, you're not running out this time, you little coward,' he said scathingly.

His eyes glittered in the shadowy light on the landing; his face was all angles, hard and menacing. Melanie swallowed, backing.

'You don't frighten me,' she lied, wishing she would stop trembling. He was so tall and powerful and the house was so empty around them. The sound of their breathing seemed very loud.

'I should frighten you, Melanie,' he said, a leashed violence in his voice. 'I'm going to make you face up to the truth.'

She had backed into one of the bedrooms; all the furniture had gone but the room still held occupants—Melanie's worried eyes caught the scuttle of a spider along a swaying silken thread on the wall.

'I don't know what you're talking about,' she said.

'Don't you?' He took another step and was far too close. 'Oh, I think you do. You knew long ago, and so did I.'

'Knew what?' she whispered, her throat rough.

'This!' he said huskily, a hand curving about her face. She could have pushed him away, he wasn't using force, but she didn't; even though she despised her own weakness. He slowly bent and she watched his mouth with a hunger that shocked her. As it touched her lips she closed her eyes and put her arms round his neck, kissing him back in helpless desire. She was going to hate herself tomorrow, but at that moment it didn't seem to matter. Nothing mattered except the hot exchange of passion; his hand moving down her spine, over her body, his hair running through her trembling fingers.

Jamie whispered something against her mouth, the words so smothered she only realised what she had heard a minute later, and she stiffened in his arms.

'What?' she asked, pulling her head back and staring at him, her dark blue eyes wide and glazed.

He stared into them, his mouth crooked, a flush on his face. 'I love you,' he repeated and she closed her eyes again, shuddering. From behind her lids tears trickled and Jamie's arms tightened.

'Melanie? What is it? Don't. Why are you crying?'

'Nothing,' she said shakily, half laughing.

She opened her eyes again and saw bewilderment and anxiety in his face.

'What do you mean—nothing? People don't cry over nothing,' he said harshly.

She pushed him away, running a hand over her wet eyes. 'You didn't mean it. You're not in love with me. You only want to use me to get back at Ross.'

Jamie stiffened, his face tense. 'What?'

'Did you think I hadn't worked it out? You're wrong. You're a lot more obvious than you think you are.'

'Oh, am I?' he said slowly, watching her intently. 'You thought I was chasing you to annoy Ellis, did you?'

'Well, weren't you?' Her chin went up, she fought not to show how much that hurt her. 'It was Liz you were really interested in . . .'

'Liz?' His brows shot up and he laughed shortly. 'Are you crazy? Liz is head over heels in love with Ellis and has been for months. If you weren't so blind you'd have noticed, long ago.'

Melanie looked at him with contempt. 'Of course, you saw it right away, didn't you?'

'Yes,' he said coolly. 'The first time I met her, we had dinner and talked and something she said suddenly made it very obvious. When I made it clear I'd guessed, she didn't deny it. I think it was relief to be able to talk openly. She'd been hiding it for too long.'

'And I suppose you guessed Ross fancied her, too, after she'd told you about the pass he'd made at her?'

'It occurred to me,' he admitted without shame.

'And so you chased both of us,' Melanie said bitterly. 'You really meant to get Ross, didn't you?'

His dark eyes held violence again. 'I ought to slap you,' he said and she backed.

'You do and I'll . . .'

'What?' he mocked, grabbing her.

This time she fought, her body struggling helplessly in his hands. He held her, watching her with an angry smile, knowing she couldn't match his strength.

'Tell me you love me,' he said in silky provocation.

She bared her teeth, hissing through them, 'No!'

'Never?' he asked, arching his brows.

'Never, never, never,' Melanie yelled, writhing in his grip.

'Not even after we're married?' he enquired lazily and she looked at him in desolation and fury.

'I could kill you! How can you? You're a bastard and I hate you.'

'Liar,' he said, pulling her inexorably towards him, her struggles completely unavailing. Her feet skidded along the bare floorboards and Jamie gave a final jerk which sent her tumbling into his arms, held too tightly to be able to escape. She turned her head from side to side, breathing thickly, but in the end his mouth closed over her lips and a moment later Melanie gave up fighting and kissed him back.

Jamie ran his hand through her ruffled hair, looking down at her flushed face, some time later.

'I love you, Melanie,' he said softly. 'And I mean it. I want to marry you.' His fingers stroked her hot cheek. 'Now, tell me . . .'

Drowsily, she lifted her lids. 'Tell you what?'

His hand closed round her throat. 'Torment.' He kissed her quickly, lightly, lifting his mouth before she could kiss him back. 'Tell me you love me.'

'You're so sure I do,' she said, grabbing a handful of his hair and tugging it. 'What makes you so sure?'

He smiled at her and her heart turned over. 'A look in your eyes.' He brushed a finger over her lids and she shut her eyes. 'The look I saw then,' Jamie said. 'It makes me think you feel the way I do. Am I wrong?'

She leaned her head on his shoulder. 'No,' she whispered. 'I love you.'

His arms held her so tightly that she could scarcely breathe. For what seemed a very long time they didn't speak, leaning against each other, their bodies still and their hearts beating together. Melanie felt a deep peace, that poised calmness which comes before sleep. The confusion, anxiety and misery of the past few weeks fell away and everything dropped into place, she understood at last.

'The first time I saw you,' Jamie murmured conversationally. 'The very first time, I fancied you, even though you were snarling at me like a wildcat because I'd taken your parking space.'

'Taken?' she retorted, lifting her head. 'Stolen, you mean. You knew I was going to back into it! Didn't you?'

He grinned. 'I didn't know whether you were coming out or going in,' he admitted shamelessly. 'But as the space was empty, I went into it. I was in a hurry, I was late meeting someone.'

Melanie remembered the girl he had been with in the bar and frowned. 'Was she someone special?' she asked with pretended indifference, and his eyes teased.

'She thought so.' Then he laughed, shaking his head. 'No, that was our second date and our last. If I hadn't met you, I might have gone on dating her for a while but it wouldn't have come to anything—she was pretty but selfish, a spoilt little rich girl. Her father is one of the directors of Ellis's firm.'

Melanie looked down, sighing at the mention of Ross. 'Oh, look at the time,' she said, catching sight of Jamie's watch as his fingers moved gently against her shoulder. 'Mr Ramsden will wonder what on earth I'm doing.'

'When we tell him we're getting married, he'll know what we were doing,' Jamie said casually, and she went pink.

'No! I couldn't . . .'

Jamie stopped smiling, his face taut and intent. 'What do you mean, you couldn't? I asked you to marry me, Melanie, I thought you . . .'

'I mean I can't tell anyone, not yet, not so soon after breaking off my engagement to Ross; it would make me feel stupid.'

He watched her, those dark eyes hard. 'Stupid to break off your engagement to him—or stupid to get engaged to me instead?' he asked harshly and Melanie looked at him with passionate impatience.

'Oh, don't be so edgy, Jamie. I didn't mean that at all. Don't you see how changeable I'm going to look? People are going to think I can't make up my mind, they'll laugh at me!'

His face relaxed and he grimaced. 'I suppose you have something there, but does it matter what people think? You made a mistake over Ellis. So what? People do, even if they don't like admitting it. None of us is perfect.'

'No, but I rushed into an engagement with Ross and it was a mistake, so I'm afraid to rush into anything any more. We ought to take some time to get to know each other before we make any snap decisions.'

He considered her wryly. 'You've got that obstinate look again. Are you serious?'

She nodded and he shrugged without heat. 'It doesn't mean I'm not sure, Jamie,' she said huskily, stroking his cheek. 'I am. But all the same, I think we ought to take it slowly. I don't want to send Aunt Dolly into hysterics.' She gave him an uncertain glance, biting her lip. 'And then there's Ross . . .'

He stopped smiling, again. 'You do regret giving him up?'

'No,' she insisted. 'But I can't help wondering if you want me simply because you hate Ross so much.' Her dark blue eyes pleaded. 'You've always been so hostile to him, about him. You would like to get back at him, wouldn't you?'

Jamie exploded, scowling at her. 'My God! You still think I'm using you? What do I have to do to convince you? I love you, you stupid woman. I've never said that to any other woman and it wasn't a glib, easy thing to say. I meant every word!'

'I'm sorry, Jamie,' she stammered, terrified by the rage in his voice.

He looked at her, violence in his dark eyes. 'So you damned well should be. You're right, we'd better not talk about marriage yet. Obviously, you don't trust me and that means you can't really care that much for me, either.'

'No,' she said shakily, clinging to him. 'I do, Jamie. I love you but I'm still confused. The way you chased me from the start made me think it was Ross you were really trying to get at, can't you see that?'

He stared into her lifted eyes, still frowning. 'Only a woman would come up with such tortuous thinking. Look, I was furious with Ellis when he fired me, but it was business, not personal. What the hell do you think I am? What makes you imagine that I'd try to use a woman to get my own back on Ellis? Revenge is petty and pointless, anyway. What good would it do me to stab Ellis in the back? If I kept trying to get you to break off your engagement, it was because I was in love with you and I had a strong hunch that it was mutual. Right from the night we spent on the fells I could see that you and Ellis weren't right for each other. I know the man, remember.'

Melanie gave a long, deep sigh of relief. 'I'm sorry, Jamie, I misunderstood.'

He framed her face between his hands, his eyes brooding on her. 'I wish I didn't love you so much.'

Staring into his eyes, she understood him for once and smiled quiveringly. 'I know, I feel the same. That's how I knew I wasn't really in love with Ross. He couldn't hurt me, the way you can.' She stared at his mouth, her throat hot. 'But then he never got to me the way you do.'

Jamie kissed her fiercely and she wound her arms around him, kissing him back with all the intense feeling inside her.

They drove back to the office ten minutes later and found Andrew coping with the late afternoon rush. While they were talking to him about the Steynsforth house Mr Ramsden came back and beamed with delight to hear that he had probably sold the old house.

'I'll put down a deposit on it now and then my sister should be here next week to confirm the sale. I'm sure the house is just what they're looking for—in the meantime, I'll get a surveyor to look at the place and give me a report on it.' Jamie followed Mr Ramsden into the inner office to discuss the details and Melanie went back to her desk, but it was impossible to work with any real concentration. Her mind kept wandering and she was absent-minded, she kept making mistakes in her typing.

By the time Jamie and Mr Ramsden emerged from the other room, it was five-thirty and Melanie was putting the cover on her typewriter. Jamie shook hands with Mr Ramsden, smiling at him. 'I'll be in touch, then. Goodnight.'

He walked out of the door and Mr Ramsden spoke to his son about another matter, giving Melanie a vague glance as she put on her jacket and collected her bag.

'Good work, Melanie. We're going to get that bonus on the Steynsforth place after all. You see, you never know what you're going to be able to sell in this business. That's what I love about it.'

She smiled, saying goodnight to both him and Andrew, and left. There was no sign of Jamie but as she reached her parked car, she saw his car purring towards her. He leaned out, his eyes gleaming wickedly.

'Want a lift, lady?'

Laughing, she got into the passenger seat. 'Mr Ramsden is going to think my car has broken down again!'

Jamie drove off with a surge of power from the sports-car's engine. 'That old thing is ready for the scrap-heap, anyway.'

'Do you mind?' she retorted defiantly. 'I love my car, even if it is old.'

'It belongs in a car museum. I'm amazed it goes at all.'

'Well, it was all I could afford,' she said, smiling at him.

'Which reminds me, I've got an interview with a big engineering firm on Tuesday,' Jamie said. 'Most

of their work is done in the UK so I won't have to
be abroad all the time, the way I was with Ellis.'
He grinned sideways at her. 'Keep your fingers
crossed that I get the job.'

She let her head slide on to his shoulder, smiling.
'They are crossed,' she murmured, showing him.

He turned into the road in which she lived and
drew up outside her home, behind another car
which they both recognised.

Jamie stared at it. 'What's Ellis doing here?'

'The last time I heard, he was in London,'
Melanie said. 'Maybe he came to see me, I rang
him several times but he was always away.'

Jamie's head turned sharply. 'You rang him?
Why?'

She looked at him with a placatory smile. 'I still
haven't managed to give him back that ring, and
it's worth a fortune—just having it in the house
makes me nervous in case I lose it or we're
burgled.'

Jamie relaxed. 'Oh, I see.'

She slid out of the car and walked with him up
to the front door. Aunt Dolly met them in the
hall, very flushed and agitated. She didn't notice
Jamie, she was so disturbed by the news she had to
give Melanie.

'Melanie, Ross is here! I didn't know what to
say to him, I was so embarrassed! He's in the
sitting-room, with Liz. She didn't want to talk to
him, either, but one of us had to! Thank heavens
you're home. Go and see what he wants.' She
pushed Melanie towards the door. 'Oh, when I saw
him outside I nearly dropped through the floor.
I'm too old for these upsets.'

That was when she saw Jamie and stopped
talking, her jaw dropping.

He smiled at her with all his considerable charm. 'Hallo, Mrs Nesbitt.'

Melanie didn't wait to hear him twining Aunt Dolly round his little finger; she pushed open the sitting-room door and Liz and Ross spun to look at her, their faces flushed.

She wasn't sure what she had interrupted—a quarrel or a very intimate talk. What she did realise was that neither of them was thrilled to see her.

'I'm glad you're here, Ross,' she said politely. 'I wanted to make sure you got your ring back safely, that was why I rang. I'll run upstairs and get it for you.'

She backed out before he could answer and closed the door again. She had never felt so unwanted in her life. There was no sign of Jamie but she heard voices in the kitchen and picked out his, smiling. Aunt Dolly was laughing. No doubt she had been a pushover for him. Aunt Dolly liked men, especially attractive ones.

Melanie didn't hurry back with the ring. She took the opportunity of changing into something rather more alluring while she was in her bedroom, and was just doing her make-up when Liz tapped on the door and put her head round it.

Melanie grinned at her. 'I was just coming down. You haven't murdered Ross, have you?'

Liz was still flushed but her eyes were bright and she was smiling. 'Not yet, but I still may.' She paused, then said uncertainly, 'Melanie, if I went out with him would it bother you? He just asked me to have dinner and I . . .'

'Idiot,' Melanie said fondly. 'Why should it bother me? I told you, it was all a big mistake, Ross and me. We both realised it in time, thank heavens.' She ran the brush over her hair, watching

Liz in the mirror. 'Anyway, I'm having dinner with Jamie, and don't suggest a foursome because I want him all to myself.'

Liz didn't seem surprised by the news, she looked amused, in fact. 'Jamie said . . .' she began and then stopped.

Melanie swung on the dressing-table stool, eyeing her suspiciously. 'What did Jamie say?'

Liz laughed. 'That he fancied you and thought you fancied him,' she said, and Melanie gave her a cross look.

'He's too sure of himself by half!'

'Aren't all men?' Liz said drily. 'On the surface, anyway. That's their ego; they're so scared of losing face that they make a big thing of being totally confident whatever happens.'

Melanie listened with a mixture of amusement and realisation. It had never occurred to her before that Jamie might not be as assured as he seemed, or that he might be vulnerable too. She nodded slowly, getting up. Collecting the box which held the sapphire ring, she slid a hand through Liz's arm, smiling at her cousin.

'We'd better go down and join our men,' she said.

Forthcoming Titles

COLLECTION
Available in October

The Carole Mortimer Collection **LADY SURRENDER**
LOVERS IN THE AFTERNOON

The Charlotte Lamb Collection **LOVE IN THE DARK**
CIRCLE OF FATE

BEST SELLER ROMANCE
Available in November

AN UNBREAKABLE BOND Robyn Donald
ONCE FOR ALL TIME Betty Neels

MEDICAL ROMANCE
Available in November

MEDICAL DECISIONS Lisa Cooper
DEADLINE LOVE Judith Worthy
NO TIME FOR ROMANCE Kathleen Farrell
RELATIVE ETHICS Caroline Anderson

Available from Boots, Martins, John Menzies, W.H. Smith
and other paperback stockists.

Also available from Mills and Boon Reader Service,
P.O. Box 236, Thornton Road, Croydon, Surrey CR9 3RU.

Readers in South Africa — write to:
Independent Book Services Pty, Postbag X3010,
Randburg, 2125, S. Africa.

A special gift for Christmas

Four romantic stories by four of your favourite authors for you to unwrap and enjoy this Christmas.

Robyn Donald   STORM OVER PARADISE
Catherine George   BRAZILIAN ENCHANTMENT
Emma Goldrick   SMUGGLER'S LOVE
Penny Jordan   SECOND-BEST HUSBAND

Published on 11th October, 1991   Price: £6.40

Available from Boots, Martins, John Menzies, W.H. Smith, and other paperback stockists.

Also available from Mills and Boon Reader Service, P.O. Box 236, Thornton Road, Croydon, Surrey CR9 3RU.

BRING YOU COMFORT & JOY FOR CHRISTMAS

Four heart-warming Medical Romances in a single volume.

CHRISTMAS PRESENT
Lynne Collins

THE WAY WE WERE
Laura MacDonald

A MIRACLE OR TWO
Marion Lennox

THE REAL CHRISTMAS MESSAGE
Sharon Wirdnam

Available from November 1991, priced at £3.99

Available from Boots, Martins, John Menzies, W. H. Smith,
and other paperback stockists.
Also available from Mills & Boon Reader Service,
P.O. Box 236, Thornton Road, Croydon, Surrey, CR9 3RU.

Mills & Boon

Next month's Romances

Each month, you can choose from a world of variety in romance with Mills & Boon. These are the new titles to look out for next month.

TEMPESTUOUS REUNION Lynne Graham

A CURE FOR LOVE Penny Jordan

UNDERCOVER AFFAIR Lilian Peake

GHOST OF THE PAST Sally Wentworth

ISTANBUL AFFAIR Joanna Mansell

ROARKE'S KINGDOM Sandra Marton

WHEN LOVE RETURNS Vanessa Grant

DANGEROUS INFATUATION Stephanie Howard

LETHAL ATTRACTION Rebecca King

STORMY RELATIONSHIP Margaret Mayo

HONG KONG HONEYMOON Lee Wilkinson

CONTRACT TO LOVE Kate Proctor

WINTER DESTINY Grace Green

AFRICAN ASSIGNMENT Carol Gregor

THE CHALK LINE Kate Walker

STARSIGN
HUNTED HEART Kristy McCallum

Available from Boots, Martins, John Menzies, W.H. Smith and other paperback stockists.

Also available from Mills and Boon Reader Service, P.O. Box 236, Thornton Road, Croydon, Surrey CR9 3RU.